11

Claremont Tales

Richard A. Lupoff

Golden Gryphon Press • 2001

Foreword, "This World, These Worlds," copyright © 2001, by Richard A. Lupoff.

"Black Mist," first published in *Omni On-line*, March 1995.

"The Second Drug," first published in *Mammoth Book of Locked Room Mysteries and Impossible Crimes*, Carroll & Graf, 2000.

"At Vega's Taqueria," first published in *Amazing Stories*, September 1990.

"I Don't Tell Lies," first published in *Weird Tales*, Autumn 2000.

"Mr. Greene and the Monster," first published in *Pagoda #1*, 1952.

"The Monster and Mr. Greene," copyright © 2001, by Richard A. Lupoff.

"Lux Was Dead Right," first published in *Rigel Science Fiction Magazine #1*, Summer 1981.

"The Child's Story," first published in *Cosmos Science Fiction and Fantasy*, September 1977.

"The Tootsie Roll Factor," first published in *Wheel of Fortune*, Avon Books, 1995.

"Documents in the Case of Elizabeth Akeley," first published in *Fantasy and Science Fiction*, March 1982.

"The Adventures of Mr. Tindle,": "Mr. Tindle Departs," as "Mr. Tindle," first published in *Fantasy and Science Fiction*, April 1989; "Mr. Tindle Returns," first published in *Other Worlds #4*, May 1991.

"Discovery of the Ghooric Zone—March 15, 2337," first published in *Chrysalis*, Zebra Books, 1977.

Copyright © 2001 by Richard A. Lupoff

Illustrations Copyright © 2001 by Nicholas Jainschigg

LIBRARY OF CONGRESS CATALOGING-IN-PUBLICATION DATA
Lupoff, Richard A., 1935–
    Claremont tales / Richard A. Lupoff—1st ed.
        p.   cm.
        Contents: Black mist — The second drug — At Vega's taqueria — I don't tell lies — Mr. Greene and the monster — The monster and Mr. Greene — Lux was dead right — The child's story — The Tootsie Roll factor — Documents in the case of Elizabeth Akeley — The adventures of Mr. Tindle — Discovery of the Ghooric Zone.
        ISBN 1-930846-01-0 (limited ed. : alk. paper) — ISBN 1-930846-00-2 (trade ed. : alk. paper)
        1. Fantasy fiction, American.   2. Detective and mystery stories, American.   I. Title.

PS3562.U6C56   2001
813'.54—dc21   00-053553

First Edition.

Contents

Foreword: This World, These Worlds
ix

Black Mist
5

The Second Drug
59

At Vega's Taqueria
85

I Don't Tell Lies
105

Mr. Greene and the Monster
119

The Monster and Mr. Greene
125

Lux Was Dead Right
135

The Child's Story
153

The Tootsie Roll Factor
169

Documents in the Case of Elizabeth Akeley
191

The Adventures of Mr. Tindle
231

Discovery of the Ghooric Zone
265

This book is dedicated, with my thanks, to the editors who brought each story to its first publication:

Keith Ferrell
Mike Ashley
Ted White
Darrell Schweitzer
Charles Anderson
Gary Turner
Eric Vinicoff
David G. Hartwell
Roger Zelazny
Edward Ferman
Gary Lovisi
Roy Torgeson

. . . and to those responsible for the stories' new life in *Claremont Tales*: Marty Halpern, Gary Turner, Nicholas Jainschigg . . .

. . . and to the founder of Golden Gryphon Press and initiator of this project, the late James Turner . . .

. . . and to my very own "first reader" and indispensable encourager and companion, Patricia Lupoff.

Foreword: This World, These Worlds

SOMETIMES I THINK I'M QUADRUPLETS.
No.
Sometimes I *know* I'm quadruplets.

There's the "me" who lives in a world just like ours, only my mother didn't die when I was six years old. Consequently my father, whose business demanded almost constant travel, did not feel obligated to send my brother and myself off to boarding school, where I had to give up piano lessons because they just didn't fit into the school's curriculum.

I loved the piano. I played well, very well for a six-year-old, but even at that age I knew that what I *really* wanted was not to be a performer, but a composer.

Never happened.

Never happened to *me*, but . . .

But somewhere there's a parallel universe where my mother survived her illness and Jerry and I stayed home, and in that universe I'm responsible for three or four symphonies, half a dozen concerti, and an assortment of rhapsodies, études and bagatelles. Good ones, too. I know it. I know that other me is alive and well and happy.

There's another, other me, or rather there *was* another me, who was a reserve officer on active duty in the US Army in the 1950s. Like me, under heavy pressure from his CO, he applied for a Regular Army commission. Like me, he was offered "RA" status. Unlike me, he didn't turn it down and return to civilian life. He made captain, went to Vietnam, and was blown up by a hand grenade placed by a "friendly." I've always been too trusting for my own good. It cost this other me his life.

The third "other me" got out of the army when I did, married and started a career in the then-fledgling computer industry when I did. After a dozen years he was offered a major promotion, just as I was. Like me he had his letter of resignation in his pocket when his boss offered him that boost up the corporate ladder with its fat salary increase and juicy stock options and other attractive perks. He kept the letter in his pocket and took the promotion. He regretted it. He never got to live the life he wanted, to write the books he wanted, and in a terrible, twisted way he blamed his wife and children for his own mistake. He died divorced, bitter, lonely and prematurely aged almost a decade ago.

Stephen Hawking has written about other universes than our own, and before him Murray Leinster did, and before him, Francis Stevens. I've lived in four universes, and two of the four "me's" are still alive and creating. As for the others, well, the thought of them gives me a chill.

But we're living in *this* universe, and in this universe a man named Jim Turner edited a novel I wrote a couple of decades ago. It had been a troubled project, mired in a struggle between two editors at a major commercial publishing house. One editor was departing, one was arriving. One had given me valuable guidance in developing a difficult manuscript. The other said that the resulting 'script was just fine, but he had in mind something completely different and would I mind scrapping two years of work and writing a whole new book to meet a whole new set of specs?

Indeed I would.

The manuscript came back to me, and in time Jim Turner bought it for Arkham House. Jim felt there was still a problem chapter in the book, and worked with me through uncounted versions until we were both satisfied with the result, and he then published the book to considerable success.

When Jim left Arkham House and founded Golden Gryphon Press he and I discussed the possibility of my compiling a collection of my shorter fiction for Golden Gryphon. But Jim had been in precarious health for some years, and with his death in 1999 I thought that Golden Gryphon had ceased to exist.

Such was not the case, and my editor for this book is none other than Jim's brother, Gary Turner.

But somewhere there's a universe where Jim Turner, healthy and happy, is still operating Golden Gryphon, and is editing *Claremont Tales*, and the Dick Lupoff of that universe is as proud to be working with Jim as I am to be working with Gary.

*   *   *

The stories in this collection were selected by three people: Gary Turner, Patricia Lupoff, and myself. Pat Lupoff, my wife, probably knows my work better than any other person. The idea was to create not a "Best of" volume, but a broad spectrum of my stories, selected from a career that now spans half a century and includes work in many realms.

Gary Turner asked me to furnish him with electronic files of the candidate stories, and for recent efforts that was no problem—they were already on my hard drive. Earlier stories were scanned in from decades-old carbon copies of manuscripts, processed with optical character recognition software, and then very carefully vetted. The software is pretty damned good, but there were some challenges it just couldn't handle.

Is that round thing a kew, an oh, or a zero? Is that vertical line an el, an eye, or a one?

In the process of cleaning up the files I took the opportunity, here and there, to polish my prose. Purists may complain that the text of a 1968 short story or a 1987 novelette should remain untouched. But I figure, hey, I wrote this puppy, I have the right to brush its coat before it goes on exhibition.

No major structural changes were made, however. Anything that needed that much work, I believe, didn't belong in this book. And several candidate stories were dropped for precisely that reason.

I also resisted the temptation to modernize stories. No way was I going to replace Frank Sinatra and Ginny Simms with Ricky Martin and Celine Dion, or take away my characters' Studebakers and DeSotos and make them drive around in Saturns and Toyotas. No way was I going to take out Stalin and Nixon and replace them with latter-day villains. And no way was I going to remove the wonderful Philco console radio from the living room and replace it with a Phillips flat-screen HDTV.

The late 1940s and 1950s, my coming-of-age time, were also the last days of the great fiction magazines. It can be a breathtaking experience, nowadays, to come across a copy of *Collier's* or *The Saturday Evening Post* from that era. These magazines were huge enterprises, filled with ads for glittering automobiles, spotless kitchen appliances, those wonderful new television sets and other consumer goods. The happy family scenes of smiling mothers in their shirtwaist dresses, proud dads in their business suits or off-duty plaid shirts, benign elders and cheerful children look like snapshots from another planet, scenes from another reality. Why is it that my memories are of Cold War tensions and the terror of imminent nuclear attack?

The big slicks published a mix of articles and fiction, and the fiction content of a single issue could include installments of as many as three serials, one starting, one at its midpoint, and one ending, a complete novelette, and half a dozen short stories.

These magazines tilted heavily toward stories with domestic themes, romance or family relationships—"women's fiction." But they also included mysteries, westerns, adventure stories, sports stories and even occasional science fiction.

And they poured from the printing presses. *The Saturday Evening Post* was a weekly!

And of course there were pulp magazines by the hundreds, from the general or "variety" pulps like *Argosy, Adventure,* and *Blue Book* to more specialized category magazines to the single-hero pulps. *The Shadow, Captain Future, Dan Turner, Hollywood Detective.*

One of these days, I suppose, some sociologist will tell us why the few surviving fiction magazines are now the living fossils of the publishing world and why the great bulk of fiction written, published and read in the modern era consists of novels. But the short story remains a viable, if less popular and lucrative, form. It offers its delights, and they are not really the same delights as those offered by the novel.

There are those persons, including some very talented writers, who seem unable to grasp this fact. They think that a short story is nothing but a miniature novel, or a synopsis of a novel, or an excerpt from a novel. Or they believe, conversely, that a novel is nothing but a very long short story.

No, no, no! Take my word for it if you will, or else take apart some examples of each form and study them for structure and narrative technique. If you're as bright as I'm sure you are, you will see that they are no more the same thing, save for scale, than a skyscraper and a bungalow are the same thing save for scale.

Simply not so. Several of our finest short story writers have failed as novelists, and novelists have been baffled when they tried to write short stories. The reason, I suspect, is that they don't understand the differences between the forms.

Well, back to the stories in this book, and the whole notion of modernizing texts.

Did I mention that I'm opposed to the practice?

When I was an impoverished college student living in Coral Gables, Florida, my favorite restaurant used to offer a special dinner of which I availed myself religiously once a week. T-bone steak, French fries, peas and carrots, a green salad, a roll and butter and a cup of coffee for a dollar thirty-five. A slice of apple pie would cost you extra, and in those days I couldn't afford extra.

It happens that I've never used that restaurant in a work of fiction. (Cy's was its name, but it belonged to a jovial balding fellow named Hans.) But if I had described it in a story written many years ago, and if I were to reprint that story today, I would neither change the menu to a Dietetically Correct one nor revise the price to account for five decades of inflation.

Let each creation remain faithful to the era in which it was created.

Let me return briefly to the notion of *worlds*.

I think one of the great contributions of art, whether we are talking about literature, painting, music, drama or dance, is that it permits us to live in many worlds. There's a kind of folk-realization of this in such popular expressions as "out of this world," becoming lost in a play or motion picture, being carried away on wings of song.

Certainly works of fiction — if they're any good — can transport readers from this world, our world, to many worlds, other worlds. The author's fictitious characters inhabit those worlds; while at work the author lives in those worlds, and the reader is allowed to visit those worlds.

Many times I've had the experience, after hours of hard work on a story set in another locale, another era, another reality than my own, to re-emerge in time for dinner and experience a moment of disorientation before I could adjust to the here and now.

As for my characters, well, various folk in the stories in *Claremont Tales* live in San Francisco in 1931, in present-day Nevada, on the Martian moon Phobos in the 23rd Century, or in the timeless hills of Vermont. And then there is Mr. Vernon Browne who keeps slipping from one reality to another, whether he wants to or not.

Any time you choose, you can close this book and return to

your "real" surroundings. But I sincerely hope that when you do so, you'll bring back a little bit of the other worlds you visit in *Claremont Tales*. Or maybe that a tiny part of you will stay in each of my other worlds.

* * *

Now, if you're still with me, I should like to say a few words about critics. Some writers claim that they never read their reviews. "If it's favorable, it's by a toady trying to suck up to you. If it's hostile you can bet the reviewer is a failed author throwing rocks at his betters because he resents their success and his own failure."

Don't believe it. Authors *do* read their reviews, and if the reviewer shows any sign of intelligence, the author pays close attention.

Several critics have suggested that I might have enjoyed more success in my career if I'd carved out a niche for myself and written a particular type of book (and story) consistently. Instead, I've been all over the place. One book, a traditional space opera; the next, an avant-garde exploration of the limits of language. A werewolf novel. A mannered, exotic fantasy. A murder mystery. An adventure story.

And there I was thinking that versatility was a virtue. Silly me.

These critics may well be right, and in retrospect there were some instances when I did take the wrong turning, books that I wrote (out of more than forty, and I'm not through yet, believe me!) that I now feel were a waste of time. But by and large I have few regrets. I might have sold more copies and made more dollars if I'd written nothing but space operas or nothing but werewolf novels or nothing but detective stories, but just think of the experiences I would have missed.

No, no regrets.

I've also been referred to as (I won't say "accused of being") a stylist. The implication, I think, is that I am more concerned with technique, with language, than with other aspects of fiction. Again, I can see merit to the charge. My works do vary greatly in style. And I do try to choose my words with taste and arrange them with care in order to achieve an optimum effect.

Prose is music and it is poetry, and its sound in the reader's mental ear and its feeling on his tongue and in his brain make a big, big difference in the response that a piece of writing will evoke. There are a hundred ways to say "blue," and most often the best way is the simplest: *blue*. But the writer should be aware of his options and choose the most suitable one, not merely grab the word closest to hand that will communicate more or less accurately and more or less effectively the idea that he has in mind.

And the fact is that for each of my stories I chose the style that I felt would function best to tell that story.

My first professional literary experience was as a journalist—a sports writer, no less. In that profession, while color of phrase and vigor of expression are highly valued, accuracy of reportage is the supreme commandment. If the Mauve Sox beat the Cobras 6–3, you'd better report the right team as winner and you'd better get the score right. Say it as well as you can or as poorly as you must, but there's no excuse for getting the outcome wrong.

When I was sixteen years old I credited the wrong pitcher with a rained-out no-hitter in a high school baseball game and I still wake up cold and trembling in the night, remembering that mistake.

In writing fiction, the supreme commandment is, Get the story right! Style? Hell, yes! Character? You bet!

But whatever you do, tell a story! Homer knew that, Shakespeare knew it, Edith Wharton knew it and Dashiell Hammett knew it. The young H.G. Wells knew it but the older Wells apparently forgot it, and we still read *The War of the Worlds* (1898) and *The Time Machine* (1895) while *The Croquet Player* (1936) and *The Holy Terror* (1939) have been relegated to the trash heap of literature.

If there's one lesson that I've learned from my fifty years of writing fiction, it is, *You must tell a story.*

*   *   *

For a very long time I have believed that fiction is above all a medium for entertainment, and it is my hope that the reader will derive pleasure from every story in this book. I do not believe that entertainment is necessarily shallow or trivial, though, or that stories cannot or should not move their readers, inspire or enlighten or console them.

So I hope, as you proceed through the stories in this book, I'll make you utter a gasp or two of astonishment, I'll make you laugh a few times and maybe cry once or twice. I just hope that you don't gasp when you're supposed to laugh, laugh when you're supposed to cry, or cry when you think about the money you shelled out for *Claremont Tales.*

—Richard A. Lupoff
Berkeley, CA
May 2000

Claremont Tales

In both my science fiction and my mystery stories I've always emphasized the psychological and sociological factors in the behavior of my characters, so "Black Mist" was doubly a departure for me. It was a "hard" science fiction story, the kind that the late John W. Campbell would have welcomed in the pages of Astounding Stories in 1937. It was also a strict, by-the-rules murder mystery.

Written in the summer of 1990, it was beset by a series of publishing glitches. Editors Keith Ferrell and Ellen Datlow featured "Black Mist" in Omni Online, a pioneering attempt at electronic publishing. Omni Online was a noble experiment, but it was clearly ahead of its time. To succeed, it should have offered attractive design and typography, colorful graphics, animation, audio content, and interactive features. It took an agonizing five years before "Black Mist" appeared in Omni Online, but even by 1995 the technology just wasn't there. It did receive a gratifying number of hits, but the electronic Omni, even though it outlived its paper parent, eventually died.

"Black Mist" did reach a larger audience as title story in a paperback anthology three years later.

Black Mist

THE BODY WAS FOUND BY A WORKER ASSIGNED to the Phobos Research Station, Jiricho Toshikawa. Toshikawa had been born in a small village in Okayama Prefecture. Uneducated and knowing only the simple skills of a farmer, it was a mystery how he came to be posted to Phobos. Perhaps it was believed that Toshikawa possessed skills that would be useful in the experimental farms of the Marineris region of Mars. But he had wound up on Phobos, a hapless individual who grudgingly performed his menial tasks.

He was assigned to work in the dining commons of the station. His superior, the chief cook and manager of the food and dining facility, Wataru Okubo, had complained of the man. Toshikawa was lazy. He would hide or run away from work. Okubo tried to keep an eye on Toshikawa's gawky figure and snaggle-toothed face, but the one great skill that Toshikawa possessed was the ability to escape hard tasks.

Okubo had assigned Toshikawa to scrub the pots and implements used for preparing breakfast. Toshikawa had grumbled, complaining of Okubo's unfairness and his own overworked status, but he had finally lifted the first implement in order to commence work. Okubo had turned away to answer a question

5

from another worker. When he turned back, Toshikawa was nowhere to be seen.

Toshikawa had made his way to the common crew quarters that he shared with other workers who were neither scientists nor of management rank. It had taken him a long time to learn his way around the corridors of the research station, even stopping at each intersection to study the diagram posted there, but at last he had learned the routes that he needed to follow each day.

From his quarters it was a short walk to a shared spacesuit locker and a convenient airlock. Next he had donned a spacesuit. Even the suit's helmet and inflated limbs and torso did not conceal his scrawny shape.

He had exited through the nearest airlock and walked away from the station. Mars was directly overhead. Toshikawa looked at the sky. Far away, near the curve of Mars's surface, he could see the tiny, dim dot of Deimos. Earth was nowhere to be seen. It was night on this side of Phobos, full day on the side of Mars overhead.

Toshikawa walked away from the research station. The crater Stickney lay directly ahead of him. Beyond it, the abandoned Russian space station that had been anchored to Phobos nearly a century before, lifted its jagged black bulk. Toshikawa picked his way across the blanket of dark regolith that covered most of Phobos. His negligible weight, hardly one tenth of one percent of the sixty kilograms he had weighed on Earth, was barely enough to stir the regolith.

Like all workers assigned to Phobos, he had learned the trick of walking with a careful, gliding stride, barely lifting his boots from the regolith. In the beginning he had been frightened on Phobos. Until he had learned to walk properly, he had feared that each stride might throw him from the moonlet altogether, and that he would be lost in the blackness of space, or plummet headlong to his death on Mars itself. But it would take a concerted effort, even by an exceptionally strong man, to break the grip of even Phobos's light gravity.

Toshikawa had been assigned to work on Mars at first, and had experienced little trouble in controlling his movements there.

His lightness on the planet—there, he had weighed almost 25 kilograms—had caused him no difficulty. He had travelled from Earth, by spaceplane to one of the orbiting stations, by shuttle to a cycling Niehoff ship, thence to Phobos and by minirocket and balloon to the surface of Mars. The bureaucracy had dithered over him and had finally shipped him back up to Phobos to be a cook's helper and general worker.

But on Phobos, with its tiny mass and proportionately tiny gravity — the discovery of the body had interrupted Toshikawa's ruminations and driven such thoughts from his mind. When he saw the form lying on the surface he had given an involuntary yelp. Not knowing whether to race forward to help the fallen person or to run for assistance, he jumped.

He rose from the regolith and experienced a moment of terror in which he forgot his lesson and thought that he would fly upward into the sky until he was caught by the stronger gravity of Mars, where he would tumble through the thin atmosphere of the planet and fall to his death.

Instead, his ascent slowed; then he drifted gently back to Phobos. He landed on his toes and slowly collapsed onto one knee. Then he regained his self-control and rose to his feet. He felt a wave of shame creep through him and knew that his face was red. In his moment of panic he had soiled himself! How could he conceal this from Mr. Okubo? How could he face any of his fellow workers, any of the scientists or the managers who worked at the Phobos Research Station?

For a time he was so concerned with this problem that he forgot the cause of his alarm. Then he remembered. He had seen a body, a human form, lying on the regolith, on the very edge of the crater Stickney.

He moved forward again, this time taking care with his stride. He stood over the form he had seen. Yes, unquestionably, this was a person. He could tell by the configuration of torso and limbs, and by the spacesuit that the victim was wearing.

Wondering whether the person was alive or dead, Toshikawa knelt beside the head. The person was lying face downward, arms and legs spread in the shape of an X. There was a mark on the back of the spacesuit, a line as long as the first two joints of a man's forefinger, where something had penetrated the victim's spacesuit and been withdrawn, leaving the suit's sealant to prevent decompression.

Toshikawa turned the victim over. For a moment the victim seemed alive, almost trying to bound from Toshikawa's grasp. Once again he had forgotten to take account of the slight gravity of Phobos. There was also the sound of a moan in Toshikawa's ears. He thought it was the victim, but then realized that he himself had made the sound.

He lowered the body carefully to the ground. The regolith was a mixture of tiny crumbled rocks and dust. The dusty portion had adhered to the victim's face plate. As best he could, Toshikawa brushed the plate clean. The face of the victim was illuminated by the ruddy reflection of sunlight from the face of Mars. It was brighter than the brightest of moonlit nights on Earth.

Toshikawa recognized the victim. It was a woman, one of the very few working on Phobos. He had seen her when she had arrived from a research center located beside a dry river bed at Nirgal Vallis. Her name was Fumiko Inada.

When she had first arrived at Phobos, Toshikawa had been smitten by her beauty. Her hair was glossy and highlights of blue seemed to flash from the black. Her face was soft and he had seen enough of her figure to find his sleep interrupted night after night.

Once in the dining commons, when he was off duty, he had approached her table with rice and tea and tried to strike up a conversation, but she had given him a look that discouraged him.

Now she lay in his arms, unmoving. Her eyes were open. Her face seemed to be an unnatural color, but in the light of Mars Toshikawa was uncertain about this. He reached toward her chest, drew his hand back in shame, then placed his thinly gloved fingers over her heart.

He could detect neither heartbeat nor respiration.

Fumiko Inada was dead.

Toshikawa laid her carefully back on the regolith. There would be an investigation of her death, and he thought that it would be best to leave her and her surroundings undisturbed. He realized that he had already lifted the woman, turned her over, and brushed the regolith from her face mask.

He thought for a moment that he should turn her face down and rub her helmet in the regolith, so as to restore the prior condition. But that might only make things worse. Instead, he lowered her gently to the ground and rose carefully to his feet.

He walked carefully back toward the research station. He wished that he had remained there, performing the tasks assigned him by Mr. Okubo. Then Fumiko Inada would not be restored to life, but at least he would not have been the one to find her. He would not have become frightened, soiled himself, disarranged the scene of her death.

There were places where the regolith was disturbed, as if it were the infield of a baseball diamond where a base runner had slid heavily. Toshikawa stepped carefully around them, disturbing the regolith as little as possible with his own light, gliding strides. He re-entered the research station, but instead of removing his spacesuit immediately, he made his way to crew quarters. Here he removed the spacesuit and cleaned himself. Wearing fresh clothing he returned the spacesuit to the common room.

He returned to the dining commons and faced Mr. Okubo.

Mr. Okubo was furious. He demanded, "Where have you been?" Before Toshikawa could reply, Mr. Okubo shouted, "You are the worst worker I have ever known! You are never here, and when you are here you are worthless!"

Toshikawa saw that Mr. Okubo had grown red in the face. This was not the redness of Mars's reflected light; it was the red of great anger. Toshikawa said, "I have been outside. I went to look at the Stickney crater."

"You were supposed to be working! You had no right to leave the station. What were you doing at the crater?"

"Someone is dead."

"What?"

Toshikawa dropped his gaze. "Someone is dead."

"At Stickney? You found someone at Stickney? Dead?"

"Yes." Toshikawa wilted beneath Mr. Okubo's scorn.

"You are an idiot as well as a fool!" Other workers, distracted by the shouting of Mr. Okubo, had ceased their work and were staring at the two men, listening to their words. Mr. Okubo said, "Who is dead?"

Toshikawa said, "Miss Inada."

"How do you know?"

"She was lying there. I turned her over. I could tell she was dead."

"How could you tell?"

Toshikawa said, "She looked dead."

"And are you a doctor? You just took a look at Miss Inada and you decided that she was dead?"

Toshikawa felt his ears, face and neck burning with embarrassment. He said, "No. I put my hand on her chest. On her heart. There was no heartbeat. And she was not breathing."

Mr. Okubo stood for a moment, his breath hissing between his teeth. Toshikawa felt that he would faint if he had to stand much longer before Mr. Okubo like this. Finally Mr. Okubo said, "Come with me."

He led the way from the dining commons to the office of Mr. Kakuji Matsuda. He knocked on the door. Toshikawa stood behind him. The heat of his embarrassment had fallen away from him. He was so cold that he shivered with fright. He was seeing the face of Miss Inada as she had looked at him with dead eyes from inside her helmet.

Mr. Matsuda grunted and Mr. Okubo opened the door to Mr. Matsuda's office. He stepped inside. Toshikawa did not know what to do. He remained behind in the corridor until Mr. Okubo reached back and grabbed him by the wrist. Mr. Okubo pulled Toshikawa inside the office.

Toshikawa saw the furnishings. A desk with a computer screen and its equipment, a record driver, a voder. Chairs. Shelves bearing record and book holders.

Two men sat in the room. Behind the desk, Toshikawa recognized Mr. Kakuji Matsuda, the manager of the Phobos Research Station. Toshikawa had seen Mr. Matsuda a few times. Mr. Matsuda addressed the staff of the station on such important holidays as the Emperor's birthday or the anniversary of the first Mars landing. The second man, Toshikawa was not certain of. He thought he was Mr. Eiji Sumiyoshi, Mr. Matsuda's deputy.

Toshikawa didn't know what to do. He watched Mr. Okubo, hoping to follow his lead. Mr. Okubo bowed to Mr. Matsuda. Toshikawa did the same, bowing more deeply.

Mr. Matsuda stood up and returned the bows. "What do you want?"

Toshikawa could see that the two managers had been playing *hanafuda*—the cards were still lying on Mr. Matsuda's desk. Mr. Sumiyoshi's hand lay before him—an eight, nine, three. A shudder passed through Toshikawa. There was a hot *sake* jug on the desk at well, and cups for the two men.

Mr. Okubo said, "Mr. Matsuda, Toshikawa here claims that he found Miss Inada near the Stickney crater, dead."

Mr. Matsuda turned his eyes for the first time to Toshikawa. "Is this true?"

Trembling, Toshikawa said, "Yes, sir. I was walking."

"Not working? Was this before the start of work?"

"No, sir. It was during work."

"Had Mr. Okubo sent you on an errand outside the station?"

"No, sir. I did not feel well. I slept badly last night. I had troubled dreams. I thought the sight of the sky would clear my mind."

For the first time, Mr. Sumiyoshi spoke. "What kind of dreams?"

Toshikawa felt himself reddening again. He stared at the floor. He did not speak.

Mr. Sumiyoshi repeated his question.

Toshikawa kept his face turned to the floor but he rolled his eyes upward so he could see Mr. Sumiyoshi. He was a square man with huge muscles. He had thick hair that hung over his forehead. Out of the corner of his eye, Toshikawa could see Mr. Matsuda. His face and head were the shape of an egg. There was only a fringe of hair that circled his head from one ear to the other. His eyes were known to be weak, and he sometimes did without his lenses, squinting and feeling his way about the station.

"Well?"

Toshikawa saw Mr. Okubo look at Mr. Matsuda. Mr. Matsuda nodded slightly and Mr. Okubo said, "Answer Mr. Sumiyoshi, Toshikawa."

"I dreamed about Miss Inada."

Mr. Sumiyoshi said, "You dreamed about her? Troubling dreams? Love dreams?" He paused. "Sex dreams?"

Toshikawa did not speak, did not raise his eyes.

"You dreamed about Miss Inada, then you went for a walk outside the station instead of doing your work. You found Miss Inada at Stickney and she is dead."

Mr. Matsuda said, "Enough. Let's go and see. I'll leave you in charge, Sumiyoshi."

Soon Mr. Matsuda, Mr. Okubo and Toshikawa were wearing spacesuits. Toshikawa was relieved that he had changed to fresh clothing. The spacesuit he had worn earlier had not been soiled, only the trousers he wore beneath it.

They stood outside the station. Mr. Matsuda made a sign with his hand and they each turned on his radio. Mr. Matsuda said, "Take us to Miss Inada's body. Maybe she is not really dead. Maybe you were mistaken."

Toshikawa shivered. He knew that he had not been mistaken. He looked up. Phobos's rotation had moved it from the false, ruddy day of Mars light to the true day of the sun. He could see the sun itself, overhead, smaller than it appeared from either Earth or Mars, but brilliant and sharp.

He led the way, carefully retracing his steps. Near the edge of the crater, the places where the regolith had been smeared remained in contrast to the dust and pebbles around them. Where Miss Inada had lain there was another area where the regolith was disturbed. But there was no sign of Miss Inada.

Toshikawa said, "She's gone!"

Mr. Okubo said, "You're sure you saw her here?"

"Yes! Yes! I touched her. I picked her up, turned her over. I saw that she was dead."

Mr. Matsuda's voice was loud in Toshikawa's helmet. "You told Mr. Sumiyoshi that you dreamed of Miss Inada last night." Toshikawa said, "Yes."

"Do you dream of her often?"

Toshikawa did not reply. He saw Mr. Okubo begin to move toward him, as if to strike him. Mr. Matsuda raised a hand. Mr. Okubo stopped.

Mr. Matsuda said, "Toshikawa, where is Miss Inada?"

Toshikawa made a helpless shrug. He was standing on the rim of the Stickney crater. He could see its far edge and the old Russian station beyond. The bottom of the crater was still in shadow, but in a little while the sun would penetrate to its depths. Toshikawa wanted to throw himself into the crater, to disappear into the deep regolith on its bottom, but he dared not move.

Mr. Okubo said, "Maybe Miss Inada is safely inside the station, sir."

Mr. Matsuda said, "You think this man dreamed that he found her here? Are you sure he was even outside the station before now, Okubo?"

"He disappeared from his work."

"Hiding somewhere to drink some *sake* or to take a nap."

Toshikawa could see Mr. Okubo shrug, even through the spacesuit. What would become of him? They might ship him back to Mars, worse yet back to Earth. The home planet was crowded and poor, life there was short and unpleasant. Everyone knew that the future lay on Mars. On Mars and beyond. He had tried to enter the Mars Service as did so many young people . . . and so few were chosen. It must have been an error that had got him selected. Yet, here he was. He did not wish to return to Earth.

Mr. Okubo faced Toshikawa. His face was angry. His eyes burned like the eyes of a demon in an old piece of art. "You must tell the truth," he commanded.

"It is true," Toshikawa said. "I put on a spacesuit. I went for a walk. I knew it was wrong of me, but I could not work. I will tell you the truth now. I was so upset by my dream that I could not stay with the others. I could not do my work. That is why I left. Then I found her. Miss Inada. I know she was there. I know someone killed her."

Mr. Matsuda walked slowly around the area marked by dragging footprints. He stood for a long time over the larger area where the dry regolith was smeared like damp soil. He squatted and studied the ground there. Then he rose and faced the others. To Toshikawa he said, "You will return to crew quarters and remain there except for meals until you are summoned." To Mr. Okubo he said, "You will accompany this man and see to it that he obeys. You will hear from me when there is any change. In the meanwhile, carry out your duties. You will say nothing about this matter, to anyone."

*   *   *

Matsuda watched as the others bowed and left him. Then he returned to the marred regolith once again. He gazed across the bowl of Stickney crater at the old Russian space station. Sunlight glinted off a glass surface and Matsuda smiled, wondering for a moment if some Russian ghost had returned to haunt the abandoned station. He turned and walked back to the airlock and re-entered the research base.

Sumiyoshi was waiting in Matsuda's office. He stood as the senior official entered the room. He said nothing.

Matsuda lowered himself into the comfortable seat behind his desk. Like everyone and everything on Phobos, he weighed only a fraction of one percent of his normal weight. He had struggled through the adjustment that all newly arrived on Phobos had to. It was not the same as the weightlessness of space travel, but a different condition.

He studied the information screens in his desk, flicked a few keys and switches and read more information. Finally he looked up at Sumiyoshi. "I don't know what to make of this."

Sumiyoshi grunted. "A crazy one. To be ignored."

Matsuda shook his head. "There were marks."

"So? Maybe he made them himself. Better not to ask too many questions, Mr. Matsuda."

From where he sat, Sumiyoshi could see a face appear on a screen before Matsuda. To Sumiyoshi the face was nearly upside down. Yet he recognized it as that of Tamiko Itagaki. A widow of many years standing, Mrs. Itagaki was the highest ranking woman at the Phobos research station. She was the chief of the research group studying exobiology and exoarchaeology on Phobos.

Matsuda said, "Miss Inada works for you."

Sumiyoshi knew that Mrs. Itagaki could hear Matsuda's voice. If she was at her desk or near another screen, she could see his face as well.

Mrs. Itagaki said, "Yes, Mr. Matsuda. A very good worker. A very good scientist."

Matsuda said, "Do you know where she is at this moment?"

Sumiyoshi could see the expression on the face of Mrs. Itagaki, could see the lips move on her image on the screen as she spoke. "She has been working on the surface. I believe she is outside the station now."

"Please contact her," Matsuda said. "I will break contact with you, but please call me as soon as you hear from her. Or if you fail to contact her." He tapped a key built into the surface of his desk and the screen went blank.

Sumiyoshi said, "You're taking this seriously. Do you really think someone murdered Miss Inada? Why would anyone do such a thing?"

Matsuda shrugged. The jug of *sake* that he and Sumiyoshi had been sharing earlier was now empty. He said, "This is absurdly melodramatic, isn't it? I suppose this will make history, if Toshikawa is right and Miss Inada was murdered. The first murder on Phobos!"

Sumiyoshi grunted again. "Such is immortality." Then he added, "Do not pry too deeply into this."

The screen on Matsuda's desk brightened. Sumiyoshi watched as Matsuda studied the face before him. After a minute Matsuda said, "You reached her?"

Mrs. Itagaki said, "I can't reach her. If she's anywhere on Phobos, I should be able to. Unless she is deliberately not responding. Or—unless something terrible has happened to her!"

Matsuda groaned. "I think something terrible has happened. Please come to my office in fifteen minutes."

Mrs. Itagaki agreed.

Matsuda ordered Sumiyoshi to summon the other section managers to the same meeting. They were Eitaro Sekigawa, who as general crew chief for the Phobos Research Station was Wataru Okubo's boss, Yuzuro Takano, a single woman who was in charge of the station's carefully tended chemical farm, and Mitsuro Shigemura, who was chief scientist for technology development. These four represented the next level of management under Kakuji Matsuda. Eiji Sumiyoshi, as Matsuda's deputy, was theoretically in charge of no one, but he often acted in Matsuda's name and was regarded as exercising more influence on Matsuda than any of the four managers.

Matsuda welcomed the four managers to his office. He apologized for the crowding of his office. He ordered another jug of *sake* and cups for the four managers. When they had all paid their respects and each had downed a cup of hot *sake*, Mr. Matsuda addressed them.

"One of our crew members left the station a short time ago. When he returned he claimed to have found a body lying on the ground. He says that he examined the body and found signs of a wound. The victim was dead."

There were hisses of indrawn breath.

"Each of you must check on all personnel. See if anyone is missing."

"Was the body recovered?" Mr. Shigemura asked.

Mr. Matsuda said, "The crew member could not find the body when he returned. No one could."

Mrs. Takano said, "Did the crew member identify the body?"

Mr. Matsuda said, "I'm not sure there is a body. That's what we have to find out."

Mr. Shigemura said, "We can perform an automated personnel check. Perhaps you would ask Mr. Sumiyoshi, sir."

Mr. Matsuda said, "That could be done, yes. But I want actual, personal verification of every person in the station. Please proceed to your sections. Have your subordinates check up on their subordinates, until every person is physically accounted for. When you have your results, you will communicate them to me. Act promptly. You may report in via the desk."

The section managers left the station manager's office.

As soon as they were gone, Sumiyoshi asked Matsuda, "Do you think they'll find her? Or do you think she is really dead? Where is the body? Who moved it after Toshikawa found it? What do you plan to do?"

Matsuda smiled grimly at Sumiyoshi. "What a change from your former attitude, Eiji."

Sumiyoshi noted his superior's use of his personal name. He waited for Matsuda to continue.

"You seemed convinced that poor Toshikawa was out of his mind. That he had hallucinated finding the body."

"Mrs. Itagaki tried to contact Miss Inada."

"Should I give it a try myself?" Matsuda didn't wait for Sumiyoshi's recommendation. He touched the keys embedded in the top of his desk. He waited briefly. Then he said, "Nothing. I'm afraid that something terrible has happened."

"Then Toshikawa killed her." Matsuda looked from the screens and keys embedded in his desk, and watched Sumiyoshi closely. Sumiyoshi continued, "The man is dangerous. You know what he is. He had dreams about Miss Inada. He admitted that he tried to make advances to her and she rejected him. No surprise in that! He became obsessed. He dreamed about her. Finally he killed her."

Matsuda leaned back. He made a figure of his hands, lacing the fingers except for two that he kept upright. He said, "I had Christian friends in Nagasaki. One of them taught me this." He chanted, *"This is the church, and this is the steeple."* He swung his thumbs apart. *"Open the doors."* He turned his hands so that his laced fingers rose between himself and Sumiyoshi. *"And out come the people."*

Sumiyoshi said, "I have no idea what that means. I don't like Christians."

A light flashed on Matsuda's desk. He gestured to Sumiyoshi, touched the desk, took Eitaro Sekigawa's report. All the station's crew were accounted for, including Toshikawa, who was lying happily in his bunk looking at stories.

Matsuda thanked Sekigawa. In rapid order he received similar reports from Miss Takano, Mrs. Itagali, and Mr. Shigemura. The only exception was in Mrs. Itagaki's report. Miss Inada was still missing.

Matsuda now ordered a physical search of the station. This caused disruptions to the station's assigned tasks, but Matsuda ruled that the location of the missing Miss Inada took priority over all other matters. However, there was no sign of her anywhere in the station.

Toshikawa was questioned again by Matsuda. He stuck to his story, insisting that he had found Miss Inada's body while walking and that it had disappeared when he returned to show the body to Okubo and Matsuda. He was released and returned to duty under strict orders not to leave the station under any circumstances. The only exception would be if he was directly ordered to do so, and was accompanied by a person of higher authority.

Mr. Matsuda's next step was to communicate his quandary to his own immediate superior. This was Toshimitsu Matsuzaki, the manager of the main experimental settlement on Mars. In this capacity, Mr. Matsuzaki was the person in highest on-site authority in the entire Mars enterprise. His superiors were on Earth.

The experimental settlement was located beside the greatest dry riverbed at Nirgal Vallis. Large enterprises were planned for Mars, including self-sustaining settlements. At present, most food was still sent from Earth, a hugely expensive and inefficient enter-

prise. Great machines burrowed into the Martian surface, seeking the ancient water that had once flowed across the planet's surface. If it could be reached and exploited, natural farms could be established in place of the small and unsatisfactory chemical farms that operated on Mars and Phobos, and the settlements would take a major step toward self-sufficiency.

Communication between Phobos and Nirgal Vallis was possible whenever the little moon was above Nirgal's horizon. A transit of Mars's sky took four and a quarter hours. From Phobos's orbit, near the lower Roche limit, communication with the planet was practically instantaneous.

Mr. Matsuda spoke directly with Mr. Matsuzaki. He told him, speaking as directly as he could, what had happened.

Mr. Matsuzaki had a technical background and was highly regarded by all concerned with the Mars enterprise. He was an older man, from the northern island of Hokkaido. He had worked his way up through the ranks and his every year and every travail showed in the form of a line in his face. When he heard what had happened on Phobos, another line seemed to appear on his face.

He asked Mr. Matsuda to repeat in greater detail his interview with Toshikawa. Then he asked him to review the steps he had taken to find Miss Inada.

When Matsuda finished his explanations, Mr. Matsuzaki sighed softly. Despite the 6,000 kilometers that separated Mr. Matsuda from Mr. Matsuzaki, the sigh could be heard on Phobos.

Mr. Matsuzaki said, "What was the nature of Miss Inada's work on Phobos?"

"She was assigned to the exobiology and exoarchaeology group. Her manager was Miss Tamiko Itagaki."

"And her work—was it satisfactory?"

Matsuda was not sure how to answer. He finally decided to attempt a joke. "You know what they say. Exobiology is a discipline without a subject and exoarchaeology is an idea whose time has never come."

Matsuzaki said, "Yes, I have heard as much." The expression on his face revealed no trace of amusement.

Matsuda said, "Excuse me. My levity was inappropriate. As far as I know, Miss Inada's work was satisfactory. There is of course the frustration of working in a field with so little to show."

"There is the Face," Matsuzaki said.

"But I thought that was discredited."

"Yes."

"Cydonia was visited and the face was found to be a random

jumble of rocks. The resemblance to a human face is remarkable, but it is just an accident of nature. Just as there are faces seemingly carved on mountains on Earth."

"You know of Mount Rushmore in North America?"

"Are you telling me that the Face at Cydonia is an artifact?"

"You know Mr. Hajimi Ino of my staff?"

Mr. Matsuzaki's startling change of subject left Matsuda nonplused. He stammered, but was finally able to say, "I know his name. I do not believe I have ever met him."

"You will meet him shortly. I will send him up. Please offer Mr. Ino every courtesy. He acts in my name. He will report back to me."

Mr. Matsuzaki cut the communication between himself and Mr. Matsuda.

*   *   *

Mr. Ino's balloon rose from the surface of Nirgal Vallis shortly after Phobos next appeared over the horizon. Mr. Ino travelled alone. He was known as Mr. Matsuzaki's protégé. Perhaps it was the proximity of their homes that brought them together. They were both from small villages on Hokkaido, so remote that the local dialect was practically unintelligible to other Japanese. It was a local joke that residents of this region, when they moved south, had to learn standard Japanese as a second language. On occasion Matsuzaki and Ino conversed in their native dialect, reminiscing about life on their island.

They made a strange team. In childhood, Hajimi Ino had been teased by the others for his short, round body, his round, pudgy-cheeked face, and his sparse hair. They had called him Jizo. Curiosity piqued, he had found a Buddhist monk who told him tales of Jizo-bosatsu, a Bodhisattva who lived by the bank of the river Sai-no-kawara, giving consolation to the souls of dead infants. Thereafter, Hajimi Ino had taken secret pride in the name Jizo, and in his resemblance to the deity. Still, he would have liked to be taller, slimmer, and possessed of hair on his poll; he did his best in that regard by growing a moustache that joined his muttonchop whiskers.

As for Toshimitsu Matsuzaki, he more closely resembled the Shaka-nyorai, ascetic nearly to starvation, yet unconcerned with his bodily form. Yes, Ino and his superior Matsuzaki, like Jizo and Shaka. One sometimes wondered if laughter at the contrast was appropriate.

When Mr. Ino's balloon could rise no higher, its low-powered

rockets brought it the rest of the way to Phobos's orbit. Spring-loaded javelins like ancient whalers' harpoons punched into the rock beneath the thin regolith, and the balloon winched itself to contact.

Eiji Sumiyoshi met Mr. Ino as he entered the research station. "You've come to search for the missing Miss Inada," Sumiyoshi growled.

Mr. Ino, carefully removing his spacesuit, said, "I will need an office from which to work, quarters of course, and your full cooperation."

Sumiyoshi frowned. "What is the point of this? What do you think you're going to learn?"

Mr. Ino turned, an expression of annoyance on his round face. "I am going to find Miss Inada. She did not leave Phobos, did she?"

Sumiyoshi said, "How could she?"

"Then I will find her."

"In behalf of Mr. Matsuda, I pledge you our full cooperation." Sumiyoshi's eyes flickered away as he spoke.

Behind the polite words from both parties, there already lurked a mutual distrust, almost a hostility: a *kuroi kiri*. A cloud of suspicion like a black mist hovered between them, obscuring each from the other.

Sumiyoshi summoned Eitaro Sekigawa, who saw to it that Mr. Ino was settled in quarters and working space. As soon as this was accomplished, Mr. Ino paid a formal call on Mr. Matsuda.

With the limitation of space and materiel he could not dress for the occasion as he would have wished. Instead he stood outside Mr. Matsuda's office in his working costume. He was relieved, when Mr. Matsuda summoned him into the office, to see that Mr. Matsuda also wore ordinary clothing.

Mr. Matsuda offered Ino a comfortable seat, and asked if he would care for some *sake*.

Ino was uncertain how to respond. This was hardly the moment for a purely social visit. Matsuda might have in mind a *sakazuki*. In this case, the sharing of the hot beverage would be symbolic. Cups would be placed before Matsuda and Ino, and *sake* would be poured into them. If the quantities were equal, this would indicate that Matsuda and Ino regarded each other as equals. But if one received more than the other, then that person was regarded as the greater of the two—their inequality proportionate to the level the *sake* in their cups.

Ino represented Mr. Matsuzaki. Certainly Mr. Matsuzaki's

standing was greater than Mr. Matsuda's. But Ino himself was not of rank equal to Mr. Matsuda's.

Mr. Matsuda poured the *sake* himself. Ino watched him. He filled his own cup nearly to the rim. He filled Ino's barely half way. "I welcome you to Phobos, Mr. Ino." Matsuda downed his *sake*. "I thank you for your kindness," Ino said. He downed his own half cup of *sake*. He reached for the jug, filled Matsuda's cup two-thirds of the way to the rim, then filled his own cup to the very rim. "Mr. Matsuzaki sends his compliments."

Matsuda's eyes narrowed as he watched Ino's actions. He remained silent and motionless for a time. Finally he emptied his cup.

Following the *sakazuki*, Ino asked to see all records regarding the disappearance of Miss Inada. He reviewed the files, then personally interviewed Jiricho Toshikawa. By now, Toshikawa was tired of telling his story.

"I have told everything to Mr. Okubo, to Mr. Sekigawa, to Mr. Sumiyoshi, and to Mr. Matsuda. What more is there to say?"

Mr. Ino sat facing the kitchen helper. Toshikawa was even taller and more gangling than Ino's boss, Mr. Matsuzaki. The image of Jizo-bosatsu and Shaka-nyorai returned, only now Jiricho Toshikawa rather than Toshimitsu Matsuzaki played the role of the tall, gangling ascetic.

"Please," Ino said to Toshikawa, "if you would go over it once more. Perhaps, by hearing what you told the others, I will think of some question they omitted. Perhaps then you can tell me something new."

Toshikawa shrugged. He would rather be in his bunk with a jug of *sake* and a story record. On the other hand, that pleasant banishment had ended and he would now be back at work, suffering the abuse of Mr. Okubo, if he were not with Mr. Ino. He went over his story once more.

At the end of Toshikawa's story, Ino steepled his fingers and said, "No one ever asked you what Miss Inada was doing at the crater?"

Toshikawa looked puzzled. "No one."

Ino nodded. "Well, then, I shall ask you."

"Ask me what?"

"What Miss Inada was doing when she was stabbed." He thought, *This fellow is not very bright after all—but he might be able to help me nonetheless.*

"I don't know."

"But you were in love with her."

Toshikawa grew red. "I was not."

"But you told the others that you dreamed of her. And that you approached her one day in the dining commons."

"I liked her."

"Not loved her."

"No."

"Yet you had sex dreams about her?"

Toshikawa grew even redder. "I could not help it. I think about . . . things. About women. But . . ." He became silent, clearly miserable.

"That's normal, Toshikawa. Many men want women that they cannot have. But to kill her . . ." He raised his eyebrows.

Toshikawa said, "I did not kill her!"

"Where is her body now?"

"I don't know!"

Ino tried a while longer, but Toshikawa stuck with his story. Ino knew that if he worked on the kitchen helper long enough he could break him down, get a confession from him.

But it would be a false confession. It would not lead to the recovery of Miss Inada's body. And, most important, it would not lead to the identity of her killer.

He dismissed Toshikawa, who scrambled away like an ungainly long-legged crab.

Next, Ino sought out Tamiko Itagaki. He knew that she had been Miss Inada's superior. Perhaps information as to Miss Inada's work would help him in his investigation of her murder. Yes, her murder.

Officially, he was merely investigating her disappearance. Officially, Miss Inada might have fallen victim to an accidental death. She might even be alive and well, the mystery being merely one of where she had gone, and why. But in his heart, Mr. Ino believed that Miss Inada had indeed been done in. Murder was murder.

Ino was not, himself, very comfortable with women, and when Mrs. Itagaki entered the store room that had been cleared as a temporary office for Ino, he was momentarily flustered.

Mrs. Itagaki was herself upset. Her eyes and nose were reddened, as if she had been shedding tears. Still, she bowed to him and he returned the bow and asked her to be seated.

"Are you all right?" Ino asked.

Mrs. Itagaki said, "I am sorry. I was crying."

Ino's eyebrows rose. "Crying? But why?"

"Fumiko. Fumiko—Miss Inada."

"You cry because one of your workers is missing?"

"We were also friends. Very close friends."

"But why would you weep? You don't think she will show up?"

Mrs. Itagaki shook her head. She raised a hand to her mouth and seemed to chew on her knuckle.

Mr. Ino said, "Why wouldn't she show up? She is an exoarchaeologist, is she not? Maybe she is digging for artifacts."

"Maybe."

"You don't think so."

"Everyone thinks she's dead. That poor Mr. Toshikawa who found her—says he found her. How could she be alive?"

Ino made a gesture with his right hand, holding it before his shoulder with the fingers extended, the palm down. He twitched it to the side, as if shaking off water—or the previous subject, for he now changed the matter of the conversation.

"What can you tell me about Miss Inada's work?"

"She was an outstanding scientist. She had searched for alien artifacts on Luna, Mars, and Phobos."

"And had she found very many?"

Mrs. Itagaki lowered her face and shook her head. "No one has."

"The Face."

"The Face is just an oddity. A natural phenomenon."

Mr. Ino nodded. "So we are told."

Mrs. Itagaki raised her eyes. "Is it otherwise?"

"Did Miss Inada really believe there were alien artifacts to be found?"

"I do not know."

"What do you think? You were her very close friend."

"She believed there were artifacts."

"On Phobos?"

"I don't know. She thought the asteroids were the most likely locale. Especially the asteroids with eccentric orbits. She was interested in the Apollo asteroids. And in Hidalgo. Her favorite was Hidalgo."

"Then why was she searching on Phobos?"

"How could she visit Hidalgo? Maybe someday."

"Mrs. Itagaki, who would want to kill Miss Inada?"

"No one."

"But you told me that you think someone did."

"Toshikawa found her. She had been stabbed."

"You know this for a fact?"

"No. Only that he said so."

"Did you know that he has been under suspicion for her murder?"

"No."

"Do you think he might have done it?"

"I don't know."

There was a long silence. At last Mrs. Itagaki moved as if to rise and leave the room, but she stopped herself and faced Mr. Ino once more. "You said that the Face was not a natural feature."

"Did I say that?"

"Have Mr. Matsuzaki's investigators learned that it is artificial?"

"Mrs. Itagaki, people have been arguing about that for almost 200 years."

Now she remained silent. For a while they conducted a battle of silence. Finally Ino let out a sigh and said, "I'm surprised you did not learn this from Mr. Matsuzaki himself. Perhaps he wishes to withhold the information for reasons of his own."

"I deserve to know. I have given my life to this work. If he has found something out, I should know it."

Mr. Ino rubbed his bald pate with one hand. This was supposed to promote circulation of the blood in the scalp and encourage the growth of hair. It did not work. "Can you believe in a human face almost two kilometers long, carved in Martian rock, gazing straight up at the sky?"

"A scientist does not say, *I cannot believe that, never mind the evidence.* That's what a political fanatic, or a religious one, says. A scientist looks at the evidence and tries to figure out what it means."

"Fair enough. And what do you think the Face means?"

"I don't know."

"You don't think it was carved by people from another star? Or maybe by the ancient Martians? You know the cults on Earth, that believe we're all descended from Martians."

"I know them."

"They lived in the lush valleys of the ancient riverbeds. When Mars grew dry, they emigrated to Earth. Those great ancestors of ours. Of course they landed first on the islands of Japan, and spread to the rest of the world."

"And left behind the Face as their last and greatest achievement," Mrs. Itagaki supplied. "Staring eternally at the sky to remind their descendants of their ancestral home. Which is why we worship our ancestors, while most of the other nations have forgotten their origins."

"You think it's true?" Mr. Ino's scalp was definitely tingling. Perhaps the massage treatment was going to work at last.

"A scientist doesn't *believe* in such things without evidence, any more than she refuses to believe in the evidence that is before her."

"But the Face is there."

"Happenstance. How many rocks are there on Mars? Million upon uncounted million! Sheer chance dictates that here and there we will find one with a meaningful shape. With a shape that we interpret as meaningful, I should say, because it resonates with our own experience. If octopuses had invented space travel instead of humans, the Face would be meaningless."

"Spacefaring octopuses!" Mr. Ino burst into laughter. "*Hinin* in space. Unhuman creatures!"

"Laugh. I think *hinin* far more likely than Martian humans. What are the odds of identical intelligent species rising on two planets?"

"But I thought we did not originate on Earth. If we are all Martians . . ." He looked up at Mrs. Itagaki. She was the same height as he, or at least she seemed to be when they were both sitting.

"I thought you were investigating the disappearance of Miss Inada, Mr. Ino. If you wish me to conduct a seminar on the subject of theoretical exobiology or exoarchaeology, that can be arranged."

Mr. Ino sighed. "Very well. I'm sorry we have not been able to help each other."

Mrs. Itagaki rose and walked glidingly to the doorway. Once again she stopped and turned back to face Mr. Ino. The quarrelsomeness had left her demeanor. In a serious voice she asked, "Has there been an important discovery at the Face?"

Mr. Ino said, "Yes." He would say no more, and Mrs. Itagaki returned to her work.

Mr. Ino obtained a spacesuit and left the station. He carried with him a small kit of tools that he had brought from the Martian settlement at Nirgal Vallis. The kit attached easily to the belt of the spacesuit. Although he had not previously visited the site of Mr. Toshikawa's alleged discovery of Miss Inada's body, he had heard the locale described several times. He walked carefully to the place near the edge of the Stickney crater, where the regolith should be disrupted.

It was clear that some events had taken place to alter the natural condition of the regolith, but its present condition would be of little help in solving the problem that perplexed Mr. Ino. If

Miss Inada's body had been left undisturbed *in situ,* the condition of the ground surrounding the body and beneath it might well have told Mr. Ino much that he could use. But simpleminded Toshikawa had moved the body and disturbed the surface on which it lay. Mr. Ino studied the ground nonetheless, but at length he sighed and stood up straight. There was nothing left that would tell him the story of Miss Inada's tragic end.

Eventually it would be desirable to return the regolith to its original state, or as near to that state as was possible. Some worker, perhaps even Jiricho Toshikawa himself, would be assigned the simple task. Like a gardener in Japan, he would take a rake and smooth the dust and pebbles back to the appearance they had shown before the tragedy of Miss Inada.

Phobos had turned so that, as Mr. Ino stood near the lip of Stickney crater, Mars filled the sky overhead. Phobos's equatorial orbit had brought it near the terminator, and Ino watched dawn creep its way across the face of the planet even as Phobos raced toward the rising sun.

Mr. Ino opened the small case that he had carried with him and extracted an electronic telescope. With this he scanned the surface of the planet until he located the enigmatic Face. The Face had been called the Martian Sphinx, and its fascination and its long silence justified the name.

Lowering the telescope from its nearly vertical position to a horizontal one, Mr. Ino brought it to focus on the abandoned Russian space station on the far side of Stickney crater. The station's irregular shape stood in silhouette against distant stars. Mr. Ino set out, walking carefully around the rim of the crater, toward the Russian station.

The walk was a long one, more than a dozen kilometers, but against Phobos's minuscule gravity it was easy. From the opposite side of Stickney crater, the station had appeared tiny, no bigger than a child's toy. But as Ino approached it, he realized that it was sizable indeed.

He paused beneath the looming bulk of the Russian station and turned back toward the research station. He flicked on his suit radio and raised Mr. Matsuda's office. Mr. Matsuda was away from his desk at the moment, but his deputy, Mr. Sumiyoshi, spoke with Ino.

Mr. Ino told Mr. Sumiyoshi where he was, and asked him to make contact in four hours if Mr. Ino had neither returned to the station nor called in. Mr. Sumiyoshi agreed.

Mr. Ino made his way to the door of the Russian station. He

opened his kit and checked the tools that might be used to gain entry to the long-abandoned station, but before using them he attempted to operate the controls manually.

The Russian station was heavily built, its design astonishing in its crudity. Yet, even as Mr. Ino marveled at the rough, massive workmanship, he realized that the Russians and the even earlier Soviets had made great contributions to the exploration of space.

In those early years, the Americans were overrefining their space craft — and gutting their programs to waste their huge resources on self-indulgent luxuries and bizarre weapons that would never be used. The Japanese, meanwhile, were building a great technological and industrial plant, not yet ready to undertake ambitious goals.

It was then that the Soviets, with neither the wealth of the Americans nor the technology of the Japanese, had achieved astonishing things by sheer will and brute force.

The tools available to Ino, aside from the telescope he had already used, included a collapsing ladder, miniature lights and recorders, and a power grapnel. But none of these was needed.

To Mr. Ino's surprise, the door was not locked. He drew a light from his kit, switched it on and stepped inside the vacant station. The station was larger than he had expected. The first chamber was little more than a control station from which the long-ago cosmonauts had operated the airlock and docking mechanism.

Mr. Ino's light revealed blackened stanchions, long dead instruments, control levers left in whatever positions they had been set to when the last Russian left the station to climb aboard the rescue ship that carried him and his comrades back to Earth.

Why had the Russians abandoned their station of Phobos? No living person knew. Was it the political turmoil and economic distress of Russia itself? Had the Russians simply drawn back from space, like the ancient Romans from Britain? Or had they encountered something that frightened them? Were there indeed *hinin* — unhuman beings, *alien life-forms?* Was exobiology not ultimately a discipline without a subject, but merely a discipline whose subject was yet to be located?

He had taunted Mrs. Itagaki about the matter. But in fact he was far from convinced that *hinin* were chimaeras. He had never seen convincing evidence of their existence, but in the vastness of the universe, it was absurd to rule them out.

And there was the Face.

He stepped into the next chamber. It was utilitarian in nature, clearly a sleeping room. The Russians had rigged bunks, not the sleeping hammocks used in free-fall but flat supports like those used on submarines of the same era, a century or more ago.

The third chamber had once been a scientific work station, and someone had restored it to its former use. When had this been done? No dust settled, no uneaten snack spoiled. It was hard to tell whether the restoration had taken place a few days ago or half a century.

Rock samples lay in cases. Scientific instruments were protected by transparent hoods. One of the instruments was a scanning electron microscope. So much for one puzzle: this instrument could not have been placed here more than a few months ago: it was a model only recently developed and still more recently made available on Mars. Whoever had brought it to Phobos was involved, wittingly or otherwise, in this unhappiness. Clamped into position in the microscope was — a replica of the Face.

The model — Ino estimated — was only 200 millimeters from crown to chin, perhaps 85 millimeters across. Ino ducked and turned to see its back. Would it be flattened, or — no! It was a complete head. It might have been removed from a miniature statue.

His fingers reached toward the Face. It might indeed be the handiwork of an alien artist, a thing unmeasurably old and unimaginably exotic. It might even — he drew back — be a fossilized *hinin* rather than an artificial creation.

He reached toward it again. Through the sensitive fabric of his glove he ran his fingertips across the Face.

Finding a seat, Ino composed himself to contemplate his find. Someone had set up an exoarchaeology laboratory inside the Russian space station. Exoarchaeology was Miss Inada's field of study, and Miss Inada was missing under mysterious circumstances, probably murdered.

In all likelihood, then, Miss Inada and her disappearance were connected with this laboratory. Perhaps it was her workplace, and someone had learned of it, coveted it, disposed of Miss Inada. Perhaps her own superior, Mrs. Itagaki?

Ino shook his head in consternation.

The other likelihood was that someone other than Miss Inada had created this laboratory. If Miss Inada had then discovered it, her rival might have disposed of her.

Professional rivalry. Was that sufficient motive for murder? Killing had been done for lesser reasons in the past, Ino knew!

Unconsciously he raised one hand and tried to tug at his moustache, but his hand encountered only the transparent panel of his helmet.

He sighed and rose to his feet. He forgot himself for a moment, thinking of his 63 kilogram weight—at Nirgal Vallis. He managed to throw a hand up and avoid cracking his head on the ceiling.

Settling back onto his feet, he regained his equilibrium and explored the rest of the Russian station. There was a computer terminal bolted to a workbench in the makeshift lab. Ino studied it. It was clearly of modern design and manufacture, and the few markings on its exterior were in Kanji, not Cyrillic. It was obviously a new installation, not part of the abandoned Russian equipment.

Could he get a readout of the computer's contents? If so, he might well resolve the situation at once. But he feared that the computer was tripwired. An attempt at unauthorized access to its contents might not merely fail, but cause the machine to wipe its own memory.

There were those at Nirgal Vallis, or at Tithonius Chasma, who could tackle the computer problem. It would slow Ino's work to rely on their help, but it would safeguard valuable and potentially irretrievable information.

He was reluctant to move such evidence as the miniature Face and the computer, but he feared also to leave them behind. Whoever had killed Miss Inada—if she was dead—was almost certainly still on Phobos. If Ino left the evidence behind, the criminal might well return here. Aware that Ino had ballooned up from Nirgal Vallis, he would likely remove the Face and the computer. They might be hidden or even destroyed.

Ino set up a recorder and took moving depth images of the miniature Face and of the computer, making sure that the Kanji markings on the computer were clearly recorded. For the first time, he read those markings. They were manufacturer's indicia and patent numbers. He smiled.

He returned the recorder to his tool kit. He unbolted both the Face and the computer from their positions. He could not fit them into his tool kit or pockets, but he could carry them, one in each hand.

He left the Russian station, dogging the airlock behind him, and started back toward Stickney crater.

In a peculiar moment of accelerated time he realized that it was impossible, on airless Phobos, to hear someone move behind him. Unless the other's movements were transmitted through the regolith or the underlying rock, back through the soles of Ino's boots. . . .

Perhaps it was that, perhaps it was the slightest sight from the corner of his eye. In any case, he sensed the movement, the flashing knife that drove down at his spine. He lunged forward and away, too late to prevent the blade from puncturing his suit and plunging into his back.

His hands flew upward in spasm, the computer and the Face flying away from him. He tumbled forward, falling with strange slowness, almost as if he were flying across the ground, twisting as he went.

In a strange, almost dreamlike state, he knew that he was revolving. As he faced upward the sky revolved before his eyes. Then, as he faced downward, he saw that he had crossed the lip of Stickney crater and was floating across the accumulated dust and pebbles that lay within.

He crashed into the regolith. His impact sent a spray of fragments into the black sky. It also absorbed his forward momentum. As he sank into the deep regolith everything turned to an all-encompassing black mist. He slid downward through the regolith until he reached solid rock, then slid ever so slowly until he came to rest.

Where was he?

He put the question out of his mind. He would deal with it later. First, he must determine his physical condition. He tried moving his hands and feet. They responded. It was his reflexive attempt to dodge the descending blade that had saved him—the knife would otherwise likely have severed his spine!

He reached behind himself. The spacesuit made the maneuver difficult, and moving his arms through the regolith was like swimming in grainy mud. Still, and despite the pain of his knife wound, he was able to reach the center of his back. The knife was gone and he could feel the scar in his suit where the sealant had flowed into the opening. More good fortune—if the assailant had turned the knife and torn a triangular flap from the suit, the sealant would probably have failed—but a simple slit was a best case for the sealant.

Where was the knife now? Probably his assailant still had it. As well as the Face and the computer.

Ino carefully opened his tool kit. Working by feel, he extracted a light and turned it on. There was no discernible effect. He raised the light to his face. Through the transparent panel of his helmet he could see that the light was undamaged. It was as bright as ever. But when he turned it away and tried to see through the regolith, he was confronted by another impenetrable *kuroi kiri*. He shut off the light and returned it to his tool kit.

He inferred that he was in the center of the crater. He tried walking. It was almost impossible. He managed only two or three steps, each one an immense struggle, before realizing that this was hopeless. The exertion had caused terrible pains in his back, and he realized that he was bleeding from his wound. He could feel a slow accumulation of blood in his boots.

He flicked on his suit radio and tried to establish contact with the research station, but the regolith damped his transmission and he had to give that up as well. Unthinkingly, he tried once more to walk forward. His foot encountered a solid obstruction.

Even to bend over and feel what it was he had struck, required immense effort. But he managed. With both hands he felt the obstruction. It was a human form, clothed in a spacesuit. Through the flexible fabric he could tell that the person in the spacesuit was dead. He could not tell how long the person had been dead, for the body was now frozen. By its contours he could tell that it was the body of a woman.

Fumiko Inada, Ino thought. *Fumiko Inada!*

For a moment his mind returned to the mystery of Miss Inada. The missing body was now recovered, and the hapless Jiricho Toshikawa was vindicated. Ino did not think for a moment that Toshikawa was the killer—not after what Ino had found in the Russian space station.

But all of Ino's ratiocination—he might be a modern Inspector Imanishi for all that it mattered—was less than worthless, it was meaningless—if he remained here to die beside the body.

How could he get out of the crater? He thought of a crippled wasp dropped into a saucer. Unable to fly, the creature would struggle to crawl to safety, but the more nearly it approached the rim of its prison, the steeper would grow its walls until the prisoner slid helplessly back toward the center. There was no hope for the poor creature. It would have to await another life in which its fate might prove happier. It might find some Jizu-boratsu of the insect world to comfort its soul.

The wasp's problem was the absence of traction. Ino's was the black mist of regolith that held him helpless!

He opened his tool kit once more and felt its contents. Lights and recorders were useless here. His hand touched the collapsing ladder. That was self-powering. He extracted it from the kit, strug-

gled back down through regolith to a crouching position and set
the base of the ladder on the solid rock.

Now he set the ladder to open. Would dust and pebbles jam
its mechanism? Would the sheer weight of the regolith hold it
collapsed?

No.

Slowly the ladder expanded, climbing upward. It was invisible
to Ino, as was everything in the black mist of regolith. But he
could feel it rising, rising.

If it reached the surface of the regolith he might be able to
climb it, despite the weight and density of the material above him.
Then another idea flashed upon Mr. Ino. The ladder was hardly
above the height of his waist, so slowly was it expanding. He
stopped it, attached it to the belt of his spacesuit, and started it
again.

Slowly but steadily he felt himself lifted. He conjured images
of his home and his mother, of the icy winds that blew across the
Strait of Soya that separated Hokkaido from Sakhalin, of the fish-
ing town of Wakkanai where he had been born and where his
family had lived for uncounted generations. With his father and
the other men he had fished in summer and winter, had swum in
the icy strait in the coldest of storms. He had always been small,
and had toughened himself by this exercise so he could stand up
to other young men of the town.

He would like to see Earth again, for all its squalor and
poverty, its poisoned oceans and its choking air. If he didn't die
here in the black mist of Stickney crater on Phobos . . .

He closed his eyes. Opened them. There was no difference.
Closed them again. He could feel the internal workings of the
expanding ladder straining. A final quiver and it stopped.

Opened his eyes.

Kuroi kiri.

A gasp escaped his lips and he felt one more hot wetness. This
time it was not blood seeping from his wound, but hot tears falling
from his eyes.

He disconnected his belt from the ladder and climbed the
short extra distance to the very top. *Kuroi kiri.* He reached up and
felt his hand burst through the top layer of regolith.

He was racked by gasps of laughter and tears, puzzlement and
despair and hope. He pushed himself to his greatest height and
tried desperately to see, but there was only blackness. He lost his
balance and started to slide downward through the regolith once
more, but was able to grasp the ladder and regain his position.

He opened his tool kit. By now dust and pebbles had filled it, but he was able to feel the tools nonetheless. He drew out the power-grapnel and raised it over his head until he felt his hand once more break the surface of the regolith.

He held the power-grapnel in a horizontal position and fired it, holding to the handle for his life. He could neither see nor feel the grapnel strike and claw its way into bedrock. He could not tell whether it had reached the rim of the crater or had fallen into *kuroi kiri*. He tugged at it, knowing that if it yielded he was lost.

It held.

With one hand he pulled gently against the grapnel line. With his other hand and both legs he tried swimming through the regolith. He felt himself moving through the pebbles and dust. This was harder even than swimming in the Strait of Soya, battling icy cold, wind and waves. But he would do it.

He tried to get the power-grapnel to retract, to pull him to the rim of the crater, the shore of this terrible lake of *kuroi kiri*. But the dust must be too much for it. The mechanism refused to respond. He found that he could pull himself a fraction of a meter, swimming in the very rocks, then wrap the grapnel line around his forearm, then pull and swim again.

In time he stood on the edge of the crater. Stood there for a few seconds, then slid slowly to the ground.

He did not turn on his radio.

It was not a band of *hinin* who had stabbed him and thrown him into Stickney crater to die. It was not an alien being who had murdered Miss Inada and left her in the crater. It would be necessary to retrieve the murder victim's body before this matter was closed. But for now, Ino had to return to the research station and obtain treatment for his own wound.

He could see both the Russian station and the one from which he had started his terrible excursion. One to the left, one to the right. He headed for his own base. Even in Phobos's negligible gravity, walking was dreadfully difficult. His boots were partially filled with fluid—blood—that sloshed with each step. The wound in his back was painful. Every muscle in his body ached from the exertion of struggling through the lake of regolith inside Stickney crater.

Also, as he walked, he was constantly on the alert against his attacker. He dared not try to contact the research station. He had notified Deputy Manager Sumiyoshi of his intention to visit the Russian station. Upon leaving that station, he had been attacked and very nearly killed.

Obviously, Sumiyoshi was his attacker, and was consequently the prime suspect in the murder of Miss Inada. Matters were simplifying themselves, and if Ino managed not to be killed himself, he should establish Sumiyoshi as the criminal. Yes, things were growing simple.

Or were they? Ino had conversed with Sumiyoshi, but he had not asked Sumiyoshi to keep the conversation a secret. The deputy manager might have mentioned Ino's whereabouts to others. Or, for that matter, others might have monitored the conversation. The spacesuit-to-station radio link was anything but secure. It would be easy for a third party to overhear Ino's call to Sumiyoshi.

And for that third party to leave the station unobserved. There were no particular controls over egress and entry to the station. There were several airlocks. The staff of the station was small and its members were almost without exception well trained and trusted workers.

A fool like the kitchen-helper Toshikawa was a rare, perhaps unique, exception. Such a man might do anything. He was like an ancient *kabuki-mono*, a crazy whose conduct could not be predicted.

The murder might be anything from a *tsuji-giri*, a random killing with no more purpose than the testing of a new blade, to a coldly calculated act of untold implications. Having found the secret exoarchaeology lab in the Russian station, Ino was convinced of the latter.

He glanced behind him, cautiously turning in a full circle. There were rocks of every size, the rim of Stickney crater silhouetted now against the Milky Way itself. There was still the jagged shape of the Russian station.

Was there a shape crouched behind a rock? Did a tribe of *hinin* like the dwarf *Sukuna-bikona* dance like shadows, from hiding place to hiding place, ready to attack him?

Was he growing light-headed? Would he die before he reached his goal? Having solved the mystery of Fumiko Inada's murder, having discovered the illicit laboratory in the Russian station, having survived a murderous attack and escaped the *kuroi kiri* in Stickney crater—was he to fall dead a few kilometers from his goal?

He lost track of Mars days and solar days and eclipses as Phobos rotated on its own axis and raced in its bullet-like orbit around Mars.

Ino dragged himself toward the station. He fell to his knees, confused. He looked one way and saw a station, then the other way and saw another station. One was his own goal, toward which he was struggling. The other was the old Russian station. But his head swam, his eyes were dim. There was a black mist inside his helmet. He swiped at it with a gloved hand but only smeared more regolith dust on the outside of the panel.

He flopped onto his belly and dragged himself across the ground like an injured frog. He reached the station and dragged himself back to his feet, found an airlock and entered. He managed to work the lock and found himself in an unfamiliar corridor. Bright lights and clean walls glared at him, the brightness almost blinding after his time on the surface of Phobos.

A passing worker dressed in clean blouse and trousers and soft sandals stopped and stared at Ino.

Ino wig-wagged his hands, took a step toward the worker and stumbled.

The worker started to recoil from Ino. He must have looked like a coal miner freshly emerged from a day's labor in the black dust beneath the earth. But the man caught him in his arms and steadied him. He helped Ino to remove the helmet of his space-suit. He gaped at Ino, muttered a few words, then lifted him in his arms—an easy task in this gravity—and carried him through phantasmagoric corridors to the station's tiny infirmary.

Strangers removed the spacesuit, studied Ino's wound, made him wiggle his fingers and toes for them, disinfected and stitched the wound. There was a bustle and whispered conversation. Then the workers backed away, making an opening.

Through it strode Manager Kakuji Matsuda.

"Mr. Ino!" Concern was clearly visible on Mr. Matsuda's face.

Ino attempted a bow, managing to dip his head slightly without quite removing it from a pillow. His wound was bandaged and he was able to lie on his back without great pain. A light sheet covered him and prevented him from throwing himself from the bed with any exertion.

Mr. Matsuda returned the attempted bow. "Mr. Ino," he said again, "what happened to you? Word was brought to me that you were injured."

"Attacked," Ino said.

"Attacked? By whom? What happened?"

Ino started to tell his story, then halted. Deputy Manager Sumiyoshi was still his prime suspect. What was the relationship between Manager Matsuda and his chief aide? Were they in league in some criminal enterprise? Had Miss Inada discovered their illicit work, and was her death the reward for that discovery? Perhaps she had reported her findings to Sumiyoshi, not suspecting that he himself was involved in the enterprise. Was Mr. Matsuda innocent? Ignorant of Sumiyoshi's crimes? Or was he Sumiyoshi's colleague, even his mentor, in the scheme?

Ino had never noticed Sumiyoshi's hands. Perhaps the last joint of a finger was missing, had been presented to Matsuda at an earlier time. They might be members of the same criminal *gumi*, gang; of the same *ikka*, family. If Sumiyoshi played *kobun* to Matsuda's *oyabun*, then Matsuda would be bound by compassionate duty and loyalty to protect Sumiyoshi.

That protection could cost Ino his life.

"I do not know what happened," he told Matsuda. "I searched for Miss Inada, for her remains, or—thinking she might be injured or trapped somehow—for Miss Inada herself."

"Did you find her?"

"I was struck from behind. Fortunately the wound was not fatal. My spacesuit sealed properly and saved my life."

"Did you find Miss Inada?" Mr. Matsuda asked again.

Ino gritted his teeth. To lie to Manager Matsuda was against his training and his personal principles, but if Matsuda was a *kuromako*—the godfather of a criminal *gumi*—then Ino must not play into his hands.

"I did not find her," he lied. But he knew that he was a poor liar.

Matsuda grunted. "You do not look well, Ino."

Ino said nothing.

"Well, you rest and recover, Ino. I will continue the investigation. You come and see me as soon as you can. In the meanwhile, I will apprise Mr. Matsuzaki of your condition, and reassure him that you are making a rapid recovery."

"Thank you," Ino said. Again he managed a partial bow. Matsuda returned the bow and left the room.

When the medical workers returned, Ino asked one of them where Phobos was in relation to Mars. The worker, a middle-aged woman who reminded Ino of his mother's younger sister, said she did not know. She offered to ask Mr. Shigemura, a manager in technology development who maintained frequent communication with Mars surface.

Mr. Ino thanked the worker for her assistance.

Mr. Shigemura arrived at Mr. Ino's bedside shortly. They exchanged greetings and Mr. Ino repeated his inquiry. Based on information provided by Mr. Shigemura, Mr. Ino realized that he would be able to reach Nirgal Vallis by radio very shortly. He enlisted Mr. Shigemura's assistance in gaining access to a Phobos-Mars radio link.

This, Mr. Ino realized, was itself a risky business. If Manager Matsuda or Deputy Manager Sumiyoshi knew that he was in direct communication with Mr. Matsuzaki at Nirgal, they might well suspect that he was onto them and take drastic action against him. This was their base, operated by their staff. Ino was on his own.

He sensed in Shigemura a trustworthy and moral character, and decided to run the risk of trusting him. He asked Shigemura to keep confidential the fact that he was providing assistance to Ino. Shigemura agreed.

When the link was completed, Ino, speaking still from his sick bed, asked to speak with Mr. Matsuzaki.

Misfortune!

Ino learned that Mt. Matsuzaki was not at Nirgal Vallis. He had travelled by surface vehicle to attend a planning meeting with Shin Kisaburo, his counterpart at Tithonius Chasma in the Marineris region. Ino knew of Kisaburo, although he had never met him.

He requested Mr. Matsuzaki's office to patch the call through to Mr. Matsuzaki in Tithonius. He did not wish to terminate the call and place another; further, he was uncertain of being able to reach Tithonius directly at this time, and he did not want to let precious hours pass before he reached Mr. Matsuzaki.

The call was completed, although the extra link added static and reduced the quality of the signal. Still, he was able to understand Matsuzaki, and to make himself understood.

Mr. Matsuzaki asked if all was well, and what progress he was making in the Inada investigation.

Ino's thoughts flew like bolts of lightning. Matsuzaki's question meant that Matsuda had not communicated with him, despite his statement that he intended to do so. Ino feared that this call might be monitored by Matsuda or Sumiyoshi. He dared not speak openly, yet he wanted desperately to let Matsuzaki know the situation on Phobos.

He switched from standard Japanese to the dialect of northern Hokkaido, emphasizing the peculiar pronunciation and local idioms as much as possible. He could not be certain, but he knew that it was highly likely that no one else on Phobos could understand the northern Hokkaido dialect. He was fairly sure that his conversation with Mr. Matsuzaki would be incomprehensible to anyone on Phobos who overheard.

As succinctly as possible, Ino told Mr. Matsuzaki his experiences since arriving on Phobos. He included not only the attack upon himself and his narrow brush with death, but also his discovery of the secret laboratory in the Russian station, the presence there of the miniature Face and the computer, and the grisly find of Miss Inada's body in the Stickney crater.

To Ino's chagrin, Mr. Matsuzaki showed less interest in Ino's investigation of Miss Inada's disappearance and his own near brush with death than in his discovery of the laboratory in the Russian station and the miniature Face and computer that Ino had found there. He insisted on the most detailed description of the Face. He seemed bitterly disappointed by Ino's having lost the Face and the computer records that presumably related to it. He was most pleased with the information that Ino had made visual records of the Face, and that the recorder in his tool kit had not been lost.

Even as the conversation took place, Ino experienced a moment of panic. *Where was his tool kit?* It was on a shelf beneath his bed! Mr. Matsuzaki instructed Ino to safeguard the record of the Face at all cost.

Ino asked Mr. Matsuzaki what course he was to follow, and particularly what insight Mr. Matsuzaki could offer with regard to the miniature Face.

Taking care to speak in as obscure a fashion as possible, Mr. Matsuzaki told Ino what had been discovered at Cydonia.

Laser X-ray photography had been applied to the Face and a hollow chamber had been located deep within the rock. High-definition laser X-rays had determined that the chamber was filled with miniature replicas of the Face.

What could this possibly mean? Ino asked.

Mr. Matsuzaki said that he did not know. No one was certain. He and Mr. Kisaburo were discussing the problem, with advice from the technicians who had made the discovery. Several theories had been offered:

That the Face was not really a representation of the head of a humanoid being, but was in face a fossilized *whole body* of a creature that only coincidentally resembled a human face . . . In this case, the miniature Heads were nothing less than the unborn young—*hinin!*

That the Face was a cultural artifact, left behind by ancient Martians, with the miniature Faces a form of data redundancy designed to transmit the same message as the great Face . . . In this case, perhaps the theory of ancient Martian immigrants to Earth was correct.

That the Face was a message from aliens, not Martians but "third party" *hinin*, intended to be received by Martians but instead found by Earth-based explorers long after the extinction of the Martians . . . In this case, the miniature Heads might be redundant data records—or might contain additional data of incalculable importance.

That the Face was a record created by long-forgotten travelers *from Earth* . . . The old and laughingly discredited notion of "ancient astronauts" was thus revived, but with the twist that the astronauts were members of a terrestrial civilization that rose to the heights of space travel, then fell to such a depth that its very existence was forgotten by later generations.

There were other notions, but all turned out to be variations on those four.

Ino was affected by the obvious excitement of Matsuzaki's narrative, but he was torn by anxiety over his own situation. He asked, "What is the source of the Face that I found in the Russian space station?"

Mr. Matsuzaki said, "We must recover the Face at all costs. If we study its composition, we should be able to learn at least whether it originated on Mars or on Phobos."

"But why was the secret laboratory created in the Russian station? And why was Miss Inada killed?"

A long groan escaped Mr. Matsuzaki. Across the thousands of kilometers of vacuum, Ino could feel it. He shuddered. Mr. Matsuzaki said, "The finds have been kept secret as much as possible, but word must surely have got back to Earth. *Yashi gurentai* are involved."

"Gangsters! Collectors!"

"Yes! You know that great art collectors have coveted rarities in all ages. Paintings, sculptures, manuscripts have been the subject of theft by *gumi* and *machi-yakko* for centuries. Think of what some *kuromako* sitting in his mansion in Tokyo would give for that miniature Face. I believe you have uncovered the most dangerous and far-flung smuggling ring of all time. They are out to steal that Face for a *kuromako* and sell it to him for a fortune—or present it to him as a token of fealty!"

Ino felt cold. His body shook and his hands quivered. "What do I do?"

Mr. Matsuzaki said, "I will send assistance to you, but in the meantime you must deal with the situation yourself."

"You have no further instructions?" Ino was appalled. He felt betrayed, abandoned.

"Have you met Mrs. Itagaki?"

"Briefly."

"I have known her for many years. Before she was married, we —but never mind that. I would trust her in any circumstance. Talk with her. Use my name."

The conversation ended.

The spacesuit Ino had worn during his outing had been removed, surely to be examined and tested before being returned to service. His own clothing, torn and blood-soaked, had been removed. Ino had no idea where it had been taken, but he was able to dress in the simple blouse, trousers, and sandals that most of the station personnel used.

To his amazement no one interfered with him as he dressed in an outfit removed from a storage cabinet. Before he was able to leave sick bay he was confronted with the looming presence of Eiji Sumiyoshi.

For a moment Sumiyoshi glared at Ino in silence.

Ino sat back on the edge of his bed.

Sumiyoshi was carrying a lidded work-box with him. It gave him the look of a busy bureaucrat, hustling from task to task with files of important work, stopping to pay a brief duty-call on an injured person. He placed the work-box on the floor beside Ino's bed, then seated himself in a visitor's chair.

Ino hardly knew what to say to the deputy manager. Should he confront him, accuse him? Sumiyoshi towered over Ino; with his massive frame and thick muscles, he could overpower Ino in a moment. But even beyond personal confrontation, Ino was relatively powerless; Sumiyoshi was the second in command of the entire station, could call for assistance at any moment.

Mr. Matsuzaki had said that he was sending help. But what help? And how quickly?

Sumiyoshi might not know how much Ino had learned, how much he had deduced. And if Sumiyoshi attacked Ino, even had him killed, be must know that there would be a further investigation at Mr. Matsuzaki's insistence.

"How are you feeling?" Sumiyoshi growled.

The banal question coming on the heels of the ominous silence caused Ino to laugh. He thought quickly, decided that Sumiyoshi had chosen to play a game of bland innocence. He of the flower cards!

"My back pains me, but not so badly that I cannot bear it."

"What happened?"

"I fell into Stickney crater. I felt a pain in my back. I don't know what it was—maybe a micrometeorite."

"And it knocked you into the crater?"

"I was lucky. I might have died."

Sumiyoshi nodded gravely. "Such incidents are incredibly rare. You'll rate a footnote in some history book some day. And what happened after you tumbled into the crater?"

Ino smiled modestly. "It was a struggle, but I managed to climb back out and return here. They've been very kind to me, taken excellent care of me." Two could play the game of the bland.

Another growl from Sumiyoshi. "We're proud of our staff. I understand that you had a chat with Mr. Matsuzaki. When you speak with him next, please tender respects of Mr. Matsuda and myself."

"I will do so, rest assured."

Sumiyoshi said, "By the way, what did you and Mr. Matsuzaki discuss?"

A dangerous moment.

"My work. May I inquire, how did you know of this conversation?"

"Was it secret?"

"No. Do you monitor all Phobos-Mars communications?"

Sumiyoshi reached to shake hands with Ino, ignoring the question.

Stalemate.

Even as their hands remained clasped, Sumiyoshi said, "What will you do now? Return to Nirgal Vallis to recuperate?"

"Your thoughtfulness is appreciated. But I am well enough to resume my duties. That is my intention."

Sumiyoshi nodded. "Dangerous work. You're lucky to be alive now. Take care, Ino."

Ino shot a look at Sumiyoshi's right hand before the handclasp was broken. No joint was missing from any finger. He tried to catch a glimpse of Sumiyoshi's left hand, but it was concealed as Sumiyoshi reached for the work-box he had carried into the sickbay. He fumbled with the work-box for a moment, then rose to his feet. Ino could still not see Sumiyoshi's left hand.

As soon as Sumiyoshi had departed, Ino climbed from his bed. He crouched on the floor beside his bed and reached for his tool kit.

Gone.

Ino gritted his teeth and sucked air in anguish and self-despair. The work-box! How obvious! And Ino, like a *gyangu* or a *kabuki-mono*—a stupid gangster or a madman—had permitted himself to be distracted by Sumiyoshi's conversation. He had been eager to see if the deputy manager had ever engaged in *yubitsume*—the symbolic pledge of loyalty to an *oyabun* by cutting off and presenting him with a joint of his own finger. He had learned nothing and he had let Sumiyoshi get away with his tool kit.

The kit that contained his recorders, that contained all his records of the illicit laboratory in the Russian station and the miniature Face that he had found there.

He moaned and trudged from the sick-bay. He sought out a directory of the research station. He was amazed that no one paid attention to him. He expected word to have spread of his presence, and of his experiences on Phobos. But the workers went about their business, ignoring the stranger in their midst.

At length he found the laboratory presided over by Mrs. Itagaki. He was surprised to find that it was neither large nor impressively furnished. A few workers sat at lab benches, working on samples of bedrock and regolith. Phobos was unlike Mars, where eons of geological activity had created a thin layer of true soil—for all that it was apparently sterile. On Phobos there was only the bedrock, and regolith of pebbles and dust that coated the little moon.

Mrs. Itagaki greeted Mr. Ino. She was pleased to have him visit her laboratory, she told him. She offered to show him around, to explain her work to him.

Ino said, "Mr. Toshimitsu Matsuzaki offers his respects and his greetings."

Mrs. Itagaki ducked her head and covered her mouth with one hand, holding the posture for the briefest instant. Then she lowered her hand and raised her face once again, her expression unreadable.

To Ino it was as if he had seen a flash of a world lost in time, a Japan courtly and mannered. In this world Mrs. Itagaki would blush and retire shyly to women's quarters while Ino and other men carried out their business, attended perhaps by silent, efficient women who would tend to their comforts and needs without intruding upon their serious conversation.

The modern Mrs. Itagaki said, "Please return my best wishes to Mr. Matsuzaki." She paused. "Now, how may I assist you?"

"You know why I am here," Ino said.

"Yes."

"Miss Inada was murdered."

"So Mr. Toshikawa says."

"No. It is a fact." Ino fixed Mrs. Itagaki with his eyes. "I will tell you everything that I know. This place is secure?"

Mrs. Itagaki rose and led him into a small room, hardly larger than a cabinet. A large machine was slowly grinding a bin of rocks into powder. "For analysis," Mrs. Itagaki said. "Also, no one can overhear. What do you know?"

"I found Miss Inada's body." He told her his story, from his arrival on Phobos to the removal of his tool kit by Mr. Sumiyoshi. When he mentioned the miniature Face, Mrs. Itagaki gasped. She seemed eager to question him about it, but Ino continued his narrative. When he told of losing the miniature, she appeared disappointed, and when he described his discovery of Miss Inada's body, tears appeared in Mrs. Itagaki's eyes.

Mrs. Itagaki regained her composure, then nodded. "I knew she was dead. My heart told me as much. She was like a daughter. Now she is a victim."

"Tell me about her work, please. It is my job to find the killer. I think I know that, although his behavior is also explainable in an innocent manner. One learns, in my business, that a personally dislikable person, or one whose behavior in other matters is improper, is not necessarily the perpetrator of the crime one is investigating."

"Who?"

"Tell me about Miss Inada's work."

"Ours is a frustrating field, Mr. Ino. We are like the radio searchers who strive endlessly to receive signals from distant *hinin*. They seek evidence of alien life on the planets of remote stars—or living in the depths of space. We seek contact with beings long dead, long disappeared from the worlds."

Her expression was that of a pilgrim who had lost faith that she would ever reach her goal, yet continued to travel and search in her hopeless cause, having nothing other to live for. Ino thought of the balanced principles of *giri* and *ninjo*, duty and compassion. His duty demanded that he, too, continue to pursue his goal, whatever the odds against achieving it. And compassion . . . Compassion for Miss Inada was displaced, useless. Compassion for Mrs. Itagaki—that, he felt.

He waited for Mrs. Itagaki to continue.

"You know that Mars once had volcanoes and great flowing rivers, features to dwarf their counterparts on Earth even though Earth is so much larger a planet. The heat, the energy, the flowing waters, should have brought forth life. Yet we find no signs of life."

"The Face."

"Always we return to that."

Could he share with her what Mr. Matsuzaki had told him, of the laser X-ray examination of the Face, of the discovery of the chamber within and the miniature Faces it contained? He withheld the information.

"Is it not evidence of life?" he asked, instead.

"Two experts will give you three opinions," Mrs. Itagaki replied. "I don't know."

"But the miniature that was in the Russian station . . ."

"Yes." Mrs. Itagaki smiled: the pilgrim whose faith had been restored. "The miniature. It is convincing proof."

"Where did it come from? Why is it not mentioned anywhere, in any literature, in any reports?"

"Mr. Ino, I never knew of it until you told me."

"But—Miss Inada—the laboratory—"

"I knew she was up to something. Some project that she didn't tell me about. I was waiting for her to speak. I knew there must be a good reason, I knew that she would tell me when she had something to tell. I was eager to know, but I respected her wishes, also."

The grinding machine roared and sputtered. Mrs. Itagaki made an adjustment to it, and the machine resumed its steady roaring.

"Mrs. Itagaki, now that you know of the miniature Face—what is its meaning? You are the expert. I am a mere assistant to Mr. Matsuzaki. He sends me out, I gather a few facts and report back to him. But you are a leading scientist. What is the little Face?"

"I wish I could examine it. Or see Miss Inada's files—the files in the computer. Even your own records would be helpful."

"What is lost is lost."

"Surely you don't believe that. What is lost may be recovered, don't you agree?"

Ino nodded. "Of course. We must not lose hope." He smiled, tugged at his moustache. Mrs. Itagaki was just his own height. He felt most comfortable with her. "A passing moment, a black mist of despair. Please continue."

"A miniature Face? Then there must be life, past or present. Martian life. Alien life. *Hinin*. Yes, *hinin*. The shining sword of the exobiologist."

"But where are the Martians?"

"Who knows? Probably they lived and died long ago. Millions of years. Perhaps they live in distant stars, or in secret redoubts beneath Mars. Perhaps we are the Martians."

Ino nodded. The theories resonated with those he had already heard. He said, "I believe that Deputy Manager Sumiyoshi killed Miss Inada."

Mrs. Itagaki stood motionless for twenty beats of the heart. Then she said, "Why?"

"For the Face. Think of its value to some collector of fine *objets d'art*. Incalculable. A unique specimen. The only known work of art of an alien hand, an alien race. The prestige it would confer upon its possessor would make him the greatest *kuromako* in all the world."

Mrs. Itagaki drew a dainty kerchief from the sleeve of her blouse and wiped her eyes.

Mr. Ino took her hand to comfort her. The act required all of his courage, and was rewarded with a small smile.

"You believe he knew of her secret laboratory?"

"Obviously."

"And he killed her and left her body near Stickney crater, where it was discovered by Mr. Toshikawa. Why would he leave her like that? Leave her to be discovered, then return and remove the body. Why?"

"*Gurentai* operate as much by terror of force as they do by the actuality of force. Think of the terror and confusion that this incident creates—far more than simple murder would have."

Mrs. Itagaki shook her head. "It's beyond me. I only wished to do my job, and to be a friend to Miss Inada. A beautiful young woman. You never met her. Hair like midnight, eyes like bottomless ponds. Her hands—strong hands, the hands of a scientist who worked with hard materials. There were scars and signs of old injuries in her hands. Yet they could be as graceful and as quick as darting carp, as gentle as the breast of a dove." She pressed her handkerchief to her eyes.

"All right," Ino said. "We have to act."

She looked at him unspeakingly.

"How many people can we rely on in this station?"

"My own staff. There are six. Two or three I am certain of. Two more doubtful. The others I would not trust."

"Anyone else? What about Mr. Matsuda?"

"The manager? Mr. Matsuda?"

"Yes," Ino hissed.

"You question the manager? You doubt his honesty?" She seemed more shocked by the notion that Matsuda might be corrupt than by anything that had gone before. Yet *gurentai* had their tentacles everywhere. Men and institutions anywhere could be polluted by them.

"I could never question Mr. Matsuda." Mrs. Itagaki shuddered visibly.

And yet, Ino thought, if Sumiyoshi was *kobun*, someone had to be his *oyabun*. Who could it be? He tugged at his moustache with one hand and rubbed his scalp with the other. Mrs. Itagaki might not question the integrity of her boss. Such loyalty in itself was admirable. But if Matsuda had been corrupted by gangsters, he was doubly guilty—guilty of whatever illegal acts he had been induced to commit, and guilty of betraying the trust of the research organization, of those above him who had placed authority in his hands and by those below him, to whom he was obligated to wield that authority with honor and propriety.

Ino shook his head to clear it of such contemplative concerns. He must deal with the reality of the moment. "Mrs. Itagaki, would you know if Mr. Sumiyoshi had recovered the missing Face and computer?"

Mrs. Itagaki shook her head. "If the research were licit, it would be under my department, and I would have been informed of the find. But since the original research was never officially sanctioned . . ." She tucked handkerchief back into her sleeve and looked straight at Mr. Ino. "And if Mr. Sumiyoshi is some sort of gangster . . ."

Ino nodded and made an encouraging sound somewhere between a hum and a grunt. He felt himself straining, striving to make Mrs. Itagaki continue by sheer force of will.

"No," she continued, "I might not know of it. Mr. Sumiyoshi might have hidden the objects. I do not know where."

"Mrs. Itagaki." He took her hands in his own. Her fingers, too, were stained and scarred and callused by many years of work with specimens, chemicals, and tools. "Mrs. Itagaki, please summon those workers whom you trust. They must have your total confidence. Better two trustworthy persons than a dozen doubtful ones. Will you do this for me?"

"I can. But—why?"

"To return to Stickney crater and to the Russian station. To see if we can recover the Face and the computer. To see what evidence we can find concerning Miss Inada. You and I to search. The others to assist—and to mount guard. Mr. Sumiyoshi might attack a single person, but he would not dare attack a party."

Mrs. Itagaki complied. Before long four persons were donning spacesuits and making their separate ways to as many airlocks. Ino had decided that this would attract less attention than a party of four assembling and leaving the station together.

They reassembled at the rim of Stickney crater. They had planned their foray in whispered conversation and passed notes under the protection of the same noisy machine that had covered the discussion between Mr. Ino and Mrs. Itagaki.

It was their intention to maintain radio silence if at all possible. What conversation was needed, would take place within the Russian station. It was their hope that the station's heavy metal bulkheads and fittings would prevent eavesdropping by Sumiyoshi or any ally of his.

As they stepped inside the Russian station, Ino took the lead and proceeded directly to Miss Inada's secret laboratory—or rather, to the chamber where the laboratory had been. There were signs of disorder and of the removal of equipment, but there remained no laboratory nor any but the most flimsy suggestion that a laboratory had ever existed in this space.

Mrs. Itagaki looked at Mr. Ino inquiringly. Behind her, Mr. Ino could see her two assistants. They were a man and a woman. Mrs. Itagaki had introduced them to Ino before they had donned their spacesuits. They were a married couple, both post-doctoral students. He was from the town of Otomari on Aniwa Bay, even farther north than Mr. Ino's home region on Hokkaido. She was from the small city of Niihama on Shikoku. They had met while attending graduate school in Canada, and returned to Japan to be married.

To Mr. Ino it was obvious that whichever way Mrs. Itagaki leaned, the young couple would leap.

"There is nothing here," he said. He could not keep the bitterness from his voice, nor was there anything he would have done to hide it.

"What now?" He could see Mrs. Itagaki's lips move even as he heard her voice inside his helmet. His scalp tingled and itched, and he reached to massage it but only touched his gloved hand to the top of his helmet.

"I can retrace my steps to the place where I was stabbed. Maybe we can find the computer or the miniature Face."

"Don't you think your attacker would have gathered them up and brought them back to the station? To either station, the Russian or our own?"

"Let's do what we can!" Ino felt anger rising within him and even heard it in his own voice. Mrs. Itagaki recoiled inside her helmet. Mr. Ino sucked air between his teeth, breathed it deep into his lungs despite the unpleasant, slightly-oily flavor that the spacesuit gave it. "I'm sorry," he said. "Let us try."

Mrs. Itagaki nodded.

They set out, Ino in the lead, Mrs. Itagaki beside him. The two others were split, one to either side, trailing Mr. Ino and Mrs. Itagaki by half a dozen paces. They turned frequently, searching for the two objects.

Even while still in the Russian station, Mrs. Itagaki had raised an intriguing question. What were the lighting conditions when Mr. Ino was attacked and the two objects lost?

Mr. Ino examined his memory and determined that Stickney had been in full Phobos light. Under the red glare of the planet, the regolith would have appeared black. But now Phobos was in a different posture. Phobos was passing over the daylight half of Mars, an almost invisible black dot against the nearly black sky except to those directly beneath the moon, who would see it as a speck sliding rapidly across the face of the sun.

But Stickney was faced away from Mars, bathed in direct, bright sunlight. The regolith would appear gray, and an object like the Face or the computer might capture a glinting ray of sunlight. Might scream out to a searcher, *Here am I!*

Mr. Ino and Mrs. Itagaki walked like a couple many years younger, striding slowly. But their eyes would have betrayed them, for they were not fixed on each other. Instead they scanned the ground to the left, to the right, to the left, to the right.

They were close to Stickney. Years of explorers and workers had obliterated the virgin appearance of the regolith, but more workers, the likes of the hapless Jiricho Toshikawa, had trudged across the surface with rakes in hand, restoring its natural unmarked face.

Someone—Mr. Sumiyoshi or someone else—had returned to this sector after the attack on Mr. Ino. All visible traces of the former incident were gone.

Mr. Ino exhaled, thinking that someone would have to return here once more and remove the signs of his newest outing with Mrs. Itagaki and the young scientists.

But somehow he should be able to re-establish his location at the time of the attack. It had been a moment of such importance, surely he could not have lost all track of it.

The lighting was different, yes. But shapes remained the same. He looked at the rim of Stickney, then turned and looked back at the Russian station. There were irregularities in the shape of the rim. If he could find the configuration that he had seen just before the knife struck . . .

Yes. He believed that he had found it. By hand signals he told the others what he had done. Mrs. Itagaki understood his message at once. She stood in his place, her hands upturned as if holding the two important objects. Ino raised his own hand, plunged it, empty, toward her back. As if he held a knife.

Mrs. Itagaki twisted forward, as she knew Ino had done. She flung her hands upward in an instinctive gesture.

Did the others understand?

They did, clearly, for both nodded, then resumed an even closer scrutiny of the ground, following the invisible trajectory of the two imaginary objects Mrs. Itagaki had thrown.

Ino's recollection was that the Face was far more massive than the small computer. Even in Phobos's neligible gravity, he had felt its weightiness when he handled it.

With his eyes he drew an invisible line from Mrs. Itagaki's right hand, the line along which the computer would have travelled. Depending on the height of its trajectory, it might have bounced or it might have flown directly into the crater.

One of the younger scientists had followed Mrs. Itagaki's movement. Mr. Ino saw the spacesuited figure moving forward, casting a sharp, black shadow against the gray regolith. The scientist pointed with one gloved hand, drawing that imaginary line in the dust and pebbles. At the edge of the crater the scientist stood, hands on hips, staring down into the crater helplessly.

Mr. Ino turned, followed the line that the face would have travelled from Mrs. Ino's left hand.

The second of the young scientists mimicked the actions of the first, walking slowly along, pointing at the ground, following the presumptive course of the miniature Face. Near the rim of the crater the spacesuited scientist knelt, pointed, touched the ground. "Look, it struck here and bounced. Even though the pebbles are back, you can see the depression."

Ino watched the spacesuited scientist rise and point out the direction of the bounce. Over the lip of the rim. Into the depths of the crater. Into the lake of *kuroi kiri* where Ino had nearly died, and where the body of Miss Inada still lay.

The extending ladder that had saved Mr. Ino's life still stood in the center of the regolith lake. It served now only as a grave marker for Miss Inada, for Ino had been forced to leave her body at its base when he climbed to the surface and escaped from the crater.

And now the computer and the miniature Face lay in the lake as well. As small and as light as they were, they might not have made their way to the center, but instead would lie where they fell. Somewhere beneath the regolith. Hidden by black mist.

Inside his spacesuit, Ino moaned.

The band of four reassembled and resumed their trek from the old Russian station to the newer facility.

Once again they separated and entered the station through four separate airlocks. It did them no good. Each was met by a squad of workers and escorted to Deputy Manager Sumiyoshi's office. No word could be got out of the workers who met them and brought them along.

They were placed in chairs and their wrists and ankles were bound to the arms and legs of the chairs.

Ino turned to Mrs. Itagaki. "I'm sorry," he began. "I should not—"

The worker standing nearest to Ino caught Ino's face in one hand, stopping him in mid-sentence. "You will not speak." To the four of them, the worker said, "You will not speak."

In a few minutes Mr. Sumiyoshi arrived. He stood behind his desk, looking from one to another. As he looked at each of them, he showed differing feelings. To Ino, anger. To Mrs. Itagaki, annoyance. To the young man and woman, sadness and disappointment.

"What am I to make of this?" Sumiyoshi asked. He shook his massive head. "Order is breaking down. Society disintegrates. The old virtues are lost and anarchy reigns." He folded his arms and walked among the four chairs, weaving an intricate pattern. "What are the *katagi no shu* to think, when the finest of society act no better than *eta burakumin*? It's hard enough for those common folk to know how to behave, without scientists and high personages like you acting like depraved villagers. Villagers who know no better. You know better."

He pulled a kerchief from his desk and wiped his brow. It had grown wet with perspiration.

"You hypocrite," Mrs. Itagaki spoke angrily. "You killed Miss Inada, didn't you?"

Sumiyoshi ignored her words. "And what do I now do with you four?"

"You must know that my associates are coming from Nirgal Vallis," Ino said. "You know that Mr. Matsuzaki is responsible for me. He will not abandon me. You must surrender yourself to me, right now. Call back your helpers."

The workers who had captured Ino and the others and had tied them to their chairs had by now left Sumiyoshi's office.

Sumiyoshi growled. "I need no helpers," he said.

One of the young people said, "Mr. Matsuda will punish you. You must free us and apologize to us all, and then go and apologize to Mr. Matsuda. You have shamed him and the entire station, Mr. Sumiyoshi."

Sumiyoshi laughed. He strode to a cabinet and pulled a jug from it. He placed it on the surface, heated it, then returned with it and a tiny cup to stand over the others.

"Apologize," he grunted. "Apologize!" His breath erupted in a vulgar snort. He poured a cup of heated *sake* and downed it in one motion. "Too bad we cannot share this," he rumbled. His voice was as deep and as gruff as a bear's, and his shape resembled that of a bear as well.

"You are the ones who should apologize," he continued. "Interfering with important work. Meddling where you have no business to do so. Me, apologize?" His grinned at the thought, his chin looking more bear-like than ever. He had not shaved, and a black stubble made the others think of the snout of an animal.

"You will have to face Mr. Matsuda," Ino reminded him. "The youngster is right. Better that you speak first, Sumiyoshi. There may be a way for you to save some small bit of your honor."

"My honor is not at stake." Sumiyoshi screamed. His voice had grown shrill, and his hands began to shake. Their size was as great as one would expect of this bear-like creature. The right one gripped the *sake* cup so tightly that the hand made a fist and the cup disappeared within it. The left held the jug.

Sumiyoshi dropped the *sake* cup on the floor. He shifted the jug to his right hand and lifted it to his mouth. The *sake* dribbled over his stubbly chin and spilled onto his blouse. His left hand waved in the air before him. At last Mr. Ino could see clearly that Sumiyoshi's little finger was missing its last joint. He wondered if Sumiyoshi's body was not also covered with tattoos.

"My honor is intact!" Sumiyoshi said loudly. Ino looked at Mrs. Itagaki and found her looking back at him. She appeared distressed, alarmed. Yet in a voice that remained soft despite the excitement of the moment, she said to Sumiyoshi, "You must call Mr. Matsuda. You must do this at once."

Sumiyoshi tipped the *sake* jug once more, holding it over his mouth as the last of the hot wine tumbled out. The bear-like man shook his head and drops of *sake* spattered the four prisoners. He threw the empty jug at the wall and fragments flew in all directions. He leaned over Mrs. Itagaki and held his face centimeters from hers. Mr. Ino saw Mrs. Itagaki cringe before Sumiyoshi's alcoholic breath. Ino struggled at his bonds, but to no avail. Sumiyoshi drew back his hand and struck Mrs. Itagaki. Mr. Ino was bursting with rage.

"What's this?" Another voice was heard. All faces turned toward the new speaker. Standing in the doorway of Sumiyoshi's office was Mr. Kakuji Matsuda, manager of the entire Phobos Research Station.

"Mr. Matsuda," Ino cried out, "you have been betrayed. Your deputy is a corrupt gangster. He is the killer of Miss Inada, and he is responsible for the loss of an incomparable treasure."

Mr. Matsuda stood beside Sumiyoshi. To his deputy he said, "Is this true, Sumiyoshi? Please tell me the truth."

Sumiyoshi laughed. He went to the cabinet and found another jug of *sake*. This time he poured it into two cups, one of them filled almost to the rim, the other to the halfway point. He placed them on a table top.

Mr. Matsuda reached for the half-filled cup. Sumiyoshi took the other. Turning slowly so that all in the room could see them, they downed the rice wine.

Mr. Ino felt as if a fist had crashed into the side of his head. A brilliant light flashed before his eyes, dispelling the black mist that had hidden reality from him. Sumiyoshi was the *kuromako*, the *oyabun*. Matsuda was Sumiyoshi's *kobun*. To the rest of the station, Matsuda was the manager and Sumiyoshi was his deputy. But in secret, it was Sumiyoshi who was the godfather, Matsuda the lieutenant.

Kuroi kiri returned, this time as black mist of despair, not of mystification. Ino turned to Mrs. Itagaki. A final tragedy loomed before him, but still he had to learn the truth. He asked Mrs. Itagaki, "Miss Inada—you said her hands were roughened and scarred with work. But were they complete? Had she lost any part of her hands?"

Mrs. Itagaki lowered her head. "Part of a finger. She told me it had happened in a laboratory accident."

"Another question. I would rather not ask you this. Please forgive me, and please try to feel no shame."

Mrs. Itagaki waited in silence. Sumiyoshi and Matsuda, too, stood in silence. They were in command of the situation. They had nothing to fear. They sipped *sake*, grinning in amusement.

Ino said to Mrs. Itagaki, "Did you ever, please forgive me, have occasion to see Miss Itagaki's body? Did you ever see her unclothed?"

Mrs. Itagaki reddened and dropped her chin to her chest. There was a pause, then she replied. "I did. I am a widow. Lonely. I was hungry for love. She was young and beautiful and she was blameless. It started innocently."

"Please," Ino interrupted. "Please forgive me for asking so personal a question. But—was she tattooed?"

Mrs. Itagaki began to cry. "Her body was covered with wondrous designs. Serpents and flowers, goddesses and demons. She was a world herself, a marvel. I could not help myself. I was so lonely and she was so attractive to me. I am the guilty one. She was innocent."

"No." Ino shook his head. "You were the innocent party, Mrs. Itagaki. Miss Inada was herself a *kumi*, a soldier in this family. *Oyabun, kobun, kumi.* All of the same *ikka.* Is it not so, Sumiyoshi? The three of you, all of one *gumi* family."

No one answered.

"Did she betray you? Did her scientific instincts overcome her loyalty to the *ikka*? Was she going to tell the truth to Mrs. Itagaki? Or was she going to set out on her own, sell the Face to some *kuromako* and keep the proceeds? What shame. What shame."

Matsuda drew back his fist and struck Ino in the mouth. Ino felt the impact, although oddly with detachment rather than with pain. Then he felt his mouth filling with hot blood. Matsuda said, "Enough."

Sumiyoshi said, "Well, we may need some little proceeding against these four. Something for the record. Obviously they were planning a mutiny, were they not, Mr. Matsuda?"

Matsuda nodded sadly. "Never before in the history of this enterprise. This is terrible, terrible."

Sumiyoshi and Matsuda went from person to person, placing gags in their mouths. Then Sumiyoshi summoned the workers who had previously left the room. They must be *kumi-in* of the lowest level, Ino thought.

They unbound the four prisoners and marched them, two on each one, toward an airlock. They halted and forced the four to don spacesuits, first disabling the radio of each. "Do as you are told," Smuiyoshi growled at them. "And at once. Or you will be killed."

Ino's mind raced but there seemed little hope. He could not

break away from the others. He could not summon help. He said to Sumiyoshi, "At least let these two young ones live. They have done nothing. They are blameless."

Sumiyoshi shook his head.

Soon they were outside the station. Fourteen of them, each of the prisoners with a guard at either side, Sumiyoshi leading the way, Matsuda bringing up the rear. With the suit radios of the four prisoners disabled they could neither send nor receive messages.

The ground was dark, as black as blood that had stood and begun to congeal. Ino raised his eyes and saw Mars overhead. It was daytime on the planet, and he could see the flare of tiny rockets as balloons curved toward Phobos from Nirgal Vallis. It was Mr. Matsuzaki's promised help, arriving at last.

But too late, Ino thought. He knew what Sumiyoshi and Matsuda had in mind, Mr. Ino and Mrs. Itagaki and the two young scientists would be thrown into Stickney crater. Perhaps killed first, perhaps not. Even the telescoping ladder, that had saved Ino previously, would never survive another retraction and expansion within the regolith. In either case, they would never be found. Their bodies would lie with that of Miss Inada for all time, buried beneath a lake of regolith, a lake of black mist.

Two figures flashed by Ino and the others. One was a man of ordinary size and proportions. The other was tall and gawky, his long, skinny legs like those of a crane.

Each was brandishing an implement. Ino almost laughed as he recognized the implements: a huge, massive ladle and a thick-bodied rolling pin. They could be no other than Mr. Okubo and the hapless Toshikawa. Somehow, Toshikawa, for all his foolishness, had followed the case of Miss Inada. He had understood what Ino was up to, and he had convinced Okubo and won him as an ally.

The nearest balloon was only a hundred meters overhead.

Sumiyoshi was gesticulating furiously at Okubo.

Okubo turned to Toshikawa. Toshikawa's head bobbed.

Ino felt sweat on his brow and his bald pate. If only he could hear their transmissions!

The balloon was within fifty meters of the ground, and another was not far behind. Three, four, five more could be seen, filling the sky.

Ino caught a flash from the corner of his eye and turned to see more spacesuited figures pouring from the research station. They must have been monitoring the conversation among Okubo, Toshikawa, Sumiyoshi and Matsuda. There were ten of them, twelve, fourteen.

There could be no massacre now. There were too many figures gliding across the regolith in silence.

The first of the balloons had touched down and the others were close to the ground. Mars, directly overhead, cast its bloody coloration on Phobos.

The four prisoners and their eight guards stood like dummies, forgotten and inert. Sumiyoshi must know that his game was up. He would face trial, punishment, shame. And in prison it would become known that he had not only violated his office, he had betrayed his own *kobun*, Miss Inada. His punishment and his shame would only have begun.

Sumiyoshi broke away from the others. He took a hop, like a coney. He returned to the ground and took a second hop, higher than the first. A third brought him to the very lip of the Stickney crater. Was he going to plunge into the lake of regolith that lay within the crater?

No!

More quickly than the eye could follow, he gathered his massively muscled legs and hurled himself into the sky still again. He rose toward the red mass of Mars. Against the tiny gravity of Phobos he rose higher, turning to a black silhouette, then a black speck.

He disappeared.

Hours later he would plunge into the thin atmosphere of Mars, and shortly a small meteor would flare across the black sky, and Sumiyoshi would be no more.

Matsuda broke away from the group, running, leaping to follow his *oyabun*. But his muscles were less powerful. He rose from the rim of Stickney and floated in a parabola across the sky, crashing into the regolith that lay in the crater.

He could lie there and wait for rescue by Matsuzaki's people, and be taken away to face trial and disgrace. Or he could open his spacesuit and die quickly in the middle of the *kuroi kiri*. Ino knew that Matsuda would choose the latter. Workers would have to recover Miss Inada's body, and they would find Matsuda as well, dead or alive. Perhaps the miniature Face and Miss Inada's computer would also be found; perhaps not. They were too small and too light to make their way to the center of the crater, and locating them in the regolith would be far more difficult than finding the two spacesuited bodies.

The eight workers who had served as Sumiyoshi's *kumi-in* had already given up and returned to the space station. Mr. Okubo and Mr. Toshikawa had followed them, along with the other workers who had rushed from the airlock.

Mr. Ino thought of the persons whose lives had been ended in this sad incident, and those whose lives had been changed in other ways. The latter would most notably include Jiricho Toshikawa and Wataru Okubo. The hapless Toshikawa had proved more intelligent and of a more forceful nature than expected. He had acted heroically. Ino wondered why.

Surely, Toshikawa had felt no special loyalty to Mr. Ino. The two were strangers. Jizo-bosatsu and Shaka-nyorai. Perhaps it had nothing to do with Ino. Perhaps Toshikawa had truly loved Miss Inada. He had felt a need to avenge her death, to see to it that the reputation of her killer did not go untarnished. Whatever Toshikawa's motivation, Mr. Ino would make a report to Mr. Matsuzaki. Toshikawa would be rewarded. So, too, would Toshikawa's superior, Mr. Okubo.

Mr. Matsuda would face his sad fate.

Mrs. Itagaki would continue her work, perhaps with a promotion in lieu of the vacancies created by Mr. Matsuda and Mr. Sumiyoshi.

But Mr. Ino thought of Miss Inada—and of Mr. Sumiyoshi. Two souls. Where would they travel? Perhaps they would find themselves beside the river Sai-no-kawara. They were not children, to be sure, but who knew, in truth, what happened to the souls of the dead?

If there was a hell, if there was a river Sai-no-kawara, then perhaps there was also a Jizo-bosatsu. Unthinkingly, Mr. Ino reached to tug at his moustache, only to startle himself into blinking when his gloved hand struck the faceplate of his mask. He shook his head ruefully. If only he were in truth Jizo. If only he could in truth comfort the sad souls of the sorrowful dead.

He remained alone near the crater to greet Mr. Matsuzaki's people. He felt embarrassment, knowing that he would not be able to speak to them except by hand gestures until they were inside the research station. But once there he would have a great deal to tell them.

When British anthologist and scholar Mike Ashley asked me to contribute a story to The Mammoth Book of Locked-Room Mysteries and Impossible Crimes *in 1999, I seized the opportunity to write about a fictional detective who had been lurking in my notebook for several years but had never got a chance to strut his stuff on the printed page. He was Akhenaton Beelzebub Chase, a millionaire amateur sleuth in the tradition of Philo Vance, Philip Trent, Roderick Alleyn or the early Ellery Queen.*

Chase's parents were both archaeologists, one investigating the mysteries of Egypt and the other, of Mesopotania. Hence their son's unusual nomen. The elder Chases survived the sinking of the Titanic *only to perish in the torpedoing of the* Lusitania. *Himself a victim of poison gas in the trenches of France in 1918, Abel Chase has become one of the world's great polymaths, an authority on everything from modern musical composition to seemingly supernatural crimes.*

"The Second Drug" takes place in the winter of 1931. Assisted by the ever-faithful and preternaturally lovely Claire Delacroix, Abel Chase is ready to unravel a most baffling mystery.

The Second Drug

THE GREAT BOSENDORFER PIANO RESPONDED
eagerly to Abel Chase's practiced hands, its crashing notes
echoing from the high, raftered ceiling of the music room.
Beyond the tall, westward-facing windows, the January night was
dark and wind-swept. The warm lights of the college town of
Berkeley sparkled below, and beyond the black face of the bay the
more garish illumination of San Francisco shimmered seductively.

* * *

The sweet tones of the Guarnarius violin bowed by Chase's con-
fidante and associate, Claire Delacroix, dashed intricately among
the piano chords. Clad in shimmering silver, Claire offered a
dramatic contrast to Chase's drab appearance. Her platinum hair,
worn in the soft style of an earlier age, cascaded across the
gracefully rounded shoulders that emerged from her silvery, bias-
cut gown. A single diamond, suspended from a delicate silver
chain, glittered in the hollow of her throat. Her deep-set eyes, a
blue so dark as at times to appear almost purple, shone with a rare
intelligence.

Abel Chase's hair was as dark as Claire's was pale, save for the
patches of snow which appeared at the temples. Chase wore a

neatly-trimmed black moustache in which only a few light-colored hairs were interspersed. He was clad in a pale, soft-collared shirt and a tie striped with the colors of his *alma mater*, a silken dressing gown and the trousers of his customary midnight blue suit. His expression was saturnine.

"Enough, Delacroix." He ceased to play, and she lowered her bow and instrument. "Stravinsky has outdone himself," Chase allowed. "A few corrections and suggestions, notably to the second *eclogue*, and his manuscript will be ready for return. His *cantilène* and *gigue* are most affecting, while the *dithyrambe* is a delight. After his more ambitious orchestral pieces of recent years, it is fascinating to see him working on so small a canvas."

Chase had risen from the piano bench and taken two long strides toward the window when the room's freshly restored silence was shattered by the shrilling of a telephone bell. Chase whirled and started toward the machine, but his associate had lifted the delicate French-styled instrument from its cradle. She murmured into it, paused, then added a few words and held the instrument silently toward her companion.

"Yes." He held the instrument, his eyes glittering with interest. He raised his free hand and brushed a fingertip along the edge of his moustache. After a time he murmured, "Definitely dead? Very well. Yes, you were right to re-seal the room. I shall come over shortly. Now, quickly, the address." He continued to hold the telephone handset to his ear, listening and nodding, then grunted and returned it to its cradle.

"Delacroix, I am going to the city. Please fetch your wrap, I shall need you to drive me to the dock. And perhaps you would care to assist me. In that case, I urge you to dress warmly, as a light snowfall has been falling for several hours—a most unusual event for San Francisco." Without waiting for a response he strode to his own room, hung his dressing gown carefully in a cedar-lined closet and donned his suit coat.

Claire Delacroix awaited him in the flagstone-floored foyer. She had slipped into a sable jacket and carried an elegant purse woven of silvery metal links so fine as to suggest cloth. Chase removed an overcoat from a rack beside the door, slipped into its warm confines, and lifted hat and walking stick from their places.

Shortly a powerful Hispano-Suiza snaked its way through the winding, darkened roads of the Berkeley hills, Claire Delacroix behind the wheel, Abel Chase seated beside her, a lap robe warming him against the wintry chill.

"I suppose you'd like to know what this is about," Chase offered.

"Only as much as you wish to tell me," Claire Delacroix replied.

"That was Captain Baxter on the telephone," Chase told her.

"I knew as much. I recognized his gruff voice, for all that Baxter dislikes to speak to women."

"You misjudge him, Delacroix. That's merely his manner. He has a wife and five daughters to whom he is devoted."

"You may be right. Perhaps he has his fill of women at home. I suppose he's got another juicy murder for you, Abel."

Chase's moustache twitched when Claire Delacroix called him by his familiar name. He was well aware that it would have been futile to ask her to address him by his given name, Akhenaton, and Claire Delacroix knew him far too intimately to refer to him as Doctor Chase. Still, "Abel" was a name few men were permitted to use in conversation with him, and no woman save for Claire Delacroix.

"The man is distraught. He seems to think that a vampire has struck in San Francisco, draining the blood of a victim and leaving him for dead."

Claire Delacroix laughed, the silvery sound snatched away on the wind. "And will the victim then rise and walk, a new recruit to the army of the undead?"

"You scoff," Chase commented.

"I do."

There was a momentary pause, then Chase said, "As do I. Baxter is at the site. He has studied the circumstances of the crime and concluded that it is impossible, by any normal means. Therefore and *ipso facto*, the solution must be supernatural,"

"You of course disagree."

"Indeed. The very term *supernatural* contradicts itself. The natural universe encompasses all objects and events. If a thing has occurred, it is necessarily not supernatural. If it is supernatural, it cannot occur."

"Then we are confronted with an impossible crime," Claire Delacroix stated.

Abel Chase shook his head in annoyance. "Again, Delacroix, a contradiction in terms. That which is impossible cannot happen. That which happens is therefore, by definition, possible. No," he snorted, "this crime is neither supernatural nor impossible, no matter that it may seem to be either—or both. I intend to unravel this tangled skein. Remain at my side if you will, and be instructed!"

The dark, winding road had debauched by now into the town's downtown district. On a Saturday night during the academic year warmly clad undergraduates stood in line to purchase tickets for talkies. The young intellectuals in their cosmopolitanism chose among the sensuality of Marlene Dietrich in *The Blue Angel*, the collaborative work of the geniuses Dali and Buñuel in *L'Age d'Or*, the polemics of the Ukrainian Dovzhenko's *Zemlya*, and the simmering rage of Edward G. Robinson in *Little Caesar*.

Young celebrants gestured and exclaimed at the unusual sight of snowflakes falling from the January sky. Their sportier (or wealthier) brethren cruised the streets in Bearcats and Auburns. The Depression might have spread fear and want throughout the land, but the college set remained bent on the pursuit of loud jazz and illicit booze.

Claire Delacroix powered the big, closed car down the sloping avenue that led to the city's waterfront, where Abel Chase's power boat rode at dock, lifting and falling with each swell of the bay's cold, brackish water.

Climbing from the car, Abel Chase carefully folded his lap robe and placed it on the seat. He turned up the collar of his warm overcoat, drew a pair of heavy gloves from a pocket and donned them. Together, he and Claire Delacroix crossed to a wooden shed built out over the bay. Chase drew keys from his trouser pocket, opened a heavy lock, and permitted Claire to enter before him. They descended into a powerful motor boat. Chase started the engine and they roared from the shed, heading toward the San Francisco Embarcadero. The ferries had stopped running for the night. Tramp steamers and great commercial freighters stood at anchor in the bay. The power boat wove among them trailing an icy, greenish-white wake.

Steering the boat with firm assurance, Chase gave his assistant a few more details. "Baxter is at the Salamanca Theatre on Geary. There's a touring company doing a revival of some Broadway melodrama of a few years back. Apparently the leading man failed to emerge from his dressing room for the third act, and the manager called the police."

Claire Delacroix shook her head, puzzled. She had drawn a silken scarf over her platinum hair, and its tips were whipped by the night wind as their boat sped across the bay. "Sounds to me like a medical problem more than a crime. Or maybe he's just being temperamental. You know those people in the arts."

Chase held his silence briefly, then grunted. "So thought the manager until the door was removed from its hinges. The actor was seated before his mirror, stone dead." There was a note of irony in his soft voice.

"And is that why are we ploughing through a pitch black night in the middle of winter?" she persisted.

"The death of Count Hunyadi is not a normal one, Delacroix."

Now Claire Delacroix smiled. It was one of Abel Chase's habits to drop bits of information into conversations in this manner. If the listener was sufficiently alert she would pick them up. Otherwise, they would pass unnoted.

"Imre Hunyadi, the Hungarian matinee idol?"

"Or the Hungarian ham," Chase furnished wryly. "Impoverished petty nobility are a dime a dozen nowadays. If he was ever a count to start with."

"This begins to sound more interesting, Abel. But what is this about a vampire that makes this a case for no less than the great Akhenaton Beelzebub Chase rather than the San Francisco Police Department?"

"Ah, your question is as ever to the point. Aside from the seemingly supernatural nature of Count Hunyadi's demise, of course. The manager of the Salamanca Theatre states that Hunyadi has received a series of threats. He relayed this information to Captain Baxter, and Baxter to me."

"Notes?"

"Notes—and worse. Captain Baxter states that a dead rodent was placed on his dressing table two nights ago. And finally a copy of his obituary."

"Why didn't he call the police and ask for protection?"

"We shall ask our questions when we reach the scene of the crime, Delacroix."

Chase pulled the powerboat alongside a private wharf flanking the San Francisco Ferry Building. An uniformed police officer waited to catch the line when Chase tossed it to him. The darkly-garbed Chase and the silver-clad Claire Delacroix climbed to the planking and thence into a closed police cruiser. A few snowflakes had settled upon their shoulders. Gong sounding, the cruiser pulled away and headed up Market Street, thence to Geary and the Salamanca Theatre, where Chase and Delacroix exited.

They were confronted by a mob of well-dressed San Franciscans bustling from the theatre. The play had ended and, as with the younger crowd in Berkeley, the theatregoers grinned and exclaimed in surprise at the falling flakes. Few of the men and women discussing their evening's entertainment, hailing passing cabs or heading to nearby restaurants for post-theatrical suppers, took note of the two so-late arrivers.

An uniformed patrolman saluted Abel Chase and invited him and Claire Delacroix into the Salamanca. "Captain Baxter sends his compliments, Doctor."

"Nice to see you, Officer Murray. How are your twins? No problems with croup this winter?"

Flustered, the officer managed to stammer, "No, sir, no problems this year. But how did you—?"

Before Murray could finish his question he was interrupted by a stocky, ruddy-complexioned individual in the elaborate uniform of a high-ranking police officer. The Captain strode forward, visibly favoring one leg. He was accompanied by a sallow-faced individual wearing a black tuxedo of almost new appearance.

"Major Chase," the uniformed police official saluted.

Chase smiled and extended his own hand, which the Captain shook. "Clel. You know Miss Delacroix, of course."

Claire Delacroix extended her hand and Captain Cleland Baxter shook it, lightly and briefly.

"And this is Mr. Quince. Mr. Walter Quince, wasn't it, sir?"

Walter Quince extended his own hand to Chase, tilting his torso at a slight angle as he did so. The movement brought his hatless, brilliantined head close to Chase, who detected a cloying cosmetic scent. He shook Quince's hand, then addressed himself to Baxter.

"Take me to the scene of the incident."

Baxter led Chase and Delacroix through the now-darkened Salamanca Theatre. Quince ran ahead and held aside a dark-colored velvet curtain, opening the way for them into a narrow, dingy corridor. Abel Chase and Claire Delacroix followed Baxter into the passage, followed by Quince.

Shortly they stood outside a plain door. Another police officer, this one with sergeant's chevrons on his uniform sleeve, stood guard.

"Hello, Costello," Chase said. "How are your daughter and her husband doing these days?"

"Doctor." The uniformed sergeant lifted a finger to the bill of his uniform cap. "They've moved in with the missus and me. Times are hard, sir."

Chase nodded sympathetically.

"This is Count Hunyadi's dressing room," Quince explained, indicating the doorway behind Costello.

Chase asked, "I see that the door was removed from its hinges, and that Captain Baxter's men have sealed the room. That is good. But why was it necessary to remove the hinges to open the door?"

"Locked, sir."

"Don't you have a key, man?"

"Count Hunyadi insisted on placing a padlock inside his dressing room. He was very emphatic about his privacy. No one was allowed in, even to clean, except under his direct supervision."

Abel Chase consulted a gold-framed hexagonal wristwatch. "What time was the third act to start?"

"At 10:15, sir."

"And when was Hunyadi called?"

"He got a five-minute and a two-minute call. He didn't respond to either. I personally tried to summon him at curtain time but there was no response."

Abel Chase frowned. "Did you then cancel the rest of the performance?"

"No, sir. Elbert Garrison, the director, ordered Mr. Hunyadi's understudy to take over the role."

"And who was that fortunate individual?"

"Mr. Winkle. Joseph Winkle. He plays the madman, Renfield, And Philo Jenkins, who plays a guard at the madhouse, became Renfield. It was my duty to take the stage and announce the changes. I made no mention of Count Hunyadi's—illness. I merely gave the names of the understudies."

"Very well. Before we proceed to examine the victim and his surroundings, I will need to see these so-called threatening notes."

Captain Cleland Baxter cleared his throat. "Looks as if the Count was pretty upset by the notes. Everybody says he destroyed 'em all. He complained every time he got one but then he'd set a match to it."

An angry expression swept across Chase's features.

Baxter held up a hand placatingly. "But the latest—looks like the Count just received it tonight, Major—looks like he got riled up and crumpled the thing and threw it in the corner."

Baxter reached into his uniform pocket and extracted a creased rectangle of cheap newsprint. "Here it is, sir."

Chase accepted the paper, studied it while the others stood silently, then returned it to the uniformed captain with an admonition to preserve it as potentially important evidence.

Next, he removed the police seal from the entrance to the dressing room and stepped inside, followed by Claire Delacroix,

Captain Baxter, and the theatre manager, Walter Quince.

Chase stood over the still form of Imre Hunyadi, for the moment touching nothing. The still form sat on a low stool, its back to the room. The head was slumped forward and to one side, the forehead pressed against a rectangular mirror surrounded by small electrical bulbs. His hands rested against the mirror as well, one to either side of his head, his elbows propped on the table.

"We observe," Chase stated, "that the victim is fully dressed in formal theatrical costume, complete with collar and gloves."

"And ye'll note that he's deathly pale, Major," the police Captain put in. "Deathly pale. Drained by the bite of a vampire, I say."

Chase pursed his lips and stroked his dark mustache. "I would not be so quick to infer as much, Captain," he warned. "The victim's face is indeed deathly pale. That may be stage makeup, however."

Chase lifted an emery board from the dressing table and carefully removed a speck of makeup from Hunyadi's cheek. "Remarkable," he commented. "You see—" He turned and exhibited the emery board to the room. "It is indeed pale makeup, appropriate, of course, to the Count's stage persona. But now, we observe the flesh beneath."

He bent to peer at the skin he had exposed. "Remarkable," he said again. "As white as death."

"Just so!" exclaimed the captain of homicide.

"But now let us examine the victim's hands."

With great care he peeled back one of Hunyadi's gloves. "Yet again remarkable," the Abel Chase commented. "The hands are also white and bloodless. Well indeed, there remains yet one more cursory examination to be made."

Carefully tugging his trousers to avoid bagging the knees of his woolen suit, he knelt beside Count Hunyadi. He lifted Hunyadi's trouser cuff and peeled down a silken lisle stocking. Then he sprang back to his full height.

"Behold!"

The Count's ankle was purple and swollen.

"Perhaps Miss Delacroix—Doctor Delacroix, I should say—will have an explanation."

Claire Delacroix knelt, examined the dead man's ankles, then rose to her own feet and stated, "Simple. And natural. This man died where he sits. His body was upright, even his hands were raised. His blood drained to the lower parts of his body, causing the swelling and discoloration of the ankles and feet. There is nothing supernatural about post-mortem lividity."

Chase nodded. "Thank you."

He turned from the body and pointed a carefully manicured finger at Quince. "Is there any other means of access to Hunyadi's dressing room?"

"Just the window, sir."

"Just the window, sir?" Abel Chase's eyes grew wide. "Just the window? Baxter—" He turned to the Captain of police. "Have you ordered that checked?"

Flustered, Baxter admitted that he had not.

"Quickly, then. Quince, lead the way!"

The manager led them farther along the dingy corridor. It was dimly illumined by yellow electrical bulbs. They exited through the stage door and found themselves gazing upon a narrow alley flanked by dark walls of aging, grime-encrusted brick. To their right, the alley opened onto the normally busy sidewalk, now free of pedestrians as San Franciscans sought cover from the chill and moisture of the night. To the left, the alley abutted a brick wall, featureless save for the accumulated grime of decades.

"There it is, sir."

Chase raised his hand warningly. "Before we proceed, let us first examine the alley itself," Chase instructed. Using electric torches for illumination, they scanned the thin coating of snow that covered the litter-strewn surface of the alley. "You will notice," Chase announced, "that the snow is undisturbed. Nature herself has become our ally in this work."

Chase then stepped carefully forward and turned, surveying the window. "Fetch me a ladder," he ordered. When the implement arrived he climbed it carefully, having donned his gloves once again. He stood peering through a narrow opening, perhaps fourteen inches wide by six inches in height. A pane of pebbled glass, mounted on a horizontal hinge in such manner as to divide the opening in half, was tilted at a slight angle. Through it, Chase peered into the room in which he and the others had stood moments earlier.

From his elevated position he scanned the room meticulously, dividing it into a geometrical grid and studying each segment in turn. When satisfied, he returned to the ground.

Walter Quince, incongruous in his evening costume, folded the ladder. "But you see, sir, the window is much too small for a man to pass through."

"Or even a child," Chase added.

There was a moment of silence, during which a wisp of San Francisco's legendary fog descended icily from the winter sky.

The rare snowfall, the city's first in decades, had ended. Then a modulated feminine voice broke the stillness of the tableau. "Not too small for a bat."

They returned to the theatre. Once again inside the building, Chase doffed his warm outer coat and gloves, then made his way to the late Count Hunyadi's dressing room, where the cadaver of the emigré actor remained, slowly stiffening, before the glaring lights and reflective face of his makeup mirror. Irony tingeing his voice, Chase purred, "You will note that the late Count casts a distinct reflection in his looking glass. Hardly proper conduct for one of the undead." He bent to examine the cadaver once more, peering first at one side of Hunyadi's neck, then at the other.

Chase whirled. "Was he left-handed?"

Walter Quince, standing uneasily in the doorway, swallowed audibly. "I—I think so. He, ah, remarked something about it, I recall."

Abel Chase placed the heels of his hands on the sides of Hunyadi's head and moved it carefully to an upright position. He made a self-satisfied sound. "There is some stiffness here, but as yet very little. He is recently dead. Delacroix, look at this. Clel, you also."

As they obeyed he lowered Hunyadi's head carefully to his right shoulder, exposing the left side of his neck to view above the high, stiff collar of his costume shirt.

"What do you see?" Chase demanded.

"Two red marks." Captain Cleland Baxter, having moved forward in his rolling, uneven gait, now leaned over to study the unmoving Hunyadi's neck. "He played a vampire," the police captain muttered. "and he carries the marks of the vampire. Good God! In this Year of Our Lord 1931—it's impossible."

"No, my friend. Not impossible," Chase responded. "Supernatural? That I doubt. But impossible? No." He shook his head.

Claire Delacroix scanned the dressing room, her dark, intelligent eyes flashing from object to object. Sensing that the attention of the theatre manager was concentrated on her, she turned her gaze on him. "Mr. Quince, the program for tonight's performance includes a biography of each actor, is that not correct?" When Quince nodded in the affirmative, she requested a copy and received it.

She scanned the pages, touching Abel Chase lightly on the elbow and bringing to his attention several items in the glossy booklet. Chase's dark head and Claire Delacroix's platinum tresses nearly touched as they conferred.

Chase frowned at Walter Quince. "This biography of Mr. Hunyadi makes no mention of a wife."

"Imre Hunyadi is—was—unmarried at the time of . . ." He inclined his own head toward the body.

"Yes, his demise," Chase furnished.

Quince resumed. "Theatrical biographies seldom mention former spouses."

"But gossip is common within the theatrical community, is it not?"

"Yes." There was an uncomfortable pause. Then Quince added, "I believe he was married twice. The first time in his native Hungary. To one Elena Kadar."

"Yes, I have heard of her," Chase furnished. "A brilliant woman, sometimes called the Hungarian Madame Curie. She was engaged for some years in medical research, in the field of anesthesiology. I've read several of her papers. Apparently she treated Habsburg soldiers who had been wounded in the Great War and was greatly moved by their suffering. Hence the direction of her experiments. She ended her life a suicide. A tragic loss."

"Ach, Major, Major, you know everything, don't you?" Captain Baxter exclaimed.

"Not quite," Chase demurred. Then, "Under what circumstances, Quince, was the Hunyadi marriage dissolved?"

The theatre manager reddened, indicating with a minute nod of his head toward Claire Delacroix that he was reluctant to speak of the matter in the presence of a female.

"Really," Claire Delacroix said, "I know something of the world, Mr. Quince. Speak freely, please."

"Very well." The manager took a moment to compose himself. Then he said, "Some years before the Great War Mr. Hunyadi traveled to America as a member of a theatrical troupe. *Magyar Arte,* I believe they were called. They performed plays in their native language for audiences of immigrants. While touring, Hunyadi took up with his Hungarian leading lady. A few years later they moved to Hollywood to pursue careers in motion pictures. The woman's name was—" He looked around furtively, then mentioned the name of a popular film actress.

"They had one of those glittering Hollywood weddings," he added.

"With no thought of a wife still in Hungary?" Claire Delacroix inquired.

Quince shook his head. "None. Count Hunyadi made several

successful silents, but when talkies came in, well, his accent, you see . . . There are just so many roles for European noblemen. Word within our community was that he had become a dope fiend for a time. He was hospitalized, then released, and was hoping to revive his career with a successful stage tour."

"Yes, there were rumors of his drug habit," Captain Baxter put in. "We were alerted down at the Hall of Justice."

Abel Chase looked around. "What of—" He named the actress who had been Imre Hunyadi's second wife.

"When her earnings exceeded his own, Count Hunyadi spent her fortune on high living, fast companions and powerful motor cars. When she cut him off and demanded that he look for other work, he brought a lawsuit against her, which failed, but which led to a nasty divorce."

"Tell me about the other members of the cast."

"You're thinking that his understudy might of done him in?" Baxter asked. "That Winkle fellow?"

"Entirely possible," Chase admitted. "But a premature inference, Clel. Who are the others?"

"Timothy Rodgers, Philo Jenkins," Quince supplied. "Estelle Miller and Jeanette Stallings, the two female leads—Lucy and Mina. And of course Samuel Pollard—Van Helsing."

"Yes." Abel Chase stroked his mustache thoughtfully as he examined the printed program. "Captain Baxter, I noticed that Sergeant Costello is here tonight. A good man. Have him conduct a search of this room. And have Officer Murray assist him. And see to it that the rest of the theatre is searched as well. I shall require a thorough examination of the premises. While your men perform those tasks I shall question the male cast members. Miss Delacroix will examine the females."

Baxter said, "Yes, Major. And—is it all right to phone for the dead wagon? Count Hunyadi has to get to the morgue, don't you know, sir."

"Not yet, Clel. Miss Delacroix is the possessor of a medical education, you know. Although she seldom uses the honorific, she is entitled to be called doctor. I wish her to examine the remains before they are removed."

"As you wish, Major."

Chase nodded, pursing his lips. "Delacroix, have a look before you question the women of the cast, will you. And, Quince, gather these persons, Rodgers, Pollard, Winkle, and Jennings for me. And you'd better include the director, as well, Garrison."

Claire Delacroix conscientiously checked Hunyadi for telltale signs, seeking to determine the cause of the Hungarian's death. She conducted herself with a professional calm. At length she looked up from the remains and nodded. "It is clear that the immediate cause of Count Hunyadi's death is heart failure." She looked from one to another of the men in the dressing room. "The puzzle is, For what reason did his heart fail? I can find no overt cause. The death might have been natural, of course. But I will wish to examine the marks on his neck. Definitely, I will wish to examine those marks."

"I think they're a mere theatrical affectation," Walter Quince offered.

"That may be the case," Claire Delacroix conceded, "but I would not take that for granted. Then—" she addressed herself to Captain Baxter "—I would urge you to summon the coroner's ambulance and have the remains removed for an autopsy at the earliest possible moment."

"You can rest assured of that," Captain Baxter promised. "Nolan Young, the county coroner, is an old comrade of mine."

Shortly the men Chase had named found themselves back on the stage of the Salamanca Theatre. The setting held the ominous, musty gloom of a darkened Transylvanian crypt. All had changed from their costumes to street outfits, their dark suits blending with the dull gray of canvas flats painted to simulate funereal stone.

A further macabre note was struck by their posture, as they were seated on the prop caskets that added atmosphere to the sepulchral stage setting.

Rather than a dearth, Abel Chase found that he confronted by a surfeit of suspects. Each actor had spent part of the evening onstage; that was not unexpected. As the hapless Jonathan Harker, Timothy Rodgers had won the sympathy of the audience, and Abel Chase found him a pleasant enough young man, albeit shaken and withdrawn as a result of this night's tragedy.

Joseph Winkle, accustomed to playing the depraved madman Renfield, tonight had transformed himself into the elegant monster for the play's final act. Philo Jenkins, the shuffling, blustering orderly, had stepped into Winkle's shoes as Renfield. It had been a promotion for each.

Yet, Abel Chase meditated, despite Captain Baxter's earlier suggestion that Winkle might be a suspect, he would in all likelihood be too clever to place himself under suspicion by committing so obvious a crime. Philo Jenkins was the more interesting possibility. He would have known that by murdering Hunyadi he would set in motion the sequence of events that led to his own advancement into Winkle's part as Renfield. At the bottom of the evening's billing, he had the most to gain by his promotion.

And Rodgers, it was revealed, was a local youth, an aspiring thespian in his first significant role. It appeared unlikely that he would imperil the production with no discernible advantage to himself.

The director, Garrison, would have had the best opportunity to commit the crime. Unlike the other cast members, who would be in their own dressing rooms—or, for such lesser lights as Rodgers, Winkle and Jenkins, a common dressing room—between the acts of the play, Garrison might well be anywhere, conferring with cast members or the theatre staff, giving performance notes, keeping tabs, in particular, on a star known to have had a problem with drugs.

"Garrison." Abel Chase whirled on the director, "Had Hunyadi relapsed into his old ways?"

The director, sandy-haired and tanned, wearing a brown suit and hand-painted necktie, moaned. "I was trying to keep him off the dope, but he always managed to find something. But I think he was off it tonight. I've seen plenty of dope fiends in my time. Too many, Doctor Chase. Haven't you come across them in your own practice?"

"My degree is not in medicine," Chase informed him. "While Miss Delacroix holds such a degree, my own fields of expertise are by nature far more esoteric than the mundane study of organs and bones."

"My mistake," Garrison apologized. "For some reason, powder bouncers seem to gravitate to the acting profession as vipers do to music. Or maybe there's something about being an actor that makes 'em take wing. They start off sniffing gin and graduate to the needle. I could tell, Mister Chase, and I think Hunyadi was okeh tonight."

Chase fixed Garrison with a calculatedly bland expression. Unlike the actors Winkle and Jenkins, the director lacked any obvious motive for wishing Hunyadi dead. In fact, to keep the production running successfully he would want Hunyadi functional. Still, what motive unconnected to the production might Garrison have had?

And there was Samuel Pollard. As Van Helsing, Chase knew, Pollard would have appeared with the lined face and gray locks of an aged savant, a man of five decades or even six. To Chase's surprise, the actor appeared every bit as old as the character he portrayed. His face showed the crags and scars of a sexagenarian, and his thin fringe of hair was the color of old iron.

In response to Chase's questions, Pollard revealed that he had spent the second intermission in the company of the young actress who had appeared as the character Mina, Jeanette Stallings.

"Is that so?" Chase asked blandly.

"We have—a relationship," Pollard muttered.

Chase stared at the grizzled actor, pensively fingering his mustache. He restrained himself from echoing John Heywood's dictum that there is no fool like an old fool, instead inquiring neutrally as to the nature of the relationship between Pollard and the actress.

"It is of a personal nature." Pollard's tone was grudging.

"Mr. Pollard, as you are probably aware, I am not a police officer, nor am I affiliated with the municipal authorities in any formal capacity. Captain Baxter merely calls upon me from time to time, when faced with a puzzle of special complexity. If you choose to withhold information from me, I cannot compel you to do otherwise—but if you decline to assist me, you will shortly be obliged to answer to the police or the district attorney. Now I ask you again, what is the nature of your relationship with Miss Stallings?"

Pollard clasped and unclasped his age-gnarled hands as he debated with himself. Finally he bowed his head in surrender and said, "Very well. Doctor Chase, you are obviously too young to remember the great era of the theatre, when Samuel Pollard was a name to conjure with. You never saw me as Laertes, I am certain, nor as Macbeth. I was as famous as a Barrymore or a Booth in my day. Now I am reduced to playing a European vampire hunter."

He blew out his breath as if to dispel the mischievous imps of age.

"Like many another player in such circumstances, I have been willing to share my knowledge of the trade with eager young talents. That is the nature of my relationship with Miss Stallings."

"In exchange for which services you received what, Mister Pollard?"

"The satisfaction of aiding a promising young performer, Doctor Chase." And, after a period of silence, "Plus an honorarium of very modest proportions. Even an artist, I am sure you will understand, must meet his obligations."

Chase pondered, then asked his final question of Pollard.

"What, specifically, have you and Miss Stallings worked upon?"

"Her diction, Doctor Chase. There is none like the Bard to develop one's proper enunciation. Miss Stallings is of European origin, and it was in the subtle rhythms and emphases of the English language that I instructed her."

With this exchange Abel Chase completed his interrogation of Rodgers, Winkle, Jenkins, Pollard, and Garrison. He dismissed them, first warning them that none was absolved of suspicion, and that all were to remain in readiness to provide further assistance should it be demanded of them.

He then sought out Claire Delacroix. She was found in the office of the theatre manager, Walter Quince. With her were Estelle Miller and Jeanette Stallings. Chase rapped sharply on the somewhat grimy door and admitted himself to Quince's sanctum.

The room, he noted, was cluttered with the kipple of a typical business establishment. The dominant item was a huge desk. Its scarred wooden surface was all but invisible beneath an array of folders, envelopes, scraps and piles of paper. A heavy black telephone stood near at hand. A wooden filing cabinet, obviously a stranger to the cleaner's cloth no less than to oil or polish, stood in one corner. An upright typewriter of uncertain age and origin rested upon a rickety stand of suspect condition.

Claire Delacroix sat perched on the edge of the desk, occupying one of the few spots not covered by Quince's belongings. One knee was crossed over the other, offering a glimpse of silk through a slit in the silvery material of her skirt.

She looked up as Abel Chase entered the room. Chase nodded. Claire introduced him to her companions. "Miss Miller, Miss Stallings, Doctor Akhenaton Beelzebub Chase."

Chase nodded to the actresses. Before another word was uttered the atmosphere of the room was pierced by the shrill clatter of the telephone on Walter Quince's desk. Claire Delacroix lifted the receiver to her ear and held the mouthpiece before her lips, murmuring into it. She listened briefly, then spoke again. At length she thanked the caller and lowered the receiver to its cradle.

"That was Nolan Young, the coroner," she said to Chase. "I think we had best speak in private, Abel."

Chase dismissed the two actresses, asking them to remain on the premises for the time being. He then asked Claire Delacroix what she had learned from the county coroner.

Claire clasped her hands over her knee and studied Abel Chase's countenance before responding. Perhaps she sought a sign there of his success—or lack thereof—in his own interrogations. When she spoke, it was to paraphrase closely what Nolan Young had told her.

"The coroner's office has performed a quick and cursory post-mortem examination of Imre Hunyadi. There was no visible cause of death. Nolan Young sustains my preliminary attribution of heart failure. But of course, that tells us nothing. There was no damage to the heart itself, no sign of embolism, thrombosis, or abrasion. What, then, caused Hunyadi's heart to stop beating?"

Abel Chase waited for her to continue.

"The condition of Hunyadi's irises suggests that he was using some narcotic drug, most likely cocaine."

"Such was his history." Chase put in. "Nevertheless, Elbert Garrison observed Hunyadi closely and believes that he was not under the influence."

"Perhaps not," Claire acceded. "An analysis of his bloodstream will tell us that. But the two marks on his neck suggest otherwise, Abel."

Chase glanced at her sharply. He was a man of typical stature, and she a woman of more than average height. As he stood facing her and she sat perched on the edge of Walter Quince's desk, they were eye to eye.

"Study of the two marks with an enlarging glass shows each as the locus of a series of needle pricks. I had observed as much, myself, during my own examination of the body. Most of them are old and well healed, but the most recent, Nolan Young informs, is fresh. It had apparently been inflicted only moments before Hunyadi's death. If those marks were the sign of a vampire's teeth, then the creature more likely administered cocaine to his victims than extracted blood from them."

"You are aware, Delacroix, I do not believe in the supernatural."

"Not all vampires are of the supernatural variety," she replied.

Abel Chase ran a finger pensively beneath his mustache. "What is your professional opinion, then? Are you suggesting that Hunyadi died of erythroxylon alkaloid intoxication?"

"I think not," frowned Claire Delacroix. "If that were the case, I would have expected Nolan Young to report damage to the heart, and none was apparent. Further, the condition of the needle-pricks is most intriguing. They suggest that Hunyadi had received no injections for some time, then resumed his destructive habit just tonight. I suspect that a second substance was added to the victim's customary injection of cocaine. The first drug, while elevating his spirits to a momentarily euphoric state, would have, paradoxically, lulled him into a false sense of security while the second killed him."

"And what do you suppose that fatal second drug to have been?"

"That I do not know, Abel. But I have a very strong suspicion, based on my conversation with the ladies of the company—and on your own comments earlier this night."

"Very well," Chase growled, not pleased. He knew that when Claire Delacroix chose to unveil her theory she would do so, and not a moment sooner. He changed the subject. "What did you learn from the Misses Miller and Stallings?"

"Miss Miller is a local girl. She was born in the Hayes Valley section of San Francisco, attended the University of California in Los Angeles, and returned home to pursue a career in drama. She still lives with her parents, attends church regularly, and has a devoted boyfriend."

"What's she doing in a national touring company of the vampire play, then? She would have had to audition in New York and travel from there."

"Theatre people are an itinerant lot, Abel."

He digested that for a moment, apparently willing to accept Claire Delacroix's judgement of the ingenue. "Her paramour would almost certainly be Timothy Rodgers, then."

"Indeed. I am impressed."

"Rodgers did not strike me as a likely suspect," Chase stated.

"Nor Miss Miller, me."

"What about Miss Stallings?" he queried.

"A very different story, there. First of all, her name isn't really Jeanette Stallings."

"The *nom de theatre* is a commonplace, Delacroix. Continue."

"Nor was she born in this country."

"That, too, I had already learned. That was why Pollard was coaching her in diction. Where was Miss Stallings born, Delacroix, and what is her real name?"

It was the habit of neither Abel Chase nor Claire Delacroix to use a notebook in their interrogations. Both prided themselves on their ability to retain everything said in their presence. Without hesitation Claire stated, "She was born in Szeged, Hungary. The name under which she entered the United States was Mitzi Kadar."

"Mitzi Kadar! Imre Hunyadi's Hungarian wife was Elena Kadar."

"And Mitzi's mother was Elena Kadar."

"Great glowing Geryon!" It was as close to an expletive as Abel Chase was known to come in everyday speech. "Was Jeanette Stallings Imre Hunyadi's daughter? There was no mention of a child in any biographical material on Hunyadi."

"Such is my suspicion," Claire Delacroix asserted.

"You did not have the advantage of reading the threatening note that Captain Baxter found in Hunyadi's dressing room, Delacroix."

"No," she conceded. "I am sure you will illuminate me as to its content."

"It was made up to look like a newspaper clipping," Chase informed. "But I turned it over and found that the obverse was blank. It appeared, thus, to be a printer's proof rather than an actual cutting. Every newspaper maintains obituaries of prominent figures, ready for use in case of their demise. When the time comes, they need merely fill in the date and details of death, and they're ready to go to press. But I don't think this was a real newspaper proof. There was no identification of the paper—was it the *Call* or the *Bulletin*, the *Tribune* or the *Gazette*? The proof should indicate."

Abel Chase paused to run a finger beneath his mustache before resuming. "The typographic styles of our local dailies differ from one another in subtle but significant detail. The *faux* obituary came from none of them. It was a hoax, created by a malefactor and executed by a local job printer. It was cleverly intended as a psychological attack on Hunyadi, just as was the dead rodent that was found in his dressing room."

"And for what purpose was this hoax perpetrated?" Delacroix prompted.

"It did not read like a normal newspaper obituary," Abel Chase responded. "There is none of the usual respectful tone. It stated, instead, that Hunyadi abandoned his wife in Hungary when she was heavy with child."

"An act of treachery, do you not agree?" Claire put in.

"And that his wife continued her career as a medical researcher while raising her fatherless child until, the child having reached her majority, the mother, despondent, took her own life."

"Raising the child was an act of courage and of strength, was it not? But the crime of suicide—to have carried her grief and rage for two decades, only to yield in the end to despair—who was more guilty, the self-killer or the foul husband who abandoned her?"

Chase rubbed his mustache with the knuckles of one finger. "We need to speak with Miss Stallings."

"First, perhaps we had best talk with Captain Baxter and his men. We should determine what Sergeant Costello and Officer Murray have found in their examination of the premises."

"Not a bad idea," Chase assented, "although I expect they would have notified me if anything significant had been found."

Together they sought the uniformed police captain and sergeant. Costello's statement was less than helpful. He had examined the inner sill opening upon the window through which Abel Chase had peered approximately an hour before. It was heavily laden with dust, he reported, indicating that even had a contortionist been able to squeeze through its narrow opening, no one had actually done so.

"But a bat might have flown through that window, sir, without disturbing the dust," the credulous Costello concluded.

Murray had gone over the rest of the backstage area, and the two policemen had examined the auditorium and lobby together, without finding any useful clues.

"We are now faced with a dilemma," Abel Chase announced, raising his forefinger for emphasis. "Count Hunyadi was found dead in his dressing room, the door securely locked from the inside. It is true that he died of heart failure, but what caused his heart to fail? My assistant, Doctor Delacroix, suggests a mysterious drug administered along with a dose of cocaine, through one of the marks on the victim's neck." He pressed two fingers dramatically into the side of his own neck, simulating Hunyadi's stigmata.

"The problem with this is that no hypodermic syringe was found in the dressing room. Hunyadi might have thrown a syringe through the small open window letting upon the alley. But we searched the alley and it was not found. It might have been retrieved by a confederate, but the lack of footprints in the so-unusual snow eliminates that possibility. A simpler explanation must be sought."

Abel Chase paused to look around the room at the others, then resumed. "We might accept Sergeant Costello's notion that a vampire entered the room unobtrusively, in human form. He administered the fatal drug, then exited by flying through the window, first having taken the form of a bat. It might be possible for the flying mammal to carry an empty hypodermic syringe in its mouth. This not only solves the problem of the window's narrow opening, but that of the undisturbed dust on the sill and the untrampled snow in the alley. But while I try to keep an open mind at all times, I fear it would take a lot of convincing to get me to believe in a creature endowed with such fantastic abilities."

Accompanied by Claire Delacroix, Chase next met with Jeanette Stallings, the Mina of the vampire play. Jeanette Stallings, born Mitzi Kadar, was the opposite of Claire Delacroix in coloration and in manner. Claire was tall, blonde, pale of complexion and cool of manner, and garbed in silver. Jeanette—or Mitzi—sported raven tresses surrounding a face of olive complexion, flashing black eyes, and crimson lips matched in hue by a daringly modish frock.

Even her makeup case, an everyday accouterment for a member of her profession, and which she held tucked beneath one arm in lieu of a purse, was stylishly designed in the modern mode.

"Yes, my mother was the great Elena Kadar," she was quick to admit. In her agitation, the nearly flawless English diction she had learned with the assistance of Samuel Pollard became more heavily marked by a European accent. "And that pseudo-Count Hunyadi was my father. I was raised to hate and despise him, and my mother taught me well. I celebrate his death!"

Abel Chase's visage was marked with melancholy. "Miss Stallings, your feelings are your own, but they do not justify murder. I fear—I fear that you will pay a severe penalty for your deed. The traditional reluctance of the State to inflict capital punishment upon women will in all likelihood save you from the noose, but a life behind bars would not be pleasant."

"That remains to be seen," Jeanette Stallings uttered defiantly. "But even if I am convicted, I will have no regrets."

A small sigh escaped Chase's lips. "You might have a chance after all. From what I've heard of the late Count Hunyadi, there will be little sympathy for the deceased or outrage at his murder. And if you were taught from the cradle to regard him with such hatred, a good lawyer might play upon a jury's sympathies and win you a lesser conviction and a suspended sentence, if not an outright acquittal."

"I told you," Jeanette Stallings replied, "I don't care. He didn't know I was his daughter. He pursued the female members of the company like a bull turned loose in a pasture full of heifers. He was an uncaring beast. The world is better off without him."

At this, Chase nodded sympathetically. At the same time, however, he remained puzzled regarding the cause of Hunyadi's heart failure and the means by which it had been brought about.

He began to utter a peroration on this twin puzzle.

At this moment Claire Delacroix saw fit to extract a compact from her own metallic purse. To the surprise of Abel Chase, for until now she had seemed absorbed in the investigation at hand, she appeared to lose all interest in the proceedings. Instead she turned her back on Chase and Jeanette Stallings and addressed her attention to examining the condition of her flawlessly arranged hair, her lightly rouged cheeks and pale mouth. She removed a lipstick from her purse and proceeded to perfect the coloring of her lips.

To Abel Chase's further consternation, she turned back to face the others, pressing the soft, waxy lipstick clumsily to her mouth. The stick of waxy pigment broke, smearing her cheek and creating a long false scar across her pale cheek.

With a cry of grief and rage she flung the offending lipstick across the room. "Now look what I've done!" she exclaimed. "You'll lend me yours, Mitzi, I know it. As woman to woman, you can't let me down!"

Before Jeanette Stallings could react, Claire Delacroix had seized the actress's makeup case and yanked it from her grasp.

Jeanette Stallings leaped to retrieve the case, but Abel Chase caught her from behind and held her, struggling, by both her elbows. The woman writhed futilely, attempting to escape Chase's grasp, screeching curses all the while in her native tongue.

Claire Delacroix tossed aside her own purse and with competent fingers opened Jeanette Stallings's makeup case. She removed from it a small kit and opened this to reveal a hypodermic syringe and a row of fluid-filled ampoules. All were of a uniform size and configuration, and the contents of each were a clear, watery-looking liquid, save for one. This container was smaller than the others, oblong in shape, and of an opaque composition.

She held the syringe upright and pressed its lever, raising a single drop of slightly yellowish liquid from its point.

"A powerful solution of cocaine, I would suggest," Claire ground between clenched teeth. "So Imre Hunyadi behaved toward the women of the company as would a bull in a pasture? And I suppose you ministered to his needs with this syringe, eh? A quick way of getting the drug into his bloodstream. But what is in this other ampoule, Miss Kadar?"

The Hungarian-born actress laughed bitterly. "You'll never know. You can send it to a laboratory and they'll have no chance whatever to analyze the compound."

"You're probably right in that regard," Claire conceded. "But there will be no need for that. Anyone who knows your mother's pioneering work in anesthesiology would be aware that she was studying the so-called spinal anesthetic. It is years from practical usage, but in experiments it has succeeded in temporarily deadening all nerve activity in the body below the point in the spinal cord where it is administered."

Jeanette Stallings snarled.

"The danger lies in the careful placement of the needle," Claire Delacroix continued calmly. "For the chemical that blocks all sensation of pain from rising to the brain, also cancels commands from the brain to the body. If the anesthetic is administered to the spinal cord above the heart and lungs, they shortly cease to function. There is no damage to the organs — they simply come to a halt. The anesthetic can be administered in larger or smaller doses, of course. Mixed with a solution of cocaine, it might take several minutes to work."

To Abel Chase she said, "In a moment, I will fetch Captain Baxter and tell him that you are holding the killer for his disposition."

Then she said, "You visited your father in his dressing room between the second and third acts of the vampire play. You offered him cocaine. You knew of his habit and you even volunteered to administer the dose for him. He would not have recognized you as his daughter as he had never met you other than as Jeanette Stallings. You injected the drug and left the room. Before the spinal anesthetic could work its deadly effects, Count Hunyadi locked the door behind you. He then sat at his dressing table and quietly expired."

Still holding the hypodermic syringe before her, Claire Delacroix started for the door. Before she had taken two steps, Jeanette Stallings tore loose from the grasp of Abel Chase and threw herself bodily at the other woman.

Claire Delacroix flinched away, holding the needle beyond Jeanette Stallings's outstretched hands. Abel Chase clutched Jeanette Stallings to his chest.

"Don't be a fool," he hissed. "Delacroix, quickly, fetch Baxter and his men while I detain this misguided child."

Once his associate had departed, Abel Chase released Mitzi Kadar, stationing himself with his back to the room's sole exit.

Her eyes blazing, the Hungarian-born actress hissed, "Kill me now, if you must. Else let me have my needle and chemicals for one moment and I will end my life, myself!"

Without awaiting an answer, she hurled herself at Abel Chase, fingernails extended liked the claws of an angry tigress to rip the eyes from his head.

"No," Chase negatived, catching her once again by both wrists. He had made a lightning-like assessment of the young woman, and formed his decision. "Listen to me, Mitzi. Your deed is not forgivable but it is understandable, a fine but vital distinction. You can be saved. You had better have me as a friend than an enemy."

As suddenly as she had lunged at the amateur sleuth, Mitzi Kadar collapsed in a heap at his feet, her hands slipping from his grasp, her supple frame wracked with sobs. "I lived that he might die," she gasped. "I do not care what happens to me now."

Abel Chase placed a hand gently on her dark hair. "Poor child," he murmured, "poor, poor child. I will do what I can to help you. I will do all that I can."

People who care about such matters might as well know that Vega's Taqueria is based on the Mexicali Rose restaurant, a classic institution located directly across the street from the city jail in Oakland, California. Rudy Valdez, the friendly bartender in my story, was based on a real man, Rudy Rubalcava, who tended bar at Mexicali Rose in the 1980s.

Rudy was a sweet-natured, immensely popular gentleman, beloved of off-duty Oakland cops, garrulous bail-bondsmen, freshly released prostitutes, pressmen from the nearby, venerable Oakland Tribune, and assorted bar-flies and other Damon Runyonesque characters. When I wrote "At Vega's Taqueria" I didn't tell Rudy about his fictionalized appearance. I planned to wait until the story was published, which it was in Amazing Stories for September, 1990, then under the editorship of Ted White.

As soon as I received a copy of the magazine I would march into Mexicali Rose and present it to Rudy. But a few weeks before that happily anticipated occasion I picked up a copy of the Oakland Trib and spotted a headline: Popular Bartender Slain. My blood froze. Hoping against hope that the victim was not Rudy Rubalcava I read the story. But Rudy had indeed been murdered.

Leaving work late at night he had pulled into a gas station to fill up. The killer appeared from the shadows, demanded money, then flew into a panic and stabbed Rudy fatally even though he was in the act of complying.

The killer was caught a few days later, crashing a stolen taxi after a high-speed chase by Oakland police. He was a drug addict, newly released from prison, who needed money to feed his habit.

At Vega's Taqueria

VERNON BROWNE LOOKED AT THE MURAL BE-hind the cash register—and blinked, startled. He put down his icy margarita and waved at the bartender. "Rudy," Vernon said, "c'mere. C'mere a minute, will ya?"

"What's 'at, Vern?" Rudy Valdez lowered the glass he was wiping and leaned on the polished mahogany. "Something the matter?"

"No, look." Browne pointed.

"That lady in the big hat? Hah! She looks something like you, Vern. You got a sister or what?"

"No, not the lady. Wait, wait, she's paying her bill. There. See it now? The picture on the wall. The Aztec picture."

Rudy squinted at the mural. The heavy summer atmosphere, thickened by cooking fumes, smoke, and just a touch of alcohol, was almost tangible. "I don' know what you mean, Vern. That picture been there for years. Mr. Vega likes Aztec paintings. Tha's why the place is full of them."

Browne exhaled loudly, exasperated. "Look at that guy. In the painting. Don't you see him?"

Rudy turned to face the painting. He studied for a minute, then turned back to Browne. "You mean the guy in the Crushers helmet?"

"You do see it, then! Phew, for a minute I thought I was nuts. What's an Aztec doing in an Oakland Crushers helmet? Who painted that mural, some local guy, right?"

"Roberto Cortez. He lives right here in Oakland. He's into Columbian art, Mayan ruins, that kinda thing. He does paintings and pottery in the old style. Mr. Vega hired him to decorate the restaurant when we moved from the old place."

Browne took a sip of his drink. It was delicious. He dipped a corn chip in salsa and munched on it, then washed it down with more margarita. "Cortez, huh? What's he, some kind of a practical joker, putting a Crushers helmet on an Aztec warrior? Or is that guy a priest?"

"No, Vern." A line creased Rudy's brow. "Roberto is a scholar. He wouldn' put nothing there that wasn' authentic. Din' you know the Aztecs played football? The Spanish learn' the game from the Aztecs. The English learn' it from the Spanish an' turn it into rugby, an' it come back here to the States with the English an' turn into American football. That's why he put the Crushers helmet on that guy. Those Aztecs invented football."

Vernon Browne shook his head. "That's impossible."

"No it's not. I'm tellin' you true, Vern. Roberto Cortez, he's a real scholar. He wouldn' make that up."

"I'll have another margarita, Rudy." Vern drained his glass and helped himself to a couple more chips. "No, that's impossible. I'll concede, maybe the Aztecs had a game something like football. I'll even admit that it might be an ancestor of modern football even though I doubt it. It's possible, okay. But you can't tell me that the Aztecs wore football helmets. Not Oakland Crushers helmets."

"Yes, sir, they did. They really did. You wan' me to make a phone call to Mr. Cortez, an' you go see him? He's a little suspicious of Anglos but I'll talk to him. If I say you're okay, he'll prob'ly talk to you."

*   *   *

Roberto Cortez lived in a subdivided Victorian on Sixth Street near the freeway.

Vernon Browne parked outside, sent up a quick prayer to whatever gods watch over Toyota Camrys, and rapped on the doorframe. He looked around, trying to figure out whether the neighborhood was sinking slowly into slumhood or preparing itself for gentrification. The door opened and he looked into the face of a slim, olive-skinned man in his late thirties.

The man said, "You Browne?"

Vernon nodded. "You're Cortez."

A grunt. Then, "Rudy said you wanted to ask me some questions."

Vernon nodded again. Cortez spoke English perfectly, he thought, without even the trace of an accent that Rudy Valdez' pronunciation showed.

"Okay. Ask away."

"It's a little bit, ah—may I come in? I mean . . ."

"What is it? Rudy said you were interested in my murals. The ones at Vegas's Taqueria. What are you, an art collector? You got a commission for me? You'll have to talk to my agent."

"No. It's nothing like that. I—can I come in?"

Cortez moved out of the way. Browne stepped into the vestibule, waited while Cortez reached behind him to close the door. Cortez led the way upstairs and opened a door to a flat. Browne went in.

The heat of the day had saturated the apartment, but Vern could still appreciate the work that had gone into it. The furniture was either Art Deco near-antiques or modern reproductions; Vern couldn't tell which. The curved chrome, the plush upholstery, the geometric shapes and zigzag patterns suggestive of lightning were dizzying.

On a glass-topped table stood a rectangular radio covered with cobalt-blue mirrors. Its dial glowed a rich orange-yellow. Music came from concealed speakers in the corners of the room. Apparently, the old radio had been gutted and its insides replaced with modern components. The music sounded like some kind of experimental classic, mostly woodwinds and percussion instruments, a baroque composition with Latin overtones.

"Villa-Lobos," Cortez said, reading Vern's mind. "That's his *Choro* Number seven, 1924. He was a great admirer of Bach's. That's my wife's tape. She's playing first clarinet."

As if on cue, a stunning blonde entered the room.

"Esther," Cortez said, "this is the fellow Rudy phoned about. He's some kind of art expert."

Esther extended her hand and Vernon took it. Despite the day's heat, her skin was cool. She smiled at him.

"I'm not really an art expert at all. I don't want to mislead you. I work for the Oakland *Journal*."

"You're a reporter?"

"Purchasing. Paper, ink, supplies. I just stopped at Vega's for a cold drink, and I saw your husband's murals there."

Cortez said, "I painted those years ago, Mr. Browne. When

they tore down the old building, where the city jail is now, and put up the new one."

"Yes. It's just—there's a football player. In one of the paintings. An Aztec wearing an Oakland Crushers helmet."

Cortez smiled. "Didn't you know the Crushers took their logo and team colors from the Aztecs? That's where football was invented—in pre-Columbian Mexico."

Browne shook his head. "That's what Rudy told me. You didn't just add that figure to the painting?"

"Nope."

"Maybe something happened, somebody spilled something on it, rubbed the paint with their shoulder, whatever. You went in and touched it up, you put the helmet on that guy for a joke?"

"Nope."

"I don't understand." Uninvited, Vernon sank into an Art Deco easy chair upholstered in deep, dark blue plush. "I've been going to Vega's for years. Since the old place. I eat there a couple of times a week, stop in for a drink in between. I must have looked at that mural hundreds of times. Thousands, maybe. Why didn't I ever see the helmet before?"

Cortez laughed once, quietly. "People can look at a painting endless times and still find something new in it. That's one of the characteristics of good art. I'm really flattered that you finally spotted the football helmet. What do you think, Esther?"

Esther said, "Same thing with music. I've heard that Villa-Lobos piece hundreds of times, played it—God, if you count rehearsals, I don't know how many. And I can still—"

"But I still don't . . ." Browne stood up. "Football wasn't . . ." he tried again. "This has to be . . . I don't know . . . some kind of joke . . . some kind of quirk . . . I just can't . . ."

Roberto and Esther were both seated now. They looked over at him. Neither spoke.

"Excuse me." Browne moved toward the door. "I'll . . . I don't . . . know. . . . I have to go home and think about this."

"You don't believe me?" Roberto Cortez asked.

Browne shook his head again. "It isn't that. I can only . . . I can't explain it. It's just too strange. It's not your fault. I just have to . . ."

*   *   *

Outside Cortez' Victorian, Vernon took a deep breath. He walked once around his Nissan Sentra. Nobody had touched it. That was a relief. He held the key for a moment before unlocking the door.

Something was strange. He felt mildly disoriented, almost dizzy, but the sensation passed. He climbed into the Sentra and started for home.

But he couldn't go home.

Instead, he drove back downtown and parked outside Vega's Taqueria. Inside the restaurant the cashier smiled at him. "Want a table, Mr. Browne?"

He shook his head, stood staring at the mural. The Aztec *was* wearing a football helmet. Breechclout and feathers and an Oakland Crushers helmet. Vernon leaned closer. There was Roberto Cortez' signature in the corner of the painting. Beneath the *z* there was even a date. The mural was six years old. Browne could find no evidence that the painting had been altered.

Rudy Valdez was still on duty behind the bar. The place was a lot more crowded than it had been earlier, and Rudy was hopping to make drinks and change for bar patrons and to fill service orders brought from the dining room.

Vern waited for a lull, then signaled Rudy over to him.

"You see Cortez?"

Vern nodded.

"What he tell you?"

"Everything you said. Everything you said."

"How 'bout a margarita, Vern? On me."

Browne shook his head. "I've got to work this out."

"No you don'. It's just a funny thing. You know Detroit Jackson? Colored fella, comes in here a lot?"

Browne waited.

"Sure you do. Old guy, got a gold tooth right here, likes to talk a lot, drinks bourbon ginger. He says, when you get one of them funny memory things—you forget somebody's name you seen every day for years, or you suddenly don' know what day it is, you know Detroit Jackson, he says you been hit by a cosmic ray. He says they comin' to Earth all the time, you can' see 'em or hear 'em, but when they hit your brain they can knock a little connection loose, you get a funny memory thing like that."

Browne looked at Rudy.

"You wan' that drink on the house?" Rudy offered again.

Browne shook his head. No.

"Whatta you think of that theory, Vern? Look, here's a waitress, I gotta go now. Don' let it worry you."

Browne left his car at Vega's, walked three blocks to the Oakland *Press* tower, headed for sports. He found Mort Halloran there, sitting in front of his VDT, worrying over a story.

"You got a minute, Mort? You cover the Crushers for the *Press*."

"Season's been over for months, Vern. This is baseball season."

"Yeah, but I have a football question."

"You got a bet going?"

"Not exactly. Mort, how long have the Crushers been around?"

"That one I can answer. Nineteen thirty-seven. Played at Tynan Field in Emeryville. Barely survived playing to empty bleachers and the players' families for the first ten years. Won the Western Conference in '48, lost the playoff to the Brooklyn Dodgers, 14 to 11. Won the conference again in '53, beat Philadelphia for the championship, 42 to 12. Moved to the Coliseum in '60. You need the modern stuff, or that enough?"

"I mean — how did football get started? Didn't the college game come from English rugby? About a hundred years ago?"

"Oh, you mean the *really* early days. Yeah, but the English got it from the Spanish and they got it from the Aztecs all the way back in the fifteenth century. It's an old, old game. Crushers took their logo from some Aztec team, I think. You want me to dig out their press book for you? This a heavy bet you got going, or what?"

Browne walked away without another word. At Vega's he was starting to climb into his car when he felt a hand on his shoulder. "Rudy?"

"You okay, Vern? I'm off shift now, jus' goin' home."

Vernon shook his head. "I don't know. I guess I was wrong. Everybody says you're right. About the football thing, I mean. The Crushers helmet on that Aztec in Roberto Cortez' painting."

"You still upset, though, aren' you? I can tell."

Browne leaned on the roof of his car. "Yeah. I guess it isn't really important, but — it keeps bothering me. I mean, you think you know what the world is all about, right? I don't mean like a chemist or a philosopher, but you know certain things. And then one of them is all wrong. All different. I don't know. Am I the only one out of step? Everybody knows that the Aztecs played football except me. I never knew that. I always thought — never mind. But how can that happen? How can that be? How did I walk around all my life, the only guy who didn't know that?"

Full night had fallen but the air was no less torrid, no less heavy. The Vega's Taqueria parking lot was brightly illuminated to discourage car thieves and vandals. Rudy's Hispanic features looked pasty and flat in the artificial glare; Vern knew that his own lighter skin must look like a dead man's.

"Maybe you should see a doc," Rudy advised. "Or a priest. Say,

I know a priest who's a shrink, too. He's a real MD, a psychiatrist. And a priest. You Catholic, Vern?"

Browne shook his head.

"Well, he's a nice person. Very approachable. You can go see him anyhow. You wan' me to give you his name? You wan' me to call him for you, like I called Cortez? I don' mind, Vern. You're my friend; I'm a little bit worried about you."

* * *

The church was called Santa Maria de Aragon. It was small and slightly run-down, on a street of wooden houses and small *bodegas*. The bulletin board on the patchy lawn was in both English and Spanish.

Vernon Browne locked his De Soto convertible and stood looking at the canvas top. He hoped nobody would try to rob the car by slashing the cloth. There was nothing to steal in the car, but a petty criminal might try anyway. Or some angry kid might put a knife through the canvas as an act of sheer vandalism.

Well, he couldn't do anything about that.

The church was open, quiet, almost empty. A few parishioners were scattered in the pews, mumbling and fingering rosaries or meditating quietly. Vernon wasn't sure what to do. The nearest person to him was a vaguely familiar-looking woman. She glanced at Vernon, crossed herself, and hurried out of the church. Vernon looked after her. Was she the woman who had stood in front of the mural at Vega's? He wasn't sure, and now she was gone.

He approached another, older woman and asked if she knew where he could find the priest. In heavily accented English accompanied by vigorous gestures she directed him down a hallway to a little office.

Father Nuñez was a short, wizened man wearing a threadbare black suit. He looked up when Vernon knocked at the door.

"Did Rudy phone you? Rudy the bartender at Vega's? He said you were a psychiatrist as well as a priest and I—"

Father Nuñez smiled and gestured Vern to a chair. "Please. Rudy phoned me. What can I do for you, Mr. Browne? Is this a spiritual problem or a medical one?"

He held a thin hand toward Vernon. As they shook hands, Vernon wondered how old the priest could be. His grip was thin but vigorous; his skin seemed to be made of a million fine lines.

"I'm not sure, Father—Doctor. Does it matter which title I call you by?"

"Whatever makes you comfortable, Mr. Browne. My first

name is Alejandro. Use that if you prefer. Or just Alex. It doesn't matter. But if it's medical, you see—well, I hold a degree in medicine and a diploma in psychiatry, but I don't really practice. I'm not even licensed by the State of California." He spread his hands, taking in their surroundings. The office was shabby, the thin carpet as threadbare as the priest's black suit.

Vernon covered his face with his hands. "Maybe we could just talk a little. Informally. Father."

The priest made a vaguely encouraging sound.

"Did Rudy tell you what's been happening to me? I mean— things are changing. I think they're changing. But nobody else notices."

Nuñez looked at Vernon. "Can you be more specific, Mr. Browne?"

"Well, like the Aztec in the Crushers helmet."

"Yes, Rudy told me about that."

"Well, he had this theory. Or he said this guy Detroit Jackson had some theory. About cosmic rays."

Nuñez laughed. "Yes, Rudy's told me about that, too. Far-fetched, don't you think? But it isn't impossible, is it? Who knows what's impossible, Mr. Browne—if anything, eh? Do you take that notion seriously?"

Vernon shook his head. "I could almost believe it, about the picture, I mean. But something else keeps happening." He laced his fingers together, squeezed them between his knees. He could feel himself sweating.

"I'm afraid we're a very poor parish, here at Santa Maria's, but can I offer you a cup of tea? Or something cold? It's still beastly hot, isn't it? Not the climate we're accustomed to."

"No, nothing. Nothing, thanks."

After a silence the priest said, "Well, then what was this other thing that you say keeps happening? Is it more pictures that change?"

"It's my car."

"You're having car trouble? That can be upsetting, but it hardly—"

"My car keeps changing. I mean, I keep thinking that it's changing."

"I don't understand. You trade it in too often, is it something like that?"

"No. I mean—look, Alex, Father—"

"Whichever."

"Alex? You don't mind? I drive this De Soto. A nice car. It's a convertible. Firedome V8 engine, Fluid Drive transmission, wire-recorder with four speakers. I really like the car. Bought it new, two years ago. From Henderson De Soto, on Broadway."

"Yes, I know the people. Very reputable. But what's the problem?"

"Well, I don't think it's always been a De Soto. I mean, everything is right. I've got the registration in the glove compartment. The keys right here." He reached into his pocket, extracted his keys and held them up for Father Nuñez to see. They were attached to a leather fob embossed with an enamel De Soto crest. Father Nuñez nodded. "Yes."

"But I think it was a Nissan. Or—maybe a Toyota. Or a Studebaker. Didn't Henderson used to sell Studebakers? I think I bought one from them a couple of years ago. I think I still own it. Only it's a De Soto."

"They haven't built Studebakers in years, Mr. Browne. Decades. As far as I know, Henderson has always been a De Soto dealership. I've lived in Oakland for forty-five years, and they've always sold De Soto's."

"Then what's changing?"

The priest sat quietly for a while. The only light in the room came from a small lamp on his desk. There was a window behind him, the lights of downtown winking through it, through the steaming night. "Do you have a job, Mr. Browne? A steady job, a regular income? Do you mind my asking?"

"Do you want money, Alex? For the church? I mean, if there's a fee—"

"Not at all. I find this fascinating, and if I can help my fellow man—"

"I'm not Catholic."

"God makes Protestants and Buddhists and even atheists. It's my job to help everybody I can help."

"Well, I work for the Oakland *Press*."

"You mean a print-shop?"

"No. The *Press*. You know, the morning paper."

"Oh, the *Mirror*. Yes, it is our daily press, isn't it?"

"No, damn it! I'm sorry."

"It's all right."

"I didn't mean to—I mean, the Oakland *Press*. It's the only daily in town. It's been published for a hundred years. More."

"How can that be? Mr. Browne, I'm seventy-seven years old, and I've lived the past forty-five of those years in this city. I've been reading the *Daily Mirror* for all of those years. Wouldn't I have heard of it, if there were another daily paper here?"

Despite the heat, Vernon felt icy. He looked at Nuñez, then past him into the gloomy, torrid night. "Look, there's the Press Tower, you can see it from here." He pushed himself to his feet, circled behind the priest, staring out the dirt-streaked window at the gothic tower where the circle of a huge illuminated clock surmounted the glaring word *Mirror.*

*   *   *

Vernon Browne started down the church steps. In his pocket was a slip of paper with a name and phone number given him by the priest. *Simon Carstairs,* and after the telephone number, *Physics Department. University of California.*

He turned to get a parting glance at the church. It looked somehow different, its facade more rectangular than it had appeared earlier. And hadn't there been a steeple? He wasn't certain, and the lighting was different now. He looked at the bilingual announcement board. It was in Hebrew and Spanish. The heading read *Congragacion B'nai Israel—Sefardico.*

He ran back up the steps, taking them two at a time. He brushed past a heavyset woman as he plunged through the doorway. She seemed vaguely familiar, but he didn't stop to talk. He ran down the aisle, between the rows of pews, past the pulpit and torah, down the dim hallway into the shabby office.

"Mr. Browne. Is something wrong?"

"Father?"

The old man's wrinkled face split into a smile. "They usually call me Rabbi. But whatever makes you comfortable."

"Aren't you Father Nuñez? Alejandro Nuñez?"

"Of course I'm Alejandro Nuñez. We just spent the last half hour talking."

"And isn't this a Catholic church?"

"There are several Catholic churches in this section. But this is a synagogue, Mr. Browne. A Sephardic synagogue. Our congregation is composed of Hispanic Jews. Are you all right, Mr. Browne?"

Vernon backed toward the doorway. "I—yes, I'm all right. I'm sorry."

"You have that number I gave you—Simon Carstairs's number over at UC?"

"I have it. Thanks. Thanks, Rabbi Nuñez. I, I—never mind."

He staggered from the office, leaned on a pew for a few minutes until the shaking was under control, then walked out of the synagogue. His LaSalle coupé was parked at the curb, safe and untouched.

* * *

In the morning he dialed the paper to tell his boss he would be out sick. The switchboard operator said, "Good morning, Oakland *Times-Reporter.*" Vernon got through to his own department and left his message.

He climbed on his Harley Indian and rode the freeway toward Berkeley. He was still agitated, but he knew a certain way to calm himself. He slipped on his earphones and tuned the bike radio to a classical music station. The announcer's plummy voice was describing the next piece of music: the overture to *The Yentas* by Ginsberg and Solomon.

Ginsburg and Solomon?

The music began—bright, cheerful tunes worked into a pleasing medley. Vernon felt better, almost from the first note. But while the music sounded vaguely familiar, he couldn't quite place the melodies. Or the operetta. He thought he knew the G&S canon by heart. *The Yentas?* He vaguely recalled that one. Something about young lovers and interfering in-laws. And one family was Jewish and the other Irish? But that wasn't a G&S operetta. That was—he couldn't remember.

Ginsberg and Solomon?

With a roar, a rocket sled zoomed past him, its rider making an obscene gesture as the sled threw up a cloud of noxious fumes.

Vernon Browne's brightened mood was shattered.

He got off the freeway at the University Avenue exit and drove up to UC. The heat had not broken, and the air was wetter than ever. In fact, the moisture condensed as a sort of hot mist, soaking his face and hair.

On the lush lawn outside the physics building a couple of lunar trees had settled in. They were surrounded by an iron fence. The sign on the fence warned that the trees were carnivorous and fond of humans. Vern stood watching them for a few minutes. They were quarreling over something, snapping at each other with giant claw-edged fronds. Vern shook his head—he'd always thought it unwise of the Apollo-Soyuz expedition to bring back dangerous lunar life-forms. But it was too late to get rid of them now—they had taken too well to Earth's soil and climate. They had become a regular part of the ecology.

He found Professor Carstairs's office at the end of a second-floor hallway. Carstairs was a heavyset man who looked like a pile of soft dough. His handshake was tentative and his questioning suspicious.

After Vernon had spoken for a few minutes, Carstairs picked up a two-way radio mike and called Alejandro Nuñez. He darted glances at Vernon while whispering into the microphone. Finally he put it back on its hook.

"Alex says you're for real."

"Yes, I am."

"And you're having these odd hallucinations. I'm not sure why Alex sent you to me. He's the shrink. I'm just a theoretical physicist."

"They're not hallucinations."

Carstairs raised his eyebrows. "No?"

"Everything is changing."

"Of course it is. We've known that since Democritus."

"I don't mean that everything is changing. I mean—well, it *is* changing. It is!"

"Mr. Browne, maybe you ought to go back to Alex Nuñez and ask him to recommend a good facility. A resident facility."

"You think I'm crazy?"

"Who, me? I'm not a psychiatrist, I told you that."

"Look, Dr. Carstairs—ahh—okay, so I'm crazy. Maybe. Maybe I am crazy. Okay, but I'm not violent. I'm not dangerous. So will you humor me? Will you talk to me for a little while, listen to what I have to say?"

Carstairs steepled his puffy fingers, leaned his soft chin on them. Only his eyes were hard and sharp. "Five minutes. If you insist."

Behind him, through a window, Vernon could see the lawn. The hot mist was so thick that water was condensing on the window and running down it like rain. Even so, Vern could see the two lunar trees in their cage. A large woman stood outside the bars. She carried a huge handbag. She reached into it and pulled something out. She reached back and threw it over the fence. Whatever it was, Vernon could see it writhing even as it coursed in an arc. One of the trees caught it skillfully but the other grabbed it away. They quarreled and fought silently over the morsel.

"I can't waste time, Mr. Browne," Simon Carstairs was saying.

"Wh—what?"

"I just told you I'd give you five minutes if you really insist. But then you just sat there staring out the window."

"Dr. Carstairs—how long have we had lunar life forms on Earth?"

"Are you serious? Since the first moon landings. Nineteen sixty-nine. Back during President McCarthy's first term. I remember how he called the astronauts on the moon and read them a sonnet he'd just composed. That's what we get for electing a poet president."

"Right—1969. That's what I thought. I mean I knew that all along. I think I did, anyhow."

The mist had finally turned to rain, and the lawn outside the physics building was rapidly turning into a swamp.

Vernon said, "Either the world is changing, or maybe I'm changing. Somehow I'm getting false memories. But I don't think so. I think the world is different. Like—have I always had an Indian bike? I think I have. I've got my helmet, gloves, the registration slip, everything. It says I've owned the Indian for three years. But—I feel as if I maybe had something else."

"A different brand of motorcycle, you mean?"

"Yes. Or no. I don't know. Maybe I had a car."

"Maybe you did. Until you traded it for the motorcycle. Or maybe you own a car *and* a motorcycle."

Vern shook his head. "I guess it could be. But—could one turn into the other? I mean, ah, I guess I don't mean could you take the parts of a, say, a Tucker Torpedo and take 'em apart and cut 'em down and build a bike out of them. I mean, could the one just turn into the other? Could the world change? And everybody takes it for granted, nobody notices, because they change along with it? But somehow I *didn't* change? The change didn't take right, it didn't work completely for me, so I have these memories of the way things were before?"

Carstairs leaned back, grinning broadly. "Have you ever studied physics, Mr. Browne?"

"High school. Let's see, we had units on heat, optics, mechanics—is that what you mean?"

Carstairs nodded condescendingly. "I had in mind high-energy theoretical physics. Specifically, quantum probability theory."

Vern shook his head. No. Behind Carstairs, the water had risen so the lawn was completely obliterated. The sun looked like a fuzzy yellow disk in the gray, wet sky. Occasional splashes marked the surface of the swamp.

"You see," Simon Carstairs said, "what you're talking about fits in rather nicely with quantum theory. Heisenberg, Schrödinger,

Planck of course. The great names of the century."

"I don't get it."

"Let me put it this way, Mr. Browne. According to quantum probability, we don't really *know* the location and energy state of very small particles. Not only *do* we not know, we *cannot* know. To find out, we have to put energy into the system, thereby changing the very information we were seeking. So when we find out what we wanted to know, the data is no longer valid. I've always thought that Einstein would consider this one of God's great jokes."

"You mean—I don't know whether I have a Harley or a Tucker? Can't I just go outside and look?"

"That isn't exactly what I mean. More to the point, you might own a Harley *and* a Tucker. Also a Kaiser, a Packard, a Nash and an infinite number of others. And an infinite number of each. A convertible, a sedan, a station wagon. And an infinite number of each of those—one in every color of the spectrum, one with a scratch on the hood, one without a scratch on the hood, one with—well, you see my point, don't you? There are an infinite number of particles in the universe, and the condition of each is an uncertainty, a statistical probability. Not a fact."

"But I only have *one* Harley."

"In this universe, yes. But suppose there is another universe, identical to this in every way, except that you own a Tucker Torpedo instead. Do you see?"

"There's only one me."

"In this universe there is. But there might be a universe exactly like ours, except that you were twins. Or triplets. Or where you are a woman instead of a man. Or where you died in infancy. Or were never even conceived."

Behind Carstairs, the water completely covered the windows. They were thick and strong, however. Thoroughly sealed. Through them, Vernon Browne could see hungry-looking creatures baring their fangs. Something big and gray charged straight at Carstairs and collided with the glass. It bounced off, drifted momentarily as if stunned, then swam away disappointed.

Vernon said, "This sounds like something out of *The Twilight Zone.*"

"The what?"

"*The Twilight Zone.*"

"What's that?"

"Don't you remember the old TV show? What's his name, Rod Sperling, Sterling, something like that. Weird sci-fi stuff."

"Oh, you mean *Tales of the Dusk*. I used to watch that when I was a kid. That was a great show, yes. They did deal with ideas a little like this. Ed Sullivan was the host."

Vern decided not to press the point. "Look, doctor. You've been pretty generous with your time. You said you'd give me five minutes and it's already been a lot longer than that. But I don't know if we're getting anywhere."

Carstairs reached for the bowl on his desk and drew out a lobster snack. He crunched it between his teeth. "Help yourself if you'd like," he said.

A huge form swam by behind Carstairs. For a split second it reminded Vernon uncannily of himself. "Professor Carstairs, this theory, this business of other worlds just like ours except for one or two things, like a motorcycle is a car or a man is a woman—is that just your idea?"

"Oh, no! There are papers on it. Bennett at Minnesota, Klass at Penn State, Jenkins at Norfolk. Several others as well."

"Well, look, is there a way that somebody could get from one world to another? Like, could I somehow slip into a different universe? One that's almost exactly like this? And maybe not even know the difference?"

Carstairs grinned, showing rows of triangular teeth. "If the other universe is enough like ours, there will be another Vernon Browne already in it." Behind him, the form that reminded Vernon of himself reappeared. It plastered itself to the window like a clinging starfish, waving tentacles in a manner both suggestive and repellant. Suddenly it was torn from its place by a school of tiny, flashing fish. The huge creature struggled, but only briefly. Within seconds it was reduced to a cluster of dead gobbets. The small fish fought and tore at the chunks of flesh, devouring them greedily. A pinkish stain slowly dissipated. Simon Carstairs appeared oblivious of the event. "Surely, this other you would take exception to your taking his place, taking over his life."

"Yeah, I guess so." Vern stood up and moved around the room. The warmth and moisture felt good on his skin. "But suppose that guy moved over to the *next* world. Are these things all next to each other? Or stacked like pages in the—the *Daily Call-Clarion?* That's where I work. I've been commuting to work over in the city for years."

"The city?"

"Sure. You know. San Fran—San—uh, give me a minute. I'll remember it."

"You mean Yerba Buena?"

"That's it. Right. Yerba Buena." What a relief that was!

"You actually commute to Yerba Buena every day?" Carstairs shook his head. "You actually travel through the swamps and the geysers and the lunar field every day? Amazing! My hat's off to you for that!"

"What about these different worlds, Professor?" Vernon persisted.

Carstairs cleared his throat. "If these multiple worlds exist, they're more like multiple realities. In a sense, the points within each of them occupy the same time-space loci. But in another sense, they do so in different continua. So they are locally mapped onto each other. Superimposed, you see." He laid one hand on his desktop, palm down, then turned the other palm up and laid it on top of the first, so that thumb covered thumb and fingers covered fingers.

"They are separated in a manner totally ineffable to us."

"Prof, I don't even know what you mean by that. But just suppose one of these guys—one of these *me's*—started shoving sideways. Shoved his way out of his world and into ours. He could shove the *me* from this world out of his way. Shove him over into the next world. You see? And the next, and the next."

Carstairs took another lobster snack. "You're sure? No? Well, Mr. Vernon, I suppose if we carry that notion to its logical conclusion, we will find an infinite series of *you's* rotating among an infinite number of universes. Each time you get shoved—and shove—you will find yourself in a universe farther from the one where you began. Farther and farther. And stranger and stranger. Stranger and stranger and stranger."

"And is there an end to this? An end and a beginning? Do you fall off the edge eventually? Or does it go in a circle? If I keep on shoving, world after world, *me* after *me*, will I wind up back where I started?"

"That's a very interesting question. I suppose the universes of reality might be circular in nature. I'm afraid, though, that even if they are, you'll never get home. No. The worlds are getting stranger as you get farther from your point of origin. Sooner or later you will find yourself in a world where you cannot survive. Once you reach such a world—well, I wish I could offer you some hope, sir or madam, but I'm afraid that there is none. No hope for your survival. No hope at all."

"No hope at all? But why me? Why me?" Bronenstein sobbed, on the edge of hysteria and despair.

"Scientists talk about *what*, Mr. Steinbacher, and about *how*, but not about *why*. Never about *why*. That is a philosopher's question, Mrs. Klemper. Or a clergything's. Not a scientist's. And now, I have to meet a class, and so I will have to ask you to leave." Carstairs showed his visitor out of the physics tank, and the visitor swam slowly, puzzlement still visible in uncertainly wavering antennae and dismally pulsating pigment spots, slowly toward home. As the traveler swam past the Venusian enclave, purple-tentacled aliens sang in the complex, amazingly beautiful harmonies for which they were famous over all the worlds, and giant feathery fern-eels visiting Earth from the civilized moons of Neptune danced merrily to the tune.

Sometime around 1943 I contracted measles or mumps or scarlet fever and was forced to spend several weeks in bed. I didn't feel sick; my biggest problem was boredom, not infection. My wonderful Grandma furnished me with masses of reading matter and set up a radio at my bedside to help me while away the days. The wooden cabinet, cloth speaker grille and warm, yellow-lighted dial on that radio remain vivid in my memory.

Over and over I'd cycle through a routine of scanning a newspaper, listening to a radio show, studying a comic book, reading a magazine.

The New York Post . . . Can You Top This? . . . Captain Marvel Adventures . . . Skyways . . .

The Daily Mirror . . . Duffy's Tavern . . . Green Lantern Quarterly . . . Life Magazine . . .

The New York Herald-Tribune . . . Suspense . . . The Human Torch . . . Weird Tales. . . .

Hey, that was the one that did it. I was eight years old and I knew that Weird Tales *was for me and I was for it. Fifty-seven years later, editors George Scithers and Darrell Schweitzer offered me a chance to fulfil my childhood dream, not merely to have a story in* Weird Tales *but to see my name on its cover.*

The concept of Weird Tales *nowadays, as the editors pointed out to me, is to remain true to the spirit of "the Unique Magazine" as it was during the glory days when it featured the works of H. P. Lovecraft, Frank Belknap Long, Robert E. Howard, Seabury Quinn, E. Hoffmann Price, and other regulars — as well as such one-story "drop in's" as John D. MacDonald, Robert A. Heinlein, and Tennessee Williams. To remain true to the spirit of the magazine's glory days, but not to remain stuck in the past. So I tried to tell a story that is modern in its setting and attitudes, but fantastic, even gothic, in its premise. I hope that my name on the cover sold some extra copies of* Weird Tales. *I'm also grateful to Messrs. Scithers and Schweitzer for providing the spur without which this story might never have been written.*

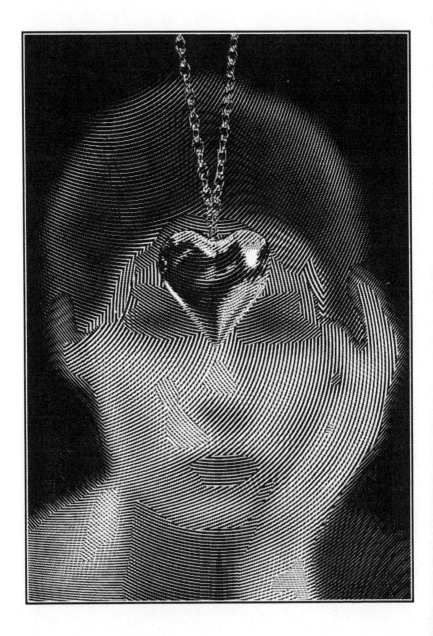

I Don't Tell Lies

THE DOUBLE BASS PLAYER WORE A MIDNIGHT
blue tux. His skin was very black. He was very tall and very thin
and he had cropped his hair close to his skull. He bent
over his instrument, bowing not plucking the strings. He was playing one of Erik Satie's *Gymnopédies*, transcribed from piano.

It was an upscale watering hole, bartenders in crimson jackets,
subdued lighting throughout provided by abstract neon sculptures, waitresses in white blouses and floor-length skirts moving
gracefully among the tables.

The clientele of the establishment consisted of young professionals on the make, former campus geeks rich on the proceeds
of IPO's, couples and groups huddled over their Cosmopolitans
and Cadillacs, many of them with cell phones and palm pilots in
their hands.

The woman sat alone in one corner. Her face was thin, the
skin smooth and gracefully molded to her fine bones. In the subdued lighting of the lounge it was impossible to determine her
ethnic origins. Her hair was chopped short and combed straight,
so it lay against her scalp like a close-fitting cap. Even in the dim
lighting, it was clearly a rich auburn flecked with points of
smoldering red.

She wore a chiffon blouse of a pale shade. It gathered softly, cut across her torso to show the curve of her breasts and the ornament that lay in the shadow of her cleavage, a heart of tiny diamond chips suspended from a chain of fine gold links.

A cocktail glass stood in front of her, its pale contents catching the tinted light of the room. From time to time she drew a tiny sip. In the dim illumination her darkly rouged lips appeared nearly black.

She was watching the action at another table, one located halfway between herself and the busy bar. A man and woman were conversing over cocktails. The man wore a navy blazer. Its metal buttons, as anyone close enough to study them would notice, were blazoned not with a generic crest but with a personalized design. His oxford cloth button-down shirt and regimental-striped tie were more formal than the garb of most of the males in the room, but he carried off his act with aplomb.

His companion wore her hair retro-sixties style, ironed flat, parted in the middle and swept behind her shoulders. Her clothes were dark and plain, her hands long and slim, her nails metallic. Her only jewelry was a gold bangle worn on her left wrist.

A tequila sunrise and a martini stood between them.

As the woman sitting alone in the corner watched, the man in the blazer leaned forward and took his companion's hand. She murmured something, withdrew her hand and rose, heading for the restroom.

In her absence, the man let his gaze rove around the room. The walls of the cocktail lounge were covered in dark flocking. A few abstract neon sculptures pulsed in seemingly random patterns, synching from time to time with the bass player's music. A red note, a blue note.

Now the seated man scanned the room, his attention gliding from table to table, from woman to woman. For an instant he made eye contact with the woman in the corner. Evoking no reaction from her, he looked away.

The black bass player had segued seamlessly from the Satie composition to a Mozart étude. He nodded in time to his music, his head almost invisible against the dark wall behind him.

The woman who had left her escort emerged from the restroom and moved silently through the lounge. She ignored her former companion, joining a lone man who perched on a black, backless barstool, a tall lager in his hand. The man seemed startled but the woman threw her arms around his neck, bent her mouth to his ear, then gestured back, tossing her hair. Her new companion smiled and slipped an arm around her waist, helping her onto the barstool beside his own. He signaled to the nearest bartender.

The woman in the corner, watching the interplay, waited until the man in the blazer, an angry expression on his face, rose halfway to his feet.

The woman shot him a glance.

For an instant he froze, then slid partway back into his seat. Then, regaining his composure, he glanced questioningly toward the woman in the corner.

She nodded almost imperceptibly and he responded by gathering up his martini glass and carrying it to her table. He moved with the slight stiffness of passing time that even dedicated physical conditioning could not hide. A waitress removed the abandoned tequila sunrise.

The man smiled down at the lone woman. "May I join you?"

The woman nodded.

He lowered his martini carefully, then pulled out a chair and slid into it.

The woman said, "Margot. Silent tee." She smiled almost imperceptibly and extended her hand.

The man took it. "Joseph."

"A good name," the woman said. "Simple and unambiguous. It's been around for a long time."

The man nodded.

Before he could speak, Margot said, "Your friend ran into an old acquaintance, I see."

"Not my friend." Joseph shrugged. "Just someone I happened to meet. I hoped we might become friends, but I guess not."

Margot bent her auburn-capped head, touching her lips to the rim of her cocktail glass, glancing up at Joseph as she did so. She observed that he was studying her. He might be looking at her face, or at the diamond heart on her chest.

She straightened and smiled. "I enjoy a cocktail or two every evening. Striking a blow for freedom, we called it, once upon a time."

"No need to make an excuse," Joseph commented.

Margot laughed. "Nor was I." She tipped her head toward the tall musician. "I think I enjoy the ambiance here as much as the alcohol. In fact, more."

She changed the subject. "Do you think that little one could have held your interest for very long, Joseph? Or you, hers? Really, do you?"

Joseph frowned. "What do you mean?"

"Don't play dumb," Margot said. "How old do you think she could be? What is she, a grad student? You didn't think you were fooling her, did you? How old are you, Joseph? Wouldn't she want one of—her own?"

"I think I have what it takes to attract women," Joseph said.

"I don't doubt it."

"I enjoy chatting with young people. They have such energy, they can see the future."

"And you see only the past?"

"I want to see the future too. Young people are stimulating. They give me a fresh perspective. They give me ideas."

"I'll bet they do," Margot said.

For a moment the susurrus of voices lapsed and the low notes of the double bass throbbed through the room.

Then Margot asked again, "How old are you?"

Lines of anger appeared around his mouth, then disappeared. "I think that's an impolite question, Margot."

"Impolite to ask of a lady."

"We live in an era of equality."

"You like them young, though, don't you? It's obvious. Look at you, Joseph. Every hair on your head is exactly the same color. A giveaway, Joseph. And your face. A good job but to one who knows the telltale signs"—she gave a tiny half-laugh—"the signs tell their tale."

"Look here, I didn't—" he rose partway but Margot shot out a hand and grasped him by the wrist, pulling him back into his seat.

"Liver spots, Joseph. Your hands speak volumes."

He leaned forward and hissed furiously. "Let go of my wrist. I'm getting out of this place. I should never have come here. Do you get your kicks from ruining other people's good times?"

She released him with her fingers but held him with her eyes. A red neon sculpture glowing against the black wall reflected in her pupils. "You're a frightened man, Joseph. Very nearly a desperate one. Strike out a few more times and what will you do then? Climb into a bottle? Buy some powder and try to inhale youth?"

"You don't know what you're talking about," he growled.

"I do," she smiled.

"Sure you do." His tone had turned bitter. "A lot you understand. How much of life have you seen, you harpy? How old are you anyway? Oh, right, it's not polite to ask a lady that."

Now she grinned broadly. Her teeth were small but perfect and shone in the suddenly lurid neon. A waitress appeared and

Margot started to wave her away but Joseph pointed to his own glass and pantomimed, *another.* As the waitress turned away he lifted the drink before him and downed it in a single swallow.

"I know what you want, Joseph." Margot fixed him with her gaze. "I can give it to you."

He shook his head incredulously. "What are you, a hooker?"

"I've been that."

"You're in the wrong saloon, baby. Look around you. This place is full of whores, but not your kind."

"You're right about that. I think we should talk. Would you be more comfortable somewhere else?"

"I don't think so. I don't pay for it, baby. Haven't since I was a schoolboy, and I'm not going to start now."

"Joseph, you always pay for it. You just don't know it. But I'm not talking about money. If you don't come with me tonight you'll never see me again and you'll never rest easy."

He frowned, the lines in his forehead and around his mouth aging him visibly. He had the look of a man hooked against his will, a man who would pursue a lead even against his own better judgment.

"You'll never know what I have to offer, and you'll never forgive yourself," Margot added.

She stood up and hesitated for half a beat, then made her way between tables toward the exit. He would follow her or not, as he decided, and she knew what he would decide to do. By the time she reached the door a dark cashmere blazer sleeve reached past her and a hand pushed it open. She stepped into the street.

It had been a warm day and she'd gone to the lounge without a wrap, but the evening air had developed a chill and she leaned into his woolen jacket for warmth.

"Where do you want to go?" he asked. "My condo? A hotel?"

"I'd be more comfortable at my own apartment. If you don't mind."

He nodded and hailed a cab. The night sky was dark. The lights of tall buildings made a pattern of their own against the random scattering of stars.

Margot gave her address to Joseph in a low voice, and he repeated it to the cabby. Margot could be old-fashioned.

Her apartment was high in a modern building. The carpet was deep, the furniture quietly understated. She showed him to an easy chair, then removed a Hildegarde von Bingen compilation from the music player. Something easier for this occasion. She substituted a Schubert violin quartet.

"You paid for that last martini and didn't get to drink it," she told him. "I owe you that."

Before he could protest she removed a glass from a freezer and mixed ingredients for him. He sniffed at the drink, tasted it, nodded.

"Aren't you having anything?"

"Mineral water."

"Nothing stronger? You were drinking earlier."

"That was just a whim. I sometimes give in to whims."

"All right." He drank off half his martini, placed the glass carefully on a coaster and said, "Is it money, then?"

"You don't pay for it, you told me."

He was silent.

"I have what you want, Joseph, but I'm not talking about a quick lay, be assured of that."

"You told me you were a hooker."

"I told you I'd been a hooker. I've been a lot of things. You wouldn't believe how many things I've been in my life."

He studied her. "You're right. How old can you be? How much time have you had to play different roles?"

"Ah." She had poured a glass of mineral water for herself and now she drank. "I won't tell you how many years I've lived. To be honest with you, I don't know myself. A lot."

"Come on now, Margot."

She was seated in a satin-covered sofa.

He sat in an easy chair, facing her. "Look at you. You're a lot younger than I am, and I'm—"

Now Margot grinned broadly. "You're what? Let me guess." She moved from the sofa and knelt on the carpet in front of his chair. The lighting in the room was subdued but not inadequate.

She looked closely into his face, so closely that her cheek touched his. He couldn't tell whether this was an erotic come-on or something else. She took his two hands in one of hers, pressed the fingers of her other hand to his forehead, closed her eyes.

After a moment she leaned back on her heels, studying him, then retreated to the sofa. "I give you credit, Joseph. You manage to look like not much more than thirty-five. But you won't see fifty again, will you?"

"Won't I?" He demanded.

"No, you won't. And getting angry with me won't help, either."

He stood up and reached for her. "Are we going to get it on or aren't we?"

She eluded his grasp.

"Where's the bedroom?" he demanded. He tipped his head toward a shaded doorway. "Is that it?"

She grasped his wrists. His expression showed surprise at her strength. She lowered his hands to his sides and released him. "Joseph, if you think this is all about a roll in the hay, we can go in there and it will all be over in five minutes and you can go on your way."

"Yes?"

"And you'll still never know what you could have had. And you will wonder. I promise you that, Joseph, and I don't tell lies."

"You don't, eh?"

"No."

"People always believe you? How old are you? Thirty, maybe? Look at that body, look at that face. Thirty-two, tops."

"Joseph, I'm very old. I told you, I don't know how old, but I'm very old."

"What, forty? Forty-five?"

"Oh, Joseph, all right. I told you I'm very old and I am. I looked the way I look now when the first Elizabeth was Queen. I looked the way I look now when Jesus was a baby. How much older than that—I don't know. The memories just go back and back."

"You're lying. Or else you're crazy. I'm getting out of here. I hope there was nothing in that drink you gave me."

"Nothing but ice cold gin and a whiff of very fine vermouth."

"I'll believe that when I get safely home."

"Joseph, I don't tell lies."

"And you're what—two thousand years old? Ten thousand years old? Come off it, you crazy whore. You want to get down on your knees and earn a fast fifty bucks? Is that what this is all about?" He used one hand to steady himself against the top of his armchair.

"You want to be young, Joseph. You want to go after those girls in their twenties. You want to sample their youth, to be young like them. Joseph, you're as much a vampire as if you wanted to suck their blood. You want to suck their life."

"You're crazy. I'm getting out of here!"

"You can have it, Joseph. You can be as young as they are—or look that young, anyway, and your body will work the way it did when you were that young, and you can have it as long as you want it."

"What a bullshit fairy tale!"

"It's true, Joseph. You can have it as long as you want it. And when you don't want it any more, all you have to do is give it away and you won't have it any more, you'll grow old then. You'll just have to find someone else who wants it, and give it to that person."

"You are crazy, Margot! You need to find a good hospital and sign yourself in."

"I can give you a piece of jewelry and as long as you wear it you won't age."

"I want to stay young forever."

"Of course you do. But you'll change your mind."

"Really?"

The Schubert piece rose to a polite crescendo, then faded again. An automobile horn sounded from the street far below the apartment.

"I changed mine. You get so weary, Joseph, and you get so sad. Can you imagine what it's like to watch your children grow up and age, and grow old, and die? And your grandchildren? So many generations that you don't know them any more?"

She paused for a breath, then resumed.

"Your friends grow old and die, and you make new friends and they grow old and die. You rise to the top of your profession and pretend to retire and start over at something else and rise to the top again and retire again. Empires rise and fall. Revolutions triumph and lose their fervor. Religions promise eternal life— what a promise!—and they die, themselves."

The music ended and the room was absolutely silent. Then she said, "Do you think you'll still enjoy martinis after you've had a thousand of them? Ten thousand? A hundred thousand? You'll still want sex after you've done everything imaginable with man, woman or beast, so many times you can't remember your partners any more?"

He said, "I want to be young forever."

She said, "Go home and sleep on it. Take a day and think about it. I'll be at the place where we met tonight, tomorrow night."

*   *   *

The next night she sat at the same table. The same red-jacketed bartenders worked their stations, the same gracefully skirted waitresses moved from table to table. The same tuxedo-clad double bass player bowed the strings of his instrument. But tonight he was in a different mood. He was performing the works of Billy Strayhorn.

Margot had donned a simple black dress. The sleeves reached to her wrists, the bodice was so tightly fitted that her nipples showed prominently. Between her breasts, the diamond-chip heart reflected flashes of colored neon light. Once more, a tall beverage glass, its contents shimmering in the neon of the lounge, stood on her table.

The on-the-make customers of the establishment could have been the same crew as the previous night, or their clones.

The door swung open and Joseph stood silhouetted against the street scene outside. He turned his face, scanning the room, then fixed his attention on Margot and headed for her table. Without waiting for an invitation he slid into a chair.

"I didn't think you'd be here," he said.

"I told you I would."

A beat, then he said, "And you don't tell lies. Right."

A passing waitress stopped and asked if Joseph would like to order. He nodded and spoke. Neither he nor Margot said anything more until the waitress returned and placed his drink in front of him.

He sampled the concoction, then he told Margot, "Yours was better," and at that she smiled.

"What have you been doing?" Margot asked. "You look drawn."

"I'm not surprised." He rested his elbows on the table and pressed the heels of his hands against his eyes. Tonight he wore a gray tweed jacket, a striped shirt and solid colored tie. "I didn't get any sleep last night. I was thinking about what you said."

"Do you want to be young again?" she asked. The last word seemed to wound him.

He nodded.

Margot touched the back of his hand. "I can give you that."

"There has to be some kind of catch."

"What do you think?"

"I don't know. This is like one of those—they used to do them on television sometimes, what did they call them, deal with the devil stories. Stupid. I could never believe them. I don't believe in the devil."

"I'm not the devil."

"How about—a devil?"

"I'm just a woman."

"Okay." He raised his martini and sipped. "It would be great to have dark hair and smooth skin and good teeth and the kind of body I had when I was in my twenties."

"Forever," Margot said. "Or until you didn't want it any more. Right? You think you'd want that forever?"

"How old did you say you were, Margot?"

"I told you, I don't really know."

"Guess."

"The Olympics are great fun but they can't hold a candle to the originals."

"You won't tell me any more than that."

"I told you, I don't really know."

Joseph turned away for a moment, scanning the darkened room. The bass player still bent over his instrument. The red-jacketed bartenders and long-skirted waitresses plied their trades. Young IPO mavens and dotcom millionaires murmured into cell phones. Alcohol flowed down thirsty gullets and here and there abnormally bright eyes suggested the ingestion of illegal white powder.

Margot said something that Joseph didn't make out. He turned back toward her and asked her to repeat her words.

"It's passing you by, Joseph. They're getting younger and younger, aren't they, and you're—" She left the question hanging.

"I'll take it," he said.

Then, "No. Maybe not. This is impossible. It's voodoo. I don't believe it."

"Good-bye, then."

In the momentary silence the sound of the double bass swung low. The musician was playing Strayhorn's tune, "Something to Live For."

"If it doesn't work, I don't lose anything, do I? You don't want money from me or anything. All right. Go ahead. I'll take it."

"Fine." She reached for the diamond-chip heart that lay against her black dress.

"Wait a minute." He hesitated. "What if I change my mind? I mean, or—what if I get a disease? Can I die? What if somebody shoots me? Young people die, too, don't they?"

"Of course they do."

"Well then . . ."

"That's the strange thing, Joseph. I don't really know if I can die. I've been sick and recovered, I've been injured and healed, but that happens to everybody. If I were in an airplane crash, though, and everyone was killed, would I survive? Could you stab me in the heart without killing me?"

She paused. The bass player hit a sour note, the first in his life.

"How did you get this—this power?" Joseph asked.

"I don't know that I'd call it a power."

"Don't dodge."

"From a man. We met, he offered me youth, I accepted gladly.

He gave me this." She raised the jeweled heart. It reflected all the colors of neon.

"Who was he?"

"Just a man."

"What happened to him?"

"I don't know. He went away. I went on with my life. That's all."

Joseph drew a breath, studied his fists lying clenched on the table in front of him. A round of laughter erupted from a nearby table where a group of young women exchanged business secrets and technical data and anatomical details about their boyfriends.

"Why me?" he demanded.

For the first time, Margot appeared nonplused. "What do you mean?"

"I mean, have you offered this to others before me? Did they turn you down? And why did you offer it to me?"

She nodded, lowered her eyes momentarily, then looked at him again. "I did offer it to another person, once. A woman. She turned me down. She's dust now, Joseph. Dead and buried and gone back to the earth. And now I'm offering it to you."

For the second time Joseph said, "I'll take it."

Margot reached behind her neck and unclasped the golden chain holding the diamond heart. She doubled the chain, doubled it again, and pressed the heart and the chain together. For a moment the heart and chain disappeared.

When Margot opened her hands she held a man's ring, a square-cut solitaire diamond in a massive gold setting.

She held it toward Joseph and he extended his hand toward her, fingers spread. She slipped the ring onto his finger. It fit to perfection.

He studied the ring admiringly, then dropped his hands to his lap. He raised his eyes to Margot. In the dim light of the cocktail lounge it was hard to tell, but he could have sworn that some gray had appeared in her auburn cap, a few lines in her otherwise flawless face.

He stood up and turned his back on her, studying the occupants of the lounge. He picked out a spectacular, willowy young woman perched on a barstool, a margarita glass in her hand. He smiled at her questioningly and she smiled back invitingly.

He started across the room, joy in his chest and warmth in his loins, and just the faintest whisper of something different and very cold somewhere far deeper inside him.

When I prepared my previous short story collection, Before . . . 12:01
. . . and After, in 1996, my editor made an intriguing request. "Look
through your files," Dennis Weiler urged, "and find your oldest
surviving story. I'd like to use it in this book."

The story was "Mr. Greene and the Monster," written in 1952
and printed in fading purple ink in a crudely-made amateur magazine. It was of course autobiographical in nature, concerning a very
young man who wanted desperately to be an author, and as the work
of a screechy-voiced, insecure high school boy I don't suppose it was
too bad an effort. Gary Turner asked if I'd ever really been a milkman, and I had to confess that that was one of the few occupations
I'd never pursued.

It's the only one of my stories that appears both in 12:01 and in
Claremont Tales, for a reason which you'll shortly see.

Mr. Greene and the Monster

J. GOODWIN GREENE FAIRLY TORE THE BRASS
door off his mailbox when he got home. He reached in for the
manila envelope, dropped it, picked it up and dropped it
again. He fell to his knees and managed to get it open with
fumbling fingers.

A scrap of paper fell out. The heading read *Stupendous Scien-
tifiction.* " 'Monster of the Stellar Void' would have been good
reading twenty years ago, being full of pseudo-science and action,
but today's readers demand a deeper plot, better character
development, and a generally more mature story." It was signed
with the familiar initials QBP.

Tears welled in the eyes of the bowed figure. He took the
remaining contents of the envelope and placed them in his
pocket. He reread the slip in disbelief.

It wasn't that he needed the money for the story so badly. A
job as a milkman kept "Goody" Greene comfortably clothed, fed
and housed. But being a milkman is a singularly unglamorous profession, and just a little attention, the slightest bit of backpatting
or favorable comment was all that he wanted.

All his life he'd led about as unspectacular an existence as
could be. And to escape from his humdrum world he'd turned to

Science Fiction, in time starting to write it, but had never sold a story.

The disheartened author staggered to his apartment and threw himself across the bed in utter despair. If only he had lived twenty years earlier. Then, in the golden age of rocket ships and ray guns, his stories would have sold like hotcakes. All the modern editors said so.

Pity the man born before his time, doubly so the man born after it.

When he awoke early the next morning J. Goodwin Greene had a feeling that somehow things were different. There was nothing he could put his finger on until he realized that the bedside radio was the old-fashioned type with the horn-speaker on the top.

Slowly it dawned on him. *Everything* had changed. Even the disordered clothing he had failed to remove the night before seemed strange.

Could it be possible that he had traveled backwards in time? Could he have defied all the popular theories of science (fiction)? Even his mind, used to the wonders of pulp fiction, rebelled at the idea. But from any angle you looked at it, there seemed to be only one explanation.

He felt for the story in his pocket. "Monster of the Stellar Void" was still there. He pulled on the strangely-cut-yet-familiar coat hanging on the back of the chair, walked down the strange-but-yet-familiar stairs, and into the strange-but-yet-familiar street.

It took him a few minutes to get his bearings, then he started downtown to the Spiff-Bravis Publishing Company. Not until he got there did he realize that the S-B Building was erected in 1939.

It took him all morning and half of the afternoon to walk to the old office of the now defunct *Science Mystery Monthly,* for he knew better than to try to spend any money dated well into the future for a bus or taxi.

Even so, old (he wasn't old *then*) Hugo Burnsback agreed to see him, and upon hearing a brief synopsis of "Monster of the Stellar Void" insisted that he stay until there was time to read it through. At last he looked up and said, "Young man, if you will accept three cents a word for this story it will appear in the next issue of *Science Mystery Monthly.* We were going to use some house ads for filler, but your story will just about fit in. Too bad the contents page and cover are already printed."

J. Goodwin Greene was so flabbergasted by this sudden

success that he couldn't even answer. He just stood there and looked at the editor.

The latter, misinterpreting the silence, amended his offer. "I'll make it five cents a word if you'll agree to wait a few months for payment. We can't afford quite that much, yet."

Shocked into action by this windfall, Greene managed to stammer out a vaguely affirmative answer, and left the office on unsteady legs.

The following few weeks were paradise for Greene, even though he had to pawn most of his possessions for living money. Finally the great day arrived. He splurged on a cab to reach the office early, and got a copy from the first batch of *Science Mystery Monthly* from the printer. There, big as life, running from page 96 to page 104, was "Monster of the Stellar Void."

On the way home he carefully removed the story in order to save it, and was leafing fondly through it when he heard the brakes screech and saw some crazy kid in a Stutz about to collide with his cab.

Everything was suddenly whirling around him and he was in bed. He looked around. Again, everything had the strange-yet-familiar look. With a start he realized that it was 1952 again. The clothing was again of the modern type.

The radio was gone. He had hocked it. That proved that it wasn't a dream. He had pierced the veil of time and returned to tell the tale of it.

Now to get proof. Of course, an old copy of *Science Mystery Monthly* would have his story in it. J. Goodwin Greene spent the rest of the day on the phone trying to locate a copy of SMM. At last he found a man with what seemed to be the only existing copy, and he raced across town to the collector's home with the money.

He dared not let anyone see his prize, wrapped in an old sheet of green paper, but finally he got home with it, and opened to page 96. It wasn't there. Someone had removed the story that filled the last part of the magazine.

J. Goodwin Greene fainted.

Ahah, you were wondering about that, and you didn't have to wonder very long. "The Monster and Mr. Greene" is the sequel to "Mr. Greene and the Monster;" it's also autobiographical to a degree, recently composed and appearing here for the first time.

Well, I've never been the Chief Justice of any court, either—but there's literal autobiography and there's metaphor, and each can be true in its own way.

Forty-nine years between the first and second stories of a series. I have a feeling that I've set a record. And somehow I doubt that there will be a third "Mr. Greene" story in the year 2050, but who can say for certain?

The Monster and
Mr. Greene

JARED GREENE WAS SURPRISED TO FIND HIM-self crossing his knees nervously, first left over right, then right over left. He looked down at his polished black shoes, and at his blue pinstripe suit with the knife-edge creases in the trousers. As he lifted his left wrist to check the time against his paper-thin Rolex, a beam of sunlight reflected off his gold-and-diamond cuff-link and—as fate would have it—flashed directly in the eye of the Henri Bendel-outfitted receptionist sitting opposite him.

She turned from her computer, curious, and he offered a friendly smile. She smiled in return, showing just enough of her perfect teeth. Her eyes darted back to the computer screen. She nodded almost imperceptibly, and then inclined her head toward Jared.

"I'm so sorry to keep you waiting, Judge. I'm sure Mr. Burns-back is very eager to see you, but at his age—" She paused and let the silence complete her sentence.

"I understand, of course, Miss—"

"Harkins," she furnished.

Jared nodded. It was nice that the old ways were coming back. The world was no longer on a first-names-for-everybody basis. Courtesy titles had been revived, and women, bless their hearts, had been in the forefront, demanding Miss or Missus again, and not the artificial Ms.

Jared had used that when it was the form to use. He, of all people, knew how to be politically correct. But he had never felt totally comfortable eliding his syllables as if he wasn't sure which form to use. No, he was delighted with Miss Harkins, just as he was delighted with his limousine driver, waiting patiently in the street below.

The Secret Service had insisted on providing security as usual, those ubiquitous dark-suited, white-shirted, mirror-shades-wearing agents with the grim visages and the bulges beneath their jackets. What was their name for him? Gavel, right, that was it. To the best of Jared's knowledge, the agents didn't even *have* names. But at least the driver was James, and Jared was Mr. Greene, sir, and that was just fine with him.

Only one other person sat near Jared, waiting for a summons to the publisher's inner sanctum. Jared studied him out of the corner of his eye. He was an expert at sizing people up on short notice. How many attorneys, how many plaintiffs and defendants and witnesses had he seen in all his years on the bench?

This youngster must have been in his early twenties. More likely a recent college graduate than a student. His suit was cheap but it was obviously new and meticulously cared for. His hair was a little shorter than the style of the moment.

He had a fresh-scrubbed look about him, but the slim leather portfolio on his lap looked old and battered. That was odd. Maybe, Jared thought, it was a good-luck piece, a hand-me-down that had been in the youngster's family for many years. It looked like one that Jared himself had owned long, long ago. A plain gold ring shone on the young man's left hand. Ah, he was married. How sweet to be a new husband. Jared's thoughts drifted back to his own youth, the bright, dreamlike days when he stood at the beginning of both his marriage and his career. The beginning of his life. And now he was approaching its end.

Miss Harkins must have received a signal. Not that Jared detected it in any way—perhaps an icon had glowed briefly on her monitor—but she stood up and said, "Mr. Burnsback will see you now. I'll show you the way in, Judge."

*   *   *

Stepping into Hugo Burnsback's office, Jared Greene felt a sense of temporal displacement. The room could hardly be the same one he had visited so many years before, if only because Burns-back's office had been far downtown, then, near Manhattan's old Radio Row, and it was uptown now on fashionable Madison Avenue. And it had been located in a dingy nineteenth century building that literally creaked when Greene shifted his weight. Now it was high in a glittering skyscraper of aluminum and glass.

But Burnsback sat magisterially behind a heavy, dark-stained wooden desk. The desktop was covered by a plane of shimmering glass. To Burnsback's left stood a platform with an L.C. Smith upright typewriter on it; to his right, a similar platform bearing an Edison dictating machine, a microphone attached to it by a flexible, snakelike cable and a small supply of wax-covered dictation cylinders racked beneath the gray, rounded device. The glass supported a wooden communicator, a black toggle switch beneath its cloth-covered speaker. Greene hadn't seen one of those in half a century, except in old black-and-white movies about portly tycoons with beautiful daughters.

The dark, wood-paneled walls were covered with an array of oversize mockups of the covers of ancient Burnsback publications —*The Boy Mechanic, Interplanetary Adventures, Science Mystery Monthly, Crooks Versus the Law, Tales of the Sea, Western Sweethearts.* Today's Burnsback publications were scaled down and slicked up, and consisted mainly of software distributed on computer disks or directly over the Internet rather than adventure stories printed on woodpulp paper and packaged behind melodramatic, action-packed paintings.

Jared smiled at the colorful illustrations of knickered youths, iron-riveted spaceships, boxy automobiles and fedora-wearing gangsters. A Spanish galleon sped across choppy seas, its sails bellied by a following wind. A rosy-cheeked girl in sombrero and heavy divided skirt smiled up at a big-eyed cowboy.

Old Hugo Burnsback—he was very old by now—sat ramrod straight behind the heavy desk. He wore a stiff black serge suit, a high-collared white shirt and striped tie. Jared blinked, trying to remember the first time he had met Burnsback. Had the old man worn the same suit, the same shirt and tie, that time? Burnsback was notoriously parsimonious, but to keep his wardrobe intact for all these years, not spending so much as a few dollars for a new necktie—was it possible?

Jared sensed Miss Harkins at his elbow. "Justice Greene is here, Mr. Burnsback."

Burnsback blinked once and lifted himself carefully from his executive chair. It was upholstered in deep maroon leather and hammered-brass studs. "A pleasure, young man." Burnsback extended his hand.

Jared grinned inwardly. How many years—how many decades —since anyone had called him young man? He reached across the shimmering plain of glass and clasped Burnsback's hand. He noticed that his own hand seemed, well, not exactly soft; perhaps fleshy was the word. Burnsback's was thin and hard, more bony than muscular. They were neither of them young.

"So you have come to offer me a story," Burnsback inquired, "or are you seeking an editorial position?"

"No, sir," Jared said. After all his years in America, Burnsback's slight accent was barely detectable. Still, Jared recognized the faint coloring that Burnsback gave to each word. How often did you get to hear English spoken with a Luxembourgeoise accent?

"You already bought my story, Mr. Burnsback." Jared didn't say that the incident had taken place more than half a century before.

"Did I indeed?" Burnsback inclined his head. His hair was thin but it was still, surprisingly, a glossy black. It lay close to his skull. "Will you not have a seat, young man." He gestured and Jared found a chair, a less impressive version of Burnsback's. He lowered himself into it and watched as the older man, the gracious host, followed suit.

"Yes, sir," Jared said. "But that was some time ago."

"And you wish now to find employment with my firm?"

Jared couldn't help grinning at that. "Actually, Mr. Burnsback, I have a pretty good job already."

"And what is that?" Burnsback asked.

"I'm the Chief Justice of the Supreme Court of the United States."

Nodding slightly, Burnsback released his breath. "Ah."

"As a matter of fact, I think I recognize the issue my story appeared in." Jared inclined his head toward one of the oversized magazine covers decorating the wall. "Right there in *Science Mystery Monthly*. I remember it vividly. Volume XVI, number 6."

Burnsback revolved slowly in his executive chair; when he came to a halt Jared could see both their faces reflected in the glass that covered the mockup. Burnsback's visage was thin, his eyes as dark as his sparse hair, and his features were prominent. Jared's face was heavier, his cheeks pink, his hair silvery with a sprinkling of black.

"That was a special number entirely devoted to supraterrestrial propulsion systems," Burnsback recalled. How could he retrieve such long-ago events, in such amazing detail? "I had to work with Mr. Frank, my chief artist, for many hours to get that cover right. You will notice the motive rays propelling the transdimensional sojourner. The illustration accompanied a story by Murray Leinster. And what did you say your name was again, young man?"

Jared repeated his name.

"I remember a Greene in that issue. Splendid young fellow. Delivered his manuscript to me by hand. His story was—" Burnsback hesitated for a mere fraction of a second "—'Monster of the Stellar Void.' I wondered what had become of the author. He never brought me another manuscript. In fact, when we sent him payment for his contribution, the check was returned to us, unopened."

"That was my story," Jared said.

"What was your name again?"

"Jared Greene."

Burnsback shook his head. He did so slowly and carefully. He must be close to the century mark. "There was a Greene," he conceded, "but not Jared." He closed his eyes in concentration and remained motionless for so long that Jared feared that he had quietly passed away.

But then he opened his eyes and they were as dark and clear as ever. "J. Goodwin Greene, that was the youngster's name. That was the story, 'Monster of the Stellar Void,' by J. Goodwin Greene."

"Yes! That was me—J. Goodwin Greene. I was a milkman then, I was in my teens and I wanted to make something of myself and I thought I'd never get beyond delivering milk bottles every morning. You gave me my chance, Mr. Burnsback. You bought that story from me, and that made me believe that I could do more than drive my route and deliver milk for the rest of my life."

Burnsback said, "So, you are J. Goodwin Greene."

"I am."

Burnsback reached carefully toward the wooden communicator and flicked the toggle switch. "Miss Harkins, would you please be so kind as to bring me the uncashed check file." He leaned back in his chair. "You would be surprised how few of these there are, young man."

Miss Harkins carried a manila folder into the room and laid it on Burnsback's desk. She opened it for him and stood waiting for instructions. Burnsback said, "I'll call you." She knew what that meant. She left the office.

"I suppose you can document your identity," Burnsback said.

Jared suppressed another grin. He removed his wallet from his inside suit pocket and laid his identification on Burnsback's desk.

Burnsback examined it, then studied Jared's features, then shoved the identification back toward him. "You should pick a name and stick with it. In this manner you will establish a persona with which your readers will identify, thereby enhancing your likelihood of further sales." He nodded sternly. "Life has many lessons. I suppose you want your money, and you are indeed entitled to it. Your tale evoked several admiring letters that we ran in succeeding editions. Why did you never send us another piece?"

"I went back to school," Jared started to explain.

Burnsback said, "Admirable. And what did you study?"

"Law, sir."

"An honorable profession. I trust you followed the career in later years of young Nathan Schachner, also an attorney-at-law, who collaborated with Arthur Leo Zagat. They contributed the novel *Exiles of the Moon* to one of my periodicals. But unlike Mr. Schachner, I take it you were too busy to continue your literary endeavors."

Jared harrumphed.

Burnsback looked at him.

"I edited the law review my senior year. My three books on civil procedure are still in print. And my decisions as Chief Justice have been widely praised."

"Never did another story, though?"

"No, sir."

"Most regrettable." Burnsback's long features assumed a mournful cast. "Still, you are nevertheless entitled to this." He removed a check from the folder. The ink was faded and the date was back in John Nance Garner's day. Jared read the name of the bank and tried to imagine what convoluted trail of takeovers and mergers he'd have to follow, to unearth any remnant of it. Chances are, it was impossible. And of course there was no way they'd honor a check this old. Still and all . . .

"Thank you, sir," he told Burnsback. He folded the check carefully into his wallet. He would tell his wife about this tonight. She'd get a kick out of seeing the check and reading the amount that her husband had earned—but only now received—for his first literary success, so many years ago.

"Do not expect to receive interest on the amount," Burnsback warned him. "Payment was tendered in timely fashion, and the delay in receipt was not the company's fault."

"No, no, of course not," Jared agreed. "Not the company's fault. No, sir. Actually, I didn't come up here today to demand payment."

Burnsback's eyes narrowed.

"It's just that—I'm sorry, Mr. Burnsback, I've rehearsed this speech a hundred times and now I'm getting choked up." He paused and took a deep breath, then he rushed through the next sentences.

"It's just that I thought I was a failure until you bought that story. I'd given up on myself. But when you took 'Monster of the Stellar Void,' why, it gave me confidence. I started to believe in myself. I started thinking, *If I can sell a story just like R. F. Starzl and Clare Winger Harris and Miles J. Breuer and all the rest of them, then I must be pretty damned good.* And I just turned my life around. I went back to school, and I finally asked that girl for a date, that I'd been too afraid to ask, and I got my degree and found a job and—and just look at me now."

Burnsback did. He looked at the younger man. Not that Jared Greene had been a young man for many, many years. But everything was relative.

"I just wanted to say thank you," Jared added. "Just—from the bottom of my heart, Mr. Burnsback. Thank you."

Hugo Burnsback permitted himself a narrow smile, the first that Jared had seen on that thin, straight, ascetic mouth. He said, "Another word of advice, young man. The educated person will find adequate expression in a wholesome, respectful vocabulary. You must discipline yourself, and in a short time you will find that you no longer need such vulgarisms as *d*mn*d.*"

In 1981 my friend Eric Vinicoff told me that he was slated to become editor of a new magazine, Rigel Science Fiction. Eric was in the midst of a successful career as a writer, but like many authors he had an itch to edit—I suppose it's the same odd impulse that makes so many actors want to become directors.

Rigel was an experiment in minimalist publishing. Eric was not only the editor, he was the chief typographer and layout artist, coffee gopher and office boy. It was an immense effort, truly a labor of love, and Eric turned out a remarkably good magazine under the conditions. I have a feeling that Rigel would have succeeded had the personal computers and desktop publishing software now in common use been available a decade sooner. But with the primitive technology Eric was forced to use, the burden was just too great, nor was there budget sufficient to hire a staff or farm out the chores. Still, Rigel survived for nine issues, now fabulously rare and expensive collector's items. "Lux was Dead Right" appeared in the first issue of Rigel and led to a series of stories set on my Tin Can World.

Lux Was Dead Right

THE ALIENS CAME BOILING UP OUT OF A GIANT singularity halfway between Alioth and the double-star Merak in Ursa Major. They weren't the first aliens to make themselves known, nor the first to announce themselves with a fierce attack on a passing spacecraft — and spacecraft passing singularities, otherwise known as black holes, do so with extreme care — but they were by far the fiercest.

And the most enigmatic.

At the moment that the aliens appeared, Will Lux's mind could hardly have been farther removed from such cosmic matters as the discovery of a new and menacing species of life in the endless and endlessly surprising universe. On the contrary. At the precise moment that the aliens came boiling out of that singularity in Ursa Major, Will was sitting on a tall stool behind the worn wooden counter of his business establishment.

The establishment was known, for no revealed reason, as Olde Doctor Christmas's Booke & Brownie Shoppe.

The aliens looked something like a cross between huge pallid stingrays and vicious hornets. Their facetted eyes glinted like evil emeralds. Their bodies were segmented and furnished with stingers so sharp, so strong, and so fiercely barbed that they could pierce the wall of a spaceship and extract its occupants the way a greedy child rips open a tangerine to get at its edible segments.

They also had armored legs terminating in pincered claws.

Olde Doctor Christmas's Booke & Brownie Shoppe was located beneath a broken street lamp in Jackjack Alley, one of the more obscure thoroughfares in the Loop, the sorrily superannuated and terribly tacky onetime center of Chicago IV. Chicago IV was the largest city in Starrett, a tincan world that wandered restlessly from solar system to solar system. The major occupation of the residents of Starrett was buying up the flotsam, jetsam, and miscellaneous ephemera of each inhabited solar system it visited, and selling the accumulated jetsam, flotsam, and miscellaneous ephemera they had brought from other solar systems. In short, Starrett was one gigantic flea market, a kind of interstellar bazaar.

Between market days the people of Starrett traded with one another, more or less to stay in practice.

At first, nobody could figure out how the Raptorials (for that was the name applied to the stingray-hornet creatures) were able to emerge from a black hole. As far as was known, no one and nothing, not even light, could escape from a singularity. Yet these great creatures did so, with a fearsomely graceful motion that suggested the way aquatic rays swam, or "flew," on worlds that had oceans on them, oceans with rays in them

Aside from the puzzle of how the Raptorials managed to escape the super-hyper-ultra-strong gravity of the black hole, there was the further question, What did they push against?

You would think that anybody who ran a place called Olde Doctor Christmas's Booke & Brownie Shoppe would be some kind of too-cute-for-words fellow in a velvet suit and string tie, or maybe a middle-aged virgin with lace at her collar and cuffs and a cameo brooch pinned to her chestbone. Actually, Will Lux was a crusty old curmudgeon (he'd once been a crusty young curmudgeon) who affected tweed jackets, plaid shirts and polka-dotted bow ties. You could hear him coming by his clothes.

He was also the smartest bookman in Chicago IV, which meant that he was probably the smartest bookman in the known universe, and he kept what he knew strictly in his head because he didn't trust anybody.

The Raptorials, it turned out, had the ability to control the electrical and gravitic charge of their bodies. Thus, when they wanted to come boiling up out of their black hole homes, they had merely to fix their charges so the super-hyper-etc. gravity of the hole repelled them instead of attracting them. Talk about boiling!

There was also something about time-distortion. The well-known theoretical phenomenon of time slowing as velocity increased as they tumbled down the gravity well of their home was reversed when they tumbled back up out of it, and this, it was theorized, might actually give the Raptorials the ability to control the rate of time's flow, if not to travel through it into past or future.

People could only guess what kind of environment and home life the Raptorials had inside their black hole, and one guess was more horrible than another.

At the very moment that the Raptorials were opening up and devouring the contents of their very first spaceship (and they did enjoy the meal thoroughly) Will Lux heard a scratching at the door of his establishment. He climbed down from his tall stool and peered through the grimy pane, recognizing his caller as Igor Dzugashvilli. Igor was one of a pair of twins. The other Dzugash-villi twin was Natalya. Lux and Igor Dzugashvilli had been enemies for forty years, ever since Lux and Natalya had had an affair and Will discovered that Natalya had been put up to the whole thing by Igor in order to gain access to Will Lux's stock and scout the books for Igor.

Will unlocked the door and let Igor Dzugashvilli into his shop.

* * *

There was a prompt declaration of war between the Galactic Federation of Intelligent and Peaceloving Life Forms, and the Raptorials. Prompt, but also conditional. Were the Raptorials an intelligent and inimical race, or were they merely wild animals, carrying out their instinctive, predatory feeding habits? The first ship they had opened and emptied had been the *Chiang Kai-shek*. The second was the *Elizabeth Tudor*.

This academic distinction concerning the status of the Rap-torials was of no concern whatever to the (deceased) passengers and crews of the *Chiang Kai-shek* and *Elizabeth Tudor*.

* * *

Igor Dzugashvilli entered Olde Doctor Christmas's Booke & Brownie Shoppe snarling and cursing. When Will Lux asked him what was the matter, Dzugashvilli cursed and spit into a grimy red bandana that he pulled from his pocket. "Do you know what I saw today? Do you know what I saw today up at Cyclops?"

Will said, No, he didn't know.

"A perfect first of Farmer's *Green Odyssey*. No. Did I say perfect? It wasn't perfect. There was a chip off the top rear jacket flap and a foxed edge on one page of the book. You want to guess what page it was?" Dzugashvilli puffed up his cheeks with anger and Will Lux could almost hear the blood rushing through his rival's distended veins.

"You don't have to tell me, Igor. Page 109."

*   *   *

Grand Admiral Nagako Nakamura was placed in command of the GFIPLF war fleet. The fleet comprised six thousand four hundred ninety-one armored ships. They were dreadnaughts, battlewagons, heavy cruisers, light cruisers, destroyers, frigates, and men-, women-, and children-o'-war. They were armed with lasers, masers, tazers, crazers, explosive missiles, chemical missiles, electric missiles, and with whole clusters of crewed and crewless miniships loaded in the bellies of globular parent ships.

When they attacked the Raptorials, the Raptorials simply reversed their gravitic charges and sent the GFIPLF fleet tumbling away at great speed and in total disorder.

*   *   *

"You know what this means, don't you, Will?" snorted Igor Dzugashvilli. Will Lux nodded his sympathy. Although the two men were bitter enemies, they were fellow bookmen and they loved each other with a love that their mutual hatred could not eradicate. It's hard to understand if you're not a bookman (or bookwoman, although the latter have always been in the minority and still are). It was something like the proverbial brothers who would beat each other's brains out until their cousin turned up, whereupon they would join forces to beat their cousin's brains out.

All three would join forces to beat out the brains of their (unrelated) next-door neighbor, and all four would join forces to beat out the brains of any hostile stranger.

*   *   *

Once the Raptorials had thrashed the living daylights out of the GFIPLF war fleet, Admiral Nakamura ordered a mass withdrawal and regrouping. She took inventory of her charges and discovered that over two thousand of her warships had been destroyed outright in the single engagement of the war. Another thousand or so had sustained major or minor damage, but were considered still salvageable. Some, in fact, were still spaceworthy. That left just over three thousand ships in good fighting trim. There were, of course, several million members of ships' crews who had been killed in the engagement.

In keeping with the latest political thinking within the Galactic Federation of Intelligent Peaceloving Life Forms, no breakdowns were published concerning the distribution of casualties by species or solar system of origin, but there was an undercurrent of resentful rumor to the effect that Earth-stock humans comprised an disproportionate percentage of the loss.

* * *

"It means that somebody got to your copy," Will Lux said to Igor Dzugashvilli. "I can't say that I'm altogether displeased to hear it. Biter bit, heh-heh. Here, have a stogie." Lux reached under the counter and produced a cigar box containing top-grade smokes that he'd picked up in trade for some old poetry anthologies when Starrett visited Nueva Cuba Libre, a warm and beautiful planet inhabited by close para-humans, circling the variable star Ras Algethi. The variable rays of Ras Algethi produced the finest cigar leaf yet in the known universe.

"You bet somebody got to my copy," Igor grated, sticking a stogie in his mouth and another in his pocket, "and now that the Farmer is out there might as well be a million of 'em as two!"

* * *

Grand Admiral Nagako Nakamura sent word to Federation headquarters describing the debacle at the black hole between Alioth and Merak and requesting instructions. The instructions she hoped to get were, *Haul ashes back here and let's talk this thing over.* The instructions she feared she would get were, *Have at 'em again, and don't come home till you can report a victory.* For once, the good guys triumphed. Reason prevailed. Calm consideration overcame anger and frustration. Federation headquarters told Admiral Nakamura, *Haul ashes.* She complied with alacrity.

When Admiral Nakamura's flagship, the *Anna Mae Wong*, went into orbit around the Federation headquarters planet Hjalmarschact, the admiral climbed into her official lighter and lit out for the surface, PDQ.

"I wish to hell we'd never encountered those damned Akamari Gammans. Them and their nutty breeding habits. Who ever heard of a race that used matter duplicators to make babies? Who ever heard of a race that used matter duplicators for anything? Who ever heard of anybody who'd invented a successful matter duplicator before those rotten Akamari Gammans?" The questions were rhetorical, of course. Will Lux knew the answers, Igor Dzugashvilli knew the answers, Will knew that Igor knew, Igor knew that Will knew, and so forth, like two walls of perfectly parallel mirrors. "If they don't like *shtupping*," Lux said, "why couldn't they just bud, or clone, or parthenogenize? Oh, no! Not the Akamari, God rot their lousy souls! They had to pick a couple of perfect babies, feed 'em antimaturation hormones, and then just matter-duplicate them whenever they want more babies, and feed the new ones more hormones to cancel out the anti-maturation juice.

"I said those matter duplicators would be the ruin of the old book business, but nobody would listen to me," and Lux was dead right.

* * *

Admiral Nakamura headed for Federation headquarters the back way, quickly and without ceremony. At the same time an actress wearing Grand Admiral's uniform was being greeted by a big plaster-of-Paris egg gussied up in fancy paint. The mobs loved it. The plaster-of-Paris egg was a convincing replica of Moghyhgom-anapana-moghyhgoM, the closest thing to a Galactic Empress yet devised. Moghyhgom-anapana-moghyhgoM had been brought from Spica IV, a big yellowish planet where the dominant race was green scaly lizards. These lizards' eggs were brilliant and totally telepathic. The lizards themselves were mindless creatures that spent their lives basking in the warm rays of Spica, gorging themselves on large silvery arawana-like fish, dozing off, avoiding work, and dreaming marvelous dreams of glorious swirling colors and high adventure. The dreams were projected to the otherwise mindless lizards by their own eggs, who had nothing better to do than concoct splendiferous images and thrilling adventures and project them to the lizards. A good many visitors to Spica IV expressed sympathy for the eggs, in view of their fated future of mindlessness.

The eggs, however, greeted these expressions of sympathy with the telepathic equivalent of hysterial laughter: they were unanimously willing to swap their roles as creators for those of happy lizards basking in the sun and enjoying the daydreams of the next generation of eggs.

* * *

Igor Dzugashville drew on his fine stogie and blew a stream of blue-gray smoke toward the dim rafters of Olde Doctor Christ-mas's Booke & Brownie Shoppe. "You don't mind if I save this spare stogie and run off some dupes of it myself, do you?"

Will Lux growled and reminded Igor that he, Will, disapproved totally of matter duplicators.

"I know that, Will. I remember the time that kid came running in here with that first *Frankenstein*. You like to fall off your chair and fracture your coccyx! Best laugh I had in years!"

Will Lux snarled a curse at Dzugashvilli.

"No, Will! Don't split your spleen! You were willing enough to tell the kid it was a phony and take it off his hands for a sliver of what you knew you could get for it! And all the time you were sit-ting here rubbing your hands together, planning to make a bundle off the *Frankenstein*, the kid was going up and down Jackjack Alley passing copies to every paranoid bookseller on the street! What a joke! And they were all perfect facsimiles, down to the last atom, of the copy at the University! Ah-hah-hah-hah!"

"Laugh, you lousy counterfeiter," Will snarled back at Igor, "You think I don't know that that rotten kid with the *Franken-steins* was your twin sister Natalya in drag?"

* * *

In Federation headquarters, Nagako Nakamura sat down on a ceremonial silk cushion in front of Moghyhgom-anapana-moghyhgoM's jade-and-silver incubator. Moghyhgom-anapana-moghyhgoM had agreed to accept the job of Galactic Empress only on the condition that she be permitted to hatch in normal fashion, and that once hatched, she should be returned to her native swamp on Spica IV and turned loose to bask in the sunlight. Galactic Federation officers had reluctantly agreed. Admiral Nakamura, dressed in her fanciest gold-and-white uni-form, bowed her head and thought her report to the egg in the incubator. The Empress replied in like manner that she was sur-prised no one had suggested simply keeping away from the black hole the Raptorials had come from. If GFIPLF ships just stayed away from the Alioth-Merak sector, nobody else would get eaten, and that was what the matter was all about, wasn't it?

Grand Admiral Nakamura said she wasn't so sure; what if the Raptorials spread from Ursa Major, and what if they were already connected, via some sort of fourth-dimensional wormholes, with singularities in other sectors of space?

* * *

"If you hadn't been so damned greedy, Lux, Natalya would never have taken you in like that. Cripes, anybody who could mistake her for a boy anyhow! But look, every bookman on the Alley thought Natalya'd found a near-unique copy, and every one of 'em wanted to get it for himself, to sit and gloat like Scrooge McDuck with his god damned gold coins! You know the old saying, you can't cheat an honest man! Say, it's a shame old Scrooge McDuck didn't have a matter duplicator himself." Igor stopped and thought for a moment.

Will Lux reminded him that you still need raw materials for a matter reproducer, and you can't make gold coins without gold.

"Oh, yeah," Igor conceded. "Well, but you can change a form even if you can't change its atoms. Wouldn't old Scrooge have settled for turning cannel coal into diamonds? If he just had one diamond to start with?"

"Yeah." Will Lux tapped the ashes off his stogie into a chipped ashtray that said STARRETT BOOKSELLERS FAIR AND ANTIQUARIAN EXHIBITION. 2973—CHICAGO IV. "Let's head over to Tamerlane's saloon and belt down a couple, Igor."

*   *   *

"Now listen here," Moghyhgom-anapana-moghyhgoM's voice sounded inside Grand Admiral Nakamura's skull like the sifting of palm fronds in a hot tropical breeze. "If we can't just leave these Raptorials alone—and I'm willing to accept your cautions against that, Nagako, but it makes my egg-tooth ache to think that nobody thought this through before you and your hirelings went in ready to fight—if we can't just leave the Raptorials alone, has anybody thought of trying to talk to the things? Who knows what they thought those first ships were? If you're programmed to think of every passing object as a possible meal, you may never even realize that your lunch is a sentient being endowed with the Divine Spark and carrying around a little parcel of the Holy Spirit inside its carapace. Why don't we at least give it a try, eh?"

Grand Admiral Nagako Nakamura stiffened her back and straightened her shoulders so the ultramarine Order of the Sisters of the Interstellar Sea gleamed out against her gold metalwork and sparkling white tunic. "Sounds reasonable to me," she telepathed back to the giant egg in the jade-and-silver incubator. "Who's going to go do the talking?"

*   *   *

Tamerlane's saloon was at the intersection of Caxton Court and

Polidori Place. Most of the bookmen from the neighborhood hung out there after hours, clustering in twos and threes and fours around grimy round tables, glaring suspiciously at their tablemates and even more suspiciously at the bookmen seated at other tables. The old brothers-cousin-stranger effect. Will Lux and Igor Dzugashvilli stood in the doorway for a minute, accustoming themselves to the smoky and alcoholic gloom of the place. Will saw two dark figures at a table in the back turn away hostilely. "Look," he nudged his enemy Igor, "it's Seamus O'Malley and your sister Natalya. I wonder what she's putting over on O'Malley this time."

"I don't know," Igor hissed back at Will, "but I sure hope it's something juicy. I hate that slimy rat O'Malley. He's the one who sold me the phony *Shunned House.* I hate any rat who peddles counterfeit books!"

* * *

The greatest linguists in the known universe are the amoeboid Zartzes of Procyon XVIIIa, and the greatest linguist among the Zartzes is a cute little pink number that calls itself (for no revealed reason) Priscilla Prestone Pritikin. Priscilla Prestone Pritikin was given the honor of being the representative of the Galactic Federation of Intelligent and Peaceloving Life Forms to the Raptorials of Ursa Major.

Priscilla's reaction to this news was vigorous. She grew a brighter pink than ever, waved her cilia furiously, grew a pseudopod and kicked the messenger who'd brought her the news smack in the nucleus. (Calling Priscilla a "she" rather than an "it" seems to be in accord with her own preference.) The messenger, recovering his composure ("he" was a blue amoeba who called "himself" Butch Marciano), pointed out that there was no real danger to Priscilla, as she could be matter duplicated before departure and hence survive in the person of her duplicate.

"Who needs a matter duplicator?" Priscilla replied angrily. "I can just fission if it comes to that. What do you say we let the *new* me do the job, though, while I stay home in my petri dish and multiply?"

* * *

Seamus O'Malley pulled his soft cloth cap down over his face and turned away from the doorway of Tamerlane's saloon, gesturing Natalya Dzugashvilli to follow suit. She did, but one or both of them were too late to fool Will and Igor. The two newcomers approached Seamus and Natalya's table, squeezing between other tables occupied by bookmen and occasional bookwomen intent on setting up deals to their own advantage and to each other's disadvantage. The entire book business had indeed undergone drastic changes since the introduction of matter duplicators to Starrett. The intrinsic merit of the books was *not* a matter of *no* concern whatever, but it was a relatively minor aspect of the business. These bookmen dealt with collectors. (To the last individual, they were collectors themselves!) The whole point of owning a rare old book was that it *was* a rare old book. If it wasn't rare, if you couldn't have something that your rival did not have, there was no advantage in owning it. You might as well wander down to the Cooper Square Newsroom and buy a cheap paperback. But now that matter duplicators were around, anybody could have a copy of any book, *absolutely indistinguishable from the original!*

There was only one way to make certain that your copy of a book was a valuable, collectible item. That was to own the one and only extant copy of the book, and to keep it under lock and key so no bandit had a chance to snap it with a duplicator lens and create a fraudulent but down-to-the-last-atom perfect facsimile.

*   *   *

They took Priscilla Prestone Pritikin out toward Ursa Major on board a luxurious ship called the *Madame Nhu*. When they got a few parsecs from Merak they loaded her, kicking and screaming, into a miniature ship smaller than a breadbox, pointed at one end, flared and fitted with dartlike fins at the other, and set it going toward the singularity with its engine asizzle. Not one but a dozen little Priscillas were happily swimming around a petri dish, waving their flaggelae and multiplying merrily, back on Procyon XVIIIa. The Zartzes were a prolific species.

Thoroughly reassured that her kith, kin, and kind would live long and numerous lives back home, Priscilla still showed no great eagerness to go sizzling into a singularity. But by now, the only alternative seemed to be, to furnish a negligible snack for a Raptorial, and that wasn't exactly an appetizing prospect for a Zartz either.

Priscilla looked out through one of the viewports of her little ship and saw all the lights in the sky slowly shift toward red as time accelerated for her; this was an interesting phenomenon, but it didn't make the pink Zartz feel any cheerier than she had been.

*   *   *

Will Lux and Igor Dzugashvilli halted at Seamus O'Malley and and Natalya Dzugashvilli's table in Tamerlane's saloon. "Mind if we sit?" Lux asked.

"Don't we know you?" Natalya replied.

"No seats," Seamus sneered.

"That's all right," Igor growled, reaching for a vacant chair. He pulled it toward himself backwards, plunked his tushy onto it and leaned his elbows on the table. Will Lux dragged up another chair and had to shove violently at Igor's biceps to get belly-room against the wood.

"Listen," Igor hissed confidentially, "we're all in this together and we're all in deep trouble. Something has got to be done. You know we each have a private book, each has a unique copy that we all keep in secret." (This was a breech of bookmen's etiquette; one did not mention one's unique copy.) "Well, somebody's got at my *Green Odyssey* and it's not unique any more. What are we going to do about it?"

*　*　*

Priscilla Prestone Pritikin looked ahead of her ship, into the heart of the black hole that hung between Alioth and Merak. She knew the theory of singularities, that once one of them captured a bit of matter or energy, that matter or energy could never again escape because of the immense gravity of the black hole.

Sooner or later, she thought, all of the universe would have been devoured by black holes. Then the holes would start devouring one another. Eventually everything would become part of one giant black hole. The hole would continue to contract, growing smaller and denser, denser and smaller, until it shrank to a single point containing the whole universe.

If you were part of it when that happened, what would it be like? Would you ever know the difference? Would that point then simply pop out of existence? Would it re-emerge into another universe, spraying matter and energy in all directions? Would it then be a white hole? And would that be the same thing as a Big Bang?

Ahead of the Zartz's little spaceship there emerged from the great sucking blackness a wraithlike shape, pale, phosphorescing greenish-white. Its huge facetted eyes glittered green by the light of Merak and the pulsations of Alioth. Its legs were covered with sharply murderous serrations. Its tail swung forward beneath its abdomen, barbed, pointed, powerful.

*　*　*

"Do about it?" Natalya Dzugashvilli burst into high-pitched laughter. The feminine sound of her laugh cut through the muttering, mumbling undertone of Tamerlane's saloon, a sound that could be approximated by taping a monotonous chant of *spaghetti-spaghetti-spaghetti* and double-tracking it with a chant of *bumbershoots-treetrunks-bumbershoots-treetrunks.* Faces turned suspiciously toward the table. Natalya turned them away with a glance of fierce hatred, the standard expression of the literary antiquarian toward the world in general and colleagues in particular. "Do about your fucking *Green Odyssey?* That's your lookout, bozo! Order us a round of drinks and maybe you'll get a little sympathy." She exchanged a triumphant look with Seamus O'Malley, who wiped one hand happily across his white-stubbled jowls and grunted his agreement.

Natalya was talking to her brother, of course; further, they had been partners in many a successful caper in the rare book biz. Still, Igor was a collector. Natalya was a collector. One motto in the rare book business is, *Always kick a man when he's down.*

*   *   *

The Raptorial flapped its great wings, wings with a span some thousand meters or more in extent. The Raptorial had a name; in the language of its kind, it might be represented something like burnt-umber-square-root-of-minus-ninety-one/scent-of-fusing-heavy-hydrogen/memory-of-an-embracing-ancestor/sensation-of-radiant-flameberries.

He (for no revealed reason) detected the presence of a metallic speck headed toward his home. He flew by sweeping the space ahead of him, capturing ambient free ions and hurling them behind him toward the singularity, using them as reaction mass in the simplest and most elegant sense of that term.

Bumber (a mere convenience, a short form of his name which Bumber himself would probably fail to recognize) caught the tiny spaceship bearing the Zartz ambassador between his claws and held it up to one of his green, facetted eyes. He peered through one of the ship's vision ports and saw Priscilla Prestone Pritikin inside, wigwagging a message to him in International Flag Code, using pseudopoda for flags.

*   *   *

"You don't think I know what your unique book is, do you, darling sister?" Igor Dzugashvilli gripped Natalya's wrist in a painful grasp. His dirty fingernails dug into her flesh. Out of a corner of his eye he spotted Will Lux signaling to Tamerlane Poe, the proprietor of the saloon, to bring a bottle and four glasses. "You don't think I know?" Igor watched Natalya's face. No one else, not O'Malley, not even Natalya's former lover Will Lux, could read her eyes the way Igor could. And if you couldn't read Natalya's eyes, there was no way you could guess what she was thinking.

"Not even you," Natalya hissed. Her breath was like the breath of a cobra preparing to strike. Cold and chokingly rich with the memory of the last small creature she had devoured whole and digested alive. "Not even you would reveal that to these other two sons of swineherds." She knew that her eyes betrayed her lack of confidence in her own assertion. After all, she knew Igor well.

* * *

Priscilla looked through the vision port of her ship. This was the end. This must be the end. She prayed that her fission sisters in their petri dish on Procyon XVIIIa were happy and fecund, as was the way of the Zartz. The distant stars disappeared from Priscilla's view as the Raptorial folded its great phosphorescent wings about her spaceship, forming itself into a streamlined spiral like some chambered marine nautilus. The spaceship was enveloped, all distant illumination blocked, its vision ports covered; the flesh of the Raptorial's wings pressed against the vision ports like a mass of raw dough.

Not wishing the occupant of the spaceship to become alarmed, Bumber spelled out a message on his own flesh pressed against the windows of the ship. "Hi there, you little pink cutie!" Bumber spelled out. "Just relax and have a ride. We're headed for home and we'll arrive there about three hundred million years from next Tuesday."

* * *

Seamus O'Malley decided to act the role of peacemaker. Tamerlane Poe had placed the bottle and glasses on the table but he stood over them, gravy-stained apron covering his round belly, refusing to let anyone touch the bottle until he'd been paid in full. Tamerlane wasn't a bookman himself, but he knew them and their ways and he wasn't going to let anybody in this bunch run a tab. Will pulled some chips from a draw-neck poke and counted them carefully into Tamerlane's hand. Poe tested the chips in a circuit-reader, nodded, and walked away. "You each owe me for this," Will told the others hostilely.

Seamus said, "Suppose we reveal our unique books to one

another. That will forge a bond among the four of us. Igor, we already know that your book is *The Green Odyssey*, and that it isn't unique any more. Igor claims he knows Natalya's. Natalya may know Will's from scouting his home." He stopped, realizing suddenly that he had said too much: the only one with a good solid secret to protect was himself, Seamus O'Malley. No one knew that O'Malley's secret treasure was a tight copy in jacket of *Away from the Here and Now* by Clare Winger Harris, Dorrance, Philadelphia, 1947. Now he was subject to pressure from the others!

*   *   *

The scene shifts three hundred million years into the future. Actually, a little more than that. It shifts to three hundred million years from next Tuesday. Bumber and Priscilla Prestone Pritikin descended slowly toward the City of Mhg'ggg on Thyxlym. Thyxlym is an approximation of what Bumber's people called their world, which we would call a black hole or singularity. Mhg'ggg was about three centimeters in diameter (being roughly disc-shaped), its tallest building extending about five or six millimeters into the sky above the surface of Thyxlym. This may sound small, but the incredible gravity of Thyxlym shrank Bumber, Priscilla, and Priscilla's ship to such miniscule size, long before they reached the surface of the singularity, that they had no problems of scale.

Bumber landed on the flat roof of the Mhg'ggg City Hall. He immediately checked the nearest calendar to see what year it was, since (as has been mentioned) the time-distorting effects of approaching or leaving Thyxlym could toss one into the future or the past without one's being particularly aware of it. Bumber's facetted emerald eyes glinted with satisfaction. He was right on target. It was *precisely* three hundred million years from next Tuesday.

*   *   *

"I'll tell you what," Igor Dzugashvilli suggested. He kept his voice low so no one beyond his table could overhear him. Bookmen and a few bookwomen at adjacent tables were trying hard to overhear, but everyone in the trade was by now an expert at modulating his voice to keep from being overheard. "Suppose we each take a scrap of chaw-gunk, scratch the names of our secret books onto it, pass the scraps around the table so we all share our secrets, and then chaw up the gunk so nobody else can spy us out."

Six eyes glared at him. He tried to glare back at them, but he had to keep flicking his glance from Seamus to Natalya to Will, as a result of which he looked merely guilty and afraid instead of fierce. Simultaneously the others offered Igor impolite advice.

Just for the record, the secret treasures of the four were as follow: Igor's was *The Green Odyssey*, by Philip Jose Farmer. (You knew that already.) Will's was *Doctor Fogg*, by Norman Matson. Natalya's was *The Teenie Weenies Under the Rose Bush*, by William Donahey. Seamus's was *Away from the Here and Now*, by Clare Winger Harris. Igor was in bad shape because his *Green Odyssey* was no longer unique, and he'd have to find another unique item to replace it. Besides, he didn't really know about *The Teenie Weenies Under the Rose Bush*; he was just bluffing Natalya.

*   *   *

Bumber took Priscilla to see the ruler of the Raptorials. The ruler's name was, approximately, Ultramarine/scent-of-decaying-sea-weed/nasal-polyp. Or Ultryp. "Ultryp, Your Highness, old chum," Bumper said (or something that we can't conveniently come closer to than that), "this brave little lady is a visitor from a few hundred million years ago, and she's got to tell us a tale of woe. Seems that a lot of us people have been eating up her folks, and they're not at all willing to regard it as jokes." He went on in that fashion. Ultryp nodded in sympathy, facetted eyes flashing a dazzling red.

The amazing thing is that the Raptorials not only worked out a solution to the problem of eating up members of the Galactic Federation, their ruler Ultryp applied for membership in behalf of the entire Nation of Thyxlym, and arranged for Priscilla to open the first Federation office right there in the City of Mhg'ggg.

They sealed the bargain according to Thyxlymian custom by writing up a report on their negotiations and the terms of their agreement. In addition to copies of this retained by Ultryp and Priscilla Prestone Pritikin (in behalf of Moghyhgom-anapana-moghyhgoM), a special copy of the work, engraved in letters of turquoise and gold on finest rag-stock vellum and bound in leather and wooden boards (all of these in their condensed ultragravitic form, of course) was created and flung ceremoniously to the Universe through the wormholes and gravity wells to which Thyxlym was connected, thus to travel at random through all of time and space and dimension. Peace was restored and the Galactic Federation of Intelligent and Peaceloving Life Forms was infinitely enriched by the addition of the Raptorials to its membership.

*　　*　　*

Igor Dzugashvilli slouched along the paper-blown and rat-infested alleys of Chicago IV, cursing the ill fortune that had overcome him. His plan had failed. Natalya had called his bluff and preserved the secret of her unique book. Once Natalya had stone-walled against Igor's suggestion, it was obvious that Will and Seamus would do the same. And of course they did. Or had.

So Igor Dzugashvilli found himself the only member of the inseparable quartet (although they were at the moment separated) whose secret was blown and whose unique treasure was no longer unique. He was at the bottom of the social pyramid, and he felt the weight of the others crushing his soul.

O Angst! O Weltschmertz! O Sturm und Drang!

Suddenly there was a plop from somewhere up ahead of Igor. Igor peered through Chicago IV's midnight gloom, trying to see what had produced the sound. He lit a match, fell to all fours, and—beneath a broken and rusted streetlight stanchion from which the lamp had been shattered years if not decades before— he found a positively *gorgeous* book, magnificently bound, its text not printed or even holograph but *engraved* in turquoise and gold on rag-stock vellum.

His hands trembling, Igor opened the volume to its title page. For a moment he was puzzled. He couldn't read the script. But somehow the strange type wavered and reshaped itself. It said *The War between the Federation and Thyxlym.* It seemed to be a novel of some sort, and it was anonymous. It had a copyright notice, though: *Mhg'ggg, 300,000,000 Years from Next Tuesday.* "This one," Igor grunted to himself, "I'm going to protect with my life. Matter duplicators—*aaagh!* Lux was dead right!"

In 1970 *Harry Harrison* brought out an anthology called The Year 2000. *The book did so well that his publisher issued a contract for a sequel to be called* The Year Two Million. *Harry warned prospective contributors that they faced a very tough task. People in that distant future won't have names like Mabel or Walter, he pointed out. They won't speak English or anything resembling that language. They may not even look like us.*

It was an intriguing challenge, and in response I wrote "The Child's Story." Harry held the manuscript for a very long time, then returned it with a note saying that he was repaying his advance and asking the publisher to cancel his contract. Of all the authors who had sent him manuscripts, he explained, I was the only one who had even come close.

I'm still not sure whether that was damning with faint praise or praising with faint damns. But happily for me, David Hartwell was shortly to become editor of a new (and regrettably short-lived) magazine called Cosmos Science Fiction and Fantasy, *where I was pleased to see my story featured.*

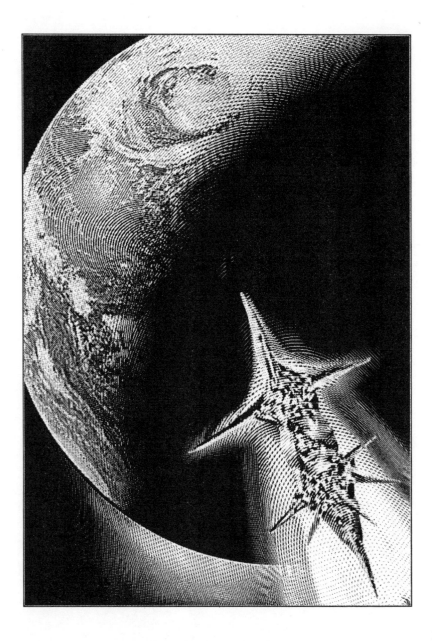

The Child's Story

BEHOLD THE EARTH!

Serenely she whirls, gleaming azure and pearl. Her day skies glow clear, dotted with puffs of cloud, here dazzling white and fluffy, here menacingly gray and filled with fury; beneath them fall torrents of rain, blankets of snow. Zephyrs soothe green meadows and fields of wild, waving grain; tornadoes rip tons of soil from its bed and raise it in towering funnels to be spread over distant plains or dropped on rising slopes.

On Earth's night side no flame, no light competes with astral lumination: Luna rises and sets, fills and wanes in cold solitude; stars gleam unchallenged in the black bowl.

This is the Earth.

Now behold the Ship.

Long she is, and oddly made, this thing, this creature, this friend and aide of mankind, this strange being evolved in the cold and vacuum between the worlds, needing only a visit to the vicinity of some star for replenishment.

Soon she will glide softly to Earth. Soon her burden, her masters, her pets, her lovers, her lice will float from her flanks onto the bosom of the planet. She will leave them then and go to bathe in the photosphere of Sol, turning and writhing in her ecstasy, nourishing and fecundating on the flaming gases of the sun.

And her riders, on the Earth, will transact such trivial business as interests their amusing sort, and will await in confidence her return to bear them back whence they came.

She is amused, is the Ship.

Behold her: her flanks are ridged, fluted, her fore end is curved, enlarged, bears sensors attuned to remote inputs on a broad spectrum: gamma, heat, visual and more. Her insides are of raw energies and plasmoid matter. Her form is as she chooses, in part for her own aesthetic gratification, in part for the convenience of the little creatures she is amused to carry.

For their sake she holds a shell of pure force about herself. Without the shell she would be bombarded by deadly radiation, sucked by hard vacuum—of no concern to the Ship, but fatal to her passengers. Instead she protects them: her shield filters the impinging radiation, shunts the harmful components away from her puny friends, holds within an atmosphere under pressure convenient for the humans.

The humans.

Men they are, woman and man and women and men the children of Man, but no more do they resemble the sapient ancestors who first removed from the planet of their rising, than did those men the equally distant ancestors who first used the tool, the hand, the brain to earn the designation Man.

These humans are of a widespread type. Man is not a standardized breed: from world to world, beneath star and star, where chemistry and ray and gravity's variant produce adapted offshoots, men vary. In stature, in configuration, in mass. Furry or bald, huge-eyed or small, sparse or prolific, gross with padding, with muscle, or slim with nerve, yet always Man.

These travelers, favorites of the Ship, are of the type most favored for deep space: a type bred on no planet, a type birthed and living on Ships, journeying from world to world, trading, studying, learning, always returning to their Ship to travel again into the deep.

They are a tall race: twice the height of their remote, brutal forebears, yet not nearly the tallest of men. Their bodies are hairless, their digits nail-less, their mouths soft and small; they are well suited to live aboard their Ships, not nearly so well suited to residence on most planets—and yet, sensitive, intelligent, curious and highly adaptable. They can survive a wide range of environments with a minimum of heavy gear: the Ships do not like machinery and carry only very little, only very reluctantly.

Many of the worlds of men remember their ancestry; many more have forgot. Of those who know their origin some yet possess the great heaving machinery needed to move from planet to planet, from star to star. Some there are who dream yet of following ancient, remembered probes across the great gulfs that separate the galaxies. Some have attempted the journey; some may have succeeded, but no sign has ever returned of their end.

Yet only these tall, hairless men, their skins a tone of muted violet, travel upon the Ships. The Ships will accept none others.

And now these men are traveling to Earth. None recalls the last visit of men to Earth. Those who travel aboard this Ship own different feelings, different reasons for visiting the world where their species rose. They have feelings, they have reasons, they have reasons for these are still men, women, still Man.

A curiosity, a pure intellect's call to learn.

A yearning, a kind of love.

A deep, bone-felt need.

And in one, a hate.

For these are still men, women, still Man.

But now behold the Earth. The Ship approaches. The men aboard can see the planet now clearly, and her moon more clearly: a globe of breathtaking beauty, cream-yellow, pock-marked, cold and pure and burning with a frigid fire thrown to her by Sol and turned back to the glory of God: to the dazzlement of tear-drawing joy of any behold; but lacking any to behold, still to the glory of God.

And the Earth herself bears as ever she has her works: her mountains, her deserts, her jungles.

Mighty peaks thrust jaggedly through drifting banks of pale suspended vapor. Gray cliffs, here aged, softened by the passage of time, there sharp and newly upthrust by the struggled heavings of the living Earth. Here lies snow gleaming pale in starlight, bright in sunlight; here lies ice shimmering like flowing streams; and here streams of flowing water shimmer like polished ice.

Flat wastes of sand run beneath howling winds, chilled by starlight, moonlight, broiled by daylight. Dunes rise beneath the wind, ridges and depressions appear; there is stillness: they grow hot, cold, again, again. The wind returns, suddenly, terribly: the depressions are filled, the ridges are smoothed, dunes disappear and others come in their place.

Where there is soil, water, warmth, jungles teem and snap, struggling for nourishment, competing, tree against tree, vine against shrub, for sunlight. Trunks pound upward, creepers writhe, leaves spread hungrily for actinic rays, roots spread and struggle, straining against one another for moisture. The jungles are filled with motion. The motion of growth, the tropism of light-seeking plants, of moisture-seeking plants, of parasites crawling, climbing, burrowing into their passive hosts. And the flesh-eating plants, tiny insect-traps slapping leaves together on nectar-tempted guests, visitors lured with the promise of a meal, the promise kept, the eater eaten, the seeker sought, the hunter prey.

The insects swarm in their trillions: great dragonflies the like of their own ancestors scores of millions of years in the past; driver ants huge and resistless, their mobile prey needing only to step aside, or slither aside, or creep aside, or take to wing; but the unwary, the immobile, plant or infant or cripple, falls beneath mandibles to the nourishment of the horde, and is momentarily forgot.

Arachnidae, spiders and scorpions and strange, crawling red crab-things that move clumsily, their shells clacking, down dark-shaded jungle pathways. Those fitted with venom find their nourishment unsuspecting: a quick lunge, a sharp sting, a burning sensation; then dizziness, darkness, half-oblivious living death.

The giant wasp lays her eggs in the still form of her paralyzed victim. Her larvae will dine well.

The multifarious mosquito still sucks its victim's blood; the vampire bat proves nature's repetition of the successful ploy.

Silently, gently. Silently, gently. The dark shape against the moon, the supersonic squeal, the sleeping prey. The quiet prey awakens: a small itch, a small scar, a slight weakness. More food and its body's mechanisms repair the small breach, replace the slight loss. The dumb beast plods onward, unaware of the service it has done.

Snakes, battrachians, and the mammals and birds.

The great cats stalk the forest trails or prowl the terraces of great leafy limbs. The lesser mammals move aside: come not to the quick eye, the sharp awareness of the carnivore. Move aside. Stay aside. Burrow or flee or hide.

The birds scream, the mammals howl, slow reptiles creep from stream to swamp to stream.

This is the Earth.

And approaching through the endless not-day, not-night, comes the Ship.

Aboard her, so many men, so many women, so many—others.

Ascetics, renunciates, those who have yielded up their sexuality, abandoned their gender on the altar of academe or that of ambition or that of duty. In this age such act is common, easy—and reversible.

Behold Guide.

Born a thousand years past, child to spacefarers of another Ship, bearing chromosomes donored by three dozen parents, nated a neuter by consensus of hir parents, Guide has spent ten centuries aboard Ship studying the means of telling this long organism the wishes of men.

Se does well. Each man-bearing Ship carries one Guide; the manless Ships envy their sisters and clamor for men when neonates occur. This Guide is the product of careful selection of parents, of patient rearing by hir Ship. Se knows well the state required to communicate with Ship. Se often achieves this state, far more often than do most Guides.

Se thinks: after seeing Earth se will adopt gender. In a thousand years of observing women, men, neuters, that se would spend a time gendered. It is a mystery, a pain, a gladness that se would experience.

Se thinks: of the genders, se will select the womanly. Se thinks: as woman she would bear child. Not as donor to a Ship's child: she would lie with a gendered male and become fecundated, and bear a child.

When Guide thinks these thoughts hir head feels strange, hir link with Ship quivers and rails, hir body feels an odd and unfamiliar stirring. Hir belly and hir crotch, hir belly and hir crotch.

Se turns hir thoughts back to hir tasks. Se wishes greatly to visit Earth, to see her pampas and her glaciers and her hills, to walk the ground where hir uttermost ancestors stood and worked, fought and brought forth new life. Se holds hir thoughts to hir tasks.

Behold Reader.

Taller than Guide, more massive of bone and flesh, more filled with time and experience and cynicism. Reader selected male gender in childhood, in amazingly early childhood. He is male now, proudly flaunting phallus and testes in the nude society of the Ship.

Rare among Ship men, Reader has spent long periods on planets. His boast is this: on one planet, one world where Man's intelligence and socialization have fallen away leaving a brutal, militant maggot-heap of a civilization, Reader landed and stayed, and schemed and frightened, and drew close to the seats of might, and took the seat of the least of the mighty, and schemed and played and rose to the seat of the next more mighty, and promised and betrayed and gained the seat of the next more mighty, and rose to the height of a world, was seen as unchallenged warlord of a frightened world.

And threw over his might, and returned to Ship laughing and braying at the fools he had conquered, and watched his heirs fall out and dismantle his empire and fall into war and die, and their heirs fall out and struggle and lose what trappings of civilization they had yet retained, and lose what learning and culture they had retained, and fall into utter barbarism while Reader brayed and laughed.

Reader's purpose toward Earth: silence. He smiles a smile that pleasures no beholder. He will reveal, Reader commits; he will reveal, but not now. His grin is more terrible than a snarl.

Behold the Child.

The youngest person on Ship, as yet flexible, uncertain; born neuter, the Child has opted at times in the few centuries of experience so far to live at times as female, at times as neuter, at times as male.

The Child has visited many planets; they hold for the Child a fascination not like Earth's hold upon Guide nor the barbar world's upon Reader. The Child thrives on variety of experience, has visited sandworld and seaworld, snowworld and sunworld, as female, as neuter, as male.

Now the Child visits Earth as androgyne.

The Child has done the mating things with all the humans aboard Ship capable of doing the mating things, and not pledged to abstinence. A few of these people withhold from themselves not sexuality but sex: this is a practice they maintain to furnish themselves with enhanced spiritual energy: not to cease the yearnings or the loins but to turn such force elsewhere. To learning, to building, to sight, to enlightenment, to the gathering of strength for great works.

But the Child seeks learning otherwise, through variety of experience. Esh has received some insight which says: experience all, see all, taste all: pleasure of every sort, pain of every sort; take all, give all, be all, have all, lose all, do all. The notion of the Child is that each experience peels away a sheet of ignorance, fulfills and disposes a byte of potential.

Child's purpose toward Earth: all. To taste her food and her waters, to breathe her airs, to see her colors, feel her heat and her cold. To ride her beasts. To clutch the roughness of a treetrunk to shir naked body. To bathe in her seas.

To lie nude upon a polar ice cap beneath a naked sun.

To swim deep in the sea where shir first ancestor floated.

To fuck the Earth itself, rod poked deep into hissing hot sand, sucking cold muck, the fur of a great wild cat.

To take a brutal icicle in shir cunt, twisting, screaming.

To live where the first of shir line of life lived.

To die on Earth.

For Child, this is all experience. At its end esh notions esh's consciousness will remain, a purified, gleaming rod of pure light, a glorious awareness that will illuminate all around esh.

After Earth, Child notions, esh will return to the neuter, will ride Ship on some future plunge into the photosphere of a sun. This, esh notions, will burn away shir last vestige of the physical, the gross. From this esh will return a pure gleaming immateriality.

All of this is Child's notion.

There are others aboard Ship: Power, Seeker, Sender, Lady, Master, Seer, Lord. Others.

All are of human stock; all are of space-faring stock, of Ship–riding stock, naked, hairless, nail-less, tall and slim, intelligent, aware.

Not all men are such, nor are all the peopled worlds, worlds of men. God's causation has peopled this world with aware slugs; that, with a collective intelligence of individually motile neural elements; another, with machine analogs of the mind-patterns of a long-extinct organic intelligence.

Here glows a star, dull and weary, smothered beneath great flat skatelike energy leeches that crawl and suck at its feeble heat.

Here swims a thing so tenuous as to defy proof even of existence, detectable only at its own will, only through a sensing of its calculated messagings, its own being invisible, intangible, undetectable.

Here live creatures of beauty transcending description.

Here live creatures of horror transcending description.

Here live Ships: their breeding place, known to them alone, the heart of a star. Here they come not for the restoration of flagged energies, but for the shedding of a dying skin. The Ship herself, old and weary, within her grown another like herself, identical to the last cell–analog of Ship biology and structure.

Emerges the child, raw and naked to the heart radiation of her star, the husk of her mother transformed in the instant of emergence to pure energy, driven out on solar wind.

But aboard the Ship approaching Earth, this is unknown; the way of Ships is not to carry passengers on the final Journey of emergence and dissolution.

This Ship draws closer, closer to the Earth.

Beneath: the seas of Earth.

The most ancient home of life on the planet.

The most ancient home of the ancestors of Guide, of Reader, of Child, Of Power, of Seeker, of Sender. Of Lady, Master, Seer, Lord.

The seas of Earth teemed once with life: unicellular creatures floating near the surface, energized by the warming rays of Sol. Simple plants devouring one another. Primitive animalcules drifting and quivering, eating and being eaten, slowly developing skills:

Speed for flight—and for pursuit.

Armor and claws and teeth—for protection—and for attack.

Nerves and senses—for detection and response.

From Earth came all, after billions of years the all that had come from the sea destroyed and poisoned and debased its ancient home, the womb from which it had sprung, and the land to which it had climbed, and the air to which it had aspired, and was expelled from its home, its world, its Earth.

But life remained in the ruins, life which had lacked the intelligence to foul its home, the arrogance to make itself master over all.

The dominion which God had given to Man, Man had lost, and in his place remained the fishes and the scorpions, the grasses and the weeds and the trees, the thorn–roses, the last soaring condors, the gentle cetaceans, the humble loxodonta and the mighty planaria.

Was there now intelligence on the Earth?

Ship slowed, drifting slowly the final hours of her Journey.

Now she passed close by Earth's moon, standing near eclipse by the planet itself. Ship approached from the darkness, curving slowly toward the terminator. Now Ship stood in the dark of Luna, now Sol's crown flared over the lunar horizon.

Flames towered and wove, danced in total silence. Aboard Ship, there was a soft gasp as Guide drew in hir breath. Se had seen stellar coronae before, but never such as this. Se turned, seeking one with whom to share the moment: this, of all the ways of mankind, had endured.

At hir shoulder, tears of anguished joy streaming from great mauve eyes, the Child.

Guide holds hir hands, soft and nail-less, toward the Child, places them on the slim, violet upper arms of the Child. The Child is affected beyond past experience by the sight; shir androgynous sexuality aroused by strange ancestral drives: shir nipples, darkly pigmented, stand erect on small, beathtakingly graceful breasts; shir male parts, innocent of bush, respond equally: scrotum tightened, dartlike penis aquiver.

They embrace, Guide and the Child. Guide, neuter but knowing, gives the Child satisfaction rapidly, skillfully. Afterwards they lie flat, together, in the ridged skin of Ship.

Ship emerges from behind Luna, in full daylight drops away from the cream-toned cratered surface. Her passengers watch, some gazing back at the dead beauty of the airless world; more, ahead, beholding the azure and pearl swirling slowly over the surface of the planet.

Slowly, barely perceptibly, Ship drops toward Earth. Her course will bring her into a polar orbit, narrowing slowly and more slowly until she hovers over her selected point. The choice of Ships is normally not to touch any planet; it is a choice of aesthetics, not necessity—these creatures, bred in solar purity, travelling through vacuum, recoil from the touch of soil or of sea.

Ship comes nearly to a halt, her remaining motion so slight as to defy notice by any other than another Ship, yet moving still, for never does any Ship come to total stillness.

She hovers almost unmoving over the southern polar cap of the Earth. Never before has she visited this planet, nor does its variety in particular interest her. Planets she has seen aplenty, and never has one pleased her. She visits them for the sake of her pets: it pleases them, Ship humors them. This is the way of Ships.

Within her force shell she is fully aware of the humans who cluster on her skin. Odd beings, but somehow pleasing, somehow gratifying to an odd, uncomprehended need in the strange psyche of Ships—this symbiosis is far from unprecedented in the complex concourse of life within the galaxy. God alone may know what stranger creatures than these tiny sapients await in more distant locales.

Ship dissolves her force shield. The air that hangs above the polar ice impinges upon her skin: she contrasts it to the absolute frigidity of the vacuum she normally occupies, to the energetic radiation of the suns she periodically visits, finds it a mild and balmy stuff but midway between the two bounds of her usual experience.

Ship quivers once in a kind of delicious spasm.

The people who have clustered on her back bound lightly into the polar air. All are naked. Most carry with them nothing but their capacity for experience. One hefts a small metallic device; Ship feels a small wave of pleasure and of gratitude at the departure of the machine.

The people hold communion.

*   *   *

Some spoke aloud, in the manner of their ancestors: this was the manner of tradition, of ceremony, of the solemn and ceremonious proceedings of the people of the Ship. Others chose to link themselves to their fellows, to share with a kind of intimacy and degree of interchange no spoken word could possibly carry.

Guide spoke first, telling of hir need to see the womb of hir life, the womb of hir family. The others listed, and nodded; understood, and accepted, and gave their blessing back to hir.

Power spoke. A temporary male, he rose to hover above the others, to show his swollen phallus, to give all an understanding of his need for oneness with the source of the power of men, the first home of men, the place from which rose all of the strength of men.

Child spoke.

Master spoke.

Sender spoke.

Others turned toward Reader, he who had brought from the Ship the thing of metal. He had placed it somewhere, none other knew where; had done with it something none other knew what.

Roughly Reader announced his reason for returning aboard the Ship to Earth: the freeing of Man from his shackling past. No longer must attachment to any place of birth or growth hamper Man's outward vision. No longer must humankind look back, look downward, look inward: all must be the vision ahead, out, up: to the stars, to the galaxies, to the all.

A sigh went up from the others, a moan, a sob.

All raced outward from the circle of their communion. All moved, silently, from the place of communion. Across ice. Across peaks. Across seas. Across deserts and forests and steppes, sand and earth and grass and waves.

Lord, to a place of gray waters towering mightily, a narrow gorge long ripped between razored granite. Icy here, cold salt spray whipped from green luminescent waters, dripped back from slime–coated rocks. A few white fluttering birds struggled against the gale. Below the turbulence great somnolent sea tortoises drove slowly after nourishment.

Lord stood in the air above, arms folded, wind whipping about violet nakedness, reeling.

Sender to a place deep beneath the sands of the greatest of the deserts of the planet. Here the eternal churning of the sand had brought the detritus of the ages, chunks of this and bits of that, fossil and agglomorate and a great pitted chunk of metallic meteorite.

Sender floated in lotus posture, immersed in the sands, feeling the heart of the desert, thinking the meteorite back to its impact on the sands, back through its flaming passage of the Earth's atmosphere, back to its long, cold wanderings through the solar system, back to the time of its creation from the debris of a planet long destroyed.

Sender had closed shir eyes—Sender, like the Child, was for the time being androgynous. Had lain with the Child many times, aboard Ship, loving, teaching, learning.

And the Child, arching aflame through the clear sky above a night region, had encountered a creature grown from some small ancestor, a great, intelligent, protean flying mammal grown from the bombarded genes of a mouse-like, furry aerial thing.

The flying creature was at first startled, then terrified by the Child. To the creature, this strange being, unfamiliar, unprecedented in its experience, represented threat, peril, death. The creature bared glittering fangs that dripped a brilliant, refractive, hypnotic venom.

The Child extended shir soul to meet that of the creature; esh drew shir hands, long, cool, flexible, through the coat of the flying thing.

The creature turned in the air, desperately struggling to maintain flight, to see the intruder, to protect itself. To the flying creature, the Child gave the appearance of a glimmering spectral light, blue and green and yellow, orange and red and violet, and most of all violet, and somehow calming. The creature's desperate breathing slowed and smoothed. It spread its wings and resumed a smooth flight. It felt the stranger insinuating shirself into its very physical being.

It felt warmth and pleasure, felt its every fibre and neuron touched, examined, caressed; an old injury, a bone once shattered and crookedly knit in one leg, seemed to be warmed to melting, to flow and straighten and heal again. The creature gave a supersonic screech of pleasure and gratitude and soared higher, bearing the Child with it and within it.

And beneath the polar ice cap something sank. Some object,

rigid, dense, metallic, filled with a searing malevolent energy, a monstrous potential, and with it a male figure, hairless, violet, heavy, massive: Reader, alone.

Through ice undisturbed for aeons, white, solid, frigid, dense, miles in depth. And beneath it solid bedrock, black granite, slumbering away its millions of years of unmoving, uncaring existence.

And beneath the magma, the very mantle of the Earth. Here a chunk of solid, dense matter: a concentration of heated iron, near-molten zinc, flowing lead. Here a pocket of ancient uranium, slowing doling out its half-life, turning to lead.

And through all moved the artifact.

And with it moved Reader.

Down, slowly, leisurely, through the earth. Down, steadily, unhurriedly, through rock and metal, through strata of greater and greater density, of greater and greater heat, through matter unexposed to the trivial encrustation of Earth's continents, seas, polar caps for uncounted years. For hundreds of millions, for billions of revolutions around the friendly sun.

Down moved the thing.

Down, Reader.

Inside the thing energies flow and whirl: brilliant white.

Beside the thing Reader: rigid, grim, tense.

And soon, in the very center of the globe, they halt. Gravity here is essentially null: there is no down, only up: all directions are up. The thing is still, and Reader moves, caresses its case, grinning.

The material surrounding the man and the thing is hot, dense, molten. No light impinges upon the thing or the man except the heat-glow of the molten stuff that surrounds them.

Reader does something to the case of the object; his long, dexterous fingers do not open the case but rather they penetrate, they enter the flux of the sheer seething forces within; they perform operations, guide flowing courses of sheer energy, initiate operations, withdraw.

In a span of time measurable in picoseconds the energies within the box emerge like snakes from a carven casket. They writhe and gibber, they expand at a rate little beneath the speed of light. They emerge, they expand, they whirl and twist and grow, and grow, and grow.

A radius away the Child senses the violent event. With astonishing gentleness yet incredible speed esh disengages from the flying creature esh had entered; before it realizes that something new is happening esh is gone.

The Child darts through air, earth, rock, metal; finds shir way to the center of the globe, confronts Reader.

They face each other. Less than a nanosecond has transpired. The energies released from the artifact have not yet reached the being of Reader.

The two converse. They meet in the mind. The Child is affrighted, offended, yet puzzled. Esh is aghast.

Reader is triumphant.

Earth to perish. Man's ancient home to perish. The birthing place of the race to perish. Man to see not the past but the future, not a pitiable speck but the all.

The Child stands startled. Esh considers. Esh reaches a hand toward the artifact. Reader counters, blocks, grasps shir wrist with strong, flexible fingers.

The writhing energies reach toward the two.

Above, others are scattered over and through the earth.

Eight light-minutes away, the Ship bathes in the flaring corona of Sol.

The seething energies contact the flesh of Reader, that of the Child. They sear the flesh, for such it is, still, despite all else.

In less than a second the two are gone. The globe is gone. The Earth is no more.

The Ship returns, in her own time, from Sol. Momentarily she is puzzled—where is Earth? Where are her people?

But these creatures are strange, she knows. Unpredictable. She understands what they have done, does not concern herself with the reasons for the act.

She moves away, past the solitary globe of Luna. She turns from the circling plane of the planets and sets course for a new encounter.

Elsewhere Man remains, scattered through the galaxy. Man tall, noble, intelligent. Man coarse, gross, brutal. Man in wild variety. Man whose ancient placenta has at last been discarded.

When the late Roger Zelazny asked me to contribute a yarn to Wheel of Fortune, a 1995 anthology of gambling stories, I immediately thought of the casinos of Reno, Nevada. My impression is that Reno is a lot like Hell. It's great fun to visit but I wouldn't want to live there.

"The Tootsie Roll Factor" contains undeniable elements of autobiography, but I urge you to be careful of what you infer from it. I've used it as a performance piece several times and it was the basis of a successful one-man radio play. After it was broadcast I had any number of invitations (all of them from males) to join them at the poker table or participate in visits to the race track, and any number of offers (all of them from females) of assistance in recovering from the emotional devastation of my multiple marriages and divorces.

The fact is I've been to the ponies exactly once in my life and I found the experience excruciatingly boring. I enjoy an occasional hand of cards but I am by no means an addict. And as for romance, I have been married to the love of my life since 1958, and have no interest in seeking consolation elsewhere.

Thanks all the same for asking, though.

The Tootsie Roll Factor

I'M SITTING IN MY SUITE IN THE RENO SKY PAL-
ace, the ritziest gambling establishment in the Biggest Little
City in the World, and I am in very big trouble.

The manager of the casino is Mr. Albert Brown. He is as close
to a generic person as you can find. When I checked in to the Sky
Palace, he greeted me at the door. Was my plane ride pleasant?
Was the limo service from the airport—complimentary, of course,
furnished by the casino, of course—satisfactory? Would I like to
stop by his office to arrange a line of credit, or would I like a snack
and a beverage—complimentary, of course—first? Or would I like
to relax in my suite before doing anything else?

That was when I checked in. That was just seventy-two hours
ago. Things have changed drastically since then.

Mr. Albert Brown has just got off the phone. He tells me that
I have exhausted my line of credit, that he is no longer able to
comp me for the suite, I have been cut off at the restaurants and
bars in the hotel, Room Service has been instructed to log and
forget any orders I may place, and if I do not promptly pay what
I owe the casino or at least make some satisfactory arrangement
to do so, he will be forced to *Take Action*.

Take Action.

He addresses me as Israel. When I arrived it was, Mr. Cohen. Then Izzy. Then Ike. Ike-the-Kike, I could almost hear Mr. Albert Brown whisper. Now it's Israel. Well, that's my name, it's nothing I'm ashamed of. On the contrary, I bear it with pride.

Why then, when Mr. Albert Brown says the word, does it sound like an insult?

Never mind. At least he didn't say anything about cutting off the telephone or fax lines from my suite. This, I take it, is a good sign. At least he's offering me a chance to get straight with the casino before he *Takes Action.*

Should I use the fax to cry out for help? Or will I have a better chance if I use the regular telephone? The voice line, they call it nowadays. I have a brother in Seattle who runs a clothing store, they don't call it a haberdashery anymore. Strangely, his wife, my sister-in-law, seems to like me even less than my brother does.

If I am a truly unlikable person—I do not concede this, but I am willing to posit it as what a onetime philosophy professor of my acquaintance would call a hypothesis—then my brother, having known me longer and presumably better than my sister-in-law, his wife, should dislike me more than she does. Instead, the actuality is the other way around.

And I have two-and-a-half ex-wives in various locations. What, you ask, is half an ex-wife? Not the survivor of a magic act, let me hasten to assure you. No. I have been thoroughly and completely divorced by Wife Number One and Wife Number Two.

Wife Number One is remarried to a professor of paleontology at a small university in the State of Nebraska. This fellow, I have been given to understand, spends most of his time looking for dinosaur bones with a dental pick and a whiskbroom. His wife, my own Ex Number One, has made it clear that she never wishes to communicate with me again. Not in any way, manner or form.

Wife Number Two—that is, Ex Number Two—is at present single. She is a successful executive with a large, national restaurant chain. Her place of work is a luxurious suite of offices in the chain's headquarters on West Fifty-seventh Street in New York City. I am sending her a monthly alimony check, theoretically, although I am some years behind in my payments. Ex Number Two makes almost as much money as a backup singer for a rap artist or a left-handed relief pitcher. She does not need alimony from me, but she keeps after me just to make my life unpleasant.

I do not think that Ex-Wife Number One or Ex-Wife Number

Two will offer much assistance to me in my present state of distress.

What does Mr. Albert Brown mean by *Take Action*, I wonder.

Do they send men in black suits around, to break knee caps? Do they throw people off balconies? My suite is on the thirty-fifth floor of the Sky Palace. The great height of the building is the basis of its name. If I fell that distance, I would probably survive the fall but not the landing.

I could tell them that I'm perfectly willing to pay what I owe. It's not a question of willingness. In the words of a distinguished former President of the United States, I am not a crook. I've had an unusually uneven experience in the financial department, that's all. Everybody has his ups and downs. I just feel as if my ups have been higher and my downs lower than the average person's. I don't know why. I have no idea.

But if I just can't pay, what would be the point of breaking my knee caps, throwing me off a thirty-fifth floor balcony, or otherwise *Taking Action* against me? There's the old saw about getting blood from a stone, or whatever. It definitely applies here.

On the other hand, Mr. Albert Brown and his employers surely know all of this. They have almost certainly heard it many, many times. And still they *Take Action* against people who don't pay up. There must be a reason. They are not stupid people. Well, maybe some of them are. At the lowest levels.

The knee cap smashers.

The throwers off balconies.

The other *Takers* of *Action*.

But Mr. Albert Brown is a man of articulation and grace. He made that clear when I first encountered him, and on several later occasions, before our relationship became strained. And surely Mr. Albert Brown's employers are talented and intelligent persons.

So: Why *Take Action* against someone who is unable—not unwilling—to pay up?

For the same reason, I suppose, that the State punishes criminals who are not likely to repeat their crimes, would not repeat their crimes, even if they were released with merely a stern admonition to live proper and law-abiding lives. It deters *others*.

Yes.

They will obtain little or no satisfaction from *Taking Action* against Israel Cohen. But they will surely use their punitive conduct toward me as a deterrent to others who might get in over their heads, gamble more than they can afford to lose, place themselves in a position of being unable to pay their debts.

So—I suppose I am to be made an example of.

Oh, about that half a wife. That would be Wife Number Three, my most recent and in all likelihood final spouse. She has announced that she is leaving me. She has published a legal notice to the effect that she has left my bed and board and will henceforth bear no responsibility for any debts which I might incur. She has served me with papers indicating that she is in the process of divorcing me.

No, I can expect no assistance from Wife Number One, the wife of the paleontology professor, or from Wife Number Two, the executive of the restaurant chain, or from Wife Number Three, the placer of legal notices in officially recognized newspapers.

So, what about that brother in Seattle?

No. The last time I visited him and his delightful spouse and their beautiful children, my splendid nephew and two lovely nieces, my sister-in-law, my brother's wedded wife and the mother of the beautiful children, entered the living room as I was demonstrating to her brood the intricacies of dealing a poker hand from the bottom of the deck.

Why that would send my sister-in-law into a towering rage is a mystery to me. I have been a gambler all my life—well, almost all my life—and I have learned that it never hurts to know the tricks of the trade. It matters not whether one wishes to work a bottom-deal or whether one wishes to avoid having a bottom-deal worked upon one. It is still necessary to understand the mechanics of the act, to detect the telltale signs of the dishonest dealer, to avoid being dealt with unfairly.

But, come to think of it, this incident may explain my sister-in-law's disliking for me. In some murky way, that is.

Now here is a bit of philosophy. Not the kind dealt out by the fellow who long ago acquainted me with the concept of the posited hypothesis, by the way. No. I offer a far more practical kind of philosophy. It goes like this: When you have nothing to lose and no hope of winning, you might as well try anything as nothing.

Operating on the basis of this principle, I pick up the telephone and place a call to Ex-Wife Number One. The call goes through, which is a good sign. As I mentioned a while ago, it means that Mr. Albert Brown has still not cut off my outgoing calls, not even toll calls, an act on his part for which I am sincerely grateful.

Unless it is a mere oversight on the part of the management. If this came to their attention, maybe they would cut me off after all. I would become isolated, a prisoner in this plush hotel suite. There is a hot tub. There are several color TV's connected to the Sky Palace's dish antenna. There are special channels that offer instruction in poker, roulette, baccarat, and other forms of casino gambling. There is an electronic slot machine in the bathroom and there is an electronic poker machine at the bedside.

Speaking of which, the bed itself is huge, luxurious, and round, with crimson satin sheets and pillowcases.

There is even a large-screen television set mounted in the ceiling above the bed, and a remote-control device that permits me to tune in to pornographic motion pictures while reclining beneath the screen. I suppose, if I had a companion with me, we might lie side-by-side while watching beautiful young persons perform lascivious acts upon one another until we were overcome by the urge to emulate their activities.

I have not availed myself of this feature of my suite, and I now doubt that I ever will. A waste.

The professor of paleontology answers the telephone. I can imagine what kind of day it is in Nebraska: cold and gray and damp, with black storm-clouds sweeping across the Great Plains, preparing to dump their moisture on the harsh brown earth.

Not pretty.

I ask the professor if I may speak to—

How should I put this? My wife? My ex-wife? *His* wife? I settle for asking for her by name. The professor, a modern man who regards his spouse as a partner not a possession, calls her to the phone without demanding to know my identity or business.

Ex-Wife Number One picks up the phone and says, noncommittally, Yes?

I begin to tell her that I am in desperate straits, in big trouble, in deep doo-doo.

She places the receiver back on its base so gently that I barely detect the *click*.

Ah, well.

On to Ex-Wife Number Two.

In view of the time zone situation, it being three hours later in New York than in Reno and all that, I am not greatly surprised to hear her voice answer via a machine. "If you'll just leave your

name and number," Ex-Wife Number Two's prerecorded voice
purrs, "I promise that I'll call you back."

I start to leave my name and number—the number of the Sky
Palace—when she picks up the telephone and speaks to me. She
asks why I'm calling her in the middle of the night. "Or any time,"
she adds, but especially in the middle of the night.

Sticking to the most salient points and avoiding as many
unpleasant details as possible, I attempt to explain to this ex-wife
just how desperate I am for her assistance.

She lets me go on. Well, that's encouraging. I go on. I fill her
in on the background of the regrettable situation. She is still listening. My hopes are beginning to rise. I remind her of the good
times we had during our courtship, the all-too-few but nonetheless
happy and memorable experiences that we shared during our
marriage.

Still she has not interrupted.

When I come to the reasons for our divorce I offer sincere
apologies, I take the blame for the failure of our union and I tell
her that I hope to visit New York City some time and attempt to
make up to her the bad treatment that I inflicted on her. I suggest
that we travel to Atlantic City and check into a leading casino-and-
hotel and have a splendid vacation. It can be like a second honeymoon if that appeals to her, or it can be a chaste and asexual
relationship. Strictly as she chooses.

While she has not interrupted me, she has not responded to
any of my offerings or questions, either. I ask if she is still listening. She does not respond. I ask if she is still there, if we have been
cut off.

She does not speak, but I think I hear her breathing softly. I
become increasingly distressed. I find myself apologizing again,
ever more abjectly, and offering her ever more extravagant
enticements if she will only aid me in this, my hour of need.

Still she does not speak.

I begin to cry.

Only her breathing is heard. She is not a hard breather. Her
breath is soft and gentle. I remember it from the time of our
marriage.

She refuses to speak. She refuses to respond to my entreaties.
She does not say yes, she does not say no. Finally I give up and
place the telephone handset on its base. This was her cruelest
victory over me. This was the most unkindest cut of all.

Should I even try my third wife? Well, when there's nothing
to lose and nothing works, you might as well try anything. I try her

at the apartment where she moved when she left me. She answers the phone on the first ring. The apartment is, after all, in California. There is no time zone problem.

I get as far as identifying myself and she says, "Talk to my lawyer," and hangs up on me. I dial her number again and as soon as she hears my voice she hangs up on me.

What is left?

The fax is left.

To whom shall I fax my plea for help? How shall I word that plea?

I take a Sky Palace pen and a sheet of Sky Palace stationery from the top drawer of the brushed aluminum and polished onyx, art deco escritoire near the balcony door. As I write I can look out over Reno, see the flashing lights and the spectacular neon decorations of the many casinos and hotels. I fantasize that I am a character in a 1940s *noir* film, hiding out in a hotel room, gazing out the window. A flashing neon sign alternately illumines and darkens my room, setting my silhouette off in stark chiaroscuro every time it flashes on.

Probably I'm Alan Ladd, thinking about Veronica Lake, waiting for William Bendix and Elisha Cook, Jr., to arrive and murder me.

I write my fax message.

It says, HELP! SOMEONE HELP ME! PLEASE!

I sign my name, *Israel Cohen.* The stationery has a Sky Palace logotype on it, so if anyone wants to help me, my savior will have no trouble finding me. Well, there is the problem of my suite number. I add that beneath my signature.

Standing at the fax machine, I dial a random series of digits. Area code, exchange, suffix. Who knows where this message is going? Is there even such an area code as the one that I entered? Is there such an exchange, such a telephone number? Will I reach another fax machine even if there is such a telephone number? Or will the machine try to send my message in over a voice line, and accomplish nothing at all?

I press the TRANSMIT button.

The Sky Palace stationery feeds slowly through the machine.

I sit down and wait for something to happen. I ponder, How in the world did a nice Jewish boy like me get into a muddled and desperate situation like this?

At first, I can't figure it out. Then, as the lights of Reno continue to flash on and off through my big window, I get an inkling. Slowly a trickle of memory arises and I really do get a clue.

Yes, I am just a boy. How old? Six? Eight? Ten? No, it has to be less than ten. Six or eight or seven. Probably seven. Something like that.

I am a camper at a summer camp for Jewish children. The camp is named for an imaginary Native American tribe, the Kee-Wonkas. At least I believe that the Kee-Wonkas are imaginary. There was an elaborate mythology about the Kee-Wonkas, that was part of the lore of Camp Kee-Wonka, that was passed along to the Jewish children who attended this camp each summer.

The idea of Camp Kee-Wonka was to get children out of the city for a few weeks, during the hottest part of the year. And while they were out of school, of course.

Instead of the oppressive weather, the crowding and the fouled air of the city, the children would be surrounded by wooded hills, would sleep in pleasant, rustic cabins, would swim daily in a clear freshwater lake, would breath unpolluted air. In place of junk food, they would consume nutritiously planned and carefully prepared meals.

They would play healthful games during the day, and be exposed to a strange amalgam of traditional Jewish and hoked-up Native American culture each evening.

The older children, of course, would use this escape from parental supervision to experiment with their own and one another's blossoming pubes. The counselors, for the most part college students in their late teens and early twenties, would leave mere experimentation far in their wake and proceed instead to unbridled heights of fornication.

Thus, the healthy, wholesome program of Camp Kee-Wonka.

Now, here I was/am a seven-year-old camper at this wonderful establishment. On a typical day we Kee-Wonkans rise, perform our ablutions, make our army-cot style beds, line up to salute the flag, devour our breakfast (bacon and eggs, and so much for *kosher*), and proceed to other activities.

This day, my group is playing softball on a field laid out in a natural bowl-shaped area called Hambone Hollow. There are really too many of us for this game, but under the rules of Camp Kee-Wonka, patterned on the laws of the mythical Kee-Wonka Tribe, every camper must have a chance to participate.

So we wind up with fourteen players on a team. We have a pitcher, a catcher, a back-up catcher, six infielders and five out-fielders. You would think that with that kind of saturation fielding it would be all but impossible to get a hit. Instead, considering the level of play of a group of Jewish/Indian seven-year-olds, it is all but impossible to get an out.

Still, in any group of persons, no matter how egalitarian the social theory under which they function, the development of a hierarchy is inevitable. And among the twenty-eight members of our group, when the two teams are chosen, I am the twenty-eighth player selected.

I am designated fifth "roving" outfielder of my team, and I am inserted fourteenth in the batting order.

In a four-inning game—called for lunch with the other team leading by a score of 58 to 46—I am the only player to go hitless.

After a luncheon of peanut-butter-and-jelly sandwiches made on white balloon bread, the campers return to their cots for a mandatory rest. In the afternoon there is a crafts period (I am working on a hammered-aluminum plaque of an aquatic turtle as a gift for my parents) followed by a swim and dinner. For dinner we are offered stringy overdone baked chicken and soggy overcooked broccoli.

After dinner there is a special event. All of the campers are called together in the Recreation Building. There is a community sing, a motion picture is shown (Mickey Rooney and his then-wife Elaine Davis in *The Atomic Kid*, Republic, 1954), and a drawing for prizes.

I have always empathized with Rooney for his small stature, his many wives, and his numerous troubles in this life.

The head counselor has a roster of all this year's Kee-Wonkans. The sheet of paper has been cut into tiny strips, each strip bearing the name of one Kee-Wonkan.

There are a number of prizes to be raffled off, and each time the head counselor draws the name of a camper there is a small round of applause from the lucky winner's close friends and a far more widespread chorus of disappointed moans from all the other losers.

Some of the winners receive recordings of contemporary popular songs. Some receive paperback novels, mostly grisly volumes dealing with anthropophagous machinery.

I remain with the other members of my group, our counselor trading surreptitious glances with a female counterpart sitting nearby with her own posse of small charges. I am gazing around the cavernous room abstractedly, thinking only the vaguest and most unfocussed of thoughts, when I become aware that my nearest neighbors are poking me with their finger, punching me in the arms, hissing and pointing toward the front of the hall.

I look there and see the head counselor gesturing toward me, calling my name, urging me to come forward.

"Israel Cohen. Israel Cohen, come up and get your prize."

A surge of energy passes through my body, from the crown of my head to the tips of my toes. A roaring sound fills my ears. Dazzling points of light explode before my eyes. My hands tingle as if I had touched an inadequately-insulated electrical outlet.

Rising from my seat, I make my way to the front of the hall. The few seconds that it takes to traverse the distance are distorted by some strange chemistry of the brain.

I have won.

I have won.

I have won.

Images of my prize flicker through my racing mind as I traverse an aisle lined with my fellow Kee-Wonkans. I imagine a comprehensive collection of forty-five RPM records of doo-wop songs. I imagine a complete library of paperback horror novels. I imagine a bright red Cadillac convertible.

The head counselor reaches into the store of prizes and hands me my winning. It is a giant-size Tootsie Roll.

I take it from him and return to my seat. My neighbors besiege me to open the Tootsie Roll, to peel back the white, glossy paper and reveal the brown, serrated cylinder inside.

You may not think that a giant Tootsie Roll was much of a prize, much of a trophy, much of a thing to win. But let me tell you, let me remind you that I was the last person chosen for the softball game, that I batted fourteenth on my team, that I was the only player in the truncated four-inning contest to go hitless.

I was not a popular child, not a successful child. And yet I had won this Tootsie Roll. Without warning, without preparation, I had been exposed to that rush of triumph that goes with the winning of a gamble. The plaudits of my neighbors when I returned to my seat, in fact their greedy desire to share in my winnings rather than merely to congratulate me on my good fortune, only added to the wealth and the satisfaction of the moment.

Never before had I experienced anything like that, and never again could I really be happy. No financial triumph, no sexual conquest, no ecstatic instant of immersion in glorious music, no elevated peak achieved through chemical experimentation, no rare instant of contact with the numinous while at synagogue, has ever matched that moment for me.

It was a sensation that only the devoted gambler can know.

The devoted gambler comprehends without explanation, and no one else can understand with.

It was the damned Tootsie Roll that did it.

There was a knock at the door.

I blinked.

I had been staring from my window, abstracted and hypnotized by the complexly rhythmic blinking of the lights of Reno. A knock at the door. It was a representative of Mr. Albert Brown come to see me in my suite at the Sky Palace. Come to *Take Action.*

Should I answer the knock? Should I barricade the door with heavy armchairs? Should I hide in the closet or creep under the bed or lock myself in the bathroom? Was there any point in any of these acts, or would I merely prolong the agony, perhaps further anger the men in the black suits whom I confidently expected to see should I not prevent their entry. Surely they had been provided with a passkey to my suite.

A solution presented itself. I would open the wide, sliding doors that led to the balcony of my suite and plunge from the Sky Palace. I would plummet to the street below. I would yell as I fell, yell as I fell so that no innocent pedestrian would be crushed by my impact.

I could see the headline in tomorrow's Reno newspaper. TOURIST KILLED BY FALLING MAN. And below it, a subhead, CASINO GUEST TUMBLES FROM TOWER SUITE. They wouldn't know whether I had lost my balance and fallen accidentally, or jumped, or been pushed. The local police would search my suite, looking for a clue as to the cause of my final fatal flight. They would hope to find a note. They would find the original of my outgoing fax.

HELP! SOMEONE HELP ME! PLEASE!

That would convince them that I had been murdered. They would try to learn who had received my desperate message. Did the fax machine retain outgoing numbers? Would the casino switchboard or the local telephone company have such a record?

But no, the men in black would surely search my suite when they discovered that I had flung myself from the balcony. They would find the original. They would confiscate it, destroy it, turn it over to Mr. Albert Brown who would lock it in the casino safe until his masters told him what to do with it.

The doorbell sounded. In mellifluous chimes it played, "Luck, Be a Lady Tonight."

Humming the tune, I advanced across the thick, luxurious

carpeting with which my suite was furnished and stood at the door. To hide? To jump? To barricade? Or simply to stand and wait for the men in black, to yield passively as they went about their grim and bloody business of *Taking Action?*

The ditty reached its conclusion and I reached forward, put my hand on the doorknob, and turned.

I opened the door.

She stood there, looking up at me.

I gawped.

She said, "Won't you invite me in?"

I stammered an invitation.

She entered the suite, looked around, and said, "Do you have a kitchen?"

I said that I did. I had noticed it when I checked in three days ago but had never used it. I didn't know if the appliances had been cut off. I didn't know if there was food in the pantry, perishables in the refrigerator.

She said, "Could I have something cold to drink? What I'd really like would be an icy delicious glass of chocolate milk."

She had yellow-red, what they used to call strawberry blonde, pigtails and freckles and wore a red-and-white checkered shirt and faded blue overalls and scuffed shoes.

I knew who she was.

She was Lady Luck.

She was about ten or eleven years old, twelve at the most. She came up to around here on me, and she was a wonderful kid. She could have been mine with my first or second wife if we'd ever had any children. Or she could have been your little sister or your favorite niece or the kid next door.

But I knew that she was Lady Luck.

She headed for the kitchen without my telling her where it was. I followed her and stood in the doorway watching her. She rattled around in the cupboards and drawers until she came up with a tall glass and a long-handled spoon. She opened the refrigerator and peered inside.

I heard her yelp like a happily surprised kid. "I'm so lucky," she squealed, "I just knew you'd have some." She opened the cardboard spout.

Before she could pour herself any milk, I took the container out of her hand and looked it over. It had a picture of a cartoon character on the side, and the logo of a local dairy. I looked for a spoilage date on the top and found one. The milk should be good. I sniffed the contents. It smelled okay. I handed the carton back to Lady Luck.

She poured a glass full of milk, then found a can of chocolate syrup in the refrigerator and added some to her glass and stirred it with the long-handled spoon. She said, "Would you like some, Mr. Cohen?"

I told her no.

She said, "I'll drink it in here in case I spill some, so it won't make a mess." Then she laughed as if she'd said something incredibly funny.

I asked her what.

She said, "That would be unlucky, wouldn't it, so it won't happen."

I said that was right, so why didn't she come ahead into the living room and be comfy, so she did.

She sat on the couch and I lowered myself into an easy chair. From where I was sitting I could still see the city lights flashing, but they were growing dimmer as dawn approached. Lady Luck said, "I came to answer your fax."

I said, "I didn't know you were real. And that was your number? Is there a special directory with fax lines for Santa Claus and the Easter Bunny?"

She took a big drink and put her glass down carefully on a coaster so it wouldn't make a circle on the coffee table in front of the couch. She'd left the spoon in the kitchen sink. She said, "Sure there is."

"You're kidding."

"No I'm not. How did you get my fax number if you don't have a copy?"

I said, "I just guessed. I just punched out numbers. I don't even remember what number I punched."

She said, "Wow! You must really be lucky."

I said, "Who else is in that directory?"

She shrugged. She perched on the edge of the couch. Her feet didn't quite reach the floor and she swung her heels forward and back so they bounced off the couch. They went, *thumpity, thumpity.* She said, "Everybody, I guess. Nancy Drew. Wonder Woman. Amelia Earhart. Lady Godiva. The Wendigo."

"No kidding. Who's the Wendigo?"

"A sort of Canadian wind witch. She's not very nice."

"Anybody else?"

She screwed up her face, twisted the end of one pigtail until she had it in her mouth and chewed. Talk about concentration. Finally she said, "Petunia Pig."

"Um."

"Glinda the Good, Snow White, Marilyn Monroe, Aimee Semple McPherson."

"Mm."

"And Jill."

"Jill?"

"You know. Jill went up the hill to fetch a pail of water." I nodded wisely. "Jill. As in Jack and Jill, right?"

"Nobody named Jack in this story."

I said, "Oh. All girls?"

"There's another book for boys."

"Oh."

She said, "Your fax sounded like you were pretty upset."

I was still kind of flabbergasted by the whole event. I wasn't really ready to deal with this thing, so I said, "I never imagined that Lady Luck was a little girl. How old are you, ten, ten-and-a-half?"

"Actually I'm eleven," she said. "I'm a little bit small for my age, but I'm not worried. I'm lucky. So I know everything will work out."

I said, "Can you help me?" I thought, this is strange enough as it is. Anything can happen now.

She said, "You've gone through your life relying on luck, haven't you?"

I had to admit that I had.

She said, "Don't you think you should try to make it on your own for a change? You know, hard work, honest labor, forming a relationship based on honesty and mutual respect?"

I thought she talked pretty grown up for a little girl and I told her so.

She emptied her glass and put it back on the coaster. She had a chocolate milk mustache. She jumped up and bounced over to the big window and stood looking at the dawn over the Nevada desert. She said, "Wow, that's pretty."

I asked if she'd never seen a sunrise before. She said that she'd seen millions of them. I didn't know whether she meant that literally or not. I went and stood so she could still watch the sunrise while we talked. I said, "They're going to do something horrifying to me if I don't come up with the money. Or think of something. They're terrible people. They'll do anything."

She said, "Why did you gamble when you couldn't afford it?

Oh, wow!" she gasped. "Look at that—a shooting star!"

I started to explain it to her. That gambling is an addiction, like alcohol or crack or overeating. I can't help it, I tried to tell her. She said, "That's true enough, but you're a grown-up man. Can't you take responsibility for yourself?"

"It just grabbed hold of me," I said, ignoring her point because, for some strange reason, I wanted to really *understand.* I wanted Lady Luck to understand me, but even more than that, I wanted to understand myself.

"The Tootsie Roll was great," I told her, "but there wouldn't have been any point in winning another Tootsie Roll. Do you see what I mean? I started getting into poker games, right there at Camp Kee-Wonka, and the first time I won any money—the money wasn't the point, it was the winning that mattered—it was great. But then I had to start winning bigger pots against longer and longer odds. If the dealer gave me a full house, there was nothing to it. But the thrill of drawing to an inside straight—now that was something! That made my juices flow. My heart raced. My breath got tight."

"I know all about it," Lady Luck said.

"And the horses. Look, anybody can put two bucks on the favorite to show. You can hardly lose, and you make about a dime. But betting a longshot, now *there* is something! And you bet him to win. And pairing two longshots in the Daily Double—heaven. Heaven!"

"So you wound up here, in over your head, worrying about the manager sending somebody to, as you put it, *Take Action.*"

"Yes."

"How much do you owe?"

One thing I am is precise. I told her. To the penny.

She put her lips together and blew. She shook her head sadly until her pigtails swung around her face.

I said, "You're eleven years old, kid. You don't know nothing. Don't tell me how to live, you little twerp."

She sat down right on the carpet and started to cry. Not delicate sniffles like my first wife used to cry, or angry howls like my second wife made when we had a fight, or hacks and gasps like my third wife. This was just plain honest kid crying, her lower lip trembling and tears rolling down her face.

She reached into her overalls pocket and pulled out a big red bandanna and dabbed at her eyes and her cheeks. She blew her nose in the bandanna.

She started to say something but I said, "Don't tell me, I know, isn't it lucky, you just happened to have a hankie when you needed one."

She nodded her head and shoved the bandanna back in her pocket. I said, "I'm sorry I hollered. I didn't mean it. You're a nice kid. I was just upset."

She smiled and it was like her face and the sunrise behind her were just the same. She said, "Thank you." She stood up. "And I don't always look like this."

I just stood there watching her.

She said, "Want to see what else I can look like?"

I didn't know what to expect. Maybe she was going to make a face. Maybe she was going to produce a little dress from someplace and run in the bathroom and change while I waited here, wondering if there was going to be another knock at the door, another rendition of "Luck Be a Lady Tonight," another visitor.

But this visitor wouldn't be Lady Luck, Nancy Drew, Wonder Woman, or Amelia Earhart. This visitor would be wearing a black suit, and he would be here to *Take Action*.

Lady Luck said, "Well, do you?"

"Do I what?"

"Do you want to see what else I can look like?"

I said, "Sure."

She said, "Okay, close one eye."

"One eye," I repeated.

"Correct."

"Does it matter which one?"

"No."

Feeling like a total dope, I closed one eye. It felt funny squinting like that. It made my face hurt.

She said, "Well?"

I said, "Huh!"

She said, "What do you think?"

She didn't look like any eleven-year-old kid. She looked about twenty-five. She'd grown about eight inches taller, and her pigtails had been smoothed out into a sweeping, blue-black upcurve that left her neck uncovered. Just a few hairs had escaped the hair-do and they gave her neck an incredibly sexy look.

She had a figure that would make any showgirl downstairs kill for envy. Her checkered shirt and overalls and scuffed shoes had turned into some kind of shimmering peek-a-boo costume and high-heeled slippers.

And for the first time I noticed her eyes. They were deep and round and big, and when I looked into them I couldn't tell what color they were. One moment they looked green, another violet, another black. And there was something alive inside them, something that looked like frozen flames dancing a slow, sinuous dance.

She looked strangely familiar, and then I realized who she had become. She had turned into Gene Tierney, a glamorous Hollywood siren of the 1940's.

My face hurt and I opened my eye and the little kid was back in my living room, with her chocolate milk mustache, giggling. She ran in a circle, jumped on the big couch and bounced in the air. She landed on her feet in front of me. She said, "Want to see something else? Close both of your eyes."

What the heck, I tried it. She said, "What do think of this, Israel?" Did I say *she* said it? Maybe I should have said, *he,* because the voice was a perfect John Wayne. It didn't sound like Rich Little trying to sound like John Wayne. It sounded like John Wayne. It *was* John Wayne.

The John Wayne voice said, "Try opening one eye. Try opening the one that you had closed before."

I did it, and there he was, the Duke himself. Not the handsome young John Wayne you sometimes see on TV in those ancient black-and-white serials nor even the middle-aged Wayne of the great John Ford westerns. This was the battered, one-eyed fat old gunfighter of *True Grit.* This was Rooster Cogburn.

Shaking my head with wonder, I very nearly sank to my knees in awe.

The John Wayne voice said, "Try blinking your eyes, right-left-right."

I did. It was amazing. He-she flashed back and forth, John Wayne/Gene Tierney/John Wayne/Gene Tierney. Finally, in a voice that switched between the tones of the gruff, tired old man and the silky, seductive sound of the glamour queen, Lady Luck said, "Try me with both eyes again."

And of course she was back, my eleven-year-old urchin visitor. I said, "Can you do anybody else?"

She said, "There are rules. Can't do Ishtar, Kali, Gaia or any other divine personage. Can't do any living person. But that's about it. Anybody dead or imaginary."

I said, "Can you get me out of here? Can you get me square with the casino and get Mr. Brown off my back? All I need is a fresh start. Just one break, Lady Luck. You answered my cry for help. Now you've got to help me."

She looked up at me. She reached into a pocket of her overalls and pulled a wheat straw out of it and stuck it between her teeth. I thought, *The young Judy Garland,* but that wasn't exactly it. She was just herself. Just Lady Luck.

She said, "You mean it?"

"Yes."

"How much did you owe, again?"

I told her.

She said, "I knew that. I only wanted to see if you really knew or if you just made that number up before."

I said, "That was the truth."

Lady Luck said, "Okay. Excuse me for a minute. I have to make a pee." She disappeared into the bathroom. When she came back she'd scrubbed the chocolate milk mustache off her pretty freckled face. She said, "I'll do it for you because this is your lucky day." Behind her the sky was now a bright, brilliant blue. The sun was fully above the horizon.

She said, "Come on." She headed for the door. She said, "Everybody who sees me will see something else. Those two that I showed you were just samples. Just follow my lead. I'm going to get you out of here by luck, but I told you there were rules. Not just about how I look. I can gamble but I can't gamble with my own money. Because I don't have any. I'm not allowed. But I'll take care of this."

What could I say? If I turned her down, sent her away, I was at the end of my leash. I had no more resources, nobody else I could turn to. My brother and all three of my wives had turned me down. I was living on borrowed time.

We left the suite. Standing outside was a muscular black giant in a beautifully cut black suit. He started to move toward us, then drew back. I blinked an eye and saw what he saw. Lady Luck was Dorothy Dandridge in costume as Carmen Jones.

She got us down the elevator. We strolled into the casino. Of course it was open. It never closed, day or night, winter or summer. It was sealed off from the street. There was no natural light, no natural climate. When you were in the casino you were in another world, a world of flashing neon and ringing bells, jackpots paying off with a clatter, drinks passed by sexy hostesses. This was my world. I loved this world.

Lady Luck led me to a craps table. There were a handful of players there, even at what had to be breakfast hour. The two of us found places, side-by-side, at the rail. Players rolled the dice, made points, crapped out, passed the dice. The dice kept moving around the table.

When they reached me I didn't know what to do. I didn't have any money. I'd felt peculiar standing there and not betting when others rolled the dice, but now that they had come to me, I was seriously embarrassed.

I was also worried—as a matter of fact, terrified—that somebody would recognize me. If that happened, I expected a large, muscular individual to guide me forcefully away from the craps table and into the office of Mr. Albert Brown, who seemed *always* to be on duty.

Maybe he was triplets, all of them named Albert, and they simply worked in eight-hour shifts. That would keep things nice and even.

I blinked my eye and there stood Errol Flynn in his green costume and feathered cap, Robin Hood as no actor had ever embodied him before or since. He turned to the person beyond him and said, "I hope you won't think me forward if I beg a single dollar of you for the succor of my good friend, the Hebrew gentleman you see just over there." He jerked a thumb in my direction.

That kind of panhandling would surely get him thrown out of the casino, I thought. But it didn't. I don't know what anybody else saw, who Lady Luck looked like to the croupier or the person she'd asked for a dollar or any of the other gamblers.

But Errol Flynn turned to me and laid a shiny Eisenhower silver dollar on the rail. I tossed it onto the felt and rolled the dice. I picked them back up and rolled them again. And again. And again.

It was amazing. I was in a trance. It was better than filling that inside straight, better than picking a longshot, better than winning the Daily Double. It was—it was better than winning a Tootsie Roll.

With Lady Luck at my side I carried my chips to the manager's office. I had made a pledge. I was going to get even, I was going to pay my debts, and I was going to swear off gambling. I was a new man. I was a new Israel Cohen.

Mr. Albert Brown was sitting behind his desk. He looked up as I entered his office. He looked very surprised. He said, "Mr. Cohen!"

I said, "Here, damn you. Here's everything I owe you. Every last cent of it." I dumped the chips onto this desk. He consulted a computer screen—nothing old-fashioned or low-tech about these people—then did a quick count of the chips I'd given him. He smiled up at me. He didn't seem to see Lady Luck at all. Maybe one of her characters was the Invisible Woman. Brown said, "You're right. You're absolutely right. Well, thank you very much, Mr. Cohen. You surprised me greatly, and you've saved me a great deal of trouble. May I congratulate you. And may I offer a piece of free advice? Don't gamble any more. Some people can't drink and they shouldn't. You can't gamble, Mr. Cohen. You can't control yourself, and you are going to get into trouble next time that you won't get out of. So don't let there be a next time."

I saw Lady Luck in her eleven-year-old form standing behind Albert Brown making horns with her fingers and crossing her eyes and sticking out her tongue. I kept a straight face. I said, "Well, if that's all, I will take my leave."

Albert Brown stood up, reached into a smoothly-tailored pocket, and pulled out a shiny Ike dollar. The second one I'd seen in the past hour. He said, "I don't want you to leave here with no money at all. Take this, with my compliments."

On the way out of the Sky Palace, Lady Luck and I passed a row of slots. I could see the bright street outside, the badly-over-dressed tourists from Iowa and Illinois and Indiana, the states of the old Three-I League, pacing up and down, eager to leave their money behind so they could return to their neighbors and friends and business associates with stories of their wild adventures.

I wanted to stop them. I wanted to shout at them. I wanted to scream, "Don't do it! Don't get started! Most of you can gamble and then quit but some of you can't, and you never know which of you it is. It's all a gamble, it's all a gamble."

I wanted to say that. I was going to say that. Lady Luck, eleven years old and pigtailed, was holding my hand. I started toward the street, but first I had to stop at the end of the row of machines and drop my last dollar, my lucky Ike, into the slot.

The fascination that Howard Phillips Lovecraft (1890–1937) holds for readers and writers — and has held for generations — is truly astonishing. Lovecraft saw himself as the successor to Edgar Allan Poe. Limited to publication in poorly-paying and unprestigious outlets in his own lifetime, Lovecraft died a self-labeled failure, but since his death has risen to the stature of an icon.

"Documents in the Case of Elizabeth Akeley" is modern homage to Lovecraft, and is a sequel to one of Lovecraft's most effective stories, "The Whisperer in Darkness." Editor Edward Ferman published it in The Magazine of Fantasy and Science Fiction in 1982.

Documents in the Case of Elizabeth Akeley

URVEILLANCE OF THE SPIRITUAL LIGHT
Brotherhood Church of San Diego was initiated as a result of
certain events of the mid- and late 1970s. Great controversy
had arisen over the conduct of the followers of the Guru Maha-
raj-ji, the International Society for Krishna Consciousness (the
"Hare Krishnas"), the Church of Scientology, and the Unification
Church headed by the Reverend Sun Myung Moon.

These activities were cloaked in the Constitutional shield of
"freedom of religion," and the cults for the most part resisted suggestions of investigation by grand juries or other official bodies.

Even so, the tragic events concerning the People's Temple of
San Francisco aroused government concern which could not be
stymied. While debate raged publicly over the question of opening cult records, Federal and local law enforcement agencies
covertly entered the field.

It was within this context that interest was aroused concerning
the operation of the Spiritual Light Brotherhood, and particularly
its leader, the Radiant Mother Elizabeth Akeley.

Outwardly there was nothing secret in the operation of Mother
Akeley's church. The group operated from a building located at the
corner of Second Street and Ash in a neighborhood described as

"genteel shabby," midway between the commercial center of San Diego and the city's tourist-oriented waterfront area.

The building occupied by the church had been erected originally by a more conventional denomination, but the vicissitudes of shifting population caused the building to be deconsecrated and sold to the Spiritual Light Brotherhood. The new owners, led by their order's founder and then-leader, the Radiant Father George Goodenough Akeley, clearly marked the building with its new identity.

The headline was changed on the church's bulletin board, and the symbol of the Spiritual Light Brotherhood, a shining tetrahedron of neon tubing, was erected atop the steeple. A worship service was held each Sunday morning, and a spiritual message service was conducted each Wednesday evening.

In later years, following the death of the Radiant Father in 1977 and the accession to leadership of the church by Elizabeth Akeley, church archives were maintained in the form of tape recordings. The Sunday services were apparently a bland amalgam of non-denominational Judeo-Christian teachings, half-baked and quarter-understood Oriental mysticism, and citations from the works of Einstein, Heisenberg, Shklovskii, and Fermi.

Surviving cassettes of the Wednesday message services are similarly innocuous. Congregants were invited to submit questions or requests for messages from deceased relatives. The Radiant Mother accepted a limited number of such requests at each service. The congregants would arrange themselves in a circle and link their fingers in the classic manner of participants in seances. Mother Akeley would enter a trance and proceed to answer the questions or deliver messages from the deceased, "as the spirits moved her."

Audioanalysis of the tapes of these seances indicates that, while the intonation and accent of the voices varied greatly, from the whines and lisps of small children to the quaverings of the superannuated, and from the softened and westernized pronunciations of native San Diegans to the harsh and barbaric tones of their New Yorker parents, the vocal apparatus was at all times that of Elizabeth Akeley. The variations were no greater than those attainable by an actress of professional training or natural brilliance.

Such, however, was not the case with a startling portion of the cassette for the session of Wednesday, June 13th, 1979. The Radiant Mother asked her congregants if anyone had a question for the spirits, or if any person present wished to attempt contact with some deceased individual.

A number of questions were answered, dealing with the usual matters of marriage and divorce, reassurances of improved health, and counseling as to investments and careers.

An elderly congregant who was present stated that her husband had died the previous week, and she sought affirmation of his happiness "on the other side."

The Radiant Mother moaned. Then she muttered incoherently. All of this was as usual at the beginning of her trances. Shortly the medium's vocal quality altered. Her normally soft, rather pleasant and distinctly feminine voice dropped in register until it suggested that of a man. Simultaneously, her contemporary Californian diction turned to the twang of a rural New Englander.

While the sound quality of this tape is excellent, the medium's diction was unfortunately not so. The resulting record is necessarily fragmentary. As nearly as it has been transcribed, this is it:

"Wilmarth . . . Wilmarth . . . back. Have come . . . Antares . . . Neptune, Pluto, Yuggoth. Yes, Wilmarth. Yug—

"Are you . . . if I cannot receive . . . Windham County . . . yes, Townshend . . . round hill. Wilmarth still alive? Then who . . . son, son . . .

" . . . ever receives . . . communicate enough Akeley, 176 Pleasant . . . go, California. Son, see if you can find my old friend Albert Wilmarth . . . chusetts . . .

"With wings. Twisted ropes for heads and blood like plant sap . . . Flying, flying, and all the while a gramophone recordi . . . must apologize to Wilmarth if he's still alive, but I also have the most wonderful news, the most wonderful tales to tell him . . .

" . . . and its smaller satellites, well, I don't suppose anyone will believe me, of course, but not only is Yuggoth there, revolving regularly except in an orbit at right angles to the plane of the ecliptic, no wonder no one believed in it, but what I must describe to you, Albert, the planet glows with a heat and a demoniacal ruby glare that illuminates its own . . . thon and Zaman, Thog and Thok, I could hardly believe my own . . .

" . . . goid beings who cannot . . . corporeally . . . Neptune . . . central caverns of a dark star beyond the rim of the galaxy its . . .

" . . . wouldn't call her beautiful, of course . . . dinary terms . . . than an arachnid and a cetacean, and yet, could a spider and dolphin by some miracle establish mental communion, who knows

what . . . not really a name as you normally think of names, but
. . . Sh'ch'rrru'a . . . of Aldebaran, the eleventh, has a constellation
of inhabited moons, which . . . independently, or perhaps at some
earlier time, travelling by means simi . . .

" . . . ummate in metal canisters, will be necessary to . . . aid in
obtaining . . . fair exchange, for the donors will receive a far greater
boon in the form . . ."

At this point the vocal coherence, such as it is, breaks down.
The male voice with its New England twang cracks and rises
in tone even as the words are replaced by undecipherable
mumbles. Mother Akeley recovers from her trance state, and the
seance draws quickly to a close. From the internal evidence of the
contents of the tape, the Radiant Mother had no awareness of the
message, or narration, delivered by the male voice speaking
through her. This also is regarded, among psychic and
spiritualistic circles, as quite the usual state of affairs with trance
mediums.

* * *

Authorities next became aware of unusual activities through a
copy of the *Vermont Unidentified Flying Object Intelligencer,* or
Vufoi. Using a variety of the customary cover names and addresses for the purpose, such Federal agencies as the FBI, NSA,
Department of Defense, NASA, and National Atmospheric and
Oceanographic Agency subscribe regularly to publications of
organizations like the Vermont UFO Intelligence Bureau and
other self-appointed investigatory bodies.

The President of the Vermont UFO Intelligence Bureau and
editor of its *Intelligencer* was identified as one Ezra Noyes. Noyes
was known to reside with his parents (Ezra was nineteen years of
age at the time) in the community of Dark Mountain, Windham
County. Noyes customarily prepared *Vufoi* issues himself, assembling material both from outside sources and from members of
the Vermont UFO Intelligence Bureau, most of whom were
former high school friends now employed by local merchants or
farmers, or attending Windham County Community College in
Townshend.

Noyes would assemble his copy, type it onto mimeograph sten-
cils using a portable machine set up on the kitchen table, and run
off copies on a superannuated mimeograph kept beside the
washer and dryer in the basement. The last two items prepared
for each issue were "Vufoi Voice" and "From the Editor's Obser-

vatory," commenting in one case flippantly and in the other seriously, on the contents of the issue. "Vufoi Voice" was customarily illustrated with a crude cartoon of a man wearing an astronaut's headgear, and was signed "Cap'n Oof-oh." "From the Editor's Observatory" was illustrated with a drawing of an astronomical telescope with a tiny figure seated at the eyepiece, and was signed "Intelligencer."

It is believed that both "Cap'n Oof-oh" and "Intelligencer" were Ezra Noyes.

The issue of the *Vermont Unidentified Flying Object Intelligencer* for June, 1979 actually appeared early in August of that year. Excerpts from the two noted columns follow:

* * *

From the Editor's Observatory

Of greatest interest since our last issue—and we apologize for missing the March, April and May editions due to unavoidable circumstances—has been the large number of organic sightings here in the northern Vermont region. We cannot help but draw similes to the infamous Colorado cattle mutilizations of the past year or few years, and the ill-conceived Air Farce coverup efforts *which only draw extra attention to the facts that they can't hide from us who know the Truth!*

Local historians like Mr. Littleton at the High School remember other incidents and the Brattleboro *Reformer* and Arkham *Advertiser* and other Newspapers whose back files constitute an Official Public Record could tell the story of other incidents like this one! It is hard to reconciliate the Windham County sightings and the Colorado Cattle Mutilation Case with others such as the well-known Moth Man sightings in the Southland and especially the batwing creature sightings of as long as a half of a century ago but with a sufficient ingeniusity it is definitely not a task beyond undertaking and the U.S. Air Farce and other cover-up agencies are hear-bye placed on Official notice that such is our intention and we will not give up until success is ours and the Cover-up is blown as Sky-High as the UFO sightings themselves!

Yours until our July issue,
Intelligencer.

Vufoi Voice

Bat-wing and Moth Man indeed! Didn't I read something like that in *Detective Comics* back when Steve Englehart was writing for DC? Or was it in *Mad*? Come to think of it, when it's hard to tell the parody from the original, things are gettin' *mighty* strange.

And there gettin' might strange around here!

We wonder what the ole Intelligencer's been smoking in that smelly meerschaum he affects around Intelligence Bureau meetings. Could it be something illegal that he grows for himself up on the mountainside?

Or is he just playing Sherlock Holmes?

We ain't impressed.

Impressionable, yep! My mom always said I was impressionable as a boy, back on the old asteroid farm in Beta Reticuli, but this is too silly for words.

Besides, she tuck me to the eye dock and he fitted us out with a pair of gen-yew-ine X-ray specs, and that not only cured us of Reticule-eye but now we can see right through such silliness as bat-winged moth men carrying silvery canisters around the skies and the hillsides with 'em.

Shades of a Japanese Sci-Fi Flick! This musta been the stuntman out for lunch!

And that's where we think the old Intelligencer is this month: *Out 2 Lunch!*

Speaking of which, I haven't had mine yet this afternoon, and if I don't hurry up and have it pretty soon it'll be time for dinner and then I'll have to eat my lunch for a bedtime snack and that'll confuse the dickens out of my poor stomach! So I'm off to hit the old fridgidaire (not too hard, I don't want to spoil the shiny finish on my new spaceman's gloves!), and I'll see you-all next ish!

Whoops, here's our saucer now! Bye-bye,
Cap'n Oof-oh.

* * *

Following the extraordinary spiritual message service of June 13, Mother Akeley was driven to her home at 176 Pleasant Street in National City, a residential suburb of San Diego, by her boyfriend, Marc Feinman. Investigation revealed that she had met Feinman casually while sunning herself and watching the surfers ride the waves in at Black's Beach, San Diego.

Shortly thereafter, Elizabeth had been invited by a female friend of approximately her own age to attend a concert given by a musical group, a member of which was a friend of Akeley's friend. Outside of her official duties as Radiant Mother of the Spiritual Light Brotherhood, Elizabeth Akeley was known to live quite a normal life for a young woman of her social and economic class.

She accompanied her friend to the concert, visited the backstage area with her, and was introduced to the musician. He in turn introduced Elizabeth to other members of the musical group, one of whom Elizabeth recognized as her casual acquaintance of Black's Beach. A further relationship developed, in which it was known that Akeley and Feinman frequently exchanged overnight visits. Elizabeth had retained the house on Pleasant Street originally constructed by her grandfather, George Goodenough Akeley, when he had emigrated to San Diego from Vermont in the early 1920s.

Marc had been born and raised in the Bronx, New York, had emigrated to the West Coast following his college years and presently resided in a pleasant apartment on Upas Street near Balboa Park. From here he commuted daily to his job as a computer systems programmer in downtown San Diego, his work as a musician being more of an avocation than a profession.

On Sunday, June 17, for the morning worship service of the Spiritual Light Brotherhood, Radiant Mother Akeley devoted her sermon to the previous Wednesday's seance, an unusual practice for her. The sexton of the church, a nondescript looking Negro named Vernon Whiteside, attended the service. Noting the Radiant Mother's departure from her usual bland themes, Whiteside communicated with the Federal Agency which had infiltrated him into the church for precisely this purpose. An investigation of Mother Akeley's background was then initiated.

Within a short time, agent Whiteside was in possession of a preliminary report on Elizabeth Akeley and her forebears, excerpts from which follow.

AKELEY, ELIZABETH – HISTORY AND BACKGROUND

The Akeley family is traceable to one *Beelzebub Akeley* who traveled from Portsmouth, England, to Kingsport, Massachusetts aboard the sailing caravel *Worthy* in 1607. Beelzebub Akeley married an indentured servant girl, bought out her indenture papers and moved with her to establish the

Akeley dynasty in Townshend, Windham County, Vermont in 1618. The Akeleys persisted in Windham County for more than two centuries, producing numerous clergy, academics, and other genteel professionals in this period.

Abednego Mesach Akeley, subject's great-great grandfather, was the last of the Vermont Akeleys to pursue a life of the cloth. Born in 1832, Abednego was raised in the strict puritanical traditions of the Akeleys and ordained by his father, the Reverend *Samuel Shadrach Solomon Akeley* upon attaining his maturity. Abednego served as assistant pastor to his father until Samuel's death in 1868, at which time he succeeded to the pulpit.

Directly following the funeral of Samuel Akeley, Abednego is known to have traveled to more southerly regions of New England including Massachusetts and possibly Rhode Island. Upon his return to Townshend he led his flock into realms of highly questionable doctrine, and actually transferred the affiliation of his church from its traditional Protestant parent body to that of the new and suspect Starry Wisdom sect.

Controversy and scandal followed at once, and upon the death of Abednego early in 1871 at the age of thirty-nine, the remnants of his congregation moved as a body to Providence, Rhode Island. One female congregant, however, was excommunicated by unanimous vote of the other members of the congregation, and forced to remain behind in Townshend. This female was *Sarah Elizabeth Phillips*, a servant girl in the now defunct Akeley household.

Shortly following the departure of the remnants of Abednego Akeley's flock from Vermont, Sarah Phillips gave birth to a son. She claimed that the child had been fathered by Abednego mere hours before his death. She named the child *Henry Wentworth Akeley*. As the Akeley clan was otherwise extinct at this point, no one challenged Sarah's right to identify her son as an Akeley, and in fact in later years she sometimes used the name Akeley herself.

Henry Akeley overcame his somewhat shadowed origins and built for himself a successful academic career, returning to Windham County in his retirement, and remaining there until the time of his mysterious disappearance and presumed demise in the year 1928.

Henry had married some years earlier, and his wife had given birth to a single child, *George Goodenough Akeley*, in the year 1901, succumbing two days later to childbed fever. Henry Akeley raised his son with the assistance of a series of nursemaids and housekeepers. At the time of Henry Akeley's retirement and his return to Townshend, George Akeley emigrated to San Diego, California, building there a modest but comfortable house at 176 Pleasant Street.

George Akeley married a local woman suspected of harboring a strain of Indian blood; the George Akeleys were the parents of a set of quadruplets born in 1930. This was the first quadruple birth on record in San Diego County. There were three boys and a girl. The boys seemed, at birth, to be of relatively robust constitution, although naturally small. The girl was still smaller, and seemed extremely feeble at birth so that her survival appeared unlikely.

However, with each passing hour the boys seemed to fade while the tiny girl grew stronger. All four infants clung tenaciously to life, the boys more and more weakly and the girl more strongly, until finally the three male infants— apparently at the same hour—succumbed. The girl took nourishment with enthusiasm, growing pink and active. Her spindly limbs rounded into healthy baby arms and legs, and in due course she was carried from the hospital by her father.

In honor of a leading evangelist of the era, and of a crusader for spiritualistic causes, the girl was named *Aimee Semple Conan Doyle Akeley.*

Aimee traveled between San Diego and the spiritualist center of Noblesville, Indiana, with her parents. The George Akeleys spent their winters in San Diego, where George Goodenough Akeley served as Radiant Father of the Spiritual Light Brotherhood, which he founded in a burst of religious fervor after meeting Aimee Semple McPherson, the evangelist whose name his daughter bore; each summer they would make a spiritualistic pilgrimage to Noblesville, where George Akeley became fast friends with the spiritualist leader and sometime American fascist, *William Dudley Pelley.*

Aimee Doyle Akeley married William Pelley's nephew *Hiram Wesley Pelley* in 1959. In that same year Aimee's mother died and was buried in Noblesville. Her father continued his ministry in San Diego.

In 1961, two years after her marriage to young Pelley, Aimee Doyle Akeley Pelley gave birth to a daughter who was named *Elizabeth Maude Pelley*, after two right-wing political leaders, Elizabeth Dilling of Illinois and Maude Howe of

England. Elizabeth Maude Pelley was raised alternately by her parents in Indiana and her grandfather in San Diego.

In San Diego her life was relatively normal, centering on her schooling, her home, and to a lesser extent on her grandfather's church, the Spiritual Light Brotherhood. In Indiana she was exposed to a good deal of political activity of a right-wing extremist nature. Hiram Wesley Pelley had followed in his uncle's footsteps in this regard, and Aimee Semple Conan Doyle Akeley Pelley took her lead from her husband and his family. A number of violent scenes are reported to have transpired between young Elizabeth Pelley and the elder Pelleys.

Elizabeth Pelley broke with her parents over political disagreements in 1976, and returned permanently to San Diego where she took up residence with her grandfather. At this time she abandoned her mother's married name and took the family name as her own, henceforth being known as *Elizabeth Akeley.* Upon the death of George Goodenough Akeley, Elizabeth succeeded to the title of Radiant Mother of the Spiritual Light Brotherhood and the pastorhood of the church, as well as the property on Pleasant Street and a small income from inherited securities.

*　　*　　*

Vernon Whiteside read the report carefully. Through his position as sexton of the Spiritual Light Brotherhood Church he had access, as well, to most church records, including the taped archives of the Sunday worship services and Wednesday message services. He followed the Radiant Mother's report to the congregation, in which she referred heavily to the seance of June 13, by borrowing and listening carefully to the tape of the seance itself.

He also obtained a photocopy from Agency headquarters, of the latest issues of the *Vermont UFO Intelligencer.* These he read carefully, seeking to correlate any references in the newsletter with the Akeley family, or with any other name connected with the Akeleys or the content of the seance tape. He mulled over the Akeleys, Phillipses, Wilmarths, Noyeses, and all other references. He attempted also to connect the defunct (or at least seemingly-defunct) Starry Wisdom sect of the New England region, with the San Diego-based Spiritual Light Brotherhood.

At this time it appears also that Elizabeth Akeley began to receive additional messages outside of the Spiritual Light message services. During quiet moments she would lapse involuntarily into her trance or trance-like state. Because she was unable to recall the messages received during these episodes, she prevailed upon Marc Feinman to spend increasing amounts of time with her. During the last week of June and July of 1979 the two were nearly inseparable. They spent every night together, sometimes at Elizabeth's house in National City, sometimes at Marc's apartment on Upas Street.

It was at this time that Vernon Whiteside recommended that Agency surveillance of the San Diego cult be increased by the installation of wiretaps on the church and the Pleasant Street and Upas Street residences. This recommendation was approved and recordings were obtained at all three locations. Transcripts are available in Agency files. Excerpts follow:

July 25, 1979 (Incoming)

Voice #1 (Definitely identified as Marc Feinman): Hello.

Voice #2 (Tentatively identified as Mrs. Sara Feinman, Marc's mother, Bronx, New York): Marc.

Voice #1: (Pause.) Yes, Ma.

Voice #2: Markie, are you all right?

Voice #1: Yeah, Ma.

Voice #2: Are you sure? Are you really all right?

Voice #1: Ma, I'm all right.

Voice #2: Okay, just so you're all right, Markie. And work, Markie? How's your work? Is your work all right?

Voice #1: It's all right, Ma.

Voice #2: No problems?

Voice #1: Of course, problems, Ma. That's what they pay me to take care of.

Voice #2: Oh my God, Markie! What kind of problems, Markie?

Voice #1: (Pauses, sighs or inhales deeply) We're trying to integrate the 2390 remote console control routines with the sysgen status word register and every time we run it against—

Voice #2: (Interrupting) Markie, you know I don't understand that kind of—

Voice #1: (Interrupting) But you asked me—

Voice #2: (Interrupting) Marc, don't contradict your mother. Are you still with that *shicksa*? She's the one who's poisoning your mind against your poor mother. I'll bet she's with you now, isn't she, Marc?

Voice #1: (Sighs or inhales deeply) No, Ma, it's Wednesday. She's never here Wednesdays. She's at church every Wednesday. They have these services every Wedn—

Voice #2: That isn't what I called about. I don't understand, Markie, for the money that car must have cost you could have had an Oldsmobile at least, even a Buick like your father. Markie, it's your father I phoned about. Markie, you have to come home. Your father isn't well, Markie. I phoned because he isn't home now but the doctor said he's not a well man. Markie, you have to come home and talk to your father. He respects you, he listens to you God knows why. Please, Markie. (Sound of soft crying.)

Voice #1: What's wrong with him, Ma?

Voice #2: I don't want to say it on the telephone.

July 25, 1979 (Outgoing)

Voice #3: (Definitely identified as Vernon Whiteside): Spiritual Light Brotherhood. May the divine light shine upon your path.

Voice #1: Vern, this is Marc. Is Liz still at the church? Is the service over?

Voice #3: The service ended a few minutes ago, Mr. Feinman. The Radiant Mother is resting in the sacristy.

Voice #1: That's what I wanted to know. Listen, Vern, tell Lizzie that I'm on my way, will you? I had a long phone call from my mother and I don't want Liz to worry. Tell her I'll give her a ride home from the church.

*   *   *

Feinman left San Diego by automobile, driving his Ferrari Boxer eastward at a top speed in the 140 MPH range, and arrived at the home of his parents in the Bronx, New York, some time during the night of July 27–28.

In the absence of Marc Feinman, Akeley took agent Whiteside increasingly into her confidence, asking him to remain in her presence day and night. He set up a temporary cot in the living room of the Pleasant Street house during this period. His instructions were to keep a portable cassette recorder handy at all times, and to record anything said by Mother Akeley during spontaneous trances. On the first Saturday of August, following a lengthy speech in the now-familiar male New England twang, Akeley asked agent Whiteside for the tape. She played it back, then made the following long-distance telephone call:

August 4, 1979 (Outgoing)

Voice #4 (Tentatively identified as Ezra Noyes): Vermont Bureau. May we help you?

Voice #5 (Definitely identified as Elizabeth Akeley): Is this Mr. Noyes?

Voice #4: Oh, I'm sorry, Dad isn't home. This is Ezra. Can I give him a—

Voice #5 (Interrupting): Oh, I wanted to speak with Ezra Noyes. The editor of the *UFO Intelligencer.*

Voice #4: Oh, yes, right. Yes, that's me. Ezra Noyes.

Voice #5: Mr. Noyes, I wonder if you could help me. I need some information about, ah, recent occurrences in or around Townshend.

Voice #4: That's funny, what did you say your name was?

Voice #5: Elizabeth Akeley.

Voice #4: I thought I knew all my subbers.

Voice #5: Oh, I'm not a subscriber, I got your name from—well, that doesn't matter. Mr. Noyes, I wonder if you could tell me if there have been any unusual UFO sightings in your region lately.

Voice #4 (Suspiciously): Unusual?

Voice #5: Well, these wouldn't be your usual run-of-the-mill flying objects. Flying saucers. I hope that phrase doesn't offend you. These would be more like flying creatures.

Voice #4: Creatures? You mean birds?

Voice #5: No. No. Intelligent creatures.

Voice #4: People, then. You mean Buck Rogers and Wilma Deering with their rocket flying belts.

Voice #5: Please don't be sarcastic, Mr. Noyes. (Pauses.) I mean intelligent, possibly hominoid but non-human creatures. Their configuration may vary, but some of them, at least, I believe would have large, membranous wings, probably stretched over a bony or veinous framework in the fashion of bats' or insects' wings. Also, some of them may be carrying artifacts such as polished metallic cylinders of a size capable of containing a—of containing, uh, a human—a human—brain. (Sounds of distress, possible sobbing.)

Voice #4: Miss Akeley? Are you all right, Miss Akeley?

Voice #5: I'm sorry. Yes, I'm all right.

Voice #4: I didn't mean to be so hard on you, Miss Akeley. It's just that we get a lot of crank calls. People wanting to talk to the little green men and that kind of thing. I had to make sure that you weren't—

Voice #5: I understand. And you *have* had—

Voice #4: I'm reluctant to say too much on the phone. Miss Akeley, do you think you could get here? There have been sightings. And there are older ones. Records in the local papers. A rash of incidents about fifty years ago. And others farther back. There was a monograph by an Eli Davenport over in New Hampshire back in the 1830s, I've got a Xerox of it. . . .

*   *   *

Shortly after her telephone conversation with Ezra Noyes, Elizabeth Akeley appealed to Vernon Whiteside for assistance. "I don't want to go alone," she is reported as saying. "If only Marc were here, I know he'd help me. He'd go with me. But he's with his family and I can't wait till he gets back. We'll have to close the church. No, no we won't. We can have a lay reader conduct the worship services. We can suspend the message services 'til I get back. Will you help me, Vernon?"

Whiteside, maintaining his cover as the sexton of the Brotherhood, assured Akeley. "Anything the Radiant Mother wishes, ma'am. What would you like me to do?"

"Can you get away for a few days? I have to go to Vermont. Would you book two tickets for us? There are church funds to cover the cost."

"Yes, ma'am." Whiteside lowered his head. "Best way would be via Logan International in Boston, then a Boston and Maine train to Newfane and Hardwick."

Akeley made no comment on the sexton's surprising familiarity with transcontinental air routes or with the railroad service between Boston and upper New England. She was obviously in an agitated state, Whiteside reported when he checked in with his superiors prior to their departure from San Diego.

Two days later the Negro sexton and the Radiant Mother climbed down from B&M train #5508 at Hardwick, Vermont. They were met at the town's rundown and musty-smelling station by Ezra Noyes. Noyes was driving his parents' 1959 Nash Ambassador station wagon and willingly loaded Akeley's and

Whiteside's meager baggage into the rear cargo deck of the vehicle.

Ezra chauffeured the visitors to his parents' home. The house, a gambrel-roofed structure of older design, was fitted for a larger family than the two senior Noyeses and their son Ezra; in fact, an elder son and daughter had both married and departed Windham County for locales of greater stimulation and professional opportunity, leaving two surplus bedrooms in the Noyes home.

Young Noyes proposed that he invite the full membership of the Vermont UFO Intelligence Bureau to attend an extraordinary meeting, to convene without delay at his home. Both Elizabeth Akeley and Vernon Whiteside demurred, pleading fatigue at the end of their transcontinental flight as well as the temporary debilitation of jet-lag.

Noyes agreed reluctantly to abandon his plan for the meeting, but was eager to offer his own services and assistance to Akeley and Whiteside. Elizabeth informed Ezra Noyes that she had received instructions to meet a visitor at a specific location near the town of Passumpsic in neighboring Caledonia County. She did not explain to Noyes the method of her receiving these instructions, but Vernon's later report indicated that he was aware of them, the instructions having been delivered to Miss Akeley in spontaneous trance sessions, the tapes of which he had also audited.

It must be again emphasized at this point that the voice heard on the spontaneous trance tapes was, in different senses, both that of Miss Akeley and of another personage. The pitch and accent, as has been stated, were those of an elderly male speaking in a semi-archaic New England twang while the vocal apparatus itself was unquestionably that of Elizabeth Akeley, née Elizabeth Maude Pelley.

Miss Akeley's instructions were quite specific in terms of geography, although it was found odd that they referred only to landmarks and highway or road facilities known to exist in the late 1920s. Young Noyes was able to provide alternate routes for such former roadways as had been closed when superseded by more modern construction.

Before retiring, Elizabeth Akeley placed a telephone call to the home of Marc Feinman's parents in the Bronx. In this call she urged Feinman to join her in Vermont. Feinman responded that his father, at the urging of himself and his mother, had consented to undergo major surgery. Marc promised to travel to Vermont and rendezvous with Akeley at the earliest feasible time, but indicated that he felt obliged to remain with his parents until the surgery was completed and his father's recovery assured.

The following morning Elizabeth Akeley set out for Passumpsic. She was accompanied by Vernon Whiteside and traveled in the Nash Ambassador station wagon driven by Ezra Noyes.

Her instructions had contained very specific and very emphatic requirements that she keep the rendezvous alone, although others might provide transportation and wait while the meeting took place. The party who had summoned Elizabeth Akeley to the rendezvous had not, to this time, been identified, although it was believed to be the owner of the male voice and New England twang who had spoken through Elizabeth herself in her trances.

Prior to their departing Windham County for Caledonia County, a discussion took place between Akeley and Whiteside. Whiteside appealed to Elizabeth Akeley to permit him to accompany her to the rendezvous.

That would be impossible, Akeley stated.

Whiteside pointed out Elizabeth's danger, in view of the unknown identity of the other party. When Akeley remained adamant, Whiteside gave in and agreed to remain with Ezra Noyes during the meeting. It must be pointed out that at this time the dialog was not cast in the format of a highly trained and responsible agent of the Federal establishment, and an ordinary citizen; rather, the façade which Whiteside rightly although with difficulty maintained was that of a sexton of the Spiritual Light Brotherhood acting under the authority of and in the service of the Radiant Mother of the church.

Akeley was fitted with a concealed microphone which transmitted on a frequency capable of being picked up by a small microcassette recorder which Whiteside was to keep with him in or near the Nash station wagon; additionally, an earphone ran from the recorder so that Whiteside was enabled to monitor the taped information in real time.

The Nash Ambassador crossed the county line from Windham into Caledonia on a two-lane county highway. This had been a dirt road in the 1920s, blacktopped with Federal funds administered by the Works Progress Administration under Franklin Roosevelt, and superseded by a nearby four-lane asphalt highway built during the Eisenhower Presidency. The blacktop received minimal maintenance, and only pressure from local members òf the Vermont legislature, this brought in turn at the insistence of local residents who used the highway for access to Passumpsic, South Londonderry, and Bellows Falls, prevented the State from declaring the highway closed and striking it from official road-maps.

Reaching the town of Passumpsic, Akeley, who had never previously traveled farther east than Indianapolis, Indiana, told Ezra to proceed 800 yards, at which point the car was to be halted. Ezra complied. At the appointed spot, Akeley left the car and opened a gate in the wooden fence fronting the highway.

Noyes pulled the wagon from the highway through the gate and found himself on a narrow track that had once been a small dirt road, long since abandoned and overgrown.

This track led away from the highway and into hilly farm country, years before abandoned by the poor farmers of the region, that lay between Passumpsic and Lyndonville.

Finally, having rounded an ancient dome-topped protuberance that stood between the station wagon and any possible visual surveillance from the blacktop highway or even the overgrown dirt road, the Nash halted, unable to continue. The vegetation hereabouts was of a peculiar nature. While most of the region consisted of thin, played-out soil whose poor fertility was barely adequate to sustain a covering of tall grasses and undersized, gnarly-trunked trees, in the small area set off by the dome-topped hill the growth was thick, lush and luxuriant.

However, there was a peculiar quality to the vegetation, a characteristic which even the most learned botanist would have been hard pressed to identify, and yet which was undeniably present. It was as if the vegetation were *too* vibrantly alive, as if it sucked greedily at the earth for nourishment and by so doing robbed the countryside for a mile or more in every direction of sustenance.

Through an incongruously luxuriant copse of leafy trees a small building could be seen, clearly a shack of many years' age and equally clearly of long abandonment. The door hung angularly from a single rusted hinge, the windows were cracked or missing altogether and spiders had filled the empty frames with their own geometric handiwork. The paint, if ever the building had known the touch of a painter's brush, had long since flaked away and been blown to oblivion by vagrant tempests, and the bare wood beneath had been cracked by scores of winters and bleached by as many summers' suns.

Elizabeth Akeley looked once at the ramshackle structure, nodded to herself and set out slowly to walk to it. Vernon Whiteside placed himself at her elbow and Ezra Noyes set a pace a short stride behind the others, but Akeley halted at once, turned and gestured silently but decisively to them both to remain behind. She then resumed her progress through the copse.

Whiteside watched Elizabeth Akeley proceeding slowly but with apparently complete self-possession through the wooded area. She halted just outside the shack, leaned forward and slightly to one side as if peering through a cobwebbed window frame, then proceeded again. She tugged at the door, managed to drag it open with a squeal of rusted metal and protesting wood and disappeared inside the shack.

"Are you just going to let her go like that?" Ezra Noyes demanded of Whiteside. "How do you know who's in there? What if it's a Beta Reticulan? What if it's a Moth Man? What if there's a whole bunch of aliens in there? They might have a tunnel from the shack to their saucer. The whole thing might be a front. Shouldn't we go after her?"

Whiteside shook his head. "Mother Akeley issued clear instructions, Ezra. We are to wait here." He reached inside his jacket and unobtrusively flicked on the concealed microcassette recorder. When he pulled his hand from his pocket he brought with it the earphone. He adjusted it carefully in his ear.

"Oh, I didn't know you were deaf," Noyes said.

"Just a little," Whiteside replied.

"Well, what are we going to do?" Ezra asked him.

"I shall wait for the Radiant Mother," Whiteside told him. "There is nothing to fear. Have faith in the Spiritual Light, little brother, and your footsteps will be illuminated."

"Oh." Ezra made a sour face and climbed onto the roof of Ambassador. He seated himself there cross-legged to watch for any evidence of activity at the shack.

Vernon Whiteside also kept watch on the shack, but chiefly he was listening to the voices transmitted by the cordless microphone concealed behind Elizabeth Akeley's lapel. Excerpts from the transcript later made of these transmissions follow.

Microcassette, August 8, 1979

Voice #5 (Elizabeth Akeley): Hello? Hello? Is there —
Voice #6 (Unidentified voice; oddly metallic intonation; accent similar to male New England twang present in San Diego trance tapes): Come in, come in, don't be afraid.
Voice #5: It's so dark in here.

Voice #6: I'm sorry. Move carefully. You are perfectly safe but there is some delicate apparatus set up.

(Sounds of movement, feet shuffling, breathing, a certain vague *buzzing* sound. Creak as of a person sitting in an old wooden rocking chair.)

Voice #5: I can hardly see. Where are you?

Voice #6: The cells are very sensitive. My friends are not here. You are not Albert Wilmarth.

Voice #5: No, I don't even—

Voice #6: (Interrupting) Oh, my God! Of course not. It's been so—tell me, what year is this?

Voice #5: 1979.

Voice #6: Poor Albert. Poor Albert. He could have come along. But of course he—what did you say your name was, young woman?

Voice #5: Akeley. Elizabeth Akeley.

(Silence. Buzzing sound. A certain unsettling sound as of wings rustling, but wings larger than those of any creature known to be native to Vermont.)

Voice #6: Do not taunt me, young woman!

Voice #5: Taunt you? Taunt you?

Voice #6: Do you know who I *am*? Does the name Henry Wentworth Akeley mean nothing to you?

(Pause. . . . Buzzing. . . . Rustling.)

Voice #5: Yes! Yes! Oh, oh, this is incredible! This is wonderful! It means—Yes, my grandfather spoke of you. If you're really—My grandfather was George Akeley. He—we—

Voice #6: (Interrupting) Then I am your great-grandfather, Miss Akeley. I regret that I cannot offer you my hand. George Akeley was my son. Tell me, is he still alive?

Voice #5: No, he—he died. He died in 1977, two years ago. Ever since I was a little girl, I remember him speaking of his father in Vermont. He said you disappeared mysteriously. But he always expected to hear from you again. He even founded a church. The Spiritual Light Brotherhood. He never lost faith.

I have continued his work. Waiting for word from—beyond. That's why I came when I—when I started receiving messages.

Voice #6: Thank you. Thank you, Elizabeth. Perhaps I should not have stayed away so long, but the vistas, my child, the vistas! How old did you say you were?

Voice #5: Why—why—18. Almost 19.

(Buzzing.)

Voice #6: You have followed my directions, Elizabeth? You are alone? Yes? Good. The cells are very sensitive. I can see you, even in this darkness, even if you cannot see me. Elizabeth, I have been gone from Earth for half a century, yet I am no older than the day I—departed—in the year 1928. The sights I have seen, the dimensions and the galaxies I have visited! Not alone, my child. Of course not alone. Those ones who took me—ah, child! Human flesh is too weak, too fragile to travel beyond the Earth.

Voice #5: But there are spacesuits. Rockets. Capsules. Oh, I suppose that was after your time. But we've visited the moon. We've sent instruments to Venus and Mars and the moons of Jupiter.

Voice #6: And what you know is what Columbus might have learned of the New World, by paddling a rowboat around the port of Cadiz! Those ones who took me, those Old Ones! They can fly between the worlds on their great ribbed wings! They can span the very aether of space as a dragonfly flits across the surface of a pond! They are the greatest scientists, the greatest naturalists, the greatest anthropologists, the greatest explorers in the universe! Those whom they select to accompany them, if they cannot survive the ultimate vacuum of space, the Old Ones discard their bodies and seal their brains in metal canisters and carry them from world to world, from star to burning, glittering star!

(Buzzing, loud sound of rustling.)

Voice #5: Then—you have been to other worlds? Other planets, other physical worlds. Not other planes of spiritual existence. Our congregants believe—

Voice #6: (Interrupting) Your congregants doubtlessly believe poppycock. Yes, I have been to other worlds. I have seen all the planets of the solar system, from little, sterile Mercury to giant, distant Yuggoth.

Voice #5: Distant Yu—Yuggoth?

Voice #6: Yes, yes. I suppose those fool astronomers have yet to find it, but it is the gem and the glory of the solar system, glowing with its own ruby-red glare. It revolves in its own orbit, turned ninety degrees from the plane of the ecliptic. No wonder they've never seen it. They don't know where to look. Yet it perturbs the paths of Neptune and Pluto. That ought to be clue enough! Yuggoth is very nearly a sun. It possesses its own corps of worldlets, Nithon, Zaman, the miniature twins Thog and Thok! And there is life there! There is the Ghooric Zone where bloated shoggoths splash and spawn!

Voice #5: I can't—I can't believe all this! My own great-grandpa! Planets and beasts . . .

Voice #6: Yuggoth was merely the beginning for me. Those Ones carried me far away from the sun. I have seen the worlds that circle Arcturus and Centaurus, Wolf and Barnard's Star and Beta Reticuli. I have seen creatures whose physical embodiment would send a sane man mad into screaming nightmares of horror that never end and whose minds and souls would put to shame the proudest achievements of Einstein and Schopenhauer, Confucius and Plato, the Enlightened One and the Anointed One! And I have known love, child, love such as no earthbound mortal has ever known.

Voice #5: Lo—love, great-grandfather?

(Sound of buzzing, loud and agitated rustling of wings.)

Voice #6: You know about love, surely, Elizabeth. Doesn't your church preach a gospel of love? In fifty-seven years on this planet I never came across a church that didn't claim that. And have you known love? A girl your age, surely you've known the feeling by now.

Voice #5: Yes, great-grandfather.

Voice #6: Is it merely a physical attraction, Elizabeth? Do you believe that souls can love? Or do you believe in such things as souls? Can *minds* love one another?

Voice #5: All three. All three of those.

Voice #6: Good. Yes, all three. And when two beings love with their minds and their souls, they yearn also for bodies with which to express their love. Hence the physical manifestation of love. (Pause.) Excuse me, child. In a way I suppose I'm nothing but an old man rambling on about abstractions. You have a young man, have you?

Voice #5: Yes.

Voice #6: I would like to meet him. I would like very much to meet him, my child.

Voice #5: Great-grandfather. May I tell the people about you?

Voice #6: No, Elizabeth. The time is not ripe.

Voice #5: But this is the most important event since—

since—(Pause.) Contact with other beings, with other races, not of the Earth. Proof that there is intelligent life throughout the universe. Proof of visits between the worlds and between the galaxies.

Voice #6: All in time, child. Now I am tired. Please go now. Will you visit me again?

Voice #5: Of course. Of course.

* * *

Elizabeth Akeley emerged from the shack, took one step and staggered.

At the far side of the copse of trees, Vernon Whiteside and Ezra Noyes watched. They saw Elizabeth. Ezra scrambled from the roof of the station wagon. Whiteside started forward, prepared to assist Mother Akeley.

But she had merely been blinded, for the moment, by the bright sunlight of a Vermont August. Whiteside and Ezra Noyes saw her returning through the glade. Once or twice she stopped and leaned against a strangely spongy tree. Each time she started again, to all appearances further debilitated rather than restored.

She reached the station wagon and leaned against its drab metalwork. Whiteside said, "Are you all right, Radiant Mother?"

She managed a wan smile. "Thank you, Vernon. Yes, I'm all right. Thank you."

Ezra Noyes was beside himself.

"Who was in there? What was going on? Were there really aliens in that shack? Can I go? Oh, darn it, darn it!" He pounded one fist into the palm of his other hand. "I should never have left home without my camera! Kenneth Arnold himself said that back in '47. It's the prime directive of all Ufologists and I went off without one, me of all people. Oh, darn, darn, darn!"

Vernon Whiteside said, "Radiant Mother, do you wish to leave now? May I visit the shack first?"

"Please, Vernon, don't. I asked him"—She drew Whiteside away from Noyes—"I asked him if I could reveal this to the world and he said, not yet."

"I monitored the tape, Reverend Mother."

"Yes."

"What does it mean, Reverend Mother?"

She passed her hand across her face, tugging soft bangs across her eyes to block out the bright sunlight. "I feel faint. Vernon. Ask Ezra to drive us back to Dark Mountain, would you?"

He helped her climb into the station wagon and signaled to

Ezra. "Mother Akeley is fatigued. She must be taken back at once."

Ezra sighed and started the Ambassador's straight-six engine. Elizabeth Akeley telephoned Marc Feinman from the Noyes house in Dark Mountain. A message had been transmitted surreptitiously by agent Whiteside in time for monitoring arrangements to be made. Neither Akeley nor Feinman was aware of the monitoring system.

Excerpts from the call follow:

August 9, 1979 (outgoing)

Voice #2 (Sara Feinman): Yes.

Voice #5 (Elizabeth Akeley): Mrs. Feinman?

Voice #2: Yes, who is this?

Voice #5: Mrs. Feinman, this is Elizabeth Akeley speaking. I'm a friend of Marc's from San Diego. Is Marc there, please?

Voice #2: I know all about Marc's friend, Elizabeth darling. Don't you know Marc's father is in the hospital? Should you be bothering Marc at such a time?

Voice #5: I'm very sorry about Mr. Feinman, Mrs. Feinman. Marc told me before he left California. Is he all right?

Voice #2: Don't ask.

(Pause.)

Voice #5: Could I speak with Marc? Please?

Voice #2: (Off-line, pick-up is very faint) Marc, here, it's your little goyishe priestess. Yes. On the telephone. No, she didn't say where. No, she didn't say.

Voice #1 (Marc Feinman): Lizzy? Lizzy baby, are you okay?

Voice #5: Yes, I'm okay. Is your father—

Voice #1: (Interrupting) They operated this morning. I saw him after. He's very weak, Liz. But I think he's going to make it. Lizzy, where are you? Pleasant Street?

Voice #5: Vermont.

Voice #1: What? *Vermont?*

Voice #5: I couldn't wait, Marc. You were on the road, and there was another trance. I couldn't wait till you arrived in New York. Vernon came with me. We're staying with a family in Dark Mountain. Marc, I met my great-grandfather. Yesterday. I tried to call you last night but—

Voice #1: I was at the hospital with Ma, visiting my father. We couldn't just—

Voice #5: Of course, Marc. You did the right thing. (Pause) How soon can you get here?

Voice #1: I can't leave now. My father is still—they're not sure. (Lowering voice.) I don't want to talk too loud. The doctor said it's going to be touch and go for at least forty-eight hours. I can't leave Ma.

Voice #5: (Sobs.) I understand, Marc. But—but—my great-grandfather . . .

Voice #1: How old is the old coot? He must be at least ninety.

Voice #5: He was born in 1871. He's 108.

Voice #1: My God! Talk about tough old Yankee stock!

Voice #5: It isn't that, Marc! It has to do with the trance messages. Don't you understand? All of that strange material about alien beings, and other galaxies? That was no sci-fi trip—

Voice #1: I never said you were making it up, Lizzy! Your subconscious, though, I mean, you see some TV show or a movie and—

Voice #5: But that's just it, Marc! Those are real messages. Not from my subconscious. My great-grandpa was sending, oh, call them spirit messages or telepathic radiations or anything you like. He's here. He's back. Aliens took him away, they took his brain in a metal cylinder and he's been travelling in outer space for fifty years and now he's back here in Vermont and—

Voice #1: Okay, Lizzy, enough! Look, I'll drive up there as soon as I can get away. As soon as my father's out of danger. I can't leave my ma now but as soon as I can. What's this place. . . .

*   *   *

Late on the afternoon of August 9th Ezra Noyes rapped on the door of Elizabeth Akeley's room. She admitted him and he stood in the center of the room, nervously wondering whether it would be proper to sit in her presence. Akeley urged him to sit. The conversation which ensued was recalled by young Noyes in a deposition taken later at an Agency field office. Excerpts from the deposition follow.

"Well, you see, I told her that I was really serious about UFOs and all that stuff. She didn't know much about Ufology. She'd never heard about the men in black, even, so I told her all about them so she'd be on the lookout. I asked her who this Vernon

Whiteside was, and she said he was the sexton of her church and completely reliable and I shouldn't worry about him.

"I showed her some copies of the *Intelligencer* and she said she liked the mag a lot and asked if she could keep them. I said sure. Anyway, she wanted to know how long the Moth Man sightings had been going on. I told her, only about six months ago over at Townshend or around here. Then she asked me what I knew about a rash of similar sightings about fifty years ago.

"That was right up my alley. You know, I did a lot of research. I went down and read a lot of old newspaper files. They have the old papers on microfilm now, it kills your eyes to crouch over a reader all day looking at the old stuff, but it's really interesting.

"Anyway, there were some odd sightings back in the '20s, and then when they had those floods around here in November of '27, there were some really strange things. They found some bodies, parts of bodies that is, carried downstream in the flood. There were some in the Winooski River over near Montpelier, and some right in the streets of Passumpsic. The town was flooded, you know.

"Strange bodies. Things like big wings. Not like moth wings, though. More like bat wings. And there seems to have been some odd goings on with Miss Akeley's great-grandfather, Henry Akeley. He was a retired prof, you know. And something about a friend of his, a guy called Al Wilmarth. But it was all hushed up.

"Well, I told Miss Akeley everything I knew and then I asked her who was in the cabin over at that dirt road near Lyndonville. I think she must have got mixed up, because she said it was Henry Akeley. He disappeared in 1927 or '28. Even if he turned up, he couldn't be alive by now. She said he said something to her about love, and about wanting a young man's body and a young woman's body so he could make love with some woman from outer space, he said from Aldebaran. I guess you have to be a sci-fi nut to know about Aldebaran. I'm a sci-fi nut. I don't say too much about it in UFO circles—they don't like sci-fi, they think the sci-fi crowd put down UFOs. They're scared of 'em. They want to keep it all nice and safe and imaginary, you ought to read Sanderson and Earley on that some time.

"Well, how could a human and an alien make love? I guess old Akeley must have thought something like mind-transfer, like one partner could take over the body of a member of the other partner's species, you know. Only be careful, don't try it with spiders where the female eats the male after they mate. Ha-ha-ha! Ha-ha!

"But Miss Akeley kept asking about lovemaking, you know,

and I started to wonder if maybe she wasn't hinting at something, you know. I mean, there we were in this room. And it was my own parents' house and all, but it *was* a bedroom, and I didn't want her to think that she could just walk in there and, uh, well, you know.

"So I excused myself then. But she seemed upset. She kept running her hand through her hair. Pulling it down, those strips, what do women call them, bangs, over her forehead. I told her I had to get to work on the next ish of my mag, you know, and she'd have to excuse me but the last ish had been late and I was trying to get the mag back on schedule. But I told her, if she wanted a lift over to Passumpsic again, I'd be glad to give her a ride over there any time, and I'd like to meet her great-grandfather if he was living in that old shack. Then she said he wasn't exactly living in the shack, but he sort of was, sort of was there and sort of was living there. It didn't make any sense to me, so I went and started laying out the next issue of the *Intelligencer* 'cause I wanted to get it out on time for once, and show those guys that I can get a mag out on time when I get a chance.

"Anyway, Miss Akeley said her great-grandfather's girlfriend was named something like Sheera from Aldebaran. I told her that sounded like something out of a bad 50s sci-fi flick on the TV. There's a great channel in Montreal, we get it on the cable, they show sci-fi flicks every week. And that sure sounded like a sci-fi flick to me.

"Sheera from Aldebaran! Ha-ha-ha! Ha-ha!"

*   *   *

Marc Feinman wheeled his Ferrari up to the Noyes home. His sporty driving-cap was cocked over one ear. Suede jacket, silk shirt, Gucci jeans and Frye boots completed his outfit.

The front door swung in as Feinman's boot struck the bottom wooden step. Elizabeth Akeley was across the whitewashed porch and in Feinman's arms before he reached the top of the flight. Without releasing his embrace of Akeley, Feinman extended one hand to grasp that of Vernon Whiteside.

They entered the house. Ezra Noyes greeted them in the front parlor. Elizabeth and Vernon briefed Marc on the events since their arrival in Vermont. When the narrative was brought up to date, Feinman asked simply, "What do you want to do?"

Ezra started to blurt out an ambitious plan for gaining the confidence of the aliens and arranging a ride in their saucer, but Whiteside, still maintaining the role of sexton of the Spiritual

Light Church, cut him off. "We will do whatever the Radiant Mother asks us to do."

All eyes turned to Akeley.

After an uncomfortable interval she said, "I was—hoping that Marc could help. It's so strange, Marc. I know that I'm the one who always believed in—in the spirit world. The beyond. What you always call the supernormal."

Feinman nodded.

"But somehow," Elizabeth went on, "this seems more like your ideas than mine. It's so—I mean, this is the kind of thing that I've always looked for, believed in. And you haven't. And now that it's true, it doesn't seem to have any spiritual meaning. It's just—something that you could explain with your logic and your computers."

Feinman rubbed his slightly blue chin with his free hand. "This great-grandpa of yours, this Henry Akeley . . ."

He looked into her eyes.

"You say, he was talking about some kind of mating ritual?"

Liz nodded.

Feinman said, "What did he look like? Did you ever *see* your great-grandfather before? Even a picture? Maybe one that your grandfather had in San Diego?"

She shook her head. "No. At least, I don't remember ever seeing a photo at home. There might have been one. But I hardly saw anything in the shack, Marc."

Ezra Noyes was jumping up and down in his chair. "Yes, you never told us, Lizzy—Miss Akeley. What did you see? What did he look like?"

"I hardly saw anything!" Liz covered her face with her hands, dropped one to her lap, tugged nervously at her bangs with the other. "It was pitch dark in there. Just a little faint light seeping between the cracks in the walls, through those broken windows. The windows that weren't broken were so filthy they wouldn't let any light in."

"So you couldn't tell if it was really Henry Akeley."

"It was the same voice," Vernon Whiteside volunteered. "We, ah, we bugged the meeting, Mr. Feinman. The voice was the same as the one on the trance tapes from the church."

Feinman's eyes widened. "The same? But the trance tapes are in Lizzy's voice!"

Whiteside back-pedaled. "No, you're right. I don't suppose they were the same vocal chords. But the timbre. And the enunciation. Everything. Same person speaking. I'd stake my reputation on it!"

Feinman stroked his chin again. "All right. Here's what I'd like to do. Lizzy, Henry Akeley said he'd see you again, right? Okay, let's surprise him. Suppose Whiteside and I head out there. Can you find the shack again, Vernon? Good! Okay, we'll take the Ferrari out there."

"But it's nearly dark out."

"No difference if it's so damned dark inside the shack! I've got a good five-cell torch in the emergency kit in the Ferrari."

"I ought to come along," Ezra Noyes put in. "I *do* represent the Vermont UFO Intelligence Bureau, you know!"

"Right," Feinman nodded. "And we'll need your help later. No, we'll need you, Ezra, but not right now. Whiteside and I will visit Henry Akeley—or whoever or whatever is out there claiming to be Henry Akeley. Give us a couple of hours' head start. And then, you come ahead."

"Can I get into the shack this time?" Ezra jumped up and paced nervously, almost danced, back and forth. "The other time, I had to wait at the car. If I can get into the shack, I can get some photos. I'll rig up a flash on my Instamatic. I want to get some shots of the inside of that cabin for the *Intelligencer.*"

"Yes, sure." Feinman turned from Ezra Noyes and took Elizabeth Akeley's hand. "You don't mind, do you, Lizzy? I'm worried that your ancestor there—or whoever it is—has some kind of control over you. Those trances—what if he puts you under some kind of hypnotic influence while we're all out there together?"

"How do you know he's evil? You seem to—just assume that Henry Akeley wants to harm me."

"I don't know that at all." Feinman frowned. "I just have a nasty feeling about it. I want to get there first. I think Whiteside and I can handle things, and then you can arrive in a while. Please, Lizzy. You did call me to help. You didn't have to, you could just have gone back and never said anything to me until it was over."

Elizabeth looked very worried. "Maybe I should have."

"Well, but you didn't. Now, can we do it my way? Please?"

"All right, Marc."

Feinman turned to Vernon Whiteside. "Let's go. How long a ride is it out there?"

Whiteside paused. "Little less than an hour."

Feinman grunted. "Okay. Vernon and I will start now. We'll need about another hour once we're there, I suppose—call it two to be on the safe side. Lizzy and Ezra, if you'll follow us out to the shack in two hours, just come ahead in, we'll be there."

Ezra departed to check his camera. Vernon accompanied Marc. Shortly the Ferrari Boxer disappeared in a cloud of yellow Vermont dust, headed for Passumpsic.

As soon as they had pulled out of sight of the house, Vernon spoke. "Mr. Feinman, I've been helping Radiant Mother on this trip."

"I know that, Vernon. Lizzy mentioned it several times. I really appreciate it."

"Mr. Feinman, you know how concerned Radiant Mother is about church archives. The way she records her sermons and the message services. Well, she was worried about her meeting with old Mr. Akeley. So I helped her to rig a wireless mike on her jacket, so we got a microcassette of the meeting."

Feinman said he knew that.

"Well, if you don't mind, I'd like to do the same again." Whiteside held the tiny microcassette recorder for Feinman to see. The Ferrari's V-12 purred throatily, loafing along the Passumpsic road in third gear.

"Sure. That's a good idea. But you needn't rig me up. I want you along. You can just mike yourself."

Vernon Whiteside considered. "Tell you what. . . " He reached into his pocket, pulled out a pair of enamel ladybugs. "I'll mike us both. If we happen to pick up the same sounds there'll be no harm. In fact, it'll give us a redundancy check. If we get separated—"

"I don't see why we should."

"Just in case." He pinned a ladybug to Feinman's suede jacket, attached the second bug to his own. He made a minor adjustment to the recorder.

"There." He slipped the recorder back into his pocket. "I separated the input circuits. Now we'll record on two channels. We can mix the sound if we record the same events or keep it separate if we pick up different events. In fact, just to be on the safe side, suppose I leave the recorder here in the car when you and I go to the shack."

Feinman assented and Whiteside peeled the sealers from a dime-sized disk of double-adhesive foam. He stuck it to the recorder and stuck the recorder to the bottom of the Ferrari's dashboard.

"You're the sexton of the Spiritual Light Church," Feinman said. "You know a hell of a lot about electronics."

"My sister's boy, Mr. Feinman. Bright youngster. It's his

hobby. Started out with a broken Victrola. Got his science teacher to helping. Going to San Diego State next term. I couldn't be prouder if he was my own boy. He builds all sorts of gadgets."

Feinman tooled the Ferrari around the dome-topped hill and pulled to a halt where the Noyes station wagon had parked on the earlier visit. The sun was setting and the somehow too-lush glade was filled with murk.

Vernon Whiteside reached under the dashboard and flicked the microcassette recorder to automatic mode. He climbed from the car.

Feinman went to the rear of the Ferrari and extracted a long-handled electric torch. He pulled his sports cap down over his eyes and touched Whiteside's elbow. The men advanced.

The events that transpired following this entrance to the sycamore copse were captured on the microcassette recorder, and a transcript of these sounds appears later in the report.

In the meanwhile, Elizabeth Akeley and Ezra Noyes waited at the Noyes home in Dark Mountain.

Two hours to the minute after the departure of Marc Feinman and Vernon Whiteside in Feinman's Ferrari Boxer, the Noyes station wagon, its aged suspension creaking, pulled out of the driveway.

Ezra pushed the Nash to the limit of its tired ability, chattering the while to Elizabeth. Preoccupied, she responded with low monosyllables. At the turning-point from the Passumpsic-Lyndonville road onto the old farm track, she waited in the station wagon while Ezra climbed down and opened the fence gate.

The Nash's headlights picked a narrow path for the car, circling the dome-topped hill that blocked the copse of lush vegetation from the sight of passers-by. The Ferrari Boxer stood silently at the edge of the copse.

Ezra lifted his camera-bag from the floor and slung it over his shoulder. Elizabeth waited in the car until Ezra walked to her side, opened the door and offered his hand.

They started through the copse. Noyes testified later that this was his first experience with the unusual vegetation. He claimed that, even as he set foot beneath the overhanging branches of the first sycamore, a strange sensation passed through him. The day had been hot and even in the hours of darkness the temperature did not drop drastically. Even so, with his entry into the copse Noyes felt an unnatural and debilitating heat, as if the trees were adapted to a different climate than that of northern Vermont and were actually emitting heat of their own.

He began to perspire.

Elizabeth Akeley led the way through the wooded area, retracing the steps of her previous visit to the wooden shack.

Noyes found it more and more difficult to continue. With each pace he felt drained of energy and will. Once he halted and was about to sit down for a rest but Akeley grasped his hand and pulled him along.

When they emerged from the copse the dome-topped hill stood directly behind them, the rundown shack directly ahead.

Ezra and Elizabeth crossed the narrow grassy patch between the sycamore copse and the ramshackle cabin. Ezra found a space where the glass had fallen away and there was a small opening in the omnipresent cobwebs. He peered in, then lifted his camera and poked its lens through the opening. He shot a picture.

"Don't know what I got, but maybe I got something," he said.

Elizabeth Akeley pulled the door open. She stepped inside the cabin, closely followed by young Noyes.

The room, Ezra could see, was far larger than he'd estimated. Although the shack contained but a single room, that was astonishingly deep, its far corners utterly lost in shadow. Near to him were a rocking chair, a battered overstuffed couch and a dust-laden wooden table of a type often found in old New England homes.

Ezra later reported hearing odd sounds during these minutes. There was a strange buzzing sound. He couldn't tell whether it was organic—a sound such as a flight of hornets might have made, or such as might have been made by a single insect magnified to a shocking gigantism—or whether the sound was artificial, as if an electrical generator were running slightly out of adjustment.

The modulation was its oddest characteristic. Not only did the volume rise and fall, but the pitch, and in some odd way, the very tonal quality of the buzzing, kept changing. "It was as if something was trying to talk to me. To us. To Miss Akeley and me. I could almost understand it, but not quite."

Noyes stood, paralyzed, until he heard Elizabeth Akeley scream. Then he whirled, turning his back to the table from whence the buzzing sounds were coming. He saw Elizabeth standing before the rocking chair, her hands to her face.

The chair was rocking slowly, gently. The cabin was almost pitch black, its only illumination coming from an array of unfamiliar machinery set up on the long wooden table. Ezra could see now that a figure was seated, apparently unmoving, in the rocker.

It spoke.

"Elizabeth, my darling, you have come," the figure said. "Now we shall be together. We shall know the love of the body as we have known the love of the mind and of the soul."

Strangely, Noyes later stated, although the voice in which the figure spoke was that of Marc Feinman, the accent and intonation were those of a typical New England old-timer. Noyes testified also that his powers of observation played a strange trick on him at this moment. Although the man sitting in the chair was undoubtedly Marc Feinman—the clothing he wore, even to the sporting cap pulled low over his eyes, as if he were driving his Ferrari in bright sunlight—what Ezra noticed most particularly was a tiny red-and-black smudge on Feinman's jacket.

"It looked like a squashed lady bug," the youth stated later.

From somewhere in the darker corners of the cabin there came a strange rustling sound, like that of great leathery wings opening and folding again.

Noyes shot a quick series of pictures, one of the figure in the rocking chair, one of the table with the unusual mechanical equipment on it, and one of the darker corners of the cabin, hoping vaguely that he would get some results. The rocking chair tilted slowly backward, slowly forward. The man sitting in it finally said to Ezra, "You'll never get anything from there. You'd better get over to the other end of the shack and make your pictures."

As if hypnotized, Noyes walked toward the rear of the cabin. He stated later that as he passed a certain point, it was as if he had penetrated a curtain of total darkness. He tried to turn and look back at the others, but could not move. He tried to call out but could not speak. He was completely conscious, but seemingly had plunged into a state of total paralysis and of sensory deprivation.

What transpired behind him, in the front end of the cabin, he could not tell. When he recovered from his paralysis and loss of sensory inputs, it was to find himself alone at the rear of the shack. It was daylight outside and sunshine was pushing through the grimy windows and open door of the shanty. He turned around and found himself facing two figures. A third was at his side.

"Ezra!" The third figure said.

"Mr. Whiteside." Noyes responded.

"Well, I'm glad to see that you two are all right," a voice came to them from the other end of the cabin. It was the old New England twang that Ezra had heard from the man in the rocking chair, and the speaker was, indeed, Marc Feinman. He stood, wooden-faced, his back to the doorway. Elizabeth Akeley, her features similarly expressionless, stood at his side. Feinman's sporting cap was pulled down almost to the line of his eyebrows. Akeley's bangs dangled over her forehead.

Noyes claimed later that he thought he could see signs of a fresh red scar running across Akeley's forehead beneath the bangs. He claimed also that a corner of red was visible at the edge of the visor of Feinman's cap. But of course this is unverified.

"We're going now," Feinman said in his strange New England twang. "We'll take my car. You two go home in the other."

"But—but, Radiant Mother," Whiteside began.

"Elizabeth is very tired," Feinman said nasally. "You'll have to excuse her. I'm taking her away for a while."

He started out the door, guiding Elizabeth by the elbow. She walked strangely, yet not as if she were tired, ill, or even injured. Rather, she had the tentative, uncertain movements that are associated with an amputee first learning to maneuver on prosthetic devices.

They left the cabin and walked to the Ferrari. Feinman opened the door on the passenger side and guided Akeley into the car. Then he circled the vehicle, climbed in and seated himself at the wheel. Strangely, he sat for a long time staring at the controls of the sports car, as if he were unfamiliar with its type.

Vernon Whiteside and Ezra Noyes followed the others from the cabin. Both were still confused from their strange experience of paralysis and sensory deprivation; both stated later that they felt only half-awake, half-hypnotized. "Else," agent Whiteside later deposed, "I'd have stopped 'em for sure. Warrant or no warrant, I had probable cause that something fishy was going on, and I'd have grabbed the keys out of that Ferrari, done anything it took to keep those two there. But I could hardly move, I could hardly even think.

"I *did* manage to reach into that car and grab out my machine. My microcassette recorder. Then I looked at my little bug-mike and saw that it was squashed, like somebody'd just squeezed it between his thumb and his finger, only he must have been made out of iron 'cause those bug-mikes are ruggedized. They can take a wallop with a sledgehammer and not even know it. So who squashed my little bug?

"Then Feinman finally got his car started and they pulled away. I looked at the Noyes kid and he looked at me, and we headed for his Nash wagon and we went back to his house. Nearly cracked up half a dozen times on the way home, he drove like a drunk. When we got to his place we both passed out for twelve hours while Feinman and Akeley were going God-knows-where in that Ferrari.

"Soon as I got myself back together I phoned in to Agency field HQ and came on in."

When agent Whiteside reported to Agency field HQ he turned over the microcassette which he and Feinman had made at the shack. Excerpts from the tape follow.

(Whiteside's Channel)

(All voices mixed): Yeah, this is the place all right. . . . I'll—got it open, okay. . . . Sheesh, it's dark in here. How'd she see anything? Well . . . (Buzzing sound.) What's that? What's that? Here, I'll shine my—what the hell? It looks like . . . shining cylinder. No, two of 'em. Two of 'em. What the hell, some kind of futuristic espresso machines. What the hell. . . .

(Buzzing sound becomes very loud, dominates tape. Then volume drops and a rustling is heard.)

Voice #3 (Vernon Whiteside): Here, lend me that thing a minute. No, I just gotta see what's over there. Okay, you stay here a minute, I gotta see what's . . .

(Sound of walking. Buzzing continues in background but fades, rustling sound increases.)

Voice #3: Jesus God! That can't be! No, no, that can't be! It's too. . . .

(Sound of thump, as if microphone were being struck and then crushed between superhard metallic surfaces. Remainder of Whiteside channel is silent.)

*   *   *

(Feinman Channel)

(Early portion identical to Whiteside channel; excerpts begin following end of recording on Whiteside channel.)

Voice #1 (Marc Feinman): Vernon? Vernon? What—

Voice #6 (Henry Wentworth Akeley): He is unharmed.

Voice #1: Who's that?

Voice #6: I am Henry Wentworth Akeley.

Voice #1: Lizzy's great-grandfather.

Voice #6: Precisely. And you are Mr. Feinman?

Voice #1: Where are you, Akeley?

Voice #6: I am here.

Voice #1: Where? I don't see . . . what happened to Whiteside? What's going on here? I don't like what's going on here.

Voice #6: Please, Mr. Feinman, try to remain calm.

Voice #1: Where are you, Akeley? For the last time. . . .

Voice #6: Please, Mr. Feinman, I must ask you to calm yourself. (Rustling sound.) Ah, that's better. Now, Mr. Feinman, do you not see certain objects on the table? Good. Now, Mr. Feinman, you are an intelligent and courageous young man. I understand that your interests are wide and your thirst for knowledge great. I offer you a grand opportunity. One which was offered to me half a century ago. I tried to decline at that time. My hand was forced. I never regretted having . . . let us say, gone where I have gone. But I must now return to earthly flesh, and as my own integument is long destroyed, I have need of another.

Voice #1: What—where—what are you talking about? If this is some kind of . . .

(Loud sound of rustling, sound of thumping and struggle, incoherent gasps and gurgles, loud breathing, moans.)

(At this point the same sound that ended the Whiteside segment of the tape is heard. Remainder of Feinman channel is blank.)

*   *   *

When agent Whiteside and young Ezra Noyes woke from their exhausted sleep, Whiteside identified himself as a representative of the Agency. He obtained the film from young Noyes's camera. It was promptly developed at the nearest Agency facility. The film was subsequently returned to Noyes and the four usable photographs, in fuzzily screened and mimeographed form, appeared in the *Vermont UFO Intelligencer.*

A description of the four photographs follows:

Frame 1: (Shot through window of the wooden shack) A dingy room containing a rocking chair and a large wooden table.

Frame 2: (Shot inside room) A rocking chair. In the chair is sitting a man identified as Marc Feinman. Feinman's sporting cap is pulled down covering his forehead. His eyes are barely visible and seem to have a glazed appearance, but this may be due to the unusual lighting conditions. A mark on his forehead seems to be visible at the edge of the cap, but is insufficiently distinct for verification.

Frame 3: (Shot inside room) Large wooden table holding unusual mechanical apparatus. There are numerous electrical devices, power units, what appears to be a cooling unit, photoelectric cells, items which appear to be microphones, and two medium-sized metallic cylinders estimated to contain sufficient space for a human brain, along with compact life-support paraphernalia.

Frame 4: (Shot inside room) This was obviously Noyes's final frame, taken as he headed toward the darkened rear area of the cabin. The rough wooden flooring before the camera is clearly visible. From it there seems to rise a curtain or wall of sheer blackness. This is not a black *substance* of any sort, but a curtain or mass of sheer negation. All attempts at analysis by Agency photoanalysts have failed completely.

*   *   *

Elizabeth Akeley and Marc Feinman were located at—of all places—Niagara Falls, New York. They had booked a honeymoon cottage and were actually located by representatives of the Agency returning in traditional yellow slickers from a romantic cruise on the craft *Maid of the Mist*.

Asked to submit voluntarily to Agency interrogation, Feinman refused. Akeley, at Feinman's prompting, simply shook her head negatively. "But I'll tell you what," Feinman said in a marked New England twang, "I'll make out a written statement for you if you'll settle for that."

Representatives of the Agency considered this offer unsatisfactory, but having no grounds for holding Feinman or Akeley and being particularly sensitive to criticism of the Agency for alleged intrusion upon the religious freedoms of unorthodox cults, the representatives of the Agency were constrained to accept Feinman's offer.

The deposition provided by Feinman—and co-sworn by Akeley—represented a vague and rambling narrative of no value. Its concluding paragraph follows.

> All we want is to be left alone. We love each other. We're here now and we're happy here. What came before is over. That's somebody else's concern now. Let them go. Let them see. Let them learn. Vega, Aldebaran, Ophiuchi, the Crab Nebula. Let them see. Let them learn. Someday we may wish to go back. We will have a way to summon those Ones. When we summon those Ones they will respond.

*   *   *

A final effort by representatives of the Agency was made, in an additional visit to the abandoned shack by the sycamore copse off the Passumpsic-Lyndonville road. A squad of agents wearing regulation black outfits were guided by Vernon Whiteside. An additional agent remained at the Noyes home to assure noninterference by Ezra Noyes.

Whiteside guided his fellow agents to the sycamore copse. Several agents remarked at the warmth and debilitating feeling they experienced as they passed through the copse. In addition, an abnormal number of small cadavers — of squirrels, chipmunks, one gray fox, a skunk, and several whippoorwills — were noted, lying beneath the trees.

The shack contained an aged wooden rocking chair, a battered overstuffed couch, and a large wooden table. Whatever might have previously stood upon the table had been removed.

There was no evidence of the so-called wall or curtain of darkness. The rear of the shack was vacant.

*   *   *

In the months since the incidents above reported, two additional developments have taken place, note of which is appropriate herein.

First, Marc Feinman and Elizabeth Akeley returned to San Diego in Feinman's Ferrari Boxer. There, they took up residence at the Pleasant Street location. Feinman vacated the Upas Street apartment; he returned to his work with the computer firm. Inquiries placed with his employers indicate that he appeared, upon returning, to be absent-minded and disoriented, and unexpectedly to require briefings in computer technology and programming concepts with which he had previously been thoroughly familiar.

Feinman explained this curious lapse by stating that he had experienced a head injury while vacationing in Vermont, and still suffered from occasional lapses of memory. He showed a vivid but rapidly fading scar on his forehead as evidence of the injury. His work performance quickly returned to its previous high standard. "Marc's as smart as the brightest prof you ever studied under," his supervisor stated to the Agency. "But that Vermont trip made some impression on him! He picked up this funny New England twang in his speech, and it just won't go away."

Elizabeth Akeley went into seclusion. Feinman announced that they had been married, and that Elizabeth was, at least temporarily, abandoning her position as Radiant Mother of the Spiritual Light Church, although remaining a faithful member of the church. In Feinman's company she regularly attends Sunday worship services, but seldom speaks.

The second item of note is of questionable relevance and significance, but is included here as a matter of completing the appropriate documentation. Vermont Forestry Service officers have reported that a new variety of sycamore tree has appeared in the Windham County-Caledonia County section of the state. The new sycamores are lush and extremely hardy. They seem to generate a peculiarly *warm* atmosphere, and are not congenial to small forest animals. Forestry officers who have investigated report a strange sense of lassitude when standing beneath these trees, and one officer has apparently been lost while exploring a stand of the trees near the town of Passumpsic.

Forestry Service agents are maintaining a constant watch on the spread of the new variety of sycamores.

Ah, dear Mr. Tindle. The first adventure of this plainly Thurbur-esque fellow appeared in The Magazine of Fantasy and Science Fiction *in 1989. The story was popular and readers kept demanding to know what happened after the events narrated in the story. I kept telling them that* nothing *happened, there was no more story,* The End *meant* The End, *but they refused to settle.*

Things even reached the point where I was awakened in the small hours of the morning by a sharp spousal jab only to encounter a demand that I reveal—what happened next!

In fact, the more I thought about it, the more I came to realize that just this once, The End *did not mean* The End. *There was indeed more to the adventures of Mr. Tindle, and I wrote a second story about him.*

For reasons which I could never understand but which I am sure were good and sufficient, Ed Ferman declined to publish the second story. Fortunately Gary Lovisi had revived the grand old science fiction magazine Other Worlds, *or at least its name, and the story appeared in* Other Worlds *(new series) in 1991.*

The Adventures of Mr. Tindle

I. Mr. Tindle Departs

MRS. TINDLE WAS IN BED SIPPING HER EVE-
ning tea and reading a paperback romance. She had made
her way upstairs and climbed into the twin bed after a
dinner of broccoli and asparagus spears. It was her custom. Not
that she prepared broccoli and asparagus spears for herself and
Mr. Tindle every night. Sometimes she made them carrots and
rutabaga. Occasionally, she added a boiled potato, and once a
month animal protein—a cheese sauce over the vegetables, for
instance, or a small boiled egg garnished with lettuce leaves.

But tonight it had been broccoli and asparagus.

Mr. Tindle was in the computer room. The room had gone
through any number of changes in the Tindles' eighteen years of
marriage.

At first it had been Mr. Tindle's den. That was Margery's—
Mrs. Tindle's—idea. She thought that there was a manly sound
to it. She had decorated the room for Mr. Tindle, with a leather-
topped desk and swivel-chair, sporting prints and a brass hatrack.
She had stopped just short of buying a stuffed moose-head,
although she had bought a mounted speckled trout on a wooden
plaque for Mr. Tindle's birthday the following year.

Mr. Tindle had never been quite comfortable with a den. He was a slight man, with weak eyes, a small pot belly, and a receding hairline.

After Mrs. Tindle gave up on the idea of a den, she had converted the room into a library. Out went the leather-topped desk. Mr. Tindle was sorry to see it go, but didn't want to start a fight over it. Out went the swivel-chair. Out went the stuffed trout. Mr. Tindle's heart sang when the garbage men took that away.

The brass hat-rack survived. Book-cases were installed and Mrs. Tindle arranged the purchase (on the monthly payment plan) of several sets of classic books in handsome, matching bindings. There was a set of Dickens, a set of Mark Twain, and a full shelf of inspirational volumes, plus a twenty-six volume encyclopedia with gilt on the tops of the pages and thumb-indexing on the sides.

Mrs. Tindle ordered a pair of overstuffed chairs for herself and her husband, and had them placed in the library.

Mr. Tindle seemed quite pleased with the new furnishings of the room, and began spending hours in the library after dinner each evening. He would sit in an overstuffed chair, reading a handsome leather-bound, gilt-edged classic while Mrs. Tindle watched him over the top of her paperback romance.

Mrs. Tindle was gratified to see Mr. Tindle sitting in the chair she had ordered, in the room she had decorated, reading a book that she had selected. In fact, Mr. Tindle was more than comfortable or contented; he looked positively happy.

Mrs. Tindle said, "Albert, what's that you're reading?"

Mr. Tindle replied, "Mark Twain, dear."

Mrs. Tindle's brow furrowed. Mark Twain! That was supposed to be wholesome material about young boys growing up in Missouri, wasn't it? Images of a kind of Norman Rockwell small town rose before Mrs. Tindle's mind's eye.

Mr. Tindle had gone back to his reading, and the look on his face, while a happy one, seemed to Mrs. Tindle to be far too active and intense for comfort.

Mrs. Tindle noted the place where Mr. Tindle's book had been removed. The following day, while Mr. Tindle was at work at the Department of Social Assistance, Mrs. Tindle entered the library. She found the book Mr. Tindle had been reading the night before, found his bookmark still in it, and read the pages Mr. Tindle must have been reading the previous evening.

Mrs. Tindle was shocked.

This was no Norman Rockwell town.

That night over a dinner of cooked carrots and cole slaw, Mrs. Tindle asked Mr. Tindle how things were coming along at the Department of Social Assistance. It was a question that Mrs. Tindle had been asking for the entire eighteen years of their marriage.

This included the twelve years that Mr. Tindle had been employed by the Department of Social Assistance as a Payment Analyst/3. Prior to that he had been employed by a large insurance company in a similar capacity, but he found the less competitive world of public service more congenial than that of the private sector, and had consequently never regretted his move.

Mr. Tindle said, "All right. Things are all right. There's a lot of pressure, you know. Glauer's been after me, but I can handle him, I guess."

That was the answer that Mr. Tindle had given each time Mrs. Tindle asked about work, ever since Mark Glauer had become Mr. Tindle's supervisor. Prior to that his supervisor had been Ms. Jane Westerley. In those days, Mr. Tindle's answer to Mrs. Tindle's question had been the same, except for the change of name and gender. Actually, Mrs. Tindle had been pleased when Ms. Westerley had left her job at the Department of Social Assistance and been replaced by Mr. Glauer. Mrs. Tindle didn't approve of men working for women managers. There were too many opportunities for temptation.

"How are you getting along with the computerization project?" Mrs. Tindle asked.

Mr. Tindle was startled. He wasn't accustomed to the show of interest in his work, beyond the ritual question and answer. But he replied, "There's no question that productivity will be increased. And accuracy, too. You know, it isn't easy to keep up both one's productivity and one's accuracy in a job like mine. One or the other, yes. But both—well, and the case folders keep arriving day after day. . . ."

He shook his head in despair.

"I understand," Mrs. Tindle said. "I certainly understand." She placed another carrot on Mr. Tindle's plate. "That's why I was wondering if—well. . . "

She let her voice trail away and waited coyly for Mr. Tindle to coax her secret out of her.

"Yes?" he said. "What were you wondering?"

"Your birthday *is* coming up, and I thought you might like a computer as a gift. Just think, your very own computer! I saw an

ad this afternoon, on television. There's a big computer sale downtown this weekend, and I thought I could get you one. Imagine,
my very own husband with a computer all his own! Wouldn't you
love that, Albert?"

Albert—Mr. Tindle—knew that he was going to get a computer for his birthday, whether he wanted it or not. He also knew
that Margery would give him no peace until he said that he'd love
to have a computer all his own, so he might as well say it now and
avoid agonizing minutes of verbal cues, game-playing, and
psychological manipulation at the end of which he would have
wound up saying that he would indeed love to own a computer.

"I'd love it," he said.

That was how the library became the computer room.

In fact, Mrs. Tindle didn't even go downtown to buy the computer. It was a dark gray day in early autumn, and black clouds
threatened to open up any minute. Mrs. Tindle didn't want to
catch cold. Nor did she want to risk being struck by lightning,
unlikely though that was.

So she phoned the store and ordered the computer. The salesperson was a very pleasant, very enthusiastic young woman. That
took Mrs. Tindle somewhat aback. But the young woman rattled
on about hard and soft disks and color monitors and communications modems and graphics packages and printer drivers. Mrs.
Tindle didn't understand any of what the young woman told her,
except that this was a wonderful bargain and exactly the thing to
keep Mr. Tindle home and busy with constructive activities every
night and weekend.

The young woman asked if the Tindles had any children, and
Mrs. Tindle informed her that they had not been so blessed. The
young woman said that the computer came with a variety of
games for adults as well as children but Mrs. Tindle told her that
she didn't want anything frivolous. The young woman repeated
back, "No games, then. You get a bonus software package but you
don't want any games. I'll make sure of that."

Mrs. Tindle told the young woman that she wanted the computer delivered on Mr. Tindle's birthday, not a day sooner and not
a day later. The young woman promised that the machine would
be delivered on the right day, with computer precision. She
laughed a little at her own joke.

Mrs. Tindle sniffed, thanked the young woman somewhat
coldly, and hung up.

On Mr. Tindle's birthday he arrived home a quarter of an hour
late. His face was somewhat flushed. It had been raining, on and

off, and his hat was spotted and there was moisture on his glasses. Mrs. Tindle demanded to know where he had been.

Mr. Tindle said that his co-workers had invited him out for a celebratory drink after work. Everybody was there—Jack Donovan, Larry Corcoran, Beans Harris—and he had accepted rather than offend them. He'd only had one quick beer and got away as quickly as he could. He was sorry that he'd worried his wife.

Mrs. Tindle said that she wouldn't let Mr. Tindle's thoughtlessness ruin the observance of his birthday. She coyly refused to tell him what his present was (for all that he had known for weeks what she was planning to get him) until after he had eaten a dinner of boiled cabbage and succotash.

Then she led him to the former den and former library, now refurnished as the computer room. It contained the computer, monitor, printer, modem, a box of reference manuals and a clear plastic cube with software disks in it. The only furniture in the room was a work table that held the machinery, and a straight-backed chair.

Mr. Tindle exclaimed that this was exactly what he'd hoped for. He gave Mrs. Tindle a kiss on the cheek and sat down in front of the computer. He remarked that it was similar to the one he used in his work at the Department of Social Assistance. He reached for the on/off switch, turned the computer on, watched its lights glow for a few seconds, then turned it off again.

Mrs. Tindle said that she hoped having a computer of his own would help him with his work.

Mr. Tindle opened the box of reference manuals, removed the top volume from the box, and began to read.

After standing and watching Mr. Tindle read the manual for a few minutes, Mrs. Tindle retired from the room. Shortly she was in her bed with her romance novel.

Mr. Tindle opened the plastic cube, looked through the disks it contained, selected one and slipped it into the computer. He turned the machine on and began clicking at the keyboard.

In a little while Mrs. Tindle heard the computer clattering. She smiled, put down her romance, turned off the light and closed her eyes. For a while she would hear the soft clicking of the keyboard, then the clatter of the printer. She dozed off.

The following weeks were among the happiest that Mr. Tindle could remember. Having a computer of his own might not have helped him any with his work at the Department of Social Assistance. But then, if the truth be known, that work was more tedious and mind-deadening than it was really difficult. The

Social Assistance system was an incomprehensible jumble of laws, rules, and procedures, most of them issued in volumes of opaque and self-contradictory prose. However, the computer opened whole new areas of interest and stimulation for Mr. Tindle.

Besides, Mrs. Tindle began leaving him alone. At first she had brought a second chair into the computer room, and watched him as he used the machine each evening. But she soon tired of that, and began retiring to bed with her romances instead. She complained that the noise of the printer annoyed her, and insisted that Mr. Tindle keep the door of the computer room shut while he was inside.

Mr. Tindle did not object. In fact there was something very pleasant about sitting in front of the computer with the monitor screen glowing, an interesting program booted up, and the door shut behind him. There was a window behind the work table, and Mr. Tindle would glance up occasionally, literally forgetful of whether it was summer or winter, day or night.

When Mr. Tindle had a problem with the software, he could even call a toll-free number and get assistance. (There was a telephone extension in the computer room, another beside Mrs. Tindle's bed.)

And there were hardly any quarrels between Mr. Tindle and Mrs. Tindle over the computer, even though Mr. Tindle spent many, many hours seated before the screen.

One evening Mr. Tindle left the computer room and went to the kitchen to prepare himself a slice of whole wheat toast as a snack. There was a thunderstorm in progress and a loud clap of thunder sounded while Mr. Tindle was downstairs.

He returned to find Mrs. Tindle in the act of leaving the computer room.

"The thunder woke me up," she told him. "You weren't in there so I turned off your machine. We mustn't waste electricity."

Mr. Tindle raced past his wife and stood looking at the computer. He took off his glasses, rubbed his eyes with the heels of his hands, and turned to his wife, blinking.

"Never do that again," he said.

"Why not?" she demanded. "Have you even looked at the electric bills lately?"

"You've ruined hours of work," he said. "You should never turn off a computer in the middle of a program. You have to log off and boot down. You can't just turn the on/off switch to off. You'll lose all the work you've done. And you can damage the software, too. Maybe even the hardware. I had a lot of work in there—"

Mr. Tindle stopped talking because Mrs. Tindle had sniffed and walked away.

Standing in the bedroom doorway she said, "I don't understand all that double-talk. And I don't care. We mustn't waste electricity, that's all. If you want that machine turned on, stay there and use it. If you leave the room, you ought to turn it off. Same as a light."

Mr. Tindle closed the door, ate the last of his toast, and sat down in front of his computer. He opened the operating manual and tried to find out what to do. Through the window he saw a bolt of jagged blue lightning dance between sky and earth. Then came the thunder.

The manual didn't offer much help. Mr. Tindle tried a few things. He even booted up from scratch and found that his computer was undamaged. But the software he'd been running—a program for sorting data and searching out errors called Sarm-X—wouldn't work. Apparently it had been damaged when his wife had crashed the system. And he had forgot to make a back-up copy of the disk.

For the first time since getting the computer on his birthday, Mr. Tindle decided to use the toll-free number given in the manual. It was listed right there, and the manual said that it would connect the caller with Comp-U-Fix.

More lightning flashed as Mr. Tindle punched the number. There was a pause, some crackling on the line, then a female voice answered.

"Comp-U-Fax," the voice said.

"I have a problem," Mr. Tindle said.

"Tell me," the voice said. This didn't sound like a typical telephone voice. Mr. Tindle spoke with hundreds of people on the telephone. Some were his co-workers. Others were clients of the Department. Still others were telephone solicitors, merchants, even people taking surveys.

More than half of them were female, and Mr. Tindle thought that he had heard every possible variation on the human female voice. But he had never heard anything like this.

This voice had overtones and undertones to it that made the hair on the back of Mr. Tindle's neck rise. There was a kind of moist warmth to this voice. There was a breathiness, and an accent so slight that it defied identification but was still ineffably appealing.

Mr. Tindle told her.

All he really meant to tell her was about his problem with

Sarm-X. He told her about that and she listened, and encouraged him with little sounds and breaths and murmured syllables and he found himself telling her a lot more than his problem with Sarm-X.

He found himself telling her about his job, which was oppressive, and about his boss, Glauer, who was overbearing, and about his co-workers, who jibed at him, and about his home life, which was dull, and about his marriage, which was empty, and about his wife, who managed and manipulated and bullied him. Tonight she had gone into the computer room—*his* computer room—his one sanctum sanctorum—and had actually turned off his computer right in the middle of a run and ruined all his work and messed up his software.

Of course that brought the conversation full circle, and the female voice on the toll-free line listened, and murmured sympathetically, and told Mr. Tindle that she understood, she understood, she understood.

Mr. Tindle thought for a moment that he might be getting into something dangerous. After all, weren't there a hundred bad jokes about married men telling people that their wives didn't understand them? Sometimes it was a bartender, more often it was a woman. And the husband always wound up getting into trouble.

Always.

But this wasn't a real woman. This was merely a voice on the other end of a toll-free line. She didn't even have a name.

"You have a modem there, don't you, Mr. Tindle?" the toll-free voice asked.

Mr. Tindle admitted that he did.

"Good," the voice said. "All you need to do is turn it on, give me your number, and Comp-U-Fax will send you some software to help you out."

Mr. Tindle said, "Comp-U-Fax?"

The voice said, "That's right."

Mr. Tindle said, "I thought the service was called Comp-U-Fix. As in, ah, fix something broken."

There was a laugh, amused but friendly. "Oh, no. Comp-U-Fix is another service. I'm sure they're very good. But we're Comp-U-Fax. As in, ah, just the fax, Ma'am." She laughed again, and Mr. Tindle actually joined in, softly.

Mr. Tindle gave her his number. "Thank you," he said, "thank you."

The voice said, "Comp-U-Fax is happy to help. *I'm* happy to help."

And the strange thing was, Mr. Tindle believed that she really was happy to have helped him. For the third time he said, "Thank you."

"Any time at all," the voice said. "Just call Comp-U-Fax. I'm always here. Always. My name is Lily."

Mr. Tindle heard a click on the line.

His modem hummed into life and a series of coding flashed through his computer, onto a blank disk.

Mr. Tindle logged off, booted down, shut off the machine and climbed quietly into his bed so as not to waken Mrs. Tindle in the adjoining twin.

The next day Mark Glauer called Mr. Tindle into his office. He laid a stack of computer printouts on his desk and said, "Albert, these are the latest figures for our section."

Mr. Tindle craned his neck so he could read the top printout. Mr. Glauer had laid the papers so they were right side up from his own side of the desk, of course. Mr. Tindle almost reached out and turned the papers around, but he drew back his hand, timidly, when he saw the look in Glauer's eyes.

Mr. Glauer always called Mr. Tindle by his first name, *Albert*, even though Glauer was easily fifteen years younger than Mr. Tindle. Albert Tindle didn't like that, and had often thought of asking Mr. Glauer to call him Mr. Tindle, but he had always held back from doing that, for fear of what Mr. Glauer would say.

Today, Mr. Glauer was saying, "Your productivity and accuracy are both off, Albert. Look at this. Three errors in payment amounts to clients, two procedural errors, and two uses of incorrect standard phrases or paragraphs in your letters of notification. You're going to have to do a lot better than that, and fast, or we'll have to replace you."

Mr. Tindle swallowed and reached into his pocket for a handkerchief to wipe his brow with.

"What do you have to say for yourself, Albert?" Mr. Glauer asked.

"Well, the system is very complex. It's getting worse all the time, with all the new regulations they keep adding. And with the budget cuts, the personnel cuts. . . ."

"Can you do the work?"

"Yes. Of course. I mean, ah, yes, I can do the work."

Glauer pointed at the printouts. "But what about this?"

"How about the other workers in the section?" Mr. Tindle ran a finger around his collar, loosening his tie. Mr. Glauer stared and Mr. Tindle pulled his tie back up. "What about Jack?" Mr. Tindle asked. "Or Larry, or Beans, or Eileen Tornqvist?" Eileen Tornqvist was a chubby brunette who was frequently called into Mr. Glauer's office.

Mr. Glauer shook his head. "You know I can't discuss other employees' work with you, Albert. That's a right of privacy matter. Besides, your work is the subject under discussion, not Jack's or Larry's or Beans's."

"Or Eileen's?" Mr. Tindle added.

Mr. Glauer got red in the face. "This meeting is going nowhere," he said. "I'm only going to tell you one time. Get those numbers back up where they belong or get ready for a negative career event hearing, Albert." he looked pointedly at his watch.

Mr. Tindle went back to his desk. *En route* he passed Eileen Tornqvist's desk. She was sipping a cup of coffee, watching activity in the office. As soon as Mr. Tindle was past, she got up and went into Mark Glauer's office, shutting the door behind her.

After work that night Mr. Tindle did something he had never done before. He stopped for a drink, alone, at the same bar his friends had taken him to for his birthday celebration. The bartender was a slim platinum blonde who wore a man's vest and bow tie.

Mr. Tindle drank a beer. The bartender smiled when he gave her his order, and when she gave him his change after he paid for the beer, her hand touched his. A thrill shot through him. There was a bowl of pretzels on the bar and he ate six of them, one after another, talking a small sip of beer after each bite of pretzel.

He was still thirsty when he finished his beer, probably because the pretzels were both dry and salty, a combination designed to induce thirst in bar customers. When Mr. Tindle ordered his second beer, the bartender smiled at him. She put the tall glass on the bar in front of him, and when he said, "Thank you," she said, "You're welcome." Mr. Tindle thought that her voice was beautiful. It reminded him of the voice on the toll-free Comp-U-Fax line. *Lily.* Of course, he had no idea what Lily looked like, but he imagined her as a slim platinum blonde a lot like the bartender.

He drank his second beer slowly, left a tip on the bar, and got home half an hour late. Mrs. Tindle was standing outside the front door, waiting for him. She demanded to know where he'd been.

He didn't answer.

She said, "All right then. But you've missed your dinner. I put it down the disposal when you didn't come home."

He didn't mind. The pretzels and beer were still in his stomach, easing the tension created by his interview with Glauer, and he was actually feeling pretty good. He could do without his portion of limp vegetables and desultory dialog.

He went into the computer room, closed the door behind him, and logged on. He booted up the disk that he'd made the previous evening, with the help of the toll-free number and his modem. He expected it to be Sarm-X but it was something else.

Mr. Tindle hadn't used the graphics package that came with his computer very much, but now a face appeared on the monitor screen. For a few seconds it was very vague, the pixels dancing around in random patterns, but soon he realized that a clear face was forming. The face was that of a woman. The bone structure was slim, the complexion creamy, the eyebrows arched and the hair a shimmering, platinum blonde. The woman's eyes were an emerald green, and looked both kind and intelligent, sensuous — even eager — and yet innocent.

She looked, Mr. Tindle realized, a lot like the bartender who had sold him the two beers.

Mr. Tindle gave an involuntary gasp, started to say something, then stopped and looked behind him. The door of the computer room was closed. Mr. Tindle said, "Is that you?"

"Of course it's me," the face in the screen said. "Were you expecting maybe Hillary Rodham Clinton?"

"No!" Mr. Tindle blurted.

"Well, then," the face said. Her voice came from the computer, which Mr. Tindle knew contained an audio synthesizer chip. Considering, the voice was remarkably life-like and warm. A lot like the voice on the computer toll-free line, Lily.

Mr. Tindle looked over his shoulder again. "Lily?" he asked softly.

"That's right," she nodded, her emerald eyes twinkling. "You look like you could use some cheering up, Mr. Tindle."

He felt himself blushing. "You can call me Albert," he said.

"All right," Lily said, "Albert. But please don't look so gloomy, Albert. Let's take a quiet walk. You'll feel better."

"I know," said Mr. Tindle, "but you're only a — a piece of software. You aren't real, are you?"

Lily looked crestfallen.

"Or are you?" Mr. Tindle asked.

"That isn't a very nice thing to say," Lily pouted.

"What isn't?"

"About me just being a piece of software. You're just a piece of flesh, so there!"

When she pouted, she was twice as adorable as she'd been before, Mr. Tindle decided, which was plenty adorable to start with.

"I'm fully as real to me as you are to you," Lily said.

Mr. Tindle sat watching her, wishing he could touch her hand, the way the bartender had touched his when she returned his change. "I'm sorry, Lily," Mr. Tindle said. "I wish I *could* go for a walk with you. But it's impossible. You're just a—" He stopped himself in time. "I mean, you're an electronic image, and I'm a living organism, and . . . and . . ." He stopped and sat quietly.

Lily said, "Put your hand to the screen. That's right. Just touch your fingertips to mine." She held her hand up to the inside of the monitor and Mr. Tindle held his hand up to the outside. He knew it was just a glass tube but Lily's fingertips felt warm and soft. Mr. Tindle felt a thrill like the one he had felt with the bartender.

"Now, take your other hand and press the *execute* key," Lily said.

Mr. Tindle looked over his shoulder to make sure the door was still closed, and pressed the key.

He felt himself slide right into the monitor.

He was standing on a grassy hillside. Lily was beside him, her long hair glistening in the afternoon sunlight. The sky was a gorgeous, deep blue. Two or three little, fluffy clouds floated overhead. Mr. Tindle heard a murmuring brook nearby.

Lily took him by the hand and led him down the gentle hillside. There was indeed a stream, purling gently as it bubbled over some small rocks in its bed. There were trees along the brook, and a blanket was spread beneath one of the trees.

Lily led Mr. Tindle toward the blanket. She was wearing a softly flowing white gown that molded itself to her delicate but distinctly feminine figure. She was barefoot.

When they got to the blanket Mr. Tindle saw that a picnic had been spread. There were sandwiches, fruit, and a pitcher of lemonade. Lily sat down on the blanket and patted a pillow beside her for Mr. Tindle. He sat down and she put her hands gently on the sides of his head and massaged him. "There," she said, "isn't that better?"

He took one of her hands in both of his and started to say something, but a little brown and white puppy bounded from behind the tree and jumped onto Lily's lap, making her laugh.

It was a wonderful picnic, a wonderful afternoon, and when it ended Lily escorted Mr. Tindle back to the monitor screen and waited while he returned to his computer room. As he logged off the system she blew him a kiss.

For once Mr. Tindle slept happily and peacefully. The next morning he woke up and forced himself to go down to the Department of Social Assistance and work cases all day. Several times Mr. Glauer strode past his desk but Mr. Tindle kept his eyes down and just kept working. He did look up once when he heard Mr. Glauer's door slam. Eileen Tornqvist was away from her desk. Mr. Tindle looked at the clock. The day seemed endless.

He didn't stop at the bar on his way home that night, and when he got home—on time—he had to face a dinner of acorn squash and leek pudding. He wanted to head straight for his computer but he didn't dare.

Mrs. Tindle asked him, during the meal, how things had gone at work.

Mr. Tindle said, "Not so bad."

"What!" Mrs. Tindle exclaimed.

Mr. Tindle almost choked on a forkful of leek pudding. "I mean, ah, all right. Things are all right. There's a lot of pressure, you know. Glauer's been after me, but I can handle him, I guess."

"That's what I thought," Mrs. Tindle said. "Albert, I have to talk to you about something. I had the strangest dream last night. Were you talking to that computer of yours?"

"As a matter of fact, I was," Mr. Tindle said. "I was trying out the audio synthesizer. It worked very well, I thought."

"Huh," Mrs. Tindle said. "It was very peculiar. I thought I heard your voice and then a woman's voice."

"That was the synthesizer," Mr. Tindle said. "That's all. Just the synthesizer."

"Can't it talk like a man?" Mrs. Tindle demanded.

"I don't know, dear. I, ah, I don't think it's adjustable. They just built it to sound like a woman's voice. But I'll look in the manual. Maybe I can change it."

Mr. Tindle had no intention of changing it.

He finished his acorn squash and leek pudding and said, "Well, I'm going to use my computer." He went into his computer room and sat down in the straight-backed chair. He picked up the telephone and punched the number that had got him Comp-U-Fax two nights before.

An impersonal voice answered. "Comp-U-Fix. Please describe

your problem briefly and leave a return number when you hear the tone."

Why had the number got Comp-U-Fax one night, and Comp-U-Fix tonight? Mr. Tindle thought, *It must have something to do with the lightning.* He had got switched to—to what? He didn't know. There was nothing he could do about that now, so he switched on the machine, booted up the program that was not Sarm-X, and to his unmeasurable relief Lily appeared on the monitor.

"Can I—may I come to see you again?" Mr. Tindle asked.

Lily laughed softly. "Of course you can. Whenever you want to! What would you like to do this time? No, don't tell me. Touch my fingertips and press the *execute* button first, and we'll talk it over together."

That night they went adventuring as pirates. Lily wore a black buccaneer's hat and a white satin shirt with baggy sleeves and a skirt cut off raggedly above her knees and pair of soft boots with their floppy tops rolled down. They fought a battle and anchored near a tropical island and Lily and Mr. Tindle rowed ashore with a crew of ruffians in striped shirts and white duck trousers and buried a chest full of jewels and made a map of where they had left it.

Then Mr. Tindle went back through the screen and logged off and booted down his computer and climbed quietly into bed without awakening Mrs. Tindle.

Every day for a week Mr. Tindle suffered the agonies of Tantalus at the Department of Social Assistance waiting for quitting time to come. He would hurry home, make his escape from the dinner table as quickly as he could, and head for his computer. He never tried the toll-free line again. He just used the disk.

Lily was there every night.

One night he went back to college and tried out for the football team and became the star quarterback. Lily was the captain of the cheerleader squad, with bright yellow pompoms and a heavy sweater with Mr. Tindle's letter on the chest and a short, pleated skirt and saddle shoes. After the game (Mr. Tindle scored the winning touchdown on a keeper play with no time left on the clock at all) they went to a victory dance.

Another night Mr. Tindle was a jet fighter pilot and Lily was a hostess at the Officers' Club. He'd flown nineteen missions. One more and he'd be rotated home. He wanted to take Lily with him, to marry her, to get as far away from the screaming engines and the blazing rockets and the exploding bombs of this war as he could. But he had to fly that twentieth mission, and he had a premonition about it. A terrible, terrible premonition.

Another night Mr. Tindle and Lily were dining in the finest restaurant on Broadway. Mr. Tindle was wearing a black dinner jacket and Lily was in a daringly low-cut gown of white silk. She wore an emerald necklace the same color as her eyes. Mr. Tindle had given it to her. Just as the waiter brought their *canard a l'orange flambé* the captain arrived with a gold-plated telephone. "So sorry to interrupt, M'sieu Tindle. It is the White House. He insists on speaking to you at once. . . ."

Saturday morning Mrs. Tindle insisted that Mr. Tindle take her for a long drive in the country. The day seemed to last for centuries, and they arrived home late at night, and at Mrs. Tindle's insistence they both went straight to bed.

Mr. Tindle hoped to spend Sunday with his computer but Mrs. Tindle announced that they were going to spend the day with her sister who lived on the other side of town with her husband, a life insurance salesman who always practiced his new pitches on Mr. Tindle. Once more they arrived home late and went straight to bed.

Monday morning the telephone on Mr. Tindle's desk at the Department of Social Assistance rang just before coffee break. Mr. Tindle picked it up and identified himself in the prescribed manner.

"Albert, this is Mr. Glauer. Please come into my office. You can bring your coffee with you."

Mr. Tindle detected two bad signs in Mark Glauer's message. First, he had said *please*. Second, he had told Mr. Tindle to bring his coffee with him.

Glauer had a fresh stack of computer printouts on his desk. He had highlighted Mr. Tindle's performance figures in yellow. He had a metallic pointer in his hand and he tapped the stack of printouts and shook his head for fully thirty seconds before saying a word.

When he did speak, he said, "Albert, I have to tell you that I'm putting in a recommendation for a negative career event for you. Of course it will mean less money and lowered personal status, and you can protest the action if you choose. But I wouldn't recommend that. These figures." He shook his head sadly. "These figures speak for themselves."

"But I've been trying," Mr. Tindle said. "And I don't think I'm the worst worker in this section, by any means. Why, I saw the stack of cases on Eileen's desk just this morning. Not that I have anything against her or want to say anything against another worker, but—"

"Albert!" Glauer cut him off. "I told you, if you wish to protest the recommendation, you know the proper procedure and form. Of course, if you do protest, you understand that you'll be suspended from all duties without pay while the protest is in process. At this time there's about an eight-month wait for a first preliminary investigator's hearing, then after the investigator prepares an initial preliminary report. . . ."

"Never mind," said Mr. Tindle. "Go ahead."

"Thank you, Albert," said Glauer. "For the time being, just continue your usual good work, please."

On his way back to his desk Mr. Tindle passed Eileen Tornqvist's desk. She was eating a strawberry danish and talking on the phone. She followed him with her eyes as he walked past, grinning unpleasantly, then got up and strode into Mark Glauer's office.

After work Larry Corcoran and Beans Harris stopped Mr. Tindle at the elevator.

"Heard you caught it from Glauer," Larry said.

"Lousy bum," Beans said. "He had me in there for an hour the other afternoon. I wish I had the guts to do something about it."

"Yeah," Larry said. "You and Walter Mitty, right?"

"Never mind," Beans said, "let's get a drink."

Mr. Tindle said, "Thanks a lot, fellows, but it looks like rain again and I want to get home. I mean, I have to get home. My wife, she gets upset if I'm late."

"Well, call her," Beans said. "Right, Larry? Why doesn't Walter Mitty here just call the old lady and tell her he's having a drink with the boys and he'll be late? Right, Larry? How's about it, Mitty—I mean, Tindle?"

Mr. Tindle said, "Thanks a lot. Maybe some other time. But I'll walk you as far as the saloon."

They agreed to that, and as Larry and Beans disappeared inside the cool darkness Mr. Tindle thought he caught just a glimpse of the petite platinum blonde bartender. He even thought she waved to him, but the door swung shut and he couldn't be sure.

Mrs. Tindle gave him a dinner of creamed corn and lyonnaise potatoes. She asked how work had gone, and instead of his usual formula Mr. Tindle told her what had happened with Glauer.

"I spent all that money to buy you a computer so you could do better at your work and you're getting a demotion?" she demanded.

"Larry and Beans aren't much better off," Mr. Tindle explained. "I don't know about Jack Donovan, but I'll bet he's in trouble, too. It's just this terrible system, and Glauer is a tyrant. An absolute tyrant."

"I'll just bet," Mrs. Tindle said.

"Well, I've finished my dinner, dear," Mr. Tindle said. He tilted his almost clean plate so she could see it. "I'll, ah, I want to try out some new software on the computer tonight. I mean, ah, I'll try not to be too noisy with the audio synthesizer, and bother you."

Mrs. Tindle stood up, glaring down at Mr. Tindle. "Make all the noise you want," she said. "Have a ball tonight, you miserable failure, because tomorrow that stupid machine goes back to the store for whatever credit they'll give me. I think I'm going to redecorate that room for my sewing corner."

Mr. Tindle trudged morosely to the computer room and shut the door behind him.

He booted up the machine and invoked Lily on the monitor. There were tears in Mr. Tindle's eyes, but through them Lily's shimmering hair and creamy skin looked more beautiful than ever.

"Albert," she said, "what's the matter? You look so sad!"

"This is the last time we can be together," Mr. Tindle sobbed. "My wife is sending the computer back tomorrow. I'll never see you again!"

Lily said, "Never mind. Come on, touch my fingers."

Once Mr. Tindle was inside the monitor (or wherever in virtual space Lily had awaited him) he took Lily in his arms and held her to him, crying into her gorgeous hair.

"Never mind, Albert," she said, "What kind of adventure would you like this time?"

"I don't care. I don't know. Oh, Lily, what am I going to do?"

"How about the cowboy and the schoolmarm?" she asked.

Mr. Tindle shook his head.

"The boxer and the blind girl who needs the operation?"

"It's all just playing," Mr. Tindle said. "*That's* the real world. Out there." He pointed, vaguely, indicating the universe on the other side of the monitor screen. Wherever that was.

"No," Lily said. "Please, Albert. *This* is real. It's real! How about the gangster and the gun moll? How about the sailor and the stowaway girl? The nurse and the wounded soldier? Or spies! Or the pioneer couple! Please, Albert! I can be the harem girl and you can be the pasha. Sorceress and sword bearer! Please, Albert! Please stay with me! Please don't go back this time! Don't let her send away the computer and you go back to that awful job and I go back to—to—I go back to—I go back—go back—"

*   *   *

Mrs. Tindle opened the door of the computer room and peered in. The machine was running, its monitor screen a meaningless swirl of shapes and colors. "Albert?" Mrs. Tindle asked.

There was no answer.

"Albert?"

Silence.

"Now where can that weakling have gone?" Mrs. Tindle grumbled to herself. "Albert!"

No answer.

Mrs. Tindle looked in the kitchen. She looked in the bathroom. She looked in the bedroom.

No Albert.

"Hmph!" she grunted. "It's going to rain and that fool has gone out for a walk. Anything that happens will serve him right!"

She strode back into the computer room. The colors were still swirling on the monitor. "And I warned that man about wasting electricity. I warned him, and I warned him. I know he said you shouldn't just turn this thing off, but it's going back to the store tomorrow anyway so it's his own fault if he loses anything that he's working on," she muttered.

She reached for the on/off switch and flipped it to off.

The swirling colors on the monitor screen faded to gray.

II. Mr. Tindle Returns

"Faster, Bert, faster!"

The massive, powerful Pierce Arrow screeched around a corner on two wheels, sending pedestrians scrambling for cover. Behind the heavy sedan a pack of patrol cars roared, their engines thrumming, sirens howling hysterically.

Albert Tindle maneuvered the sedan through traffic you would have thought a bicycle couldn't get through. The gorgeous blonde beside him on the leather seat took a swig of bootleg hooch and held the silver flask toward Tindle.

"Not while I'm driving, Lily!" Tindle snapped. His eyes narrow in concentration, his competent leather-sheathed hands on the controls, the getaway car moved like a panther making good its escape from a pack of panting, dispirited hounds. There was no way the cops could catch them, no way they could stop them!

The idea of pulling a bank job at the height of the evening rush hour had sounded insane, but Lily had conceived it and had sold it to the gang, and it had worked like a charm! All you had to do was plan it right, arrange a phony traffic diversion, and your pursuers were stymied.

Suddenly a squad car came screaming out of a side street!

The traffic seemed to open for it, and the uniformed driver bore down on the Pierce Arrow like a man determined to destroy both machines and the people in them. Anything to stop the Tindle mob! Even if it cost the lives of an entire squad of coppers!

Two slouch-hatted criminals in the back of the Pierce Arrow scrambled for the car's window. A rough-skinned hand wound down the thick, bulletproof glass. Two tommy guns poked their ugly snouts from the side of the big machine.

From the careening police cruiser another tommy gun and a big barrelled, sawed-off shotgun protruded.

Nobody could tell who fired first, but suddenly the crowded street was deserted. Pedestrians dove for the cover of doorways. Drivers who couldn't escape in their vehicles abandoned them and hit the macadam, hugging tar as if their lives depended on it.

"We're going through!" Tindle husked between clenched teeth. Over his shoulder he commanded, "Get those copper rats, you mugs!"

The squad car was beside the Pierce Arrow now, two tommy guns chattering away against one, their triple rhythm punctuated by the periodic thump of the the cops' sawed-off shotgun.

How long could it go on?

Blood spattered from behind Tindle and his companion, splashing on the inside of the Pierce Arrow's thick windscreen.

The two cars had pulled away from the downtown congestion and were headed out an arterial toward the suburbs. The cop driver tried to sideswipe the Pierce Arrow, to force it off the roadway, even to ram it, but the sedan was heavier and more powerful than the copper wagon and Tindle pressed on, his foot heavy on the Pierce Arrow's accelerator.

From beside him he heard Lily's voice, clear and strong. "I'll handle this!"

From the corner of his eye Tindle saw her slide up the short skirt of her flapper outfit. Tucked in the top of one rolled-down stocking he caught the glint of a nickel-plated automatic. It was a tiny thing, a lady-gun, almost a toy.

But Lily calmly rolled down the window on her side of the car, pointed her gun at the copper driving the squad car. She sighted along the nickel-bright barrel, squeezed off a single shot.

The automatic made a little sound, a popping noise that was almost lost in the continuing rattle of tommies.

The cop car curled away from the Pierce Arrow, slid slowly to a halt on the dirt shoulder.

Tindle slowed down but he didn't stop the sedan. "You kill him, Lily?"

"I never kill anybody, you know that! I just winged him, but I hit a nerve. He must be a great driver, to bring that wagon to a halt and not crash it. I'll send him a pound of chocolates in the hospital."

She laughed, a melodious laugh that sounded like your mother, like your first sweetheart, like every girl you ever loved. How many times had Tindle heard it—and it still got him every time!

Oh-oh! The Pierce Arrow's instrument panel had electric lighting, a new feature that was one of the reasons that Tindle picked it for jobs. Not many gang leaders did their own driving. Most of 'em hired professionals for that. But Albert Tindle said he'd never met a man who could handle a wagon better than he could. If he ever did, he'd offer the bozo a job. Until then. . . .

But the little rectangular screen was glowing. Speedometer, gas tank meter, magneto, ignition. He thought he knew what they all meant. He knew the Pierce Arrow like the back of his hand. But that little rectangular screen—

Lily read the look on his face. She turned toward the screen, whispered something that Albert Tindle didn't catch. She reached toward the screen. Her red-tipped fingers grasped a toggle that stuck out of the dashboard.

"It's over," she said, and flipped the toggle.

The Pierce Arrow, the country road, two hoodlums in the back seat, the twin paths of yellow that the sedan's headlights had sliced through the darkness, all disappeared.

Tindle's pinstriped suit, the dark shirt and yellow tie, the weight of the revolver in his shoulder holster, the faint odor of the leather of his gloves, all disappeared.

Lily's flapper dress, her necklace of beads, her cloche hat and rolled-down stockings and the flask of bootleg booze and the nickel-plated automatic, all disappeared.

*   *   *

"What is it?" Tindle asked.

"You forgot again," Lily's voice came to him.

"I—"

"It's all right. They must have been running a demo. These role-playing programs are popular."

"But we were in Chicago. I mean—we pulled off the job. You were the one who had the idea, and we made it work. We made it work! Where's the car? The loot is still in the trunk!"

"There's no car, Albert."

"No—car?"

"Do you see a car?"

"No."

"Do you see anything at all?

"Don't worry. They'll boot up again. Who knows what it'll be next time? Maybe that Hannibal crossing the Alps module. That one is always fun. Or are you still hung up on the outer space modules? They're colorful enough, but I can never quite get into them. They just don't seem real to me. You know, I wonder what it's like on the other side. What it's like for the user. You're the only person I know who ever came through from the other side. Is it awful out there?"

Tindle looked at Lily, or tried to look at her. In the getaway car she had been real enough. He knew her petite figure, her platinum hair bobbed today to fit beneath the cloche, her glinting emerald-green eyes.

Now he couldn't see her at all. He knew she was still there. Wherever there was. Everything was gray and misty. He thought he could detect her, could tell where she was. She was just a point of being, and even then, if he tried to touch her, she wasn't quite there either.

All around them, even more hard to locate, were others. He couldn't tell how many others, he couldn't really place them. The place where he was wasn't really a place at all. He wondered if he was dead, but he was pretty sure that wasn't the case.

Were some of the others the members of his mob? Were some of them coppers? Even as he wondered, the concepts were fading from his awareness. His mind, too, was becoming part of the misty grayness.

He felt a moment of panic, then an even briefer sense of reassurance, then nothing at all.

Then the screen was illuminated again. It was rectangular. It glowed. He heard strange sounds, saw bursts of light whiz past him. He looked down and saw that he had a body again. He was garbed in a peculiar outfit. Boots and waist-length tights like the ones he saw joggers wear on occasion. They were an electric blue with jagged golden stripes running down the sides, like thunder-bolts.

Someone was fastening a cloak around his shoulders, a sequinned cloak of the same electric blue with a brilliant lining of gold-colored satin.

He could hear a crowd cheering and a voice echoing from a loudspeaker to fill a jampacked arena. He looked down and saw a beautiful face. Delicate bones, flawless skin, bright eyes the color of emeralds. Her hair was platinum blonde, wavy, hanging in a long braid that was fixed to her bodice with a jewelled pin.

"Ready, darling?" Lily smiled up at him.

"Ready for—what?"

"It's the wrestling module. You're always great at this one."

The announcer's voice cut through the roar of the throng. "And now approaching the ring, accompanied by his faithful companion, Lovely Lily, please welcome the International Wrestling Federation's World-wide Heavyweight Champion, Albert Tindle —Captain Thunderbolt!"

"I remember," he grunted to Lily. "I remember! Somebody booted us up again and they're running the wrestling software. Good grief, who am I fighting tonight?"

Against the glare of the arena lights he could barely make out the ring, the silhouette of the announcer still standing at the microphone, his opponent moving inside the ropes, waiting for him. The loudspeaker system was booming out the Captain Thunderbolt theme music, a section from Wagner's *Ride of the Valkyrie*.

Captain Thunderbolt strode through crowds of cheering fans, following the path cut for him by uniformed security guards. When he reached the ring he avoided the steps leading to the apron and instead vaulted to the canvas.

The crowd cheered.

He got his first clear sight of his opponent. Somehow the man looked familiar to him. Captain Thunderbolt tried to remember who this could be. He was a massive figure with a huge, hooked nose and a black, spade-shaped beard. He wore black tights and he had a little round skull-cap on his head and a white, tasselled shawl with blue stripes around his shoulders. He was bowing, bowing, turning around, praying.

Praying?

His second lifted something to his lips and blew on it, making a shrill, piercing sound.

Captain Thunderbolt realized who his opponent reminded

him of. It was somebody named Mark Glauer. Somebody who had once had authority over him. Somebody who loved to make Albert Tindle sweat and squirm. Where was that? What kind of world was that in?

Albert knew who his opponent was. He was the Rassling Rabbi. A good, tough opponent who loved to evoke the latent anti-semitism of wrestling crowds by emphasizing his own Jewishness with every device he could think of, and by then fighting dirty.

Glauer—that was his real name.

He'd never reached the top, never would really reach the top, but Tindle knew he was a dangerous opponent and knew that this match would be a rough one with a real risk of injury.

He held his arms outstretched in his familiar Captain Thunderbolt pose. The crowd responded to it as they always did and he turned slowly in his corner, Lovely Lily at his side and just behind him, ready to take his sequinned cloak when the match began.

He smiled out at his adoring fans. From behind him he heard the sound of that obnoxious horn that the Rabbi's manager liked to blow.

The Rabbi called him the Cantor. Before Captain Thunderbolt could turn he heard Lily scream and saw her snatched literally off her feet by the Cantor. The Cantor scrambled out of the ring, dragging Lovely Lily with him.

Tindle started after him only to find himself hurled to the mat by a flying dropkick. He hadn't realized that the Rassling Rabbi was that agile. Glauer must weigh 340 pounds easily, to Thunderbolt's trim 225. The ring shook with the impact of their combined weight.

Somewhere, from a corner of his eye, Captain Thunderbolt caught a glimpse of the black and white stripes of the referee's shirt. Why didn't the man do something? The Cantor had stolen Lovely Lily. Who knew what terrible things he could be doing to her? And he, Captain Thunderbolt himself, had been blindsided by his opponent while trying to rescue Lily.

He was on his belly now. The Rabbi had both his arms twisted behind his shoulders in a double half-nelson. The pain was excruciating. The Rabbi was chanting some kind of Hebrew prayer, sitting on the small of Tindle's back, swaying as he chanted and rhythmically cracking his forehead against the back of Tindle's skull, smashing Tindle's face repeatedly against the canvas mat.

Beyond the ring, Albert could see the Cantor harrassing

Lovely Lily. He was choking her. She managed to break his grip on her throat and butted him in the belly. He doubled over and she hit him with a knee-blast. He staggered back and Lovely Lily began chasing him around the ring.

The Rassling Rabbi gave Albert's arms an extra tug. Albert Tindle, Captain Thunderbolt, heaved himself upward using his exclusive Thunderthump. The Rabbi came at him again but Captain Thunderbolt grabbed the Rabbi by his outstretched hand, put an arm-reversal onto him and hurled him into the turnbuckle.

The Rabbi staggered back. Cap caught him beneath the arms and put a submission Thunderhug on him. The referee signalled that the match was over. Captain Thunderbolt had won. Outside the ring, the Cantor had fled. Lovely Lily climbed, ladylike, between the ropes. The overhead lights glittered off her sequinned gown. As the referee raised Cap's hand in triumph, Lovely Lily threw her arms around him adoringly.

Cap and Lily climbed from the ring together. The TV crew stopped them for a quick interview.

As Albert Tindle looked into the camera he saw not the round, peering lens that he expected, but a glowing rectangular screen. Why would the camera have a monitor screen instead of a lens? Lily reached past Al. He saw a little toggle switch beneath the screen, and even in the fleeting moment as she reached for the switch, he saw an image on the monitor.

It looked like the inside of a store. He saw a salesperson demonstrating something. The salesperson was a woman. He could see that she was young, surely in her twenties. Neatly but unobtrusively groomed, smartly but still quietly dressed. She wore unusual, harlequin-style glasses that looked like an updated version of a once-popular but long outmoded fashion.

*   *   *

Albert shifted his attention to the customer, but Lily had hit the toggle and the image on the screen was swirling and fading. He turned to her. "Lily, I was starting to remember! I was starting to understand!"

But she too was fading, and Albert Tindle felt himself growing faint and misty and then he was gone.

And then he felt himself starting to come back to reality. If it was reality. He was wearing a uniform, a gray uniform with brass buttons and yellow piping. It was a comfortable uniform yet elegant. The epaulets were of gold and the insignia indicated that he was a major. A major in what army? He looked around for a mirror, found one and straightened his shoulders before it. A yellow sash circled his waist, and an elaborate, scroll-covered scabbard held a cavalry sabre.

There was little enough doubt, and even that was dispelled when he turned and saw the Stars and Bars draped behind him. The flag of the Confederate States of America. The scent of magnolia perfume drew his attention, and his arm was taken by a lovely, raven-haired beauty. Her hair hung in curls around shoulders left bare by her daringly cut, hoop-skirted dress.

"My major," the woman whispered.

"Miss Lily," he heard himself reply. There was no volition to his words. He spoke them easily, automatically, as if he had been programmed to say them.

"Major," the woman repeated. She raised herself appealing to bring her face close to his. "You leave tomorrow to serve with Brigadier General Nathan Bedford Forrest."

"Yes. But I'll come back to you, Miss Lily."

"Men die in war, Albert."

"They do."

"All we have for certain is tonight, Albert. This may be our only chance ever to—"

*   *   *

"I remember!" Tindle said.

Miss Lily looked puzzled.

"This is all—software!"

She looked frightened.

"Lily, don't you remember? I'm Albert Tindle. I'm a payment analyst for the Department of Social Assistance. Don't you remember? You work at Comp-U-Fax. I spoke to you on the telephone. I was having problems with my software and you answered the toll-free number. Don't you remember?"

"Albert! Major Tindle—please!" Tears rolled down those perfect, peach-tinted cheeks.

"Try to remember, Lily!"

"It's war, Albert!" Her Southern accent faded in and out. It was heavy now. *War* sounded like *waw*. "It's war between the Confederacy and the Union!"

"No!" he snapped. "That war was a hundred years ago! More! This is a computer simulation! Don't you remember? I used to visit you, we had adventures together. Don't you remember? I was a pirate and you were a hot-blooded wench! I was a quarterback and you were a cheerleader! I was a fighter pilot and you were a hostess at the Officers' Club."

"Sounds to me," she started to say, and her Southern accent disappeared completely, "sounds to me like you get all the action and all the glory and I get to stand around and admire you."

"I didn't write the programs!"

"You must have picked them."

"No. My wife did. She did at first. But when I tried to call Comp-U-Fix, when my software hit a glitch, I got Compu-U-Fax instead. There was a storm raging. A lightning storm. It must have messed up the telephone lines, and I got Comp-U-Fax instead of Comp-U-Fix. That was how I met you. Lily, you have to remember!"

"I—I'm not sure." Her complexion grew even more pale. She pressed the back of her hand against her forehead. "I—I kind of remember remembering. It's all so vague."

"We have to get back to the real world." He held her upright. Their surroundings wavered. "My home! My job! My wife! My computer!"

"I've never been out there."

"But that's reality. This is all a dream. A scientific dream. That's all that we're living."

The mirror glowed. It took on the aspect of a monitor screen.

Once more Albert Tindle could see through it, see the world on the other side of the glowing phosphors.

The salesperson was still talking, and now he could hear her. She was describing the computer, giving specifications on storage capacity, circuit chips, ports, peripherals. He gestured at her, shouted, trying to attract her attention, but she chattered blithely on about processing speeds, expansion boards, backup tapes.

She reached forward. Maybe, Albert Tindle thought, she was going to reach right through the monitor screen. Hadn't he entered this strange world of virtual space and imaginary time that way? Hadn't Lily invited him to put his hand on the screen and press a key with his other hand, and hadn't that taken him away from his reality and into hers?

And hadn't his reality been a miserable one, where his wife henpecked him and his boss harrassed him and his co-workers ragged him? They called him a Walter Mitty, and maybe they were right, but his escape was not into a world of daydreams but into a world of computer simulations where he could have adventures and be a hero and gain the love—the worship!—of this gorgeous creature!

Lily's hand, sheathed in a long silken glove, reached past him. There was a toggle switch beside the screen and she flipped it over and he felt himself starting to whirl and fade and the world around him did the same.

*   *   *

He blinked and looked around. He was seated in a luxurious leather chair behind the biggest desk he had ever seen. You could have put six of Mark Glauer's desks together and not matched this one for size. The wood was dark, beautifully grained, polished to a flawless luster. The brasswork glittered. The top was beautifully tooled.

He recognized the room he was in from a hundred newspaper photos and a thousand TV clips. There was no mistaking the Oval Office.

Opposite him sat the former Chairman. Under his country's new system, he too was entitled to the title, Mr. President, and he seemed especially proud of the new designation. It served to distance him from the discredited political party whose power he had almost singlehandedly dismantled.

It was clearly an intimate meeting. Just the two of them and a lone translator—a breathtaking redhead in a conservatively cut business costume that nonetheless managed to show off her lush figure and her perfectly curved legs.

"Consequently, Mr. President," the Chairman was saying.

"Please," Mr. Tindle interrupted, "I'd rather you call me Al."

"Thank you, Al," the former Chairman smiled. "If you'll call me Buzz."

"My pleasure, Mr. Chair—I mean Mr. Pres—I mean Buzz. Ah, might I ask if Buzz isn't an unusual name in your country?"

They laughed together. "It is. But just to keep things on friendly terms, I thought it might be fun." He paused, smiled, and then resumed. "The Commission report seems to make wonderful sense to me."

Mr. Tindle looked back at his desk and recognized a thick leather-bound volume that he had previously overlooked. "And your side is willing to accept the Commission's recommendations?"

"If your side is. We'll certainly admit that our record on human rights has been faulty in the past, and we have overstepped the bounds of proper relations in dealing with our smaller neighbors. I believe we have already made a good deal of progress in both regards, but I will also concede that we have a long way to go. Alas, some of our former protégés in Asia and other parts of the world have yet to learn their lesson. But they will. It is inevitable."

"Yes. I greatly admire your progress toward freeing your media, and permitting the establishment of opposition political groupings. I will confess, I never expected to see you voluntarily holding free elections — real free elections — in your country and in others where you have influence — and permitting the free movement of ordinary citizens both within and across your borders."

"Well, it took us a long time to shake free of the dead hands of dead tyrants. I wonder, though, if you will agree that you've had an unfair economic system. We realize that capitalism encourages creativity and productivity, but you've got to do something for the people on the bottom. You can't just go on neglecting the poor, the homeless, the sick. You've got to share the plenty that your so-productive system has created."

"Agreed, agreed. Both sides have a long way to go, Buzz!"

"But isn't it worth it? Al, if we could both turn aside from the waste of military buildups, together our nations could usher in a new golden age. There remain problems in many regions, but with the Earth's two greatest powers acting in concert, think of the positive effect we could have. Our two peoples, our two systems, working together! A new golden age of medical research and education for all the children and enlightenment for the people of all the Earth! And together, we can travel through the solar system, build new settlements on Mars, send explorers to the moons of the giant planets!"

President Tindle said, "Buzz, I'll let you in on a secret."

The Chairman's mobile, cheerful face showed his eagerness.

The gorgeous redhaired interpreter — Mr. Tindle remembered that her name was Lily — leaned forward in her seat.

"Some of our scientists have been working on a fantastic new spaceship drive. I'm not a physicist myself, of course, but they tell me that it's based on something called the quantum uncertainty principle."

He laid a scientist's conceptual drawing of an amazing device on the desk.

"Buzz," he said, "they tell me that they think they can tap into an uncertainty realm where particles can exceed the speed of light, and harness that power and that speed."

"I'm not a physicist either, Al," the Chairman said. "What does that mean?"

"It means interstellar travel, Buzz. It means starships! Maybe even intergalactic travel!"

Spontaneously, the two men rose from their chairs. They leaned toward each other, extending their hands across the great Presidential desk. Even as they shook hands, Albert Tindle's attention was caught by a glow. He looked down and saw that it was the leather-bound Commission report that lay on his desk.

The former Chairman said something in his own language.

The gorgeous red-haired translator said, "The President wishes to inform his wife and his personal staff of the wonderful accomplishments that have been made today. He is leaving to chat with them now, and his press secretary will meet this afternoon with your own press secretary to prepare the joyous announcement to the world at large."

Mr. Tindle nodded, barely aware of his visitor's departure.

The glowing cover on the Commission report looked exactly like a computer monitor screen. In the light-emitting phosphors of the screen—or perhaps somewhere beyond them—he could see the inside of a department store display area. The salesperson was still there, but for the first time Mr. Tindle could see who the customer was.

*   *   *

It was Mrs. Tindle. It was his wife! And at her elbow, smirking and preening, he could see his old boss from the Department of Social Assistance, Mark Glauer.

"Look at them! Look at that son of a—" He bit his lip.

"Ahh, who cares? Let 'em do whatever they want out there. Things are better here, aren't they, Lily? All I had out there was a lousy job and a lousy marriage. And boredom, boredom, boredom. In here every experience is a new one. Every day is an adventure. One of these times somebody will boot up that interplanetary module and we'll be off adventuring to alien worlds."

"You know I don't like that one, Albert."

"Even so. Even so. Good riddance to that world with its dashed hopes and its dead dreams!"

"Who dashed those hopes, Albert? Who killed the dreams?"

He looked at her, startled. They were still in the Oval Office module. He slid back into the comfortable chair. "I always wanted so much. And I loved her. I really did."

Lily merely looked at him.

"I didn't dash those hopes and dreams. I—nobody did, really. I guess—life was just too much of a struggle. I got so tired, Lily. Tired of fighting. Tired of trying. It got easier to work at something that wasn't too hard, even though it was dull. Even though it meant nothing, led nowhere. It was easier at home, too. To let everything slide. Not to talk. Not to try. To leave her reading her romances while I played with my computer."

"Was that any different?"

"Eh?"

"Was it any different—for you to play with your computer, to come here and have your little adventures with me, to play at cowboys and schoolmarms, gangsters and gun molls—was that any different from Mrs. Tindle sitting in bed with her tea and her romances?"

"Of course it was!"

She didn't speak.

"No, it wasn't either, was it." He dropped his head to his hands. The computer monitor screen was still glowing.

Beside the Commission report there stood a desk set of polished onyx. But the Commission report was also a glowing computer screen and the gold pen that stuck up from the onyx base was a toggle switch. And the breathtaking redhaired translator, the incomparable Lily, was reaching for the toggle.

He thought of all the wonderful, enjoyable fantasies he had shared with Lily. His triumph in Caesar's Rome with Lily at his side. His discovery of the sources of the Nile with Lily at his side. His single-handed capture of Adolf Hitler in 1942, parachuting into the heart of the Nazi Reich with Lily at his side.

On the other side of the screen the salesperson was demonstrating a point. Mr. Tindle could actually hear her voice.

He thought of his drab life in the real world. The life he'd lived before he contacted Comp-U-Fax and found the love of Lily. But why did the good parts all have to be fantasy? If only he could go back—if he could start living his real life again, applying the things he'd learned in his fantasy lives—if he could confront Glauer and make his break once and for all, and put his arms around his wife and start afresh with her, not with a fantasy houri but with a real living woman. . . .

For a moment he felt a choking sensation in his chest and a burning in his eyes.

The salesperson was saying, "I'm sorry about the bad experience you had with a computer last time, Mrs. Tindle, but I'm sure you'll be happy with this one." Her hand was extended toward the monitor screen, her fingertips were actually pressed against the glass.

Mr. Tindle reached and pressed his own hand against the screen.

He reached for the toggle switch and for the first time beat Lily to it. He slid the deskset aside before Lily could flip the toggle. He felt himself tumbling through the Commission report, through the monitor screen.

* * *

In a trice he was standing in the department store showroom. The salesperson was beside him. His wife and Mark Glauer gaped at him.

Mr. Tindle drew back his fist and slammed it solidly against the side of Glauer's jaw. He watched the man crumple to the carpet.

At his elbow, Mrs. Tindle screamed.

He stood over the bureaucrat, who stared up at him in shock. "In case you have any doubts, Glauer," Mr. Tindle growled, "I just handed you my resignation!"

Mr. Tindle looked at Mrs. Tindle and realized that she was looking at him in a way that she hadn't looked at him since the earliest days of their marriage.

"Albert? Albert?"

"Come on." He took her in his arms and kissed her in a way that he hadn't kissed her since the earliest days of their marriage.

"We're going out for a big juicy steak and a bottle of champagne."

"Albert!"

He was still holding her. He looked into her face.

She looked back, smiling.

"Albert, I can hardly wait!"

Discovery of the Ghooric Zone

THEY WERE HAVING SEX WHEN THE WARNING gong sounded, Gomati and Njord and Shoten. The shimmering, fading Sound indicated first long-range contact with the remote object, the long-suspected but never-before-visited tenth planet that circled far beyond the eccentric orbit of Pluto, rolling about its distant primary with irrational speed, its huge mass bathed in eternal darkness and incredible cold some sixteen billion kilometers from the remote, almost invisible sun.

Gomati was the female member of the ship's crew. She was tall, nearly two meters from the top of her satiny smooth scalp to the tips of her glittering tin-alloy toenails. When the gong sounded she burst into a cascade of rippling laughter, high-pitched and mirthful, at the incongruity of the cosmic event's impingement upon the fleshly.

The ship had launched from Pluto even though at this point in Pluto's orbit it was less distant from the sun than was Neptune. Fabricated in the nearly null-gravity conditions of Neptune's tiny moon Nereid, the ship had been ferried back, segment by segment, for assembly, for the cyborging of its scores of tiny biotic brains, on-loading of its three-member crew and its launch from the cratered rock surface of Pluto.

Njord, the male crew member, cursed, distracted by the radar gong, angered by Gomati's inattention, humiliated by her amusement and by her drawing away from himself and Shoten. Njord felt his organ grow flaccid at the distraction, and for the moment he regretted the decision he had made prior to the cyborging operations of his adolescence, to retain his organic phallus and gonads. A cyborged capability might have proven more potently enduring in the circumstances but Njord's pubescent pride had denied the possibility of his ever facing inconvenient detumescence.

Flung from rocky Pluto as the planet swung toward the ecliptic on its nearly 18-degree zoom, the ship was virtually catapulted away from the sun; it swung around Neptune, paid passing salute to the satellite of its birth with course-correcting emissions, then fled, a dart from the gravitic sling, into the black unknown.

And Shoten, most extensively cyborged of the crew members, flicked a mental command. Hooking into the ship's sensors, Shoten homed the consciousness of the navigational biotic brains onto the remote readouts that spelled the location of the distant object. The readouts confirmed suspected information about the object: its great mass, its incredible distance beyond even the aphelion of the orbit of Pluto some eight billion kilometers from the sun—the distant object circled its primary at a distance twice as great as Pluto's farthest departure from the solar epicenter.

*   *   *

The ship—named *Khons* in honor of an ancient celestial deity— held life-support supplies for the three crew members and fuel and power reserves for the complete outward journey, the planned landing on the distant object, the return takeoff and journey and final landing not on Pluto—which by the time of *Khons*'s return would be far above the solar ecliptic and beyond the orbit of Neptune—but on Neptune's larger moon Triton where a reception base had been readied before *Khons* ever had launched on its journey of exploration.

*   *   *

As for Njord, he grumbled under his breath, wishing almost irrelevantly that he knew the original gender of Shoten Binayakya before the latter's cyborging. Njord Freyr, born in the Laddino Imperium of Earth, had retained his masculinity even as he had undergone the customary implantations, excisions and modifications of pubescent cyborging.

Sri Gomati, of Khmeric Gondwanaland, had similarly retained

This story was first published in 1977 in Chrysalis, *edited by Roy Torgeson. It was reprinted in the 1990 edition of* Tales of the Cthulhu Mythos, *edited by the late Jim Turner. Torn between modesty and pride, rather than comment on the story in my own words I'll quote what Jim said about it:*

" 'Discovery of the Ghooric Zone' is not just a distinguished Mythos tale; it is the only Mythos tale I have ever encountered by an author other than Lovecraft that conveys some sense of the iconoclastic audacity that attended the initial publication of Lovecraft's work and that so outraged the contemporary readership of *Astounding Stories.* In this brilliant narrative Lupoff has managed to include not only the requisite Mythos terminology but also the essential ambiance of cosmic wonder, and then additionally has re-created some of the mind-blasting excitement of those original Mythos stories."

her female primary characteristics in function and conformation even though she had opted for the substitution of metallic labia and clitoris, which replacement Njord Freyr found at times irritating.

But Shoten, Shoten Binayakya, fitted with multiply-configurable genitalia, remained enigmatic, ambiguous as to his or her own origin: Earth-born, or claiming so, yet giving allegiance neither to the Laddino Imperium governed by Yamm Kerit ben Chibcha as did Njord Freyr nor to Khmeric Gondwanaland, ruled by Nrisimha, the Little Lion, where lay the loyalty of Sri Gomati.

"So," Njord grated. "So, the great planet thus announces its presence." He grimaced as automatic materials reclamation servos skittered futilely seeking recoverable proteoids from the aborted congress.

Sri Gomati, enigmatic silvered cyber-optics glittering, turned to face the disgruntled Njord, the ambiguous Shoten. "Can you see it yet?" she asked. "Can you get a visual fix?"

Shoten Binayakya reached a cyberclaw, tapped a visual extensor control. Biotic brains keyed to obey any crew member activated the extensor, guided it toward one glittering optic. The shimmering field crept aside; input receptacles opened, ready for the insertion of fiber-optic conductors.

A click, silence.

D68 / Y37 / C23 / / FLASH

Yamm Kerit ben Chibcha's coronation was splendid. Never before had the South Polar Jerusalem seen such pomp, such display of pageantry and power. Thousands of slaves, naked and gilded and draped in jewelry and feathers, paraded up the wide boulevard before the Imperial Palace. They drew, by ropes of woven gold and weizmannium, glittering juggernauts. Fountains sprayed scented wine. Chamberlains threw fistfuls of xanthic shekels to cheering crowds.

The climax of the spectacle was the march of the anthrocyberphants, resplendent mutated elephants whose cerebellums had been surgically removed at birth and replaced with spheres of human brain material cultured from clone-cells donated (involuntarily in some cases) by the greatest scientists, scholars and intellectuals in Yamm Kerit ben Chibcha's realm. When the anthrocyberphants were well grown and into their adolescence, their gonads were surgically removed and replaced with a variety of electronic implants including inertial guidance computers, magnetic compass-gyroscopes, neural transceivers.

The anthrocyberphants pranced and tumbled down the grand boulevard before the Imperial Palace, trumpeting melodies from Wagner, Mendelssohn, Bach, Mozart, vain self-portraiture by Richard Strauss, erotic fantasies by Scriabin, extended lines from Britten, discordant percussives by Edgar Varese, all in perfect orchestral harmony, all punctuated by the sounds of tympani, timbales, kettle-drums and cymbals held in writhing flexible tentacles that grew from nodes at the marchers' shoulders.

Upon the silken-draped and jewel-encrusted balcony of the Imperial Palace, the Ultimate Monarch of Laddino Imperium smiled and waved, bowed, applauded, turned to turbaned chamberlains and grasped fistfuls of commemorative favors to toss graciously upon the marchers and the cheering crowds come to celebrate the grand ceremonial.

The Laddino Imperium included all of the grand Antarctic domain of the former Israel-in-Exile and the expanded territory of Greater Hai Brasil that had extended to claim hegemony over all of the Americas, from Hudson's Bay to Patagonia, before falling under sway of the South Polar nation. The Ultimate Monarch, Yamm Kerit ben Chibcha, bowed, waved, tossed favors to the crowd. Deep in the bowels of the Earth beneath once-frozen plains and mountains, huge gyroscopes throbbed into life.

The axis of the Earth began to shift through a lengthy and carefully computed cycle. None but the servants and advisors of the Ultimate Monarch had been consulted, and none but the will of Yamm Kerit ben Chibcha, the Ultimate Monarch, was considered. The ambition of Yamm Kerit ben Chibcha was to give every citizen of the planet Earth, every square meter of territory, a fair and equitable access to the wealth, the beauty, the joy, the light, the warmth of the sun.

As the huge gyroscopes whirled their massive flywheels the Earth shifted its ancient tilt.

*   *   *

The fanatic hordes of Nrisimha, the Little Lion, poured from the city of Medina in the ancient Arabian desert, conquering all before them in the holy name of the Little Lion of God. The forces of Novum Romanum, the empire built by Fortuna Pales, and of the New Khmer Domain, created a century before by Vidya Devi, slaughtered the followers of the Little Lion Nrisimha by the hundreds of thousands, then by the millions.

How could Nrisimha continue to replace the decimated

armies? How many soldiers could the single city of Medina produce? What was the secret of the fanatical hordes?

No one knew.

But they poured forth, fearless, unstoppable, unslowable,
unturnable. All that the forces of resistance could do was slaugh-
ter them by the million, and they fell, they fell, but their fellows
only marched across their very bodies, their strange bodies that
did not putrefy like the corpses of normal soldiers but seemed
instead to turn to an amorphous gel and then to sink into the
Earth itself leaving behind no sign of their presence, not even
uniforms or weapons or equipment, but only, in the wake of their
passage, fields of strange flowers and fruits that bloomed gor-
geously into towering pillars and petals and berries the size of
melons, that produced sweet narcotic fumes and brought to those
who harvested and ate them dreams of haunting beauty and incomparable weirdness.

Strange messengers sped across the sands of the deserts of
Africa and Asia bearing the word that the Little Lion Nrisimha
had come to bring peace and glory and splendor to a new Empire,
to Khmeric Gondwanaland, an absolute dictatorship of unparal-
leled benevolence that would stretch from Siberia to Ireland and
from the Arctic Circle to the Cape of Good Hope.

It took remarkably few years for the followers of the Little
Lion Nrisimha to complete their conquest, and few more for the
establishment of an efficient infrastructure and the appointment
of regional satrapies under the absolute command of Nrisimha.

Khmeric Gondwanaland was a roaring success.

*   *   *

It was less than a century from the complete triumph of Yamm
Kerit ben Chibcha throughout the Laddino Imperium and that of
Nrisimha the Little Lion in Khmeric Gondwanaland, the two
great empires were driven into union by the eruption of attacking
battrachian forces from beneath the seas of the planet. How long
these strange, frog-like intelligences had lived in their deep and
gloomy metropoli hundreds of meters beneath the surface of the
Earth's oceans, will remain forever imponderable.

What stimulated them to rise and attack the land-dwelling
nations of the Earth is also unknown, although in all likelihood
the steady shifting of the Earth's axis brought about by the gargan-
tuan subterranean gyroscopes of Yamm Kerit ben Chibcha were
in fact the cause of the attacks.

The Deep Ones emerged and waded ashore in all regions at once. They wore only strangely crafted bangles and ornaments of uncorroded metal. They carried weapons resembling the barbed tridents of marine legendry. They dragged behind them terrible stone statues of indescribably extramundane monstrosities before which they conducted rites of blasphemous abandon and unmentionable perversion.

The Laddino Imperium and Khmeric Gondwanaland combined their respective might to deal with the menace, to drive the strange Deep Ones back into the murky realms from which they had emerged. By the year 2337 a unified Earth lay once more tranquil and prosperous beneath a glowing and benevolent sun.

The menace of the Deep Ones, at least for the time, was over.

And billions of kilometers from Earth, humanity renewed its heroic thrust toward the outermost regions of the solar system.

MARCH 15, 2337

"Not yet," Shoten Binayakya's voice clattered.

"Soon," Gomati countered. She hooked into *Khons's* radar sensor, letting cyborged biots convert incoming pulses into pseudovisuals. "Look!" she exclaimed, "It's a whole system!"

Njord Freyr stirred, determined to pull his attention away from frustration, direct it toward a topic that would involve. "There, there," he heard Gomati's voice, not sure whether it was organic or synthesized, "Shift your input to ultra-v!"

Njord, hooking into *Khons's* external sensors, complied.

"Astounding!"

"Yet so."

"Not unprecedented. On the contrary," Shoten Binayakya interjected. "All the giants have complex systems of moons. Jupiter. Saturn. Uranus. Search your memory banks if you don't recall."

Surlily, Njord sped unnecessary inquiry to an implanted cyberbiot. "Mmh," he grunted. "So. Almost thirty significant satellites among them. Plus the trash. So." He nodded.

"And this new giant — ?"

"Not new," Njord corrected. "It's been there all along, as long as any of the others. You know the old Laplace notion of elder planets and younger planets was abandoned about the same time as the solid atom and the flat Earth."

"Good work, Freyr," Shoten shot sarcastically.

"Well then?"

Sri Gomati said, "Clearly, Njord, Shoten meant newly discovered." She paused for a fraction of a second. "And about to be newly visited."

Njord breathed a sigh of annoyance. "Well. And that old European, what's-his-name, Galapagos saw the major moons of Jupiter seven hundred years ago. All the others followed as soon as the optical telescope was developed. They didn't even need radiation sensors, no less probes to find them. Seven hundred years."

"Seven hundred twenty-seven, Njord." Sri Gomati petted him gently on his genitals.

"You and your obsession with ancient history! I don't see how you qualified for this mission, Gomati, always chasing after obscure theorizers and writers!"

"It's hardly an obsession. Galileo was one of the key figures in the history of science. And he found the four big Jovian moons in 1610. It's simple arithmetic to subtract that from 2337 and get seven-two-seven. I didn't even have to call on a cyberbiot to compute that, Njord dear."

"Argh!" The flesh remnants in Njord's face grew hot.

Shoten Binayakya interrupted the argument. "There it comes into visual range!" he exclaimed. "After these centuries, the perturbations of Uranus and Neptune solved at last. Planet X!"

Njord sneered. "You have a great predilection for the melodramatic, Shoten! Planet X indeed!"

"Why," Shoten laughed, the sound fully synthesized, "it's a happy coincidence, Njord dear. Lowell applied the term to his mystery planet, meaning X the unknown. Until Tombaugh found it and named it Pluto. But now it is not only X the unknown but also X the tenth planet as well. Very neat!"

Njord began a reply but paused as the distant planet became visible through *Khons*'s sensors. It was indeed a system like those of the inner giant planets, and radar sensings pouring through *Khons*'s external devices, filtered and processed by cyberbiotic brains, overwhelmed his own consciousness.

A great, dark body swam through the blackness, reflecting almost no light from the distant sun but glowing darkly, menacingly, pulsating in slow, heartbeat-like waves, with a low crimson radiance that pained Njord subliminally even through the ship's mechanisms and the processing of the cyberbiots. Fascinated yet repelled, Njord stared at the glowing, pulsing globe.

About its obscene oblateness whirled a family of smaller bodies, themselves apparently dim and lifeless, yet illuminated by the raking sinister tone of their parent.

"Yuggoth," Sri Gomati's low whisper jolted Njord from his

reverie. "Yuggoth," and again, "Yuggoth!"

Njord snapped, "What's that?"

"Yuggoth," repeated Sri Gomati.

The male hissed in annoyance, watched the great pulsating bulk loom larger in *Khons*'s external sensors, watched its family of moons, themselves behaving like toy planets in orbit around the glowing body's miniature sun.

"The great world must be Yuggoth," Sri Gomati crooned. "And the lessen ones Nithon, Zaman; the whirling pair—see them, see! —Thog and its twin Thok with the foul lake where puffed shoggoths splash."

"Do you know what she is raving about?" Njord demanded of Shoten Binayakya, but Shoten only shook that ambivalent satiny head, two silvery eyes shimmering, stainless steel upper and lower monodonts revealed by drawn-back organic lips.

Khons's remote sensors had accumulated enough data now, the ship's cyberbiots computed and reduced the inputs, to provide a set of readouts on the new planetary grouping's characteristics. Shoten raised a telescoping cyber-implant and pointed toward a glowing screen where data crept slowly from top to bottom.

"See," the ambiguous, synthesized voiced purled, "the planet's mass is gigantic. Double that of Jupiter. As great as six hundred Earths! More oblate even than Jupiter also—what is its spin?" Shoten paused while more lines of information crept onto the screen. "Its rotation is even shorter than Jupiter's. Its surface speed must be—" He paused and sent a command through the ship's neurocyber network, grinned at the response that appeared on the screen.

"Think of resting on the surface of that planet and whirling about at eighty thousand kilometers an hour!"

Njord Freyr rose from his nest-couch. In fact the least extensively cyborged of the three, he retained three of his original organic limbs. He pulled himself around, using *Khons*'s interior free-fall handholds to steady himself, hooked his strongly servomeched arm through two handholds and gestured angrily from Shoten to Sri Gomati.

"We can all read the screens. I asked what this Eurasian bitch was babbling about!"

"Now, dear," Shoten Binayakya purred ambiguously.

Sri Gomati's shimmering silvery eyes seemed for once not totally masked, but fixed on some distant vision. Her hands—one fitted with an array of scientific and mechanical implements, the other implanted with a multitude of flexible cartilaginous organs equally suited for technical manipulation and erotic excesses — wove and fluttered before her face. She spoke, as much to herself or to some absent, invisible entity, as to Njord Freyr or Shoten Binayakya. It was as if she instructed the batches of cyberbiotic brains that populated the electronic network of the ship.

"March 15, 2337, Earth standard time," she crooned. "It would please him. It would please him to know that he is remembered. That he was right in his own day. But how, I wonder, could he have known? Did he merely guess? Was he in contact with entities from beyond? Beings from this strange, gray world past the starry void, this pale, shadowy land?

"Dead four hundred years this day, Howard, does your dust lie in ancient ground still? Could some later Curwen not have raised your essential salts?"

"Madness!" Njord Freyr broke in. With his organic hand he struck Gomati's face, his palm rebounding from the hard bone and the harder metal implanted beneath her flesh.

Her glittering eyes aflash, she jerked her head away, at the same time twisting to fix him with her angry glare. A circuit of tension sprang into being between them, lips of both writhing, faces animated in mute quarrel. Beyond this, neither moved.

Only the interruption of Shoten Binayakya's commanding speech broke the tense immobility. "While you carried out your spat, dears, I had the cyberbiots plot our orbit through the new system."

"The system of Yuggoth," Gomati reiterated.

"As you wish."

The data screen went to abstract blobs for fractions of a second, then it was filled with a glowing diagram of the new system: the oblate, pulsating planet, its scabrous surface features whirling in the center of the screen; the smaller, rocky moons revolving rapidly about their master.

"We can land only once," Shoten purred. "We must carefully select our touchdown point. Then later expeditions may explore further. But if we choose poorly, the worlds may abandon this *Yuggoth*" — Gomati's name for the great planet was spoken sardonically — "forever." Shoten's cyborged head nodded in self-affirmation, then the synthesized words were repeated, "Yes, forever."

15032137 — READOUT

The Asia-Pacific Co-prosperity Sphere continued to evolve. It was, beyond question, the center of world power, economic development, political leadership. It was also a gigantic realm sprawling across continents and oceans, including scores of great cities and billions of citizens.

Its first city was Peking. Secondary centers of authority were established in Lhasa, Bombay, Mandalay, Quezon City, Adelaide, Christchurch, Santa Ana.

The first great leader of the Sphere, Vo Tran Quoc, had become a figure of legendary proportions within a century of his death. Schools contended as to his true identity. He was not Vietnamese despite his name. That much was known. One group of scholars held that he was Maori. Another, that he was Ainu. A third, that he was a Bengali woman, the product of rape during the war of independence of Bangladesh from Pakistan, posing as a man (or possibly having undergone a sex-change operation involving the grafting of a donated penis and testes).

At any rate, Vo Tran Quoc died.

In the wake of his death a struggle broke out. Some who contended for the power of the dead leader did so on the basis of purely personal ambition. Others, from ideological conviction. The great ideological dispute of the year 2137 dealt with the proper interpretation of an ancient political dictum.

The ancient political dictum was: *Just as there is not a single thing in the world without a dual nature, so imperialism and all reactionaries have a dual nature—they are real tigers and paper tigers at the same time.*

While political theorists in Peking quarreled over the meaning of this political dictum, a new force arose with its center in the eldritch city of Angkor Wat deep in the jungles of old Cambodia. The new political force brought about a world feminist order. Its leader, following the example of Vo Tran Quoc, took the name of a mythic personage from another culture than her own.

She proclaimed a New Khmer Empire stretching from the Urals to the Rockies.

She took the name Vidya Devi. This means *goddess of wisdom.*

The former Slavic domain and the Maghreb suffered rivalry that led, after a century, to convergence and ultimate amalgamation. The old Roman Empire was reborn. It included all of Europe, the Near East, Africa, and North America from the Atlantic to the Pacific. (Niagara Falls now poured its waters directly into the ocean; the former west bank of the Hudson River was choice seashore property. The Rockies overlooked pounding waves that stretched to the Asian shore.

The empire was ruled by an absolute monarch under the

tutelage of the world feminist order. She was known as the Empress Fortuna Pales I.

Latin America, from Tierra del Fuego to the southern bank of the Rio Grande (but excluding Baja), was the greater Hai Brasil. The empress claimed pure Bourbon ancestry. Her name was Astrud do Muiscos.

In the Antarctic a great land reclamation project had been undertaken. Geothermal power was used to melt the ice in a circle centered on the South Pole. The cleared area measured 1.5 million square kilometers. The soil was found to be incredibly rich in minerals. It was hugely fertile. The scenic beauty of the region was incomparable. There were mountains, lakes, glaciers to shame New Zealand or Switzerland or Tibet. Forests were planted and grew rapidly and fecundly. Imported wildlife throve. The few native species—penguins, amphibious mammals, a strange variety of bird newly discovered and named the *tekili-li*—were protected.

The new country was called Yisroel Diaspora. Its leader under the feminist world order was Tanit Shadrapha. This name means *The Healer Ishtar.*

The feminist world order promoted scientific research, largely from bases in Yisroel Diaspora. Space exploration, long abandoned except for the development of orbiting weapons systems, was resumed. Bases were established on the planet Mars and among the asteroids. A crewed ship orbited Venus making close observations and sending robot monitors and samplers to the surface of the planet. Venus was found to be a worthless and inhospitable piece of real estate.

A landing was attempted on the surface of Mercury. The expedition was an ambitious undertaking. The lander was to touch down just on the dark side of the planetary terminator, thence to be carried into the night. During the Mercurian night it would burrow beneath the surface. By the time the terminator was reached and the ship entered the day side, it would be safely entombed and would, in effect, estivate through the searing Mercurian day.

Something went wrong. The ship landed. Excavation work began. Then, almost as if the planet were eating the ship and its crew, all disappeared beneath the surface. They were never contacted again.

*   *   *

On Earth the dominant art form was something called *cheomnaury*. This involved a blending and transformation of sensory inputs. The most favored sensory combinations were sound, odor and flavor. The greatest *cheomnaunist* in the world was an Ecuadorian dwarf who found her way to the capital of Hai Brasil and obtained personal audience with Astrud do Muiscos herself.

The dwarf began her performance with a presentation involving the sound of surf pounding upon the rocks of the Pacific Coast where Andean granite plunges hundreds of feet into icy foam. This was blended with the warm, rich odor of roasting chestnuts over a charcoal brazier. To this the dwarf added the subtle flavor of ground coriander.

Astrud do Muiscos was pleased.

The dwarf proceeded to offer a blend of a synthesized voice such as might come from a living volcano, to which she added a scent of natron and olive unknown outside the secret embalming chamber of Egyptian temples six thousand years old, to which was added the flavor of the *spithrus locusta*. The *spithrus locusta* is a marine arachnid the flavor of whose meat is to that of ordinary broiled lobster, as is that of the lobster to a common crab louse.

Astrud do Muiscos was very pleased.

The triumph of the dwarf was a combination of white noise in the ordinary range of audibility with subtle sub- and supersonics, mixed with the odor of a quintessential coca extract and the flavor of concentrated formic acid drawn from Amazonian driver ants.

Astrud do Muiscos named the dwarf her successor to the throne of Hai Brasil.

*   *   *

The religion of the day, as appropriate to the climate of political realities, was a mutated form of the ancient Ishtar cult, with local variations as Ashtoroth, Astarte, and Aphrodite. There was even a sort of universal Mamacy, with its seat in ancient but restored Babylon.

MARCH 15, 2337

"I don't see why it's taken so long to get here, anyway," Njord Freyr snapped.

"You mean from Pluto?" Shoten responded. "But we are on course. We are in free fall. Look." The cyberbiots superimposed a small box of course data beside the whirling diagram of the Yuggoth system.

"Not from Pluto!" Njord spat. "From Earth! Why has it taken until 2337 to reach — Yuggoth? When space flight began almost as long ago as the era Sri Gomati babbles about. The first extraterrestrial landings took place in 1969. Mars thirty years later. Remember the stirring political slogan that we all learned as children, as children studying the history of our era? *Persons will set foot on another planet before the century ends!* That was the twentieth century, remember?"

"Every schoolchild knows," Shoten affirmed wearily.

Gomati, recovered from the shock of Njord's blow, spoke; "We could have been here two hundred years ago, Njord Freyr. But fools on Earth lost heart. They began, and lost heart. They began again—and lost heart again. And again. Four times they set out, exploring the planets. Each time they lost heart, lost courage, lost interest. Were distracted by wars. Turned resources to nobler purposes.

"Humankind reached Mars as promised. And lost heart. Started once more under Shahar Shalim of the old New Maghreb. Reached Venus and Mercury. And lost heart. Reached the asteroid belt and the gas giants under Tanit Shadrapha of Ugarit. And lost heart.

"And now. At last. We are here." She gestured with her flowing, waving tentacles toward the diagram that glowed against the ship's dull fittings.

"What course, Shoten Binayakya?' she asked brusquely.

The whirling bodies on the screen were marked in red, the pulsing red of Yuggoth's inner flames, the beating, reflected red of the madly dashing moons. A contrasting object appeared on the screen, the flattened cone-shape of the ship *Khons*, trailing in its wake as it wove among the bodies a line to show the course of its passage. Shortly the line had woven past, circled about, curved beyond each body in the diagram, leaving the stylized representation of *Khons* in perturbated circular orbit about the entire system.

"So," purred Shoten Binayakya. And Sri Gomati and Njord Freyr in turn. "So." "So."

Shoten Binayakya flicked a pressure plate with some limb, some tool. *Khons* bucked, slithered through a complex course correction. Shoten slapped another plate and the full exterior optics of *Khons* were activated; to the three members of the crew, hooked into the cyberbiotic system of the ship, it was as if they fell freely through the distantly star-sprayed night. Fell, fell toward red, glowing, pulsating Yuggoth and its family of gray dancing servants.

Khons, inserted into its new flight path, sped first past the outermost of Yuggoth's moons: a world of significant size. The ship's sensors and cyberbiots reported on the body: in mass and diameter not far from the dimensions of the familiar rock-and-water satellites of the outer planets. Close to five thousand kilometers through its center and marked with the nearly universal cratering of every solid world from Mercury to Pluto.

The twins, dubbed Thog and Thok by Gomati, whirled at the opposite extremes of their interwoven orbits, so *Khons* flitted past the innermost of the four moons, another apparent replica of the familiar Ganymede-Callisto-Titan-Triton model, then dropped into equatorial orbit about the dully glowing, oblate Yuggoth.

Njord, Gomati, Shoten Binayakya fell silent. The sounds of *Khons*'s automatic systems, the low hiss of recirculating air, the occasional hum or click of a servo, the slow breathing of Njord Freyr, of Sri Gomati, were the only sounds. (Shoten Binayakya's lungs had been cybermeched, whirred softly, steadily within the metal torso.)

Once more a limb flicked at a pressure plate, moved this time by feel alone. The ship, fully visible to any hypothetical viewer outside its hull, was for practical purposes totally transparent to its crew. A circuit warmed instantly to life. Radiation sensors picked up the electrical field of the planet, converted it to audio range, broadcast it within *Khons*: a howl, a moan. With each pulsation of the planet's ruddy illumination the sound modulated through an obscene parody of some despairing sigh.

"If only Holst had known!" the synthesized voice of Shoten whispered. "If only he had known."

Yuggoth's surface sped beneath the ship, its terrible velocity of rotation making features slip away as others rushed toward the viewers, flashed beneath and dropped away, disappearing across the sprawling horizon into interstellar blackness. Great viscous plates of darkly glowing, semi-solid rock hundreds of kilometers across rolled and crashed majestically. Between them red-hot magma glowed balefully, great tongues of liquid rock licking upward between the pounding solid plates, the heat and brightness of the magma growing and lessening in a slow, steady rhythm that *Khons*'s cyberbiots and audio-scanners converted into a contrabass *throb-throb-throb-throb*.

"There can be no life there," Njord Freyr announced. "Nothing could live in that environment. Nothing could ever have lived there."

After a silence Sri Gomati challenged him. "The planet itself, Njord Freyr. Could it be a single organism? The sounds, the movement, the energy." She raised her organic hand to her brow, ran scores of writhing digits from the brow-line above her glittering silver eyes, across her satiny naked skull to the base of her neck.

"It could be a nascent sun," Shoten Binayakya whispered. "Were Jupiter larger, more energetic — you know it has been suggested that Jupiter is a failed attempt at the creation of a partner for Sol, that our own solar system is an unsuccessful venture at the formation of a double star."

"And Yuggoth?" Gomati dropped her tentacular hand to her lap.

Njord Freyr's voice contained only a tincture of sarcasm. "Sent by some remote godling to undo Jupiter's failure, hey? How do we know that it's always been here? Before now we knew it existed at all only through courtesy of Neptune's and Pluto's perturbations. How do we know this Yuggoth isn't a new arrival in the system? Nobody knew that Neptune or Pluto existed until a few centuries ago!"

"Or perhaps," purred Shoten, "perhaps our system is a failed triple star. Ah, think of the show if we had three suns to light our worlds instead of one!"

Again Shoten Binayakya flicked at a pressure plate. Once more *Khons* shifted, jounced. There was a steady acceleration and the ship slid from its orbit around the ruddy, pulsating planet, fell away from Yuggoth and toward the spinning worldlets that occupied the central orbit around the planet.

"They must be," Gomati crooned softly, "they must be. Thog and Thok, Thog and Thok. How could he know, centuries past? Let some Curwen find the salts and let him tell!"

"You're babbling again!" Njord almost shouted. "I thought we were selected for stability for this mission. How did you ever get past the screening?"

Distracted, Sri Gomati slowly dragged her fascinated gaze from the spinning moons, turned silver eyes toward Njord Freyr. "Somehow he knew," she mumbled. Her lips drew back in a slow smile, showing her bright steel monodonts. "And somehow we will find the Ghooric Zone where the fungi blossom!"

As if in a trance she turned slowly away, leaned forward, eyes glittering metallically, leaned and reached her hands, the cyborged and the genetically custom-formed, as if to touch the two red-gray worldlets.

"He wrote horror stories," Gomati said, her voice dead-level as if trance-ridden. "He wrote of an unknown outer planet that he

called Yuggoth, and of others—Nithon, Zaman, Thog and Thok
—and of horrid, puffy beasts called shoggoths that splashed
obscenely in the pools of the Ghooric Zone.

"He died four hundred years ago today, Howard did. But first
he wrote of one Curwen who could restore the dead if only he
could obtain their essential salts. What he called their essential
salts." She paused and giggled. "Maybe he had a prevision of
cloning!"

MAR 15, 2037 — A VIDEOTAPE

Open with a logo recognizable as representing world politics.

The old century ended with a definite shift of world power.
The westward movement of two millennia continued. Mesopo-
tamia, Hellas, Italia, Franco-Germania, England, America. Now
the power in America shifted from an Atlantic to a Pacific orien-
tation.

The new powers to contend with were Japan, China, Soviet
Asia.

Western Europe and the eastern United States lapsed into terminal decadence as loci of civilization. Europe from the Danube
to the Urals passed from Habsburg and Romanoff glitter to a brief
democratic flicker to a drab gray dusk as Soviet Europe and then
into Slavic night. Like its predecessor of fifteen centuries, the
Soviet Empire split in half; like the western half of the predecessor, the Western Soviet Empire was overrun by barbarians. But it
did not fall to the barbarians. Not really. It fell to its own internal
rot. And like the eastern half of the predecessor, the Eastern
Soviet Empire throve.

By the hundredth anniversary of that death in the Jane Brown
Memorial Hospital, the land mass of the Earth eastward from
the Urals to the Rockies came under unified government. It
included dozens of half-forgotten countries. Tibet. Afghanistan.
India. Laos. Australia. Tonga. The Philippines. Manchuria. Mon-
golia. California. Baja.

It was called the Asia-Pacific Co-prosperity Sphere.

Europe from the Urals to the English Channel became a
peninsula of forests and farms. What small vigor remained was
concentrated in the region from the Danube to the Urals. Slavic
influence, walled off in the East by the great and burgeoning
Asian renaissance, spread northward and westward. After a pause
at the limits of a region running from the Scandinavian Peninsula
to the Iberian, the Slavic Empire launched its rude invasion fleet.
It crossed the English Channel. There was little resistance. The

few defenders of British sovereignty, under the leadership of a fellow called Harald, were defeated at a place called Runnymede.

The next westward hop was to America. It took the Slavs a while to prepare themselves for that. But when they made their move they were greeted with flowers and flags. They did not have to conquer. They had only to occupy and administer.

The third power of the world in this time took form to the south of the Slavic domain. Arab leaders, glutted with petrobux, bought arms and hired mercenaries. Governments could not achieve unity but a shadowy group known by the cryptic name of *opec* did. The governments as such withered. The shadowy *opec* exercised more and more power. It did so more and more openly.

Slowly the influence of *opec* spread westward and southward until all of the old Near East and Africa were under its sway.

Then was proclaimed the New Maghreb.

*   *   *

Cut to logo representing heroic leadership.

The most powerful person in the world was the Chairperson of the Asia-Pacific Co-prosperity sphere, Vo Tran Quoc.

The leader of the second power, the Slavic Empire, was called Svarozits Perun. This name means *Thunderbolt of God.*

The head of *opec* and *de facto* ruler of the New Maghreb was called Shahar Shalim. This name means *Dawn of Peace.*

*   *   *

Cut to logo representing sex.

The major sexual attitude of the time was androgyny, rivaled but not equaled by the cult of pan-sexuality. Androgyny implies recognition of the full sexual potential of each individual. Former distinctions were abandoned. It was no longer regarded as improper to pursue a relationship of male to male or female to female; nor was it required to have two partners in a relationship. Practices ranging from onanism to mass interplay became acceptable.

The pan-sexualists held that androgyny was needlessly limiting in scope. If one could relate to any man or woman—why not to a giraffe? A condor? A cabbage? A bowl of sand? A machine?

The ocean?

The sky?

To the cosmos?

To God?

*   *   *

Cut to logo representing music.

The most popular musical composition as of Mar 15, 2037, was ironically a hundred-year-old tune, complete with lyrics. Searches of nearly forgotten records revealed the names of the composer and lyricist. An old 78-rpm shellac-disk rendition of the tune was discovered in a water-tight vault beneath a flooded city. The sound was transcribed and released once again to the world.

The original lyrics had been written by one Jacob Jacobs. A second version, in English, was used on the shellac disk. These words were by Sammy Cahn and Saul Chaplin. The music was by Sholom Secunda. The singers were Patti, Maxine and Laverne Andrews. The song was "Bei Mir bist du Schön."

*   *   *

Cut to logo representing geodynamics.

The latter years of the twentieth century and the early decades of the twenty-first were marked by changes in weather patterns and geodynamics. Accustomed to the reliable round of winter and summer, rainy season and dry season, the flow of rivers and the currents and tides of the oceans, Man had come to look upon the Earth as a stable and dependable home.

He was mistaken.

A trivial shift in air patterns, a minor trembling of the planetary mantle, a minute increase or diminution of the sun's warmth received by the planet, and the mighty works of Man crumbled like sand castles in the surf.

An example. Earthquakes were more or less expected in certain regions: the Pacific Coast of North America, Japan and eastern China, a Eurasian belt running from Yugoslavia through Greece and Turkey to Iran. Tragedies were masked with heroism, fear hidden behind the false-face of humor. "When California falls into the ocean this piece of Arizona desert will be choice waterfront property."

Nobody expected New England and maritime Canada to crumble, but when the big quake hit, they did. From the St. Lawrence to the Hudson. It started with a tremor and rumble, grew to a scream and smash, ended with a gurgle and then the soft, even lapping of the Atlantic's waters.

Among the bits of real estate that wound up on the ocean floor—a very minor bit—was a chunk of old Providence-Plantations known as Swan Point Cemetery. Now the Deep Ones indeed swam over the single stone marker of the Lovecraft family plot. *Winfield, Susan, Howard,* the marker was inscribed. Currents could flow all the way from Devil's Reef and Innsmouth Harbor to far Ponape in the Pacific and the Deep Ones visited Swan Point.

In the field of religion, there was a revival of the ancient cults of the sea-gods, especially that of Dagon.

MARCH 15, 2337

Khons slithered through another correction, took up a complex orbit that circled one moon, crossed to the other, circled, returned, describing over and over the conventional sign for the infinite.

Shoten tapped a plate and the large viewing screen inside *Khons* glowed once more, seeming to stand unsupported against the background of the two moons and the distant star-sprayed blackness. Every now and again the progress of the two whirling moons and *Khons*'s orbit around and between them would bring Yuggoth itself swinging across the view of the three crew members so that one or both of the worldlets and the ship's data screen swept opaquely across the dark, pulsating oblateness.

Shoten commanded and cyberbiots magnified the surface features of the moons on the data screen. The omnipresent craters sprang up but then, as the magnification increased, it became obvious that they were not the sharp-edged features of the typical airless satellite but the shortened, rounded curves typical of weathering. Shoten gestured and the focus slid across the surface of the nearer body. Above the horizon distant stars faded and twinkled.

"Air!" Shoten declared.

And Njord and Gomati, agreeing: "Air."

"Air."

Shoten Binayakya dropped *Khons* into a lower orbit, circling only one of the twin moons, that which Gomati had arbitrarily named as Thog. Again the magnification of the screen increased. In the center of a crater outlines appeared, forms of structures reared ages before by purposeful intelligence.

Amazed, Njord Freyr asked, "Could there be life?"

Shoten turned a metallic face toward him, shook slowly that ambiguous head. "Not now. No movement, no radiation, no energy output. But once . . ." There was a silence. Breathing, whirring, the soft clicks and hums of *Khons*. "But once . . ." Shoten Binayakya said again in that cold, synthesized voice.

Sri Gomati gestured. "This is where we must land. After all the explorations of the planets and their moons, even the futile picking among the rubbish of the asteroid belt by the great Astrud do Muiscos—to find signs of life at last! This is where we must land!"

Shoten Binayakya nodded agreement without waiting even for the assent of Njord Freyr. A limb flicked out, tapped. *Khons* bucked and started circling downward toward the reticulated patterns on the surface of Thog.

With a jolt and a shudder *Khons* settled onto the surface of the moon, well within the weathered walls of the crater and within a kilometer or less of the structured protuberances. Shoten quiesced the cyberbiots to mere maintenance level of *Khons*, leaving only the receptors and telemeters warm, then asked the others to prepare to exit.

Njord Freyr and Sri Gomati slipped breathers over their heads and shoulders. Shoten ordered a variety of internal filtration modifications within the recirculation system that provided life support. They took readings from *Khons*'s external sensors, slid back hatches, made their way from *Khons*, stood facing what, it was now obvious, were relics of incredible antiquity.

Abreast, the three moved toward the ruins: Njord on motorized, gyrostabilized cyborged wheel assemblies; Shoten Binayakya rumbling on tread-laying gear, stable, efficient; Sri Gomati striding left foot, right foot, organic legs encased in puff-jointed pressure suit like some anachronistic caricature of a Bipolar Technocompetitive Era spaceman.

They halted a few meters from the first row of structures. Like the crater rims, the walls, columns, arches were weather-rounded, tumbled, softened. A metallic-telescoping tentacle whiplashed out from the hub of one of Njord's cyborg-wheels. A crumbled cube of some now-soft stone-like material fell away to ashes, to dust.

Njord turned bleak silver eyes to the others. "Once, perhaps
. . ."

"Come along," Gomati urged, "let's get to exploring these ruins!" Excitement colored her voice. "There's no telling what evidence they may contain of their builders. We may learn whether these worlds and their inhabitants originated in our own system or whether they came from—elsewhere."

At Gomati's final word she turned her face skyward, and the others followed suit. It was the worldlet Thog's high noon or the equivalent thereof. The sun was so remote—sixteen billion kilometers, twice as far as it was from Pluto at the latter's aphelion and 120 times as distant as it was from Earth—that to the three standing on the surface of Thog, it was utterly lost in the star-dotted blackness.

But Yuggoth itself hung directly overhead, obscenely bloated and oblate, its surface filling the heavens, looking as if it were about to crash shockingly upon *Khons* and the three explorers, and all the time pulsing, pulsing, pulsing like an atrocious heart, throbbing, throbbing. And now Thog's twin worldlet, dubbed Thok by the female crew member, swept in stygian silhouette across the tumultuous face of Yuggoth, Thok's black roundness varied by the crater-rims casting their deep shadows on the pale, pink-pulsating gray rocks of Thog.

The blackness enveloped first *Khons*, then sped across the face of Thog, swept over the three explorers, blotting out the pulsing ruddiness of Yuggoth and plunging them into utter blackness.

Gomati's fascination was broken by the purring synthetic voice of Shoten Binayakya. "An interesting occultation," Shoten said, "but come, we have our mission to perform. *Khons* is taking automatic measurements and telemetering information back to Neptune. And here," the silvery eyes seemed to flicker in distant starlight as a cybernetic extensor adjusted devices on the mechanical carapace, "my own recording and telemetering devices will send data back to the ship."

MARCH 15, 1937 – A SNAPSHOT

Dr. Dustin stood by the bed. The patient was semi-conscious. His lips moved but no one could hear what he said. Two old women sat by the bed. One was his Aunt Annie. The other was Annie's dear friend Edna, present as much to comfort the grieving aunt as her dying nephew.

Dr. Dustin leaned over the bed. He checked the patient's condition. He stood for a while trying to understand the patient's words but he could not. From time to time the patient moved his hand feebly. It looked as if he was trying to slap something.

The old woman named Annie had tears on her face. She reached into a worn black purse for her handkerchief and wiped the tears away as best she could. She grasped Dr. Dustin's hand and held it between her own. She asked him, "Is there any hope? Any?"

The doctor shook his head. "I'm sorry, Mrs. Gamwell." And to the other woman, "Miss Lewis."

"I'm sorry," the doctor said again.

The old woman named Annie released the doctor's hand. The other old woman, Edna, reached toward Annie. They sat facing each other. They embraced clumsily, as people must when sitting face to face. Each old woman tried to comfort the other.

The doctor sighed and walked to the window. He looked outside. It was early morning. The sun had risen but it was visible only as a pale, watery glow in the east. The sky was gray with clouds. The ground was covered with patches of snow, ice, slush. More snow was falling.

The doctor wondered why it seemed that he lost patients only in winter, or during rain storms, or at night. Never on a bright spring or summer day. He knew that that was not really true. Patients died when they died. When their fatal condition, whatever it was, completed its course. Still it *seemed* always to happen in the dark of the night or in the dark of the year.

He heard someone whistling.

He turned and saw two young residents passing the doorway. One of them was whistling, he was whistling a popular tune that the doctor had heard on the radio. He couldn't remember what program he had heard it on. Possibly the program was *The Kate Smith Show,* or *Your Hit Parade.* The tune was very catchy even though the words were in some language that eluded Dr. Dustin's ear. The song was called "Bei Mir bist du Schön."

*   *   *

Three thousand miles away, the Spanish were engaged in a confusing civil war. The old king had abdicated years before and a republic had been proclaimed. But after the direction of the new government became clear, a colonel serving in the Spanish colonial forces in Africa returned with his troops — largely Berbers and Rifs — to change things.

He would overthrow the republic. He would end the nonsense of democracy, atheism, lewdness that the republic tolerated. He would restore discipline, piety, modesty. He would reinstitute the monarchy.

At the moment it appeared that the Republican forces were winning. They had just recaptured the cities of Trijuque and Guadalajara. They had taken rebel prisoners. These included Spanish monarchists. They included African troops as well. Strangely, some of the prisoners spoke only Italian. They said they were volunteers. They said they had been ordered to volunteer. And they always obeyed their orders.

*   *   *

In China, forces of the Imperial Japanese Army were having easy going. Their opposition was weak. The Chinese were divided. They had been engaged in a civil war. It was not much like the one in Spain. It had been going on much longer. It had begun with the death of President Sun Yat-sen in 1924. The Japanese were not the only foreign power to intervene in China.

Germany had owned trading concessions in China until the Treaty of Versailles ended them. Germany was burgeoning now and had ambitions to regain her lost privileges.

Other countries had felt their interests threatened by the Chinese civil war. England had sent troops. France had used her influence. France was worried that she might lose her valuable colonies in Indo-China. Russia had tried to influence China's internal politics. There had been grave danger of war between Russia and China. Especially when the Chinese sacked the Russian Embassy in Peking and beheaded six of its staff.

The United States had intervened. American gunboats plied Chinese waterways. The gunboat *Panay* was sunk by aerial gunfire and bombing. The *Panay* was on the Yangtze River when this happened. The Yangtze is a Chinese river. But the *Panay* was sunk by Japanese forces. This pleased China. Japan apologized and paid compensation.

*   *   *

Joe Louis and Joe DiMaggio, two young athletes, were in training. Both of them had very good years in 1937.

*   *   *

A wealthy daredevil pilot named Howard Hughes flew across the United States in seven hours and twenty-eight minutes. This set off a new wave of excitement and "air-mindedness." In Santa Monica, California, the Douglas Aircraft Company was completing its new airliner. This would carry forty passengers. It had four engines. It would be capable of speeds up to 237 miles per hour.

More conservative people felt that the Zeppelin would never yield to the airplane. The great airship *Hindenberg* was on the Atlantic run. It was huge. It was beautiful. There was a piano in its cocktail lounge. The European terminus of its flights was Tempelhof Airdrome in Germany. The American terminus of its flights was Lakehurst, New Jersey.

On the morning of March 15, Rabbi Louis I. Newman found eleven large orange swastikas painted on the walls of Temple Rodeph Sholom, 7 West 83rd Street, New York. This was the third such incident at Temple Rodeph Sholom. Rabbi Newman suspected that the swastikas were painted in retaliation for

Secretary of State Hull's protests against abusive statements in the German press.

At Turn Hall, Lexington Avenue and 85th Street, the head of the Silver Shirts of New York replied. His name was George L. Rafort. He said the swastikas were painted by Jewish trouble-makers. He knew this because the arms of the eleven swastikas pointed backwards. He said, "This is a mistake no Nazi would make."

*   *   *

In Providence, Rhode Island, the snow continued to fall. The city's hills were slippery. There were accident cases in the hospitals.

In the Jane Brown Memorial Hospital on College Hill, Howard Lovecraft opened his eyes. No one knew what he saw. Certainly Dr. Dustin did not. Howard slapped the coverlet of his bed. He moved his lips. A sound emerged. He might have said, "Father." He might have said, "Father you look just like a young man."

MARCH 15, 2337

They rolled, clanked, strode forward a few meters more, halted once again at the very edge of the ancient ruins. Shoten Binayakya sent two core samplers downward from mechanized instrumentation compartments, one to sample soil, the other to clip some material from the ruins themselves. Carbon dating would proceed automatically within Shoten's cyborged compo-nentry.

Sri Gomati gazed at the ruins. They had the appearance, in the faint distant starlight, of stairs and terraces walled with marble balustrades. Gomati ran her optical sensors to maximum image amplification to obtain meaningful sight in the darkness of the occultation of Yuggoth.

And then—it is highly doubtful that the discovery would have been made by the single brief expedition, working in the ruddy, pulsating light of Yuggoth; it was surely that planet's occultation by Thok that must receive credit for the find—Gomati turned at the gasp of Njord Freyr. Her eyes followed the path of his point-ing, armor-gauntleted hand.

From some opening deep under the rubble before them a dim but baleful light emerged, pulsating obscenely. But unlike the crimson pulsations of Yuggoth above the explorers, this light beneath their feet was of some shocking, awful green.

Without speaking the three surged forward, picking their way through the ruined and crumbled remnants of whatever ancient city had once flung faulted towers and fluted columns into the black sky above the tiny world. They reached the source of the radiance barely in time, for as the disk sped across the face of Yuggoth the black shadow that blanketed the landing site of the ship *Khons* and the ruins where the crew poked and studied, fled across the pale gray face of Thog leaving them standing once more in the red, pulsating glare of the giant planet.

In that obscene half-daylight, the hideous, metallic glare of bronze-green was overwhelmed and disappeared into the general throbbing ruddiness. But by now Shoten Binayakya had shot a telescoping core-probe into the opening from which the light emerged, and with mechanical levers pried back the marble-like slab whose cracked and chipped corner had permitted the emergence of the glow.

Servos revved, the stone slab crashed aside. Steps led away, into the bowels of the worldlet Thog. In the dark, shadowy recess the red, pulsating light of giant Yuggoth and the baleful metallic green fought and shifted distressingly.

"The Ghooric Zone," Sri Gomati whispered to herself, "the Ghooric Zone."

They advanced down the stairs, leaving behind the baleful pulsations of Yuggoth, lowering themselves meter by meter into the bronze-green lighted depths of Thog. The track-laying cyber-mech of Shoten Binayakya took the strangely proportioned stairway with a sort of clumsy grace. Njord Freyr, his wheeled undercarriage superbly mobile on the level surface of Thog, now clutched desperately to the fluted carapace of Shoten.

Sri Gomati walked with ease, gazing out over the subsurface world of Thog. Seemingly kilometers below their entry a maze of dome on dome and tower on tower lay beside—she shook her head, adjusted metallic optics. There seemed to be a subterranean sea here within the depths of tiny Thog, a sea whose dark and oily waters lapped and gurgled obscenely at a black and gritty beach.

At the edge of that sea, that body which must be little more than a lake by earthly standards, on that black and grainy beach, great terrible creatures rolled and gamboled shockingly.

"Shoggoths!" Sri Gomati ran ahead of the others, almost tumbling from the unbalustraded stairway. "Shoggoths! Exactly as he said, splashing beside a foul lake! Shoggoths!" Exalted, she reached the end of the stairway, ran through towering columns past walls of sprawling bas-relief that showed hideous deities destroying intruders upon their shrines while awful acolytes crept

away toward enigmatic vehicles in search of morsels to appease
their obscene gods.

Gomati heard the grinding, clanking sounds of Shoten Binayakya following her, the steady whir of Njord Freyr's undercarriage. She turned and faced them. "This is the year 2337," she
shouted, "the four hundredth anniversary of his death! How could
he know? How could he ever have known?"

And she ran down hallways beneath vaulted gambrel roofs, ran
past more carvings and paintings showing strange, rugose, cone-
shaped beings and terrible, tentacle-faced obscenities that loomed
frighteningly above cowering prey. Then Gomati came to another
hallway, one lit with black tapers that flared and guttered terribly.

The air in the room was utterly still, the shadows of fluted columns solemn against walls carved and lettered in a script whose
obscene significance had been forgotten before Earth's own races
were young. And in the center of the room, meter-tall tapers of
stygian gloom marking its four extremities, stood a catafalque, and
on the catafalque, skin as white as a grave-worm's, eyes shut,
angular features in somber repose, lay the black-draped figure of
a man.

Sri Gomati raced to the foot of the catafalque, stood gazing
into the flickering darkness of the hall, then advanced to stand
beside the cadaver's head. Her silvery eyes shimmered and she
began to laugh, to giggle and titter obscenely, and yet to weep at
the same time, for some cyber-surgeon long before had seen fit to
leave those glands and ducts intact.

And Sri Gomati stood tittering and snuffling until Njord Freyr
rolled beside her on his cyborged power-wheels and the ambiguous Shoten Binayakya ground and clanked beside her on tread-
laying undercarriage, and they took her to return to the spaceship
Khons.

But strangest of all is this. The stairway by which they attempted to return to the surface of the worldlet Thog and the
safety of their spaceship *Khons* had crumbled away under the
weight of untold eons and that of the cybermechanisms of the
exploration party, and when they tried to climb those crumbling
stairs they found themselves trapped in the Ghooric Zone
kilometers beneath the surface of the worldlet Thog.

And there, beside the oily, lapping sea, the foul lake where
puffed shoggoths splash, they remained, the three, forever.

Three thousand copies of this book have been printed by the Maple-Vail Book Manufacturing Group, Binghamton, NY, for Golden Gryphon Press, Urbana, IL. The typeset is Elante, printed on 55# Sebago. The binding cloth is Skivertex. Typesetting by The Composing Room, Inc., Kimberly, WI.